DEATH'S DARK VALE

DINEY COSTELOE

LARGE PRINT

Oxford

First published in Great Britain 2007
by
Castlehaven Books

Published in Large Print 2009 by ISIS Publishing Ltd.,
7 Centremead, Osney Mead, Oxford OX2 0ES
by arrangement with
The Author

British Library Cataloguing in Publication Data
Costeloe, Diney.
   Death's dark vale [text (large print)].
   1. World War, 1939–1945 - - Underground
   movements - - France - - Fiction.
   2. Convents - - France, Northern - - Fiction.
   3. France - - History - - German occupation,
   1940–1945 - - Fiction.
   4. Historical fiction.
   5. Large type books.
   I. Title
   823.9'14–dc22

         ISBN 978–0–7531–8356–4 (hb)
         ISBN 978–0–7531–8357–1 (pb)

Printed and bound in Great Britain by
T. J. International Ltd., Padstow, Cornwall

CHAPTER
ONE

9th September 1937

Adelaide Anson-Gravetty drifted awake with the feeling that today something special was going to happen. And then she remembered. Today she was twenty-one. Today she was an adult and could decide things for herself. Today was the beginning of the rest of her life. Today, though she didn't yet know it, her life was going to be turned upside down.

She swung her legs out of bed and, crossing the room, threw back the curtains. The morning sun streamed in and her heart lifted with pleasure as she opened the window and, leaning out, looked down into the gardens of the square below. There were already plenty of people about, and she watched them going about their business as she often did, but for some reason today it was as if she were seeing them all for the first time. Footmen exercised dogs in the gardens, a newsboy sold papers from a stand at the end of the square, old Mrs Harriman had already taken her seat on her favourite bench. All was the same and yet all was different for now, today, Adelaide looked at it all through adult eyes.

There was a knock at her bedroom door and Florrie, the housemaid, came in with her morning tea.

"Oh, Miss Adelaide, you're up already," she said, setting down the tray and catching up Adelaide's dressing gown from a chair. "Here, Miss Adelaide, put this on. You'll catch your death there at the open window."

"Don't worry, Florrie," Adelaide laughed. "It's not cold, it's a beautiful morning."

"So it may be, miss, but you shouldn't be leaning out the window with only your nightdress on. What would the master say?"

"He won't know," Adelaide said, adding conspiratorially, "if you don't tell him."

Florrie sniffed. She had known Miss Adelaide since she was three years old, and never once had she given her away to the master. "Come and drink your tea while it's hot," she instructed, "and I'll draw your bath for you."

"Thank you, Florrie," Adelaide said meekly, though her eyes still gleamed with mischief.

"And may I be the first to wish you many happy returns of the day, miss," Florrie added as she turned to leave the room.

"Thank you, Florrie." Adelaide smiled at the maid with genuine affection. She took her cup to a chair by the window and continued to watch the comings and goings in the square below as she dutifully sipped the tea.

Twenty-one! she thought. Father can't stand in my way now!

It wasn't strictly true of course. Her father, Richard Anson-Gravetty, could always stand in her way while he held the purse strings, but now she was of age she could decide for herself if she wanted to get a job, and if she did she could, perhaps, support herself. She need no longer rely on him. It was a heady thought. She gave it further consideration as she lay in the bath a few moments later. She loved her father, of course she did, but he liked to make all the decisions, and when he had there was no going against him. Quick of temper, any opposition put him in a towering rage, and she and her mother had both learned that the most comfortable way to live was to keep her father happy; to do what he required of them and to ask permission before doing anything that was the least bit out of the ordinary.

Mummy. Darling Mummy. Adelaide thought of her mother, so pretty, so timid, so . . . what? Irresolute? Docile? Weak? Heather Anson-Gravetty had lived all her married life in her husband's shadow, biddable, eager to please, and when she had died when Adelaide was sixteen, Richard had hardly seemed to miss her. Adelaide missed her dreadfully. She had been away at school and summoned at the last moment, had come home to find her mother lying in bed, her once-auburn hair faded and in disarray about the gaunt parchment of her face. Adelaide knew that her mother had been ill for a while, but no one had warned her how quickly Heather was wasting away. When she came into the bedroom and saw her lying, a frail waif against the white pillow, Adelaide gave a cry of distress, bitten off as her father gripped her shoulder with an iron fist.

They had been together, the three of them, for the last time, but it was Adelaide, not Richard who sat holding her mother's hand. When her mother's grasp finally slackened, it was Adelaide who laid her head on the counterpane and wept. Richard simply turned and walked out of the room, leaving his grieving daughter sobbing by the bed.

Still, Adelaide thought now as she lay back in the warm water of the bath, that's Father's way. He never shows his emotions . . . except when he's cross of course!

In the days that followed her mother's death Adelaide had always felt that Richard wasn't so much saddened by it as angry that she had dared to die without his permission. He seldom mentioned her and if he did it was never, it seemed to his daughter, with affection.

"It's as if he's put her in a cupboard and forgotten about her," Adelaide confided to Grand'mère one day.

"That's how he copes with the loss," Adelaide's grandmother replied gently. "Some people find it easier to cope by hiding the loved one away, by not thinking about them, or talking about them. Some people find that too painful." She had smiled at her granddaughter. "I miss her, too, you know, so we can talk about her together, you and I, *hein?*"

Life from then on had not been easy for Adelaide. Although her mother had never made a stand or taken her side against her father, Adelaide had known that on occasion she had sympathised with her and had done what she could to make up for Richard's rigid rule.

4

After the funeral Adelaide had been sent back to school, and during the holidays she had spent most of her time staying with Grand'mère, Heather's French mother. Richard's parents were both still alive, but Adelaide found them less sympathetic. She had always been closer to her mother's mother and it was she who helped Adelaide through the difficult days after Heather died. It was Grand'mère who championed Adelaide's cause, who stood out against her son-in-law when she thought he was too harsh, who gave her the warmth and love her father seemed unable to express.

When Adelaide had wanted to go to university, Richard had been adamant that it was a waste of time and money, even though there was a place for her at King's College, London. Adelaide had never discovered what Grand'mère had said to make him change his mind, but eventually her father had simply shrugged. "Do what you like, though why a woman would want a degree is beyond me."

Adelaide had read French, a subject she found easy as she was already almost bilingual. Grand'mère had always insisted on speaking to her in French, even when she was quite a little girl, and Adelaide had responded with enthusiasm. She had spoken French to her mother, too, but never when Richard was there. He had forbidden them to speak it in front of him as he spoke none and refused to be excluded from the conversation in that way.

No more college, thought Adelaide as she finally emerged from her bath and set about getting dressed. She had taken her degree earlier in the year and was now, unwillingly, a lady of leisure again. She had no mother to "bring her out", and anyway she despised the debutante scene. Adelaide was a girl of action. She wanted to be up and doing. She wanted to get out into the world and earn her own bread, to be responsible for herself.

Richard Anson-Gravetty was not at home on the morning of the day that his daughter attained her majority; he was away on business and wouldn't be back until the evening. So, when she finally made it down to the dining room, it was to breakfast alone, to open the cards from her grandparents and her cousin Andrew, in solitary state; to open the unexpected letter that waited beside her plate with no one there to see her do it.

The envelope, typewritten, was addressed to her and had a Belcaster postmark, but she had no idea from whom it came. Leaving it till last, she finally slit open the envelope and drew out the contents. It was from a firm of solicitors, Brewer, Harben and Brewer, with an office in Cathedral Road, Belcaster. She skimmed through it, but, as its significance penetrated her mind, she started to read again from the beginning.

Dear Miss Anson-Gravetty,

Allow me to congratulate you on attaining the age of majority. I write in pursuance of the wishes expressed in the will of your late grandfather, Sir George Hurst. As you know he died in 1920 and left you a substantial legacy to become yours on your twenty-first birthday.

As Sir George's only grandchild, you were named as the residual legatee, the money to be invested and held in trust until you came of age.

This happy day is now upon us and I respectfully suggest that you make an appointment with me to go through the terms of the will. I am sure your stepfather has a financial advisor who will take over from me now that I am no longer your trustee, but I should certainly like to meet with you and explain my stewardship to date. I hope you will be satisfied with it.

If you would write to my secretary and arrange a time convenient to yourself I shall look forward to meeting you at last.

I remain, madam, yours very sincerely,

Arthur Brewer

Adelaide stared at the letter and then looked at the envelope again to make sure it was really addressed to her. It was. She read it through yet again. Her grandfather, Sir George Hurst? She hadn't got a grandfather called George Hurst. Her grandfathers were called Gilbert Anson-Gravetty and Norman Driver. Norman Driver, Grand'mère's husband, had been dead now for ten years or more, but her other grandfather, Father's father, was alive and well and living in Winchester. So who was this George Hurst? And why did the letter refer to her father as her stepfather? None of it made any sense. Had she been adopted? Were Mummy and Daddy — she seldom called him Daddy anymore but when thinking of them together it sometimes still slipped out — were Mummy and Daddy not her real parents then?

Adelaide left the last of her breakfast and went out into the hall to telephone Grand'mère.

"Adelaide, my darling," Grand'mère cried when she came onto the line, "many happy returns of the day!"

"Thanks, Grand'mère," Adelaide said. She paused and then asked, "Can I come and see you? We need to talk."

"Of course. But we shall see each other this evening at your birthday dinner."

"I know, but I need to speak to you before that. Before Father gets home. I've had a letter."

"Ah, I see." Antoinette Driver sounded suddenly serious. "Yes, well in that case I think you'd better come round this morning and we can have a nice chat in private. I have a luncheon engagement, but that is not until 12.30."

"Can I come now?" Adelaide asked.

"Of course. Just ask Davies to show you up as soon as you arrive."

Within half an hour, Adelaide was knocking on the front door of her grandmother's house just off Eaton Square.

"Good morning, Miss Adelaide." Davies greeted her with a smile. "May I wish you many happy returns of the day."

8

"Thank you, Davies," Adelaide replied, returning his smile. "Indeed you may. Is my grandmother still upstairs?"

"Yes, miss, she is, but she said to tell you to go on up as soon as you arrived."

Adelaide thanked him and hurried up the wide oak stairs to the old lady's bedroom. She knocked loudly and in answer to a call to come in she opened the door. Her grandmother was sitting up in bed, a breakfast tray on a table beside her, the post opened and strewn across the bed covers.

"Adelaide, my darling, happy birthday!" Antoinette Driver held out her arms and, as always, addressed her granddaughter in French.

Adelaide crossed the room for a birthday hug and a kiss and then drew up a chair beside the bed. Grand'mère removed her pince-nez and smiled. "So, now you are quite grown up. Feel any different?"

Adelaide shook her head. "No, not really."

"Nor I," the old lady said equably. "I haven't felt any different since the day I left the schoolroom."

"I got your birthday card," Adelaide said, not quite knowing where to begin, "and one from Granny and Grandpa. Andrew remembered, too."

"Well done, Andrew," said her grandmother, "but I think you had some other post, yes? Another letter?"

Adelaide pulled it out of her bag and handed it over. Mrs Driver replaced the pince-nez on her nose and pulling the letter from its envelope, read it slowly. Adelaide watched her face as she did so, but the old lady showed no signs of surprise or disbelief. When she had finished she handed the letter back to Adelaide.

"So . . ." she said and waited.

"So, what is it all about?" demanded Adelaide. "Firstly, is this letter really meant for me, and if so who on earth is George Hurst?"

"It is definitely meant for you," confirmed Mrs Driver, "and Sir George Hurst was your grandfather, your paternal grandfather."

"But . . ." began Adelaide.

"Your mother, my Heather, was married before. She married a man called Frederick Hurst at the very end of 1915. He was killed on the Somme in July 1916. You were born posthumously."

Adelaide stared at her. "You're saying my mother was married before . . . and she never told me?"

"Richard wouldn't allow her to."

"What do you mean, he wouldn't allow her to?" demanded Adelaide.

"Darling, you know your father. People do what he says. He didn't want her to tell you, so she didn't."

"But she was married to this Frederick Hurst for nine months?"

Mrs Driver sighed. "Not really, no."

Adelaide looked shocked. "You mean I'm illegitimate?"

Mrs Driver shook her head with a laugh. "No, of course not, darling. What I meant was that they were never together as a married couple. Freddie was a friend of Uncle Johnny's. Freddie and Heather met in London and corresponded while he was away in France."

10

"Freddie, is that what he was called?" Adelaide interrupted. "I think I like that better than Frederick. So what happened?"

"Freddie came home on leave and they decided to get married."

"Just like that?"

"Just like that," agreed her grandmother. "We tried to persuade them to wait, but it was no use. They were difficult times, the war years; people snatched their happiness where and when they could.

"So, he had ten days' leave over Christmas. They got married by special licence on 29th December and had a four-day honeymoon in London before he went back." Mrs Driver gave a sad sigh. "He never came home. She never saw him again. He was killed on the first day of the Somme. You were born two and half months later."

Silence fell between them as Adelaide struggled to take it all in. Grand'mère reached out and took her hand and together they sat thinking about what Adelaide had just heard.

"When did she marry Father? Richard, I mean."

"Two and a half years later. We gave her all the support we could, but your mother, God rest her soul, was the sort of woman who needed a man to lean on. And anyway it would have been wrong for her to turn down another chance of happiness. Besides, she had you to consider. Richard was happy to take you on and bring you up as his child. All he asked was that it be done legally, so, when they got married he also adopted you legally and gave you his name. He said it would be better when they had more children that the family should all have the same name and grow up together with no ghosts lurking in the background."

"But Mummy must have wanted to tell me about Freddie, when I got older I mean. Old enough to understand."

"I think she did, but Richard asked for her promise and she gave it."

Adelaide shook her head in confusion. "It is most peculiar," she remarked, "to grow up thinking you are one person and suddenly discovering you are someone quite different!"

"You are you," Grand'mère pointed out gently. "You are the same you as before. Your father was Freddie Hurst, but to all intents and purposes your father is Richard Anson-Gravetty. He is the one who's brought you up as his own, loved you as a daughter, given you everything. It is no mean task to take on another man's child and he has done his best. All he asked was that you should think of him as your real father . . . and you do, don't you?"

"Of course, it's just . . . well, just such a shock to find out that he isn't. Especially when everyone else knew it all along."

"Not everyone at all," said her grandmother. "Only Norman and I, Richard's parents and Johnny. Others may have known, but in the chaos that surrounded the end of the war everyone was too concerned with their own affairs to remember other people's."

Adelaide was still holding the letter and now she looked at it again. "This solicitor, this Arthur Brewer, says I've been left money by my real grandfather, Sir George. He must have known about me."

"Yes, of course he did, but when he died there was no one left on that side of the family to have any claim to you."

"Was Freddie an only child then? Didn't he have any brothers or sisters?"

"There was a sister, Sarah I think she was called. She went to France to nurse the wounded. Took her maid and upped and went to nurse in a convent or some such. Anyway, the maid later came home in disgrace, but the sister stayed on and became a nun, of all things."

"A nun?" Adelaide was startled.

"Well, we are a good Catholic family, remember," said Mrs Driver, her face entirely serious.

That made Adelaide burst out laughing. "Oh, Grand'mère, how can you say such a thing? When was the last time you went to Mass?"

"Be that as it may," her grandmother answered serenely, "Freddie was brought up a Catholic and so was your mother. So were you, come to that. At least Heather won that battle!"

"So this Sarah is my aunt. Where is she now?"

"Still in her convent, I imagine," replied Mrs Driver, pushing aside the bedclothes and preparing to get up. "They don't let them out, you know."

"Grand'mère, why didn't you tell me before?" Adelaide asked softly.

Her grandmother gave her a rueful smile. "It wasn't my secret, my darling. Heather asked us to keep the promise she had made and so, with many misgivings, we have."

"Does Andrew know?" Adelaide was very close to her cousin, and the idea that he should have known something of this importance when she had not, would hurt.

Mrs Driver shook her head. "I don't know for sure, but I doubt it. I imagine Johnny was sworn to secrecy too. Now shoo, I have to get up."

"Grand'mère, what shall I do about this letter?" Adelaide asked.

"I should do what it asks you to," was the reply. "Go and see the man and find out about your legacy. I should imagine you have become quite a wealthy woman."

"What about Father? What do I tell him?"

"You don't need to tell him anything. He already knows. He's always known that it would all come out the day you were twenty-one. He's simply been putting it off." She looked speculatively at her granddaughter. "Why do you think he was away for your birthday morning, *hein?* He didn't want to be there when you found out. Never forget, darling, that he loves you in his own way. He's afraid of losing you to some ghostly father from the war. You must reassure him that he is truly your father and you are truly his daughter." The old lady reached for her robe and went on, "And now, my darling, I really do have to get up. You may go downstairs and wait for me there if you like. Ask Davies for coffee. We can talk some more once I am ready to go out."

The rest of her birthday passed in something of a blur. Adelaide had arranged to meet her friend Sophie for lunch, and it was all she could do not to tell her of the amazing discoveries she had made that morning. However, she knew she owed it to her father, her adoptive father that was, to talk things through with him first. The lunch was thus somewhat difficult, as Adelaide could think of very little else.

"Addie, you're miles away," laughed Sophie when she had made the same remark twice and received no answer.

Adelaide smiled apologetically. "Sorry," she said, "I was thinking about this dinner party Father is giving for me this evening. What did you say?"

"I said, shall we go shopping this afternoon? I want to buy some shoes."

"Oh Sophie, do you mind if we don't?" she said. "I really ought to go home. My grandparents are driving up from Winchester for this evening and I really should be at home to greet them when they arrive." She smiled across at Sophie and added, "Andrew's coming too. He's going to stay the night. Do you want to come round tomorrow morning for a cup of coffee?" Adelaide was well aware how Sophie felt about her cousin and she tried to bring them together whenever she could.

Sophie looked at her affectionately. "Thanks," she said. "I might." And they both laughed, knowing wild horses would not keep Sophie away.

Richard Anson-Gravetty arrived home only an hour before the dinner guests were due to assemble.

Adelaide knocked on his dressing-room door and when he called her in, she crossed the room and put her arms round him in an unusual gesture of affection.

"Welcome home, Daddy," she said. "Granny and Grandpa are here and getting changed. Everything's ready for the dinner."

He returned her hug and then held her away from him and looked into her face. "Happy birthday, Adelaide. And congratulations!"

She looked at him quizzically. "Congratulations on what?"

"On coming of age, of course."

"The years of discretion . . . when I can be told everything."

"I imagine you have already been told, if I know anything about your grandmother." He raised his eyebrows questioningly.

Adelaide laughed. "You're right, of course. Today I discovered that I am lucky enough to have two fathers. But you do Grand'mère an injustice, Daddy. She kept the secret until I had learned of it from another source."

Her father grunted. "You heard from old Brewer, I suppose."

"I did, so of course I went to Grand'mère to find out what it was all about."

"You didn't think of waiting until this evening and asking me?"

Adelaide hadn't thought of doing so, but now she prevaricated. "I didn't think you wanted to tell me, or you'd have done it before . . . or let Mummy tell me,"

16

she said. "Wasn't that why you were away this morning?" It was after all what Grand'mère had suggested.

Richard shrugged. "Perhaps," he said. His hands dropped from her shoulders and he turned to the mirror to knot his evening tie.

Adelaide moved towards the door where she turned and said softly, "Thank you, Daddy, for all you've done for me."

"It was my duty," he replied without turning round. "I'm your father."

On this rather unsatisfactory note Adelaide left the room to put the finishing touches to her own evening dress.

Later that night, as she lay in bed, her birthday dinner over, she thought about the extraordinary revelations of the day. She had left her curtains open so that the light from the street lamp below gave an eerie green glow to the room. The familiar shapes of her room were comforting as she confronted her world turned upside down. Her father wasn't her father and her mother had never told her. All of a sudden she was somebody different. It was all very well for Grand'mère to say that she was still the same person herself, but she didn't feel it. She wasn't the same person who had woken up that morning, sure of who she was and where she came from. Now she felt that part of her was made up of someone else. Parts of her, physical and mental, had been bequeathed to her by someone whom she didn't know anything about. And she wanted to know; who he was, what he was like, where he came from.

Dinner had passed off quite well. Her favourite foods had been served, a birthday cake ablaze with twenty-one candles had been brought in and the assembled family had sung "Happy Birthday" and "Twenty-One Today". Not by the slightest glance did Grand'mère, elegantly attired in a black chiffon evening dress with a corsage of tiny white roses, indicate that she and Adelaide had anything else on their minds but the birthday celebrations. No sign came from Richard that anything untoward had happened between them and to all intents and purposes the family party was a great success. He had presented her with her birthday gift in the drawing room where they had all gathered for drinks before dinner. Inside the parcel was a beautiful gold elbow bracelet, broad and heavy, chased with swirling patterns. There were gasps of admiration as she held it up to be admired before she slid it over her elbow where it nestled comfortably, fitting perfectly and drawing attention to the slender shape of her arm.

"It's really beautiful, Daddy," she said and kissed his cheek. "Thank you so much. I love it. And you've put my initials inside and the date. That makes it really special." But she wondered as she spoke if the "A A-G 9th September 1937" was some sort of statement, a declaration that whoever had been born on 9th September 1916, she was Adelaide Anson-Gravetty now.

As she caught Grand'mère's eye, she saw a look of approval and shot her a smile.

When her father had stood and raised his glass to propose her health, he had said, "We wish you every happiness, Adelaide. I only wish your mother were here with us tonight to see what a beautiful daughter we have. We wish you health, and happiness for the rest of your days."

Everyone had stood up and dutifully repeated, "Health and happiness!" as they clinked their glasses, but Adelaide had been touched by Richard's words, not only was it the first time he had mentioned her mother in months, but also the nearest he had ever come to saying he was proud of her. Perhaps Grand'mère was right; perhaps he had been afraid he might lose the battle against a ghostly, heroic father about whom she might fantasise.

Everyone had stayed overnight, so there was no rush to leave as the hour got late. They sat around in the drawing room talking companionably, at ease as they always had been. No one mentioned the subject that was churning round Adelaide's brain, though they all must have known that she knew by now.

It was strange, Adelaide thought. Was she the only one whom the revelation affected?

She had looked across at Andrew, who was chatting to Grand'mère, but there had been no chance to have a private word with him.

If he really doesn't know I'm not Richard's daughter, what will he say when he finds out, she wondered? I wish I could talk to him.

At last she fell asleep and didn't wake again until Florrie was tapping on the door with her early tea.

By the time she got down to breakfast, her father was about to leave the table.

"I've got something for you," he said. "Come and find me in the study when you've had your breakfast."

"Yes, of course, I won't be long," Adelaide replied. As she ate her toast she wondered what on earth it could be. After all, she'd had her present last night.

When she knocked on the study door twenty minutes later, she found her father at his desk.

He looked up as she came in. "Ah, there you are. I've looked this out for you. Your mother wanted you to have these things when you reached twenty-one."

He pointed to an envelope on the desk, but Adelaide did not pick it up. She said softly, "I know I'm not your real daughter, by blood I mean. But I *am* your daughter, you know. *You* are my father, not the man who died in 1916."

Richard looked up from what he was writing as she spoke but said nothing. Adelaide went on, "You're the one who's looked after me all these years. It was you sitting with Mummy by my bed when I came round from having my appendix out. It was you who ran in the fathers' race at my first school sports." She paused and when he continued to say nothing she added, "I just wish you'd told me, that's all."

Richard shrugged. "I thought it better not to. Your mother agreed. However, we both knew you'd learn in the end, when you came into Sir George's money."

"I still wish you'd told me yourself, not left me to discover from a complete stranger," Adelaide said. She sighed. "I suppose I must get in touch with this Mr Brewer, now."

20

"You must do what you think fit," Richard replied calmly. "You're of age now." He turned back to what he had been writing when she'd come in, saying as he did so, "Don't forget to take your envelope."

It was her dismissal and Adelaide picked the envelope up. "Thank you, Father." Quietly she turned and went out of the room; clearly he wanted no displays of affection. He felt he had done his duty by her and now she was on her own.

Adelaide took the envelope to her room, locked the door and sat down in the chair by the window. For a moment she looked down on the square. Only twenty-four hours since she had looked down on it in such hope yesterday morning, the first day of her adult life and yet it seemed a lifetime away.

She slipped her finger under the flap of the envelope and tore it open. Inside there were two documents and another, smaller, sealed envelope. The first of the documents was her birth certificate, naming her Adelaide Sarah, daughter of Heather Hurst and Captain Frederick Charles Hurst (deceased). Born 9th September 1916 at Greyling House, Chalfont St Giles. The second was the certificate of adoption in which she, Adelaide Sarah Hurst, became the legal daughter of Richard David Anson-Gravetty, and her surname was changed to his. It was dated 12th June 1919. She had never asked which year her parents got married. Although she knew that their anniversary fell on 21st April it was never celebrated in any style and it had never dawned on her that they might not have been married until she was nearly three.

Adelaide set the two certificates aside and opened the other envelope. Inside was a letter, written in her mother's handwriting. The sight of her mother's neat hand made tears spring to Adelaide's eyes. She dashed them away and started to read.

My darling Adelaide,

I know I haven't very long to live. This awful disease has got the better of me, and my time is nearly over. My only real regret is that I shan't see you grow up into the beautiful young woman I know you will be. You'll know by now that Richard is my second husband and not your natural father, though he has been as real a father to you as is in his nature. He made me promise not to tell you about Freddie. I know that he was always jealous of the place Freddie might hold in my heart, though he had no need to be, and he was afraid that Freddie might usurp his place with you as well. He also hoped to have children of his own and he thought it would be easier, for you and them, if it were assumed that he was your natural father.

When Freddie was killed, I was on my own. Even with the help of my parents, life was a struggle. I was still very young, with you to consider, and when Richard finally asked me to marry him it was a chance of security for us both and I took it. He is a kind man and even though he doesn't show his emotions, he loves us both. We've both learned to love him too, haven't we, and thanks to him we've had happy and contented lives.

Freddie was a wonderful man; honourable and courageous. He had a wonderful smile, which I've seen on your face on many an occasion, and a really infectious laugh, just like yours. You are like him in so many ways, not just in looks, which indeed you are, but mannerisms and character, too.

However, when I look back now I realise I hardly knew him as a husband. We had a whirlwind romance and then three days of married life and that was all. To me he was a figure of great romance, straight from a young girl's dreams. Handsome and debonair, he swept me off my feet . . . a brave soldier off to do his bit for King and country. I loved him and he loved me, don't ever doubt that, but we never had our own home, never delved deeper into each other than our few days together allowed. Richard is my true husband and believe me when I say that despite all the outward signs to the contrary, Richard is a vulnerable man.

On your twenty-first birthday you will come into the money put in trust for you by your grandfather, Freddie's father, Sir George Hurst. Then you will have to be told about Freddie, but if you feel the need to find out more about him, please be gentle about it. Remember, even though Freddie gave you life, it is Richard who has watched over you as you have lived it. Look after him for me.

God bless you, my darling.

With my love, Mummy

The writing blurred in front of her eyes as Adelaide read. Sitting with the letter in her lap, Adelaide thought about her mother.

Dearest Mummy. She knew she was dying and she wrote to me, even though she knew that I wouldn't read the letter for another five years.

Adelaide wondered briefly if Richard had read the letter before giving it to her and then chided herself for such an uncharitable thought. It was not in Richard's nature to do such a dishonourable thing.

Adelaide considered what to do for several days before she finally put in a call to trunks and spoke to Mr Arthur Brewer in Belcaster.

"My dear Miss Anson-Gravetty," said the voice over the crackling line. "I would be delighted to meet you on Thursday. Will you catch the 10.30 train from Paddington and perhaps you would take luncheon with me after we have concluded our business?"

Adelaide took a taxi from the station to the offices of Brewer, Harben and Brewer and was greeted by a lady of middle years, smartly dressed in a grey suit over a pale blue twin set.

"How do you do, Miss Anson-Gravetty. I am Miss Davenport, Mr Brewer's secretary. He is expecting you and asked me to show you straight up." She led the way up some narrow stairs to a room on the first floor. With a brief knock she opened the door and ushered Adelaide in.

"Miss Anson-Gravetty, Mr Brewer."

An elderly man rose from behind the desk at which he had been sitting and came forward to meet her, his hand outstretched.

"Miss Anson-Gravetty," he beamed, "how delightful to meet you at last!"

Adelaide shook his hand and was shown to a comfortable seat in front of a smouldering fire. Having asked Miss Davenport to bring coffee, Mr Brewer took a chair opposite her.

"I like to have a fire, even though the days aren't that cold yet," he said. "When you get to my age, you know, you feel the cold so much more." He looked across at her. "May I ask you something, Miss Anson-Gravetty? Did you know about your inheritance before I wrote to you?"

"No, Mr Brewer. It came as a complete shock," Adelaide replied. "I didn't know until I received your letter that my father wasn't my father, if you see what I mean. I knew nothing of Freddie Hurst."

"Ah," Mr Brewer sucked his breath in through his teeth. "I was afraid that might be the case. I had hoped that Mr Anson-Gravetty might have told you himself before the letter arrived. It certainly must have come as a shock."

"That's putting it mildly," Adelaide agreed. "I had no idea that he wasn't my real father."

"It was his wish that we didn't communicate directly with you and as he is, was, your legal guardian, we had to respect his wishes. However, now you are twenty-one you are responsible for your own affairs."

"I see," said Adelaide. "And what are those affairs?"

"Well, apart from a few small bequests, your late grandfather, Sir George Hurst, made you his sole beneficiary. I must tell you, Miss Anson-Gravetty, that you are an extremely rich young woman. The capital has been invested in trust for you and all the accruing interest has been reinvested. It amounts to a tidy sum."

Adelaide stared at him. "How much?" she asked him softly.

"Well, let me see now," Mr Brewer reached for a file on his desk and opened it. He pulled out a sheet of figures. "At the last evaluation your portfolio was worth some £75,000." He glanced at her face and saw the colour had drained from her cheeks. "My dear Miss Anson-Gravetty, are you all right?"

"How much?" whispered Adelaide.

"As I said," Mr Brewer went on, "you are an extremely rich young woman. The money is now yours to do with as you wish. At present it is invested fairly conservatively, and I suggest, if I may, that you leave things as they are until you've had the benefit of some professional advice."

"Yes, yes, of course. Sorry, Mr Brewer, but I can't quite take all this in." Adelaide smiled at him weakly. "Sorry."

"Don't worry, my dear, we can sort out all the paperwork and then you can take everything with you. I expect you want to discuss things with your father, hmm?"

"Before we do any of that," Adelaide said, "may I see the actual will?"

Mr Brewer delved in the file again and producing a document, passed it over to her.

Adelaide read it slowly, trying to take in the meaning through all the legal jargon. There was a small bequest of £200 to his housekeeper, a Mrs Norton, and another to the head gardener of £100, and £50 to every person in his employ at the time of his death.

The village green of Charlton Ambrose, where the Hursts lived, was part of The Manor estate, and this plus another parcel of land beyond it was left to the Parish Council to be used for the benefit of the village.

The residue of my estate is left to my granddaughter, Adelaide Sarah Hurst (now Anson-Gravetty) to be held in trust until she attain the age of twenty-one years, when it shall pass to her absolutely. My trustees, the partners in Messrs Brewer, Harben and Brewer, shall administer the trust in any way they see fit during her minority, including the sale of any property, real or otherwise that I own at the time of my death.

Adelaide looked up at Mr Brewer. "I don't see any mention of his daughter, Sarah, I think she was called. Why didn't he leave any money to her? Surely she was entitled to half, even if I had Freddie's half."

"I believe Sir George did have a daughter called Sarah, but as you say there is no mention of her in the will. It was my father who drew it up. He may know why. He knew Sir George quite well of course, our firm has been his family's lawyers for three generations."

"I see," said Adelaide. But she didn't. Why would Sir George have neglected to provide for his only daughter? "It doesn't sound fair," she said, shaking her head. "There's so much money there, she should have had some of it."

"I'm sure there was a good reason," Mr Brewer said gently. "Sir George knew what he was doing." When Adelaide made no comment, he went on, "I hope you will find our stewardship satisfactory. We have been in contact with your stepfather on occasion over the years, but once The Manor at Charlton Ambrose had been sold, he left us to manage everything.

"I'm sure you won't want to take all these documents back with you on the train," Mr Brewer said when he had been through them with her. "I'll have them all delivered to you, or your solicitor in London. Our man Dickens will bring everything up by the end of the week. Would that suit you?"

"I haven't got a solicitor," Adelaide said. "I think it would be far better if you continued to handle everything for me. You know exactly what there is. All I would like at present is a regular income if that's possible."

Mr Brewer looked delighted and assured her that it was.

On the way home on the train Adelaide tried to imagine having seventy-five thousand pounds. The sum was astronomical.

Father knows that I've an inheritance, she thought, but does he know the extent of it, I wonder?

CHAPTER
TWO

Mother Marie-Pierre sat at the desk in her office and stared at the letter. Sister Celestine had just brought it in with the other post that had arrived at the convent. It was addressed to Miss Sarah Hurst, a name Mother Marie-Pierre had given up twenty years ago. Seeing it written on the envelope gave her a jolt. She did not recognise the writing. The stamps were English but she had had no contact with England in the last eighteen years. Miss Sarah Hurst. Whoever had written to her clearly did not know her convent name, maybe did not even know that she had one.

Mother Marie-Pierre picked up the letter and, holding it between her two forefingers, spun it gently. There was no name or return address on the back. It was just a white envelope addressed in a well-formed hand. Miss Sarah Hurst. Convent of Our Lady of Mercy. St Croix. The postmark was London and the date many days ago.

Probably because the address was incomplete, thought Mother Marie-Pierre, as she stared at the envelope. It's been so long since I've had a personal letter, I hardly dare open it.

The rest of the post, all addressed to the reverend mother, was convent business, and setting aside the intriguing letter to Miss Hurst, she had concentrated on that business first. Now there was only this one letter unopened. Mother Marie-Pierre closed her eyes in a moment of unspoken prayer and then reaching for her paper knife slit the envelope and drew out the contents.

The single sheet of paper was headed with an address in London, and signed with a flourish, *Adelaide Anson-Gravetty*.

Dear God, Mother Marie-Pierre thought, it's from Freddie's daughter.

She turned back to the top of the letter.

34 Northumberland Square

Kensington

12th October 1937

Dear Aunt Sarah

I hope you don't mind me addressing you as that even though we have never met. I am your brother Frederick's daughter and so you are indeed my aunt. I expect you will be surprised to hear from me out of the blue like this, but until my birthday in September, I didn't know of your existence. On the 9th September I became twenty-one and discovered that I had an inheritance that I knew nothing about, from a grandfather I had never even heard of. I also discovered to my amazement that my father, or rather the man I have believed to be my father all my life, is not. My mother died when I was sixteen and had never told me that she had been married before. I understand from my grandmother that my mother's second husband adopted me as a two-year-old, but until I came of age I had no knowledge of that either. I have questioned Grand'mère at some length, but she knows little of my father's family. She simply said that she thought he had a sister in France who was a nun. Mr Arthur Brewer, the solicitor who dealt with my legacy, knew nothing about you but suggested that I speak with his father who used to deal with the family business. He is now retired, but I went to see him. He thought he remembered where the convent was and gave me this address, so I hope he was right and that this finds you.

What I would like to do, Aunt, is to come and see you. Please do say that I may. Until last month I had never heard of either you or my natural father, Frederick. I would love to meet you and hear about him now.

I will await your reply in hope that we shall be able to meet before very long.

Yours sincerely,

Adelaide Anson-Gravetty

Mother Marie-Pierre read and reread the letter and tears came to her eyes. Freddie's daughter.

She thought back to the last day she had seen Freddie just before he left for Christmas leave in England in 1915. He'd been so young and handsome, and though his face had been drawn and his eyes were weary from his time at the front, while they had been together it was as it had always been while they were children. They had lunched together in the embattled town of Albert and bought each other Christmas presents. She still had the pendant on the silver chain, which he had chosen for her as they wandered the town. She had worn it until the day she took her first vows, the day she ceased to be Sarah Hurst and became Sister Marie-Pierre. Now the pendant lay in its box with her only other private possessions, two photographs, one of her parents on their wedding day and the other of Freddie himself.

Freddie had returned to the front from that leave married to the sister of John Driver, a brother officer. His bride's name was Heather, but Sarah had never met her.

"I'll come and see you, sis, as soon as I get any local leave," Freddie had promised. "I want to show you my wedding photo. I want you to see Heather . . . I know you'll love her, too."

Freddie had never come. He was given no leave in the weeks that ran up to "the big push", the battle of the Somme, and she never saw him again. Freddie had led his men into the mayhem of the 1st July 1916 and had not returned. Sarah had known that Heather was expecting Freddie's child and it was with a bitter-sweetness that she heard of the birth of her niece, Adelaide, in September. "A tiny piece of Freddie is living on," she had written to her father.

In the last months of the war her father had asked Sarah to change her mind about entering the convent where she had been nursing, and come home to him.

"I've lost my son," he wrote, "I've lost my granddaughter now that her mother is going to remarry and that man is planning to adopt her. I need you, Sarah. You're all I have left. At least come home for a while."

When the war had finally drawn to a close and she could be spared from the convent hospital Sarah decided that she must go and see her father once more. She sought out her aunt, Sister St Bruno, and explained the situation to her. Aunt Anne was sympathetic. She, too, had left home to take up her vocation in the face of a disapproving and reproachful family.

"I think you should go and see him, just once more," she advised. "He has indeed lost all those most dear to him, and he will be feeling very lonely. I know you will be strong enough to withstand his wishes that you come home, but if you are not, well so be it. Maybe the Lord intends you to stay with him for a while. Go and see Mother. Talk to her about it. She is very wise. She will understand and know what is the best thing for you to do. You are, after all, only a novice. If you wanted to leave the convent, releasing you would not be difficult."

Sarah took her advice and explained the situation to Reverend Mother.

"I know that God wants me here with you in the convent," Sarah said, "but I need to see my father once more and explain to him, face to face, why I can't go home as he wants me to."

"You must certainly go, Sister," Reverend Mother said. "If you are sure of your vocation, a trip to England will not change that, and if it does, then you were mistaken in your vocation. You may be absent from the convent for one week. Then you must come back and if necessary we will review the situation."

Sir George had expected her to return home to Charlton Ambrose, but Sarah had vetoed that. She knew that despite her vocation to be a nun, it would be more difficult to refuse her father if she were back in her childhood home. So it was agreed that they should meet at the home of Sir George's sister, Lady Horner, in Carver Square.

The last time Sarah had been to stay with her aunt was on her way to France in 1915. When she arrived at the house this time, nothing had changed. She paused on the windswept doorstep and looked round the rather shabby square. It all looked the same and yet her last visit seemed an eternity away. When the door was opened, Roberts, the butler, greeted her in the hall, addressed her as "Miss Sarah" and showed her into Lady Horner's drawing room, without a flicker of surprise at her unusual dress.

Her father was waiting for her alone in the room. As she was announced he rose unsteadily to his feet and looked across at his daughter, his beloved Sarah, swathed in a floor-length black robe and her face framed by a starched wimple and headdress.

She paused on the threshold, smiling uncertainly. "Pop . . . ?" She held out her hands and then as he still made no move, she crossed the room to him, and took his hands in hers. For a moment her eyes searched his face. He looked older, much older. His eyes had sunk into their sockets, his skin was parchment, his grey hair wispy and thin.

"Pop," she said again. "Dearest Pop, aren't you pleased to see me?"

"Sarah." His voice was hoarse and he cleared his throat. "Sarah, I can't bear to see you dressed like that."

"It's still me inside, Pop," she said gently, and reached up to kiss his cheek. Her hood got in the way and he made an impatient exclamation.

"For God's sake, Sarah," he said, "can't you take that damned headgear off so I can get a proper look at you?"

Sarah had known it would be difficult for him, but she hadn't realised just how difficult. With trembling hands she unbuttoned her collar and removed the starched headdress, revealing her hair cropped short underneath, a ragged urchin cut, kept short with an unconcerned slash of the scissors.

"Oh Sarah, what have they done to your beautiful hair?" he cried.

"It's more comfortable to keep it short, Pop," she said shakily, "and no one can see how it looks." It had taken Sarah, herself, some time to come to terms with the loss of her hair. When she had first gone to the convent it was long and thick, and had to be bundled up out of the way under her nurse's cap.

She had put her arms round him then, an awkward embrace until he had suddenly returned it with a crushing hug.

"If you would like me to change, Father," Sarah said softly, "I have permission to wear my old skirt and blouse within the house."

"Permission!" Sir George almost shouted the word, and then as suddenly his shoulders sagged and he said quietly, "It would please me to see you once more as you were when you left . . . except for . . ." he waved a hand in the direction of her hair.

Sarah went to her room and removed the long black habit, replacing it with the white blouse and grey skirt that she had worn for nursing in the convent hospital. She stared at herself in the mirror. She hadn't seen her face since she had taken the veil of a novice. She looked much the same, she decided, though her short hair gave her face a different shape from when it had been crowned with a tumble of dark curls. In the days before the war she could look very sophisticated with her hair swept up off her face, emphasising her slender neck. Now she looked like a scrubbed-up charity child.

Feeling almost undressed in her plain skirt and blouse, she returned to the drawing room where her father awaited her and where Roberts had brought in the tea tray.

They had sat down and talked then, mostly about Freddie and the wife and child he had left behind.

36

"Heather is marrying again," Sir George told her. "Some chap in the city. I understand he's planning to adopt little Adelaide."

"Perhaps that's the best thing for them both," Sarah replied. "Freddie wouldn't have wanted Heather to spend the rest of her life alone, would he?"

Sir George sighed. "Maybe not, but it's hard to see your son replaced so quickly."

"It's not that quickly, Pop," Sarah answered gently. "It's almost three years since he died. Adelaide will be three in September, she needs a father. Freddie wouldn't have wanted to deny her that."

"She needs a grandfather, too," said the old man bitterly, "but they never come down to Charlton Ambrose to see me. The only times I've seen my granddaughter are when I've come up to London expressly to do so. I am allowed to visit her at her maternal grandparents' home for half an hour, always in their company. It's as if they thought I was going to run off with her."

"Shall I be able to meet Heather and Adelaide while I'm here?" asked Sarah eagerly.

Sir George shook his head. "No, I'm afraid not. They're visiting friends in Derbyshire."

"Didn't you let them know I was coming?" asked Sarah in dismay. "Didn't you tell them I was coming? You must have known I'd want to see Adelaide."

"I told them," Sir George said heavily. "I said that you'd want to see Adelaide, but they said they were engaged to join a house party for a week in Derbyshire and felt it would be rude to cry off."

"The very week that I am able to come home?" asked Sarah, incredulous.

"Precisely," said Sir George. "This is what I am saying. We are to be cut out of that child's life. This Richard Anson-Gravetty is to be her father now. Freddie is to be forgotten." His voice cracked as he spoke, and he looked away. Sarah longed to hug him and comfort him, but she knew that he might break down and would be ashamed of such weakness, so she simply waited in silence for him to regain his composure.

Sarah stayed for five days in Carver Square. She didn't leave the house as that would have required her to don her habit once more, and she knew her father hated to see her in it. They spent their days talking, talking as they had never talked in all their years. Both of them realised that this would be the last time they saw each other in this world, and each of them clung to every minute.

Then, at last, on her final evening in London Sir George grasped the nettle. "You won't be coming home again, will you, Sarah?"

They were sitting on either side of the fireplace and Sarah looked across at him with tears in her eyes. "No, Pop darling, I shan't."

The endearment, so unusual between them, was nearly his undoing, but he managed to maintain his countenance. "Then we must discuss what will happen when I die."

Sarah stared at him uncomprehendingly. This turn of conversation was entirely unexpected.

"There is no one to inherit the title. I suspect if Adelaide had been a boy they wouldn't have been so quick to change her name. Still, be that as it may, I intend to make her my heir in everything else. You will be provided for now. I am going to give you a dowry for your convent, and that will be now, not in my will. Everything else I shall leave in trust for young Adelaide, to be hers absolutely on her twenty-first birthday, but I shall choose the trustees. That man shall not get his hands on her money at any stage."

"Is he really as bad as you make him out to be?" asked Sarah.

"Probably not," admitted her father, "but he's a damned cold fish. I am sure it is he that prevents Heather bringing the child to see me. He wants nothing to do with her former husband's family. He'd probably prefer Heather without the child, but even she wouldn't hear of that, meek little thing though she is. Can't think what Freddie saw in her!"

"Pop," said Sarah, "you must do whatever you think is right for Adelaide. It is very generous of you to give me a dowry for the convent. I know you don't want me to go back, but it's where I belong."

Sir George looked away again and murmured, "On that we shall have to agree to differ, my child."

Wanting to change the subject, Sarah said, "Do you know how Molly is? Molly Day and her baby?"

"I have no idea," replied Sir George brusquely. "She came home in disgrace, and as far as I know she lives with her parents. She was very lucky they didn't throw her out. Not only was she expecting, it turned out that the father was a coward and a deserter. Did you know that, Sarah? The man was shot; shot for running away in the face of the enemy. What sort of man is that? What sort of father is that for a child?"

Sarah knew that this was not an accurate account of events, but realised it would be no use to explain what had really happened to the father of Molly's child. She had been going to ask Sir George if he could see his way to giving Molly a little cash, but it was clear from his expression that he would never entertain that idea. It had been an unfortunate choice of subject and Sarah tried to turn him to another.

"How are things generally in the village?" she asked. She knew he took his duties as squire very seriously, and cared about the people of Charlton Ambrose.

"I'm making a memorial to Freddie and the other men who went to the war from the village and didn't come back," he told her. "I'm going to plant some trees on the village green, at the far end. One for each man who died. That way they'll never be forgotten. It'll be a living memorial. What do you think of that idea?"

Tears sprang to Sarah's eyes. "I think it's a wonderful idea, Pop. A living memorial."

Sarah had left the next day, dressed in her nun's habit. Sir George did not accompany her to the station, they took their leave in Lady Horner's drawing room. Their final embrace was an awkward one, cut off as she was inside her wimple and headdress, but as she finally pulled away, Sir George said gruffly, "You're as darned obstinate as your mother, but she'd have been proud of you, Sarah, as proud of you as I am." With that he

40

strode out of the room, leaving Sarah to carry her small bag out to the taxi he had called to take her to Victoria. She knew she would never see him again, and tears streamed down her face all the way to the station.

She had been right, within eighteen months Sir George had been dead, and she had made her final vows. When the news of her father's death came, Sarah wrote to Adelaide, but she received no reply. She had heard from no one in England since that day.

Now she had this letter from Adelaide herself, asking to meet her, asking about Freddie.

Sarah drew a sheet of paper towards her and began to write: "My dear Adelaide . . ."

CHAPTER
THREE

The train chuffed fussily through the flat French countryside, stopping at small stations along the way. Adelaide looked out of the window. It was the first time she had travelled abroad by herself and she felt it was quite an adventure. She had considered hiring a car and driver when she got off the boat, after all, she could well afford to do so now, but she decided it would be more fun to take the local train and soak up the flavour of the country and its people.

As the fields and villages passed by, a living tapestry of French life, she thought about her aunt, living in her convent at St Croix. She had turned out to be the reverend mother, for goodness' sake! Would she be very religious? Would she understand why Adelaide wanted to see her, cut off as she had been from the world for more than twenty years? Adelaide was longing to meet her father's sister, but it was a longing touched with a certain amount of trepidation.

At last the train drew into the station at Albert, and clutching her suitcase, Adelaide got off and made her way outside. In the station yard, she managed to find a taxi to take her to St Croix. It was an elderly Citroën driven by a stout man, his coat stretched across his midriff and a black beret perched on his bald head. He put her small suitcase into the boot and then held the door as she climbed into the car.

"St Croix, you say?" he asked as he squeezed himself in behind the steering wheel.

"Yes, please," Adelaide said, settling herself into the battered seat. "To the convent."

The driver eyed her curiously in the mirror. "You wish to join the sisters?" he asked.

Adelaide laughed. "No, Monsieur. I am merely visiting!"

The taxi drove into St Croix, passing through the square and then along a winding lane to the convent itself, which stood four storeys high overlooking the village below.

What a forbidding place, thought Adelaide as she looked up at the bleak, grey stone walls towering above her. Almost like a fortress.

The taxi dropped her at the main entrance and she walked up the steps to the old oak front door. With its iron hinges and grille, it looked more like a castle gate than the entrance to a convent. Adelaide paused for a moment, and then, drawing a deep breath, tugged on the iron bell-pull. She could hear the bell clanging away in the distance, but almost at once the grille in the door opened and a face peered out.

"May I help you?" The question was, of course, posed in French and Adelaide happily answered in the same.

"Oh, yes please. My name is Adelaide Anson-Gravetty, I've come to see Reverend Mother."

There was a scrape of bolts being drawn, the door swung open and Adelaide was greeted by a small nun who peered at her anxiously. "Mademoiselle Adelaide? I am Sister Celestine. Yes, Mother is expecting you. Please come this way."

Adelaide followed Sister Celestine across the stone-flagged hall and along a corridor. There was no decoration on its stone walls and despite her warm overcoat, Adelaide felt even colder than she had outside. The nun led her up a flight of stairs and opened the door to a small room at one end of a long corridor.

"Here is your room, Mademoiselle. I have put hot water in the jug so that you may wash after your journey. There is a lavatory at the other end of the passage. If you will make yourself comfortable, I will come back in fifteen minutes and take you to Mother. In the meantime, I will tell her you have arrived." So saying Sister Celestine stepped aside to allow Adelaide into the cell-like bedroom, and then closed the door behind her.

Adelaide tossed her case onto the narrow bed, and having shed her hat and coat, crossed to the window to look out. Below her was a courtyard, circled by a high stone wall. Outside this was a field with woodland beyond and over to one side another, walled area, with a tall stone cross at its gate; a cemetery perhaps. The sky was grey and overcast and the view rather depressing. Shivering, Adelaide turned back into the room to find the jug of water Sister Celestine had promised. It stood on the top of a chest of drawers, steam rising from it, and folded neatly beside it was a small white towel. Adelaide washed her hands and face, brushed her hair and paid a quick visit to the lavatory at the end of the corridor. There was no mirror in the room, but she squinted into the small mirror on her powder compact and smiled encouragingly at her reflection.

It's ridiculous to be nervous, she told herself firmly. She's your father's sister, and even if she has turned out to be Reverend Mother, she's your aunt, Sarah.

She chewed on her lips to give them a little more colour, not liking to wear lipstick within the convent, and awaited the return of her guide.

She did not have long to wait. There was a tap on the door and on her calling "Come in," Sister Celestine peered round the door.

"Mother is ready to see you now," she said and led the way into the depths of the huge, grey building.

Eventually the nun paused outside a door and knocked gently. A bell sounded from within and she opened the door.

"Mademoiselle Adelaide is here, Mother," she said and stood aside for Adelaide to enter.

"Thank you, Sister." The voice was soft, with an interesting lilt. "Would you bring us some tea, please."

Adelaide walked into the room and found herself facing a middle-aged nun, rising from a desk and smiling across the room at her.

"Adelaide," she said, her eyes alight with pleasure. "You've really come."

"Aunt Sarah?" began Adelaide and then hesitated. "I'm sorry, perhaps I should call you Reverend Mother?" Her voice rose interrogatively as she paused just inside the door.

"Just Sarah, I think," replied the nun cheerfully. "You're almost the only one in the world who can call me by that name. Come in, come in and sit down. I've had them make up the fire so we can be comfortable." She indicated two chairs, one on either side of a tiny fireplace in which smouldered a small log. Despite the fire, the room was chilly, but Sarah did not seem to notice. "I hope Sister Celestine has shown you your room and made you comfortable." She added with a laugh, "It's a tiny room I'm afraid, but you're luckier than I was when I first arrived, I had to share it!"

"It's fine, thank you," Adelaide replied, still standing a little awkwardly by the door.

"Come here, my dear. Let me look at you," Sarah said. She took Adelaide's hands in hers and turned her face to the light of the window. "My dearest girl," she said with a break in her voice, "you could be your father."

They stared at each other for a moment, Sarah with tears in her eyes, then as if suddenly recollecting herself she said, "I'm sorry, Adelaide, do come to the fire and sit down. Sister Celestine will bring us some tea directly, I'm sure you'd like something warm to drink after your long journey. Tea is the one thing I have allowed myself as a treat since I became Reverend Mother. The sisters indulge me, and, I think, smile at my English ways behind my back."

Adelaide suddenly realised that they had, quite naturally, been speaking in French. She said, "Aunt . . . Sarah, how do you come to be a nun in a French convent?"

"That, my child, is a long story and bound up with the story of your father, too. I will tell you, of course, but let's have our tea first. I think I hear Sister Celestine at the door." Sure enough there was a light tap on the door, which swung open, and Sister Celestine struggled in with a tray, which she set down on the desk. On it were a teapot and two cups and saucers.

"Thank you, Sister," Reverend Mother said, and with a bob of her head the nun left the room.

"I hope you can drink tea without milk," Sarah said as she poured them each a cup of tea. "If the French ever drink tea it is almost always without milk!"

When they were sitting on either side of the fire, Sarah stared across at her niece, her eyes drinking her in as if she couldn't get enough of her. Adelaide sipped her tea, and said nothing, allowing her to look.

"Adelaide, I am so glad you wrote," Sarah said at last. "I have had no news from England since my father died in 1920. That's a very long time. I did write to you at the time, but of course you were only a tiny child then and you wouldn't remember the letter."

Adelaide smiled ruefully. "I doubt if I ever got it, Aunt Sarah," she said. "I think my father . . . my adoptive father . . . didn't want me to know that he wasn't my natural father. As I explained in my letter, I only found out about Freddie and you on my twenty-first birthday."

"I can understand that he wanted you to think of him as your real father," Sarah said. "But I think he was misguided. A person needs to know where she comes from."

"I think so too," agreed Adelaide, "which is why I am here now. I want to know about Freddie's family. I am afraid I've come to think of him as Freddie in the last few weeks. Father still means the father I've grown up with."

"Of course it does," Sarah agreed, "and so it should. He has been your father all your life. But Freddie is there too." She smiled across at Adelaide again, saying, "You really are so like him, especially when you smile. Did your mother see it, I wonder?"

"She said so," Adelaide replied, "in the letter I was given on my birthday. I've brought it with me, in case you wanted to read it."

Sarah shook her head. "No, Adelaide, I'm sure it is far too personal, but I am so glad so much of Freddie lives on in you."

The late afternoon light began to fade as they sat and drank their tea and Sarah lit the lamp that stood on a stand behind her desk. A bell began to toll in the distance and Sarah got to her feet. "I have to go to the chapel now for vespers. If you would like to join us, please do. If not, you can wait here and after vespers I will come and fetch you for the evening meal. After that, in recreation, we'll be able to talk properly for a while."

48

"I think I would like to come to the chapel with you, if that's all right. My mother was a Catholic too, and though I don't go to Mass as often as I should, I have been brought up in the faith."

Reverend Mother smiled. "I'm glad," she said simply. "Follow me."

She led the way through the winding corridors of the convent, joining with a flow of sisters heading towards the chapel. Adelaide was shown to a seat at the back, and she watched with interest as the sisters filed into their stalls. Before the nuns began to sing their office, there was a scuffling of feet and five children were led into the chapel by a flustered-looking novice. They sat down on a row of chairs just in front of Adelaide. Four of them were girls and all dressed the same in grey skirts, white blouses and pinafores. Each had her hair tied back off her face and each wore a white cap on her head. The fifth was a boy, aged about seven, with closely cropped hair that stood in a tuft at the back of his head.

"They're our orphans," Sarah told her when, after a supper of soup, bread and cheese, they repaired once more to her office. "After the war there were several children in the village who were left without fathers. One poor mother asked if we would accept her nine-year-old daughter as a novice. She had five other children and nothing to feed them with.

"Reverend Mother at the time refused to take the child as a novice, she was far too young, but she did agree to give her a home until she was old enough to make up her own mind. That made other families want

49

to do the same. Three of our children were truly orphans, passed on to us by an aunt who couldn't cope. Once the word got round that we accepted children, several have been deposited on our doorstep . . . what my father would have called children of shame!"

"And you took them all in?"

"Of course. Where else could the poor mites go? I was asked by Mother to look after them, to see to their day-to-day care and teach them, so that one day, should they choose to leave the convent, they would be able to earn their living in the world."

"Did you want to do that?" asked Adelaide with interest. "I thought you were a nurse."

Sarah laughed. "I was, after a fashion, but never a good one. Oh, I could scour bedpans and make beds, but the real nursing was left to those much more skilled than I. Anyway, as the wounded soldiers finally went home there was less call on our little hospital. No, I was delighted to take on the children. Our mother house in Paris also has an orphanage, and so it was well within the work of our order."

"And you've had orphans ever since?" asked Adelaide.

Sarah sighed. "They still turn up on our doorstep from time to time. We've never turned one away. I don't have the daily care of them now. That is the work of Sister Danielle. She, and one of the novices, Sister Marie-Joseph, take care of them now, and they go to the village school, so that they are part of the local community."

50

"And the hospital? Has that gone? Are you no longer a nursing order?" asked Adelaide.

"After the war, when the last of our wounded had been sent home, a new, small hospital was built just outside the walls. Just two wards, one for men and the other for women. That is where we still nurse the local people, and look after the dying. During the war there were huts in the courtyard outside, dreadful, ramshackle affairs, but we needed the space then and they were better than nothing. Those, I'm glad to say, have gone. They were pulled down when the new hospital was built." She sighed. "We're kept busy enough, but nothing like the flood of wounded that came back from the front."

"Tell me about my father," Adelaide said. "Tell me about Freddie."

Sarah smiled reminiscently. "Dear Freddie. He was the best of brothers. Our mother died when our younger brother, James, was born. He didn't survive either, so there was my father and just the two of us. We were very close. When Freddie joined up in 1914 I missed him dreadfully, and when he wrote to us telling us of the dreadful state of affairs in the hospitals behind the lines, I persuaded my father to let me come, with my maid, Molly, to help nurse the wounded."

"But why here?" asked Adelaide.

"Because nowhere else would have me! I was too young to join the VAD and anyway they wouldn't have let me come to France for years. I wanted to be there straight away, to help. I'd done some Red Cross training and I thought I could be of use." She gave a short laugh. "It turned out that my maid, Molly, was far more useful than I was. She knew how to make a bed, to do laundry, to scrub floors. And as it happened, she turned out to be a natural nurse."

"But why here?" persisted Adelaide. "Why this convent?"

"Because my aunt was already here. My mother's younger sister had joined the convent while I was still a child. It was she who persuaded the reverend mother that I could come and help. Persuading my father was the hardest part, but I finally managed it. So Molly and I came, and I've been here ever since."

"What happened to Molly? Is she a nun too?"

Sarah laughed. "No, not Molly! She was decidedly Protestant. She didn't approve of all this Popery at all. She only came with me because I pressed her to. My father really wouldn't have allowed me to come completely alone." Sarah sighed. "No, poor Molly fell in love with one of her patients, and when he . . . died . . . she was sent home in disgrace because she was expecting his child."

"How sad!" Adelaide said. "What happened to her?"

"She went home to her parents and had the baby there. It wasn't a happy household. When I took my vows I sent her all the money I had left. It wasn't much, but I hoped it would give her a chance to break free and live her own life."

"So where is she now?" asked Adelaide, fascinated by this story.

Sarah shook her head. "I don't know. I've had no news of her since my father died. I have written of course, but I've never received a reply. I don't think she can have received my letters or I am sure she would have answered." She gave a shake of the head. "Now, I have something else to tell you, which I hope will please you. Your great-aunt, my mother's sister, is still alive and here in the convent. She is almost bedridden now, poor dear, but her mind is as sharp as ever. I've told her you're coming and she asked me to bring you up to see her before compline."

Adelaide stared at her for a moment. "You mean I've another aunt alive that I knew nothing about?"

Sarah nodded and rose to her feet. "Sister St Bruno. Your Great-Aunt Anne. Come and meet her."

Together they went through the convent, past the common room where Adelaide heard several of the nuns gathered for their hour of recreation and upstairs to a small room on the first floor. Sarah tapped on the door and then opened it, peeping round before going in.

"Are you awake, Sister?" she asked softly.

"Of course, Mother, please come in."

Sarah opened the door wide and ushered Adelaide into the room. An elderly woman was sitting up in bed, a shawl over her head and another round her thin shoulders. Glasses were perched on her nose and she had an open Bible on the bed beside her.

"I've brought Adelaide to see you, Sister. You know, Freddie's daughter. Adelaide, this is your Great-Aunt Anne."

"Freddie's daughter . . . Charlotte's granddaughter." The voice was so soft that Adelaide could hardly hear the words, but she crossed the room to the old woman's bedside and reached for her hands. Thin and papery though they were, they gripped hers fiercely as the old nun peered up into her face. "You have the look of Charlotte," she said.

"Sarah . . . Reverend Mother . . . says I look like Freddie," said Adelaide.

"She may be right," agreed her aunt, "but I hardly knew him. No, you have Charlotte's eyes, though your colouring is not quite the same." She patted the bed and said, "Will you sit with me for a few minutes? Mother, I'm sure you can spare her."

"Of course," Sarah said. "I'll come and collect you just before compline." She smiled at her aunt. "Now don't tire yourself, Sister, Adelaide will come and see you again tomorrow, I promise. She's staying with us for three days."

Adelaide sat on the bed as directed and smiled at the old lady. "It must be very strange to call your niece 'Mother'," she said.

"Not really," replied Sister St Bruno. "There is always a reverend mother, just now it happens to be my niece. She has only just been elected, but I think she will make a good job of it. She is well respected by the sisters, despite the fact that she's English. Most of them have forgotten that by now anyway. She is strong and stands up for what she believes." The old lady laughed. "She wouldn't be here at all if she hadn't stood up to her father on more than one occasion. No, I think the convent is in good hands while she is Reverend Mother, and that is how I address her . . . in public."

Adelaide smiled. "And she calls you Sister."

"She has done so ever since she took the veil. It is as it should be." The old lady gave a conspiratorial smile. "Except when we're alone, then we're Sarah and Aunt Anne."

"Will you tell me about my grandmother, your sister, Charlotte?"

"Ah, Charlotte, she was another very strong-minded one . . ."

When Sarah came back to collect her, Adelaide could hardly believe she had been sitting by the old nun's bedside for nearly half an hour.

"She'll come and see you again tomorrow, I promise," Sarah said as she took her aunt's hand and tucked it under the covers. "God bless you, Sister."

That night Adelaide lay in the narrow bed in the room her aunt had shared with her maid Molly all those years ago and thought about all she had learned that day. What a day! Two new relations, both full of stories about their family . . . her family. Telling her of Freddie, her father, the man with dark hair and dark eyes so like her own; whose smile matched her own.

Sarah had shown her a faded snapshot of Freddie, not in his uniform, but in comfortable country clothes in the garden of his own home, petting his dog and grinning up at the camera. Even Adelaide could see the likeness between them, and she felt an ache in her heart that she had never known this laughing man, her father.

She heard of a man with all his life before him, who had led his men into the trenches and beyond. Of the war; of the courage of two young women, setting off to a foreign hospital to "do their bit" for King and country; of the horrors they had found and the wounded they had nursed. Adelaide was amazed by their courage, their stamina, their devotion to duty. She wondered as she drifted off to sleep, could she have ever done something like that?

The next two days Adelaide spent exploring the village and surrounding countryside. Although it was November and the days were short, it was relatively mild and the wintry sun still probed the drifting clouds. She walked along the riverbank, and drank coffee in the little café called Le Chat Noir on the village *place*. She attended several services in the convent chapel. She talked to the orphans when they came home from the village school, playing ludo and snakes and ladders and telling them stories. After the midday meal she spent some time with Sister St Bruno, her Great-Aunt Anne, and heard childhood stories of her grandmother. During recreation she sat with Sarah and listened to tales of her father, his exploits as a boy, his experiences in the trenches, his brief courtship of her mother, and wished that she had had the chance to know them all. It was on such an evening as this that she brought up the question of the money she had inherited.

"I've seen the will," she told Sarah, "and it worries me. There's no mention of you in it. Surely your father should have left half what he had to you."

Sarah took her hand. "Bless you," she said, "but there's no need to worry about that. My father provided for me when he was still alive." And she told Adelaide about her trip to London at the end of the war. "He was determined that the money should come to you and that no one else should have any control over it once you were of age. So, my dear, have it, enjoy it, use it for good. That's what he really wanted for you. Remember, he was a charitable man. Follow in his footsteps and he would be proud of you."

On the last morning, when she was due to leave the convent, Adelaide sat with Sarah for the last time.

Sarah opened a drawer in her desk and pulled out a box. Inside it was the photo of Freddie that Adelaide had already seen. Sarah held it out to her niece.

"You must take this," she said. "It is important that you have a picture of your father to keep."

Adelaide didn't take the snapshot, but shook her head. "No, thank you. You must keep it," she insisted. "It's yours."

"No," Sarah said firmly. "I can remember what he looked like very well. You must have it . . . and this, too." She took something else out of the box and held it out to Adelaide. It was a silver pendant on a chain. Sarah placed it in Adelaide's hand and closed her fingers over it.

"Freddie gave it to me on the last day that I saw him," she said. "I would like you to have it now." And, as Adelaide began to protest, she went on, "I can't wear it, Adelaide, it is a waste for me to keep it in a box. It gave me great pleasure when he gave it to me, and I wore it all the time, but since I can't wear it and enjoy it anymore I would like you to wear it for me. See, the pendant is a St Christopher . . . to keep you safe."

"Sarah . . . what can I say?" Adelaide looked at the photo and the pendant, all she had left of her father, all Sarah had left of her brother."

"They're yours," Sarah said firmly. "And don't worry," she added with a twinkle, "I've kept the one of my parents . . . and that's as it should be."

As Adelaide went down the steps to the waiting taxi, she turned back to see her aunt, the reverend mother of the convent of Our Lady of Mercy, watching her go. Her final words still rang in Adelaide's ears. "Remember, my dearest girl, that though we may see very little of each other, you are very dear to me and will be in my prayers. Write to me, Adelaide, and tell me of your life. Let me know when Freddie has grandchildren."

Adelaide had laughed at that. "That's a long way off, I'm afraid," she said.

"Even so, keep in touch so that I have news of you and can pass it on to Sister St Bruno."

As the taxi drew away Adelaide found she had tears in her eyes. She dashed them away. How stupid to cry, she thought. I've found a new family. That's nothing to cry about!

CHAPTER
FOUR

All day long there had been the distant sound of aeroplanes, the thunder of artillery and the rattle of machine guns from the advancing armies of the Reich combined with the last desperate efforts of the allied armies to hold them at bay.

The sound of gunfire reverberated across the countryside, and on every road there were retreating troops, ambulances carrying the wounded, and adding to the confusion of the retreat were the civilian refugees. These straggled along the roads, a slow-moving stream of humanity heading westward, pushing their worldly goods in prams, wheelbarrows and handcarts. Mothers wheeled small children perched on the saddles and crossbars of ancient bicycles; older children carried babies or led their younger brothers and sisters by the hand as they struggled along the road. The very old and the very young, the most vulnerable, trudging together in the vain hope of outrunning the invading Germans. The air was alive with Heinkels, harrying those in retreat, so that the retreating soldiers and the fleeing refugees continually had to dive in panic for the scant cover of hedge or ditch at the roadside. With no opposition, the planes screamed out of the sky, their machine guns strafing the columns winding slowly along the roads, tracer ripping through civilians and military alike.

Dead and wounded littered the road. The dead left to lie where they had fallen, the wounded struggling on as best they could, supported by their comrades or their friends. Few had any doubts as to the outcome of the German advance; many had already tasted their merciless brutality as they had torn through towns and villages, the Panzers advancing, clearing the road in front of them with indiscriminate shells.

The Leon family was among the refugees. They were making for Bordeaux where Mathilde Leon had cousins. Her husband, Marc, was in the army, but she hadn't heard from him for weeks and didn't even know if he were alive or dead. As the Germans flooded over the border, she had decided that they must leave their home, taking only what they could pile into the baby's pram and try to get to what she hoped was the safety of her cousin Jacques' home. She had heard what had been happening to the Jews in Germany, and she knew that if they remained where they were, they would be in the most desperate danger when the Germans arrived. Already their little shop had had its windows broken and daubed with paint, and that wasn't even by Germans but by one of their French neighbours. Mathilde didn't know who had done it, none of her neighbours had appeared to care before that the Leons were Jews, but now? She decided it was a sign of the times, and the times to come, and for the children's sake she felt that they should try and get away to safety.

She could only hope that they would be safer with Jacques, but in any case she couldn't think of anywhere else to go.

They had tried to stay off the main roads. Mathilde didn't want her little family to become mixed up with the columns of soldiers who seemed to be in full retreat before the oncoming German tanks. She would have preferred to have travelled at night, but it was hard enough to keep moving in the daylight along roads they didn't know, through villages where they were greeted with hostile stares. David, her eldest, was doing his best to be the man of the family, but he was only nine and could do little to help except hold his younger sister, Catherine's, hand and sing her songs to keep her going. Mathilde herself had baby Hannah hoisted on her hip in a sling, and was pushing the pram that contained their scant supply of food and water and a few clothes for each of them.

When they reached the town of Albert, they found it seething with refugees like themselves, and Mathilde decided that they might do better to travel in a larger group. There were other Jewish families and, even in the crowd, there was mutual recognition. They huddled together, aware that they were being eyed suspiciously by those around them. That night they all slept together in the bus station. There were no buses, but at least it gave them some shelter from the drizzle that had been drenching them all day.

Mathilde gave her children some bread and a sliver of cheese each, and tried to beg some milk for the baby.

61

The little she had been able to bring with her had soon run out, for Hannah had a healthy appetite.

One woman, who seemed to be alone, took pity on her and poured a little milk into a cup.

"Here you are," she said as she handed it over. "It's all I can spare, but it'll give the poor little mite something in her stomach."

"Thank you, you are so kind," said Mathilde. "Let me give you this in return." And she passed over the crust of bread that would have been her own supper.

The other woman took it, thanking her gravely. "We must hope we can find more food tomorrow," she said. "Albert is quite big. There must be some shops that still have food to sell."

Very early in the morning, with hunger gnawing at her insides, Mathilde took the children away from the others into a small park. Here she told David to sit with his sister and not to move while she went to try and find some food.

The little boy nodded solemnly and sat on the ground with his back against a wall, Catherine on the grass beside him. Mathilde dare not leave the pram in the sole charge of a nine-year-old boy, anyone might take it from him, so with some misgivings she placed Hannah in the pram on top of their worldly goods, and made ready to push it ahead of her as she went in search of food.

"Whatever happens, don't move," Mathilde told him. "Stay here until I get back. Promise me now. I shan't be long."

David promised and, with an anxious glance over her shoulder, Mathilde set off into the town to find them something to eat.

She was gone the best part of an hour, but when she returned there was a loaf of bread tucked into the pram beside Hannah. This she tore into pieces and gave to the two older children. For Hannah she tore the crumb out from the crust and soaking it in a little of their precious water, made it into a soggy pap that Hannah could suck from her mother's fingers. The crust she ate herself.

The town was awake now and people were going about their business. Many of the other refugees had already moved on, and Mathilde was anxious to leave as well. While searching for food she had become aware of the sidelong glances people were giving her, not exactly open hostility, but obvious mistrust. It was time to get out of this terrified town. She knew they had to travel westwards, so with the sun at her back she took the road out of town. The going was slow, the road uneven and very bumpy for the pram. With Hannah on her hip, she let the other children take turns riding in the pram, and that way they moved a little faster than the previous day. Even so, she knew that they had to keep stopping to rest or the children would never keep going.

Once they heard planes high overhead, and Mathilde looked round wildly for some cover, but there was none. The land stretched away in all directions, flat and almost featureless except for a line of poplar trees away in the distance and the occasional straggling farm buildings. However, the planes were quite high and droned away into the clouds to the north of them. She could hear intermittent gunfire from that direction too, and once there was a big boom as if something had blown up, but it seemed some distance away and she tried not to think about it.

As the morning progressed they began to catch up with other refugees who had set out earlier than they had. Old men and women, young mothers like her with children at their skirts, all plodding along the same straight road. Far ahead they could see the roofs of a village, above which towered a tall, grey stone building with a turret on one end, a chateau perhaps.

We'll stop there for a proper rest, Mathilde thought, and try to get something else to eat. Maybe there's a farm that will be able to sell us a little milk for Hannah. But it would be at a price, she knew that, and her small supply of cash was dwindling at an alarming speed. Everything cost so much . . . and the price tended to rise when the person who was selling knew you were desperate.

They were travelling in a much larger group now, about forty or fifty people strung out along the lane leading into the village. The road was edged with shallow drainage ditches, and above these were low hedges on either side to keep the cattle safely in their fields.

Thank God, Mathilde thought fervently. If there are cattle in the fields there must be milk to buy.

Suddenly the air seemed to explode around them and from nowhere two planes screamed out of the sky, guns blazing as they dived low, skimming the hedgerows and strafing the meandering line of refugees. With a scream Mathilde grabbed Catherine from her place in the pram, and, shrieking David's name, flung herself to the ground, rolling towards the illusory shelter of the hedge. Tracer bullets, bouncing, fiery red, ricocheted off the road, ripping through the panicking people. The planes roared up and away, spiralling into the sky, only to turn again and make another murderous pass low over the people scattered in the road. The rattle of the guns and the howl of the engines created a terrifying blast of sound, drowning the shrieks and cries of their victims below. Mathilde had rolled onto Hannah who had been riding on her hip and the baby, now beneath her in the ditch, was screaming. Catherine fell from her mother's arms landing head first in the hedge, and David, who had been walking a little way ahead, had turned to stare up at the planes, until his mother's agonised scream had made him too dive for cover. The planes came in low, spraying their helpless victims with gunfire, the shriek of their engines almost more terrifying than the barrage of bullets. This time when they were clear, they did not come back, but thundered off into the sky leaving chaos on the ground behind them. In less than two minutes they had reduced the line of refugees to a confused mass of dead, dying and wounded.

People were screaming and crying as the agonies of the wounded rose in their throats. David could hear Hannah howling, and whimpering himself, he crawled to where he could see his mother sheltering in the hedge. Only his mother made no move to calm or quiet the bellowing baby, she lay on her side, her body on top of Hannah, and beside her lay Catherine, one arm flung out as if she were reaching for something.

"Maman, Maman," he wailed, pulling at his mother's arm. She rolled over and looked up at him, but her eyes didn't look right. They were staring at him, but they weren't smiling at him or even crying with shock or pain. The crying was coming from Hannah, still crushed under her mother's body, the body that had saved her life at the cost of its own. Still not understanding what had happened, David continued to shake his mother to make her look at him properly and not in that staring way. But she didn't move and her eyes still gazed up into his face.

"Maman, you must move, you're squashing Hannah," he told her. "You're making her cry!" When his mother still didn't move, he pulled at her and managed to move her shoulders so that she tipped to one side and he was able to pull Hannah from the sling on her mother's hip and drag her clear. Hannah continued to scream, her little face scarlet and contorted with fury, her cheeks tear-stained and filthy from the ditch.

David tried to shush her, but it was useless, so he laid her carefully on the ground and bent down to look at Catherine. She lay half in the ditch, half in the hedge, with blood running down her face. She was moaning softly, but her eyes were shut and she didn't look at him. He tried shaking his mother again but it was no good, she wouldn't get up. Her head was turned away now and she wasn't looking at him anymore. That was when David saw the blood coming from a hole in her neck. He stared at it for a moment as he began to take in what it meant. It meant that Maman wasn't going to get up again . . . ever. It meant that she had been hit by the bullets from the planes and that she was dead. David let out a wail and gathering up the still screaming baby in his arms he sat on the ground, rocking backwards and forwards, backwards and forwards, backwards and forwards.

Gradually the carnage left by the Heinkels resolved itself into those who, miraculously, were not hurt, those who were wounded and those who were dead. The unhurt and the wounded struggled to their feet again, wanting to move on, away from this place of death. Those with dead companions knelt beside them and wept, before dragging them clear of the road to be left behind. All the time swivelling their eyes skywards, watching for the aircraft, straining their ears for the throb of the engines that would herald their return. But the sky was empty, the air was quiet except for the cries of the wounded and the wails of the children. The hunters, having wreaked their havoc on this little company of refugees, were searching prey elsewhere.

Slowly, those who could began to walk again, on towards the village that lay so close around the corner. Those too badly injured to walk were heaved onto handcarts, carried or supported by their friends . . . or simply left behind.

Some tried to gather up their scattered possessions, taking them into their arms, or if their handcarts or barrows had survived the onslaught, piling their and other peoples' goods onto those and pushing them away. One old man edged towards the upturned pram beside the three children, but David screamed at him.

"Go away! That's our pram! Go away! Go away!" Dumping the still screaming Hannah unceremoniously on the ground beside him, David picked up a stone and hurled it at the man. It hit him in the midriff and the man hesitated, squinting at the small boy who was already reaching for another stone. David continued to yell at him and hurl stones until the old man turned away and went in search of easier pickings.

David flopped down panting with fright and having looked once more at his mother, realised that it was up to him now. Papa had said when he went away to the war that David must look after Maman for him, that he must be the man of the house and help Maman with the girls.

"They're only little girls, David," said Papa. "You can help Maman by looking after them when she's busy."

David thought of Papa now and the tears welled up in his eyes. He didn't know where Papa was, and now Maman was dead . . . he knew that . . . so he, David, had to do something.

He crawled over to where Catherine still lay unmoving. She didn't seem to be bleeding now, but she was still moaning in a very frightening way. He knew he had to get help and that they had to get away from here before the planes came back to find them again. Unsteadily, he got to his feet and went to the overturned pram. Most of the things inside had been flung out and he noticed that there were holes in the bottom of it, but with a struggle he was able to right it again. He looked round and found some of their clothes strewn across the road. Under a jersey he found the photo of his father and mother getting married. Maman had brought it with her and wrapped it up in a shirt. Carefully he put it with the other things back in the pram and then made a sort of nest in the clothes for Hannah. She had stopped bawling now and was making a sort of whimpering noise, her fist stuck in her mouth. Carefully he picked her up and lifted her into the pram. Then he covered her with a towel and turned his attention to Catherine. He was just wondering how on earth he was going to move her, when a voice spoke behind him.

"Is she dead?"

David spun round and grabbed the handle of the pram. A woman was standing at the edge of the road looking down at him. David thought she looked a bit familiar, but he didn't know who she was. He held tight to the handle of the pram so that she couldn't take it.

"Is she dead?" the woman asked again, nodding at Catherine.

"No." David's voice came out in a husky whisper, not sounding like him at all. "Maman, she doesn't move and her eyes are staring at me. I think she's dead, but Catherine isn't. She's got blood coming out, but she's making a funny noise, so she isn't dead."

"What will you do?" asked the woman. "Do you want to come with me? I am going on now."

"No. I have to bring Catherine. She's hurt. She's bleeding. I have to find a doctor."

The woman gave a sharp laugh that didn't sound like a real laugh at all, and David took a step back.

"Don't think there's much chance of that," the woman said, "but if you want me to help you get your sister to the village over there, I'll do that."

When David didn't answer she said, "Well, do you? We can't just stand here and wait for those buggers to come back."

David nodded dumbly. He didn't know what to do, but perhaps there was someone in the village that might help if he could only get there.

"Right, then," the woman said, and bending down she scooped Catherine up into her arms and laid her on top of the pram.

Hannah gave a squawk and the woman said, "Lift the baby out. You can carry her. I'll push the pram with the little girl on top."

"What about Maman?" David looked anxiously down at his mother still lying on her side with her face in the hedge.

"You'll have to leave her," the woman replied brusquely, "like everyone else." Then she added, "Did she have any money on her? You ought to look. You'll need money whatever happens to you."

David knew that his mother had her money in a little leather bag tied round her waist under her skirt. Should he take it? Suppose this strange woman took the money away from him. He didn't want to touch his mother again. He didn't want to rummage through her clothes to find the moneybag, but they did need the money.

Losing patience, the woman said, "Here, hold onto the pram. I'll look. Do you know where she hid it?"

David told her and within a moment she was handing him the little leather pouch. "Put it somewhere safe," she instructed. "Not everyone's as honest as I am."

David hoisted Hannah up onto his hip as he had seen his mother do and managed to stuff the bag into his pocket. Then returning the baby to his arms, he looked at the woman again. This time he remembered where he'd seen her.

"You gave Hannah some milk," he said. "Last night."

She didn't answer that, but simply said, "Come on, let's get away from here."

David turned to look at his mother once more and then with a shuddering sob turned to follow the woman who was already wheeling the pram, with Catherine draped across it, along the road towards the next village.

It was still a mile or so, but they made steady progress and half an hour later they trailed into the village square. It was already seething with refugees trying to find shelter for their wounded, food and drink for themselves. The woman kept walking, pushing the pram with the injured child in it, and David was now afraid of losing his new friend. Hannah had at last fallen asleep in his arms, and she lay heavy against his shoulder, but although his arms ached he clutched her to him with one arm and held fast to the woman's skirt with his other hand, so that they should not become separated.

The woman pushed her way through the crowd and headed for a small café that opened off the square. An old lady was sitting in the window looking out at what was happening. The café door was closed, and when she pushed it, as many others had before her, the woman found that it was locked. Undeterred she banged on the window.

"Let us in," she bellowed. "I've an injured child here."

The old lady inside continued to stare, but made no effort to open the door. A young girl came round the side of the café and said, "You can't come in. We've no spare food here."

"It's a doctor we need," snapped the woman. "Which is the doctor's house?"

"He's not there, he's at the hospital."

"Hospital! Where's that, then?"

"Up at the convent," the girl pointed vaguely out of the square.

"Come on," the woman said, and plucking Hannah from David's aching arms, tucked her under her own. She rested her other hand on the handle of the pram. "You'll have to help me push."

Together they skirted the square and headed in the direction of the tall, grey stone building that dominated the village.

Sitting in her small office, the convent accounts spread out on the desk in front of her, Mother Marie-Pierre had been listening to the sound of gunfire. It had seemed a long way off at first, but now it

72

sounded much closer, and planes had twice roared low over the convent before spiralling away into the sky.

It's happening again, she thought bitterly. The Germans are coming, and this time there's no line of trenches to hold them back.

She was right. Even in the comparative seclusion of the convent, news and rumour, often intertwined and indistinguishable, were circulating. News came in from the village with the lay workers. A steady procession of refugees straggled through St Croix, each with his tale to tell. The Germans were coming. The Allies were running. The advance had been stopped. The English were swinging south to save Paris. The English were scuttling back across the Channel to save themselves, leaving France to the mercy of her enemies. Perfidious Albion!

To try and curtail speculation, Mother Marie-Pierre allowed the nuns who wanted to, to listen to one broadcast on the radio each day, and what they heard made desperate listening.

The German Panzer divisions were racing across the country, sometimes as much as thirty or forty miles a day, forcing the allied armies to retreat, squeezing them back to the Pas de Calais. Many of the retreating soldiers, both French and English, had been overtaken, blasted by the tanks, machine-gunned from the air, captured or left wounded or dead at the side of the road. Bridges were blown up, roads destroyed as the Allies retreated, and still the Germans came on, shells flying, guns blazing, unstoppable.

All this they had heard, piecing together the snippets they gleaned, blending them with the official news broadcasts.

It sounds very close today, Mother Marie-Pierre thought. Too close. I must send someone to the village to find out what has happened.

She got to her feet and went in search of Sister Henriette. Sister Henriette was one of the sisters who went visiting regularly in the village, never afraid to go into a house where there was sickness, always with a basket of food on her arm. She was well known and well liked and the people would talk to her.

"See if you can find out what's happening," Mother Marie-Pierre said. "That gunfire sounded very close. It may be that the Germans have arrived in the village. If they have there may be those who need our help. Come straight back once you know what's going on, and we can decide what we need to do. In the meantime I will call all the sisters together so we can discuss it when you get back."

"Yes, Mother." Sister Henriette flung her cloak over her habit and let herself out of the kitchen door. She took the footpath to the village, cutting down through a copse and out onto the lane, which wound down towards the square. As she reached the lane she saw a strange little group of people coming towards her, a dishevelled woman pushing a pram with a child stretched across it, a small boy helping her to push, and tucked wriggling under the woman's arm, a wailing baby.

74

Sister Henriette hurried forward. "Good gracious!" she cried. "What has happened? What's the matter with the little girl? Here, let me take the baby."

The woman relinquished the baby readily into the nun's arms, and detached the boy's fingers from her skirt. "There was a raid on the road. Air attack. These children lost their mother. I don't know how bad the little girl is, but I'll leave them with you now." She let go of the pram and started to turn away.

"Wait! You can't . . ." began Sister Henriette.

"Look, Sister, or whatever you're called. They're nothing to do with me, OK? The mother's lying dead in a ditch along with several others. I just helped them get to you. Now they're your responsibility. They'll be safer with you than they'd ever be with me. I'm on the road . . . and I'm a Jew. They're Jews too, for that matter, but you wouldn't know it to look at them . . . not if you keep the boy's trousers on, that is." She stared into Sister Henriette's astonished face. "I'm telling you, if the Germans find them with me they'll be far worse off. And my chances are better if I travel alone."

"But wait, maybe we can help you . . ." cried Sister Henriette.

"No one will be able to help me if I'm caught by the Germans," the woman said flatly. "Jews disappear, and I don't intend to be one of them."

"At least just come into the convent for a while and rest," urged Sister Henriette.

"If I rest before I'm safe, I'm dead," the woman replied. "If you want to help people, there are plenty that need it in the village square down there." She waved her hand in the direction of the village. "Go down and help them. I'm getting away from here," and turning on her heel she strode on along the lane.

David, staring after her, saw the last link with his mother disappearing and his face crumpled, tears streaming down his cheeks.

Sister Henriette, still holding Hannah, reached out her other hand to him. "Don't cry, little one. You're safe now. Let's go and find you something to eat. I bet you're hungry, aren't you? And we can get a nurse to look at your sister. She is your sister, isn't she? Come along now, I need you to help push the pram like you were before."

She reached for the handle of the pram and started to push it along the lane to the convent. David tugged at her habit, and struggling manfully against his tears said fiercely, "Give me Hannah."

The nun handed him the baby and, giving her full attention to pushing the pram, led them back up the lane to the convent.

CHAPTER
FIVE

Mother Marie-Pierre had summoned the entire community to the recreation room where they squeezed in and listened with growing horror to the news that Sister Henriette brought with her.

When she had arrived back at the convent with three small children and a pram, Mother Marie-Pierre had hurried out to meet them.

"These children have been bombed by the Germans," Sister Henriette told her briefly. "I was told their mother is dead at the roadside, and the little girl," she indicated Catherine still prostrate on the pram, "has been wounded, though I don't know how badly." Hannah was by now making her presence known to Mother Marie-Pierre with ear-splitting wails. Sister Henriette took her from David once more and putting her up over her shoulder, patted her soothingly on the back to quieten her.

Mother Marie-Pierre looked at the small boy with the dirty, tear-streaked face, and crouching down so that their eyes met easily she said softly, "What is your name, *mon brave?*"

David stared at her for several moments, his eyes huge and dark in his pale face taking in another strange lady wearing peculiar clothes. At last, as if he'd come to some sort of decision, he whispered, "David."

"Well, David, I think you are a very brave boy to look after your sisters. Would you like something to eat, while I get the doctor to look at your sister?"

David nodded and when Mother Marie-Pierre reached for the handle of the pram, he grabbed it from her shouting fiercely, "No! You can't have Catherine!"

Mother Marie-Pierre stepped back, lowering her hand. "It's all right, David. You can push the pram, but we do need to get poor Catherine to the doctor, you know. And the little one, she'd like some milk, I'd expect. What's her name?"

David, still grasping the handle of the pram possessively, murmured, "Hannah."

"Well let's go inside and find a doctor for Catherine, some milk for Hannah and perhaps some bread and cheese for you?" She ended on an interrogative note and David nodded again.

"Come along then." Mother Marie-Pierre led the way to the front door where Sister Celestine was waiting, peering anxiously round the doorpost. Mother Marie-Pierre despatched her to the infirmary to fetch the doctor, telling her, on her way, to ask Sister Danielle to come immediately.

Sister Danielle arrived almost at once and Sister Henriette handed Hannah into her care with some relief. Hannah was very hungry and was making her displeasure at the fact very clear.

"Give her some milk and get her clean and dry, please, Sister, while Sister Henriette finds David something to eat. Then we'll see what else needs to be done. Ask Sister Marie-Joseph to come to me as well, please." Mother Marie-Pierre turned back to the little boy, still clinging onto the handle of the pram. She spoke gently. "When the doctor comes we'll get Catherine into bed and make her comfortable. Will you go with Henriette to the kitchen?"

David shook his head. It was clear he did not want to leave Catherine. "Papa said look after the girls," he whispered.

"Was your papa with you?" asked Mother Marie-Pierre.

The boy shook his head again. "Just Maman . . ." His face crumpled and Sister Henriette dropped onto her knees beside him and putting her arms round him, gathered him against her.

For a long while he leaned against her, his sobs muffled in her habit. Sister Henriette looked over his head at Reverend Mother, who nodded briskly and gently lifted the little girl from the pram, carrying her indoors to find the doctor.

At last David's tears began to lessen and he pulled himself free of the nun's arms. "Maman is dead," he said on a sob. "The planes came and shot her. She's in the ditch. We had to leave her in the ditch. I couldn't carry her." He added pitifully, "She'll get cold."

"I know, I know," soothed Sister Henriette. "We'll find her for you. We won't leave her in the ditch, I promise you. You've been so brave, David. We'll help you now. You did what Papa told you to. You've been very strong. He'll be proud of you."

Tentatively Sister Henriette reached for the boy's hand and when he didn't draw away, she went to lead him up the steps, saying as he looked back anxiously at the pram, "Don't worry about your things, they will be quite safe here, I promise you." Still he dragged his feet, so she said brightly, "Tell you what, David, let's go in through the kitchen door and you can leave the pram safely in the yard."

Together they pushed the pram round the building and on reaching the courtyard, Sister Henriette helped him put it into the small shed there before leading him indoors.

Sister Marie-Joseph joined them in the kitchen as David was tucking into bread and cheese and a glass of milk, clearly very hungry.

"Mother wants you in the recreation room," she said to Sister Henriette. "I'm to take David over to the infirmary to see his sisters and to have him checked over by Dr Felix." She smiled down at the boy sitting at the table. "If you come with me, David, you can see your sisters. Catherine is awake now. She had a bump on the head, but the doctor says she'll be fine very soon."

She held out her hand, and David slid off the stool and took it. He found her less intimidating because, although she wore peculiar clothes too, her hat wasn't as big as the other ladies' and she didn't peer at him from underneath it.

When Sister Henriette reached the recreation room she found many of the sisters assembled there. At

Reverend Mother's request she quickly put them in the picture.

"All that gunfire we heard earlier and the planes; that was the Germans firing on a group of refugees," she told them. "Aeroplanes dive bombing them. When I went down, I met a woman who was bringing three children up here. She said their mother was dead at the roadside. There are people in the village who have been wounded. We need to send help at once and prepare beds in the infirmary for the most badly injured." She looked round at her assembled sisters and noticed that most of those who worked in the infirmary were not there.

"Sister Jeanne-Marie has already set off for the village with three others. Sister Eloise is making ready in the hospital," Mother Marie-Pierre said. "The rest of us need to prepare for an influx of injured and frightened people," adding with the ghost of a smile, "just like before."

Mother Marie-Pierre was very glad that some of the nursing sisters who had worked so hard during the last war, caring for the wounded ferried back from the trenches, were still able to work in the infirmary. She would need to rely on their experience and expertise to help them all through this crisis and the many more she expected to come with the arrival of the Germans.

Mother Marie-Pierre was a young reverend mother, but one of her great strengths was to use the gifts of those around her. When Mother Marie-Georges had died a few years after the war, her place had been taken by Sister Magdalene, the sister who had run the convent hospital so efficiently throughout the war. The new reverend mother had at once seen the potential in the newly professed Sister Marie-Pierre, and had put her to work in the growing orphanage. She had not been disappointed in her choice. Before long Sister Marie-Pierre had been given charge of the orphans and over the years Mother Magdalene had come to rely on her, respecting her judgement and seeking her opinion on matters which arose. Mother Magdalene had also been a comparatively young reverend mother, and had supervised the running of the convent for almost fourteen years before she had been summoned to the order's mother house in Paris. Despite her youth and the fact that many of the other sisters were technically more senior than she, it was Sister Marie-Pierre she left in charge while she was away. Again her confidence was not misplaced. The strange English girl, who had arrived of her own volition to help nurse the wounded during the Great War, had proved her worth as a member of the community, and Mother Magdalene knew that she would one day be capable of taking over from her.

Now in her mid-sixties, Mother Magdalene had moved to the Paris convent permanently as the overall mother superior of the order, leaving the community in St Croix in little doubt as to whom she wanted them to elect as her successor. There had been those who doubted the wisdom of her choice and one or two who resented that such a young sister — Sister Marie-Pierre was not much more than forty — had been placed over them, demanding their unquestioning obedience. On the whole, however, the choice had been considered a good one. She was always ready to listen to what anyone had to say, welcomed discussion, and when she finally made a decision her reasons were explained so that everyone understood her action. Thus, she soon had the complete loyalty of most of her sisters.

Now, in a crisis, her unquestioned authority paid dividends as she quickly organised the sisters to deal with the emergency. Sister Danielle who, with Sister Marie-Joseph, now looked after the orphans, quickly took the Leon children into her domain and tried to make them comfortable. Catherine had been kept in the infirmary under the careful eye of Sister Eloise; David and Hannah were washed and dressed in clean clothes. Their few possessions had been retrieved from the pram, stored safely in the shed in the courtyard. David had visited Catherine in the ward and found her sitting up in bed with a large white bandage round her head with one of the lay workers, Marthe, spooning warm soup into her mouth. Catherine smiled when she saw him. "David," she called out, "David, I bumped my head and they've put it in a bandage!" Marthe spooned in another mouthful of soup and then Catherine asked, "Where's Maman? Why isn't she here? My head hurts."

"Now then, Catherine," Marthe said hastily, "eat your soup like a good girl," adding as she turned to David, "poor Catherine can't remember how she hurt her head."

"We'll tell her all about it when she's feeling a bit better," Sister Danielle said quietly. She was still holding the little boy's hand. "We want her to try and sleep as soon as she's had her soup."

David understood what they were saying. Catherine didn't know Maman was dead. The sudden picture of his mother lying, staring up at him with empty eyes and blood oozing from holes in her neck made him cry out in despair; a primordial sound that wrenched at the heart. Sister Danielle scooped him up into her arms and sitting on a chair rocked him like a baby as he wept.

Later, when he had been checked over by Dr Felix and was finally asleep in one of the tiny bedrooms usually kept for visitors, Sister Danielle went to consult with Mother Marie-Pierre.

"We must bring their mother in for Christian burial," she said. "It is very hard for children as young as David and Catherine to take in what has happened. The baby, of course, will remember nothing. As long as she's fed and dry she will do very well, but the little boy . . ." The nun shook a regretful head.

"I'm not sure about the Christian burial," replied Mother Marie-Pierre. "I have been talking to Sister Henriette, and she says the woman who brought the children here said that they are Jews. That's why they were on the road, I imagine." She looked across at Sister Danielle. "I think it would be wiser to keep this piece of information to ourselves. Sister Henriette knows too, of course, but it could be very dangerous for those children if it leaked out."

"You mean to the Germans?" Sister Danielle was wide-eyed. "What would they do?"

Mother Marie-Pierre shrugged. "Probably nothing with children this young. They'd be no use in one of their work camps, but there is no need to draw attention to the fact that they are Jewish."

"Would anyone guess?" wondered Sister Danielle.

"Again, probably not," Mother Marie-Pierre said, "but the woman who brought them did remind Sister Henriette that there would be a physical sign on the boy."

"A physical sign?" Sister Danielle looked puzzled.

"Jewish boys are circumcised," Mother Marie-Pierre said, adding with a faint smile, "you remember Our Lord in the temple when he was a baby?"

"Oh!" Colour flooded up into Sister Danielle's face. She knew the story well enough, everyone did, but the actuality, the physical side of it had never dawned on her and the thought of her Lord Jesus having such a thing done to him brought a hot flush to her cheeks.

Seeing her confusion, Mother Marie-Pierre said gently, "Don't worry about it, Sister, all we have to do is see that it is you who gives him his bath. He's only a little boy, you know." Then to change the subject onto less embarrassing ground she went on. "However, their mother, and all the other dead, must be brought to the village for burial. Father Michel will say Mass for them and they will be buried in the churchyard. I will speak to him about the children's mother."

It wasn't just the Germans Mother Marie-Pierre was worried about, though she could hardly say so to Sister Danielle. Marthe, one of the lay workers at the convent, was also a Jew. Her family had lived in St Croix since before the first war and were part of the village community. Her father, Claude, was a farm labourer and her mother, Rochelle, kept a tiny store that sold everything from buttons and lace to billhooks and lamp oil. Marthe had come to the convent looking for work to help maintain the family . . . there were four children younger than she . . . and Mother Marie-Pierre had agreed to let her help with the rough work in the infirmary. Sister Marie-Paul, the novice mistress, had come to her in outrage.

"How can you let a Jew into the convent?" she demanded, red-faced. "It is no place for Jews. We are a Christian community!" Her anger had made her outspoken, but Mother Marie-Pierre did not reprove her for that. She simply said, "But Sister, we have a Jew living with us permanently."

Sister Marie-Paul stared at her. "Who?" she asked, dismay on her face. "Who here is a Jew?"

Mother Marie-Pierre replied gently, "Our Lord, Sister."

Sister Marie-Paul had been silenced, but she had not been reconciled to Marthe coming to the hospital each day, and Mother Marie-Pierre rather thought that she gave the girl a hard time. Luckily it was Sister Eloise who ran the hospital now, and she, recognising not only a hard worker, but someone with an instinctive flare for nursing, was pleased to have the girl and protected her much of the time from Sister Marie-Paul's spite.

The rest of the day and much of the night was spent providing care for the others who had been hurt in the

German raid, food for those who had survived and somewhere to sleep for the night.

Mathilde Leon was found still lying at the roadside and carried in on a makeshift stretcher along with ten others who had also been killed. They were laid out in the village school to be identified and then buried in the little churchyard.

The curé, Father Michel, was to say Mass for them and then they would be buried in a corner of the churchyard already set aside for strangers. When friends and families had identified the bodies, it turned out that two more of the casualties, a man and a little boy, were also Jews. Their family did not want them included in the requiem Mass, nor buried in a Christian churchyard. A weeping woman had claimed the man as her husband and a bleak-eyed man said the boy was his son. They begged that they be buried somewhere separate.

The curé had shrugged and said that they certainly couldn't be buried in the churchyard if they were not baptised and told them to ask the mayor, Monsieur Dubois, who was trying to organise the refugees in the square.

The mayor had shrugged helplessly when applied to, but Mother Marie-Pierre had spoken to him and suggested the little copse beyond the graveyard wall, which was quiet and secluded, might be a suitable resting place. The mayor, anxious to be done with the whole thing, agreed and sent a gravedigger there as well.

With the aid of the photograph that had been among the things in David's pram, Mother Marie-Pierre had identified the children's mother.

"This woman is also Jewish," she had murmured to the priest. "I think she should be buried with the other Jews."

"How do you know?" demanded the curé suspiciously. "No one has claimed her."

"No, but I have her children safely at the convent. One is injured and in the hospital and one is a baby." She produced the photo and showed him. "This picture was in their things. You can see it is the woman lying here." She did not mention David, and afterwards wondered why. She was glad that she hadn't and actually regretted mentioning the girls, but it was too late now, and anyway the curé was hardly a risk.

She walked over to the families of the Jewish dead and said, "There is another Jewish woman over here. She should be buried with her own people. Will you see to her as well? She has no one else to say the prayers."

With a desolate nod, the father of the dead boy followed her to where Mathilde lay, and, picking her up, carried her to where his son and the other man lay awaiting burial.

Mother Marie-Pierre considered giving them Mathilde's wedding picture to place in the grave with her, but decided it would be better to keep it for her children, and for her husband if he should ever return home to find them.

Gradually, over the next two weeks the convent returned to its normal routine. The news continued going from bad to worse. Despair and anger flooded through the demoralised French army as it continued to retreat, a defeated force. Fear and anguish enveloped the civilians they had failed to protect. Everyone knew that within days, barring a miracle, the Germans would be at the gates of Paris and Paris would fall.

Belgium had already fallen and King Leopold, surrendering, had sued for peace. The Allies were left with an unprotected flank as they were backed steadily towards the sea. Considering them now a defeated army with no stomach for the fight and no prospect of escape, the Panzers turned south, towards Paris. With their eyes fixed on the glorious capture of the French capital, they allowed the British Expeditionary Army and many of their French allies to be rescued by the Royal Navy, along with an armada of tiny ships crossing the Channel that snatched the cornered men from under the German artillery fire and dive-bomb raids.

Rumours of the disasters around Calais and Dunkerque spread through the people like wildfire. All had heard of the English army's escape, but the despondent talk in the cafés and village squares was of the English deserting their allies, of failing to send enough planes, and when Paris fell on 14th June everyone knew it was only a matter of days before France would formally surrender and the Nazis would take control.

However, the nuns kept to the comforting routine of daily office and went about their normal tasks as if disaster were not just around the corner. The hospital continued to care for the wounded refugees who had been brought in after the raid. Several had left to continue their flight to places where they thought they would be safe from the Germans, two more had died, and the task began to assume more manageable proportions.

The Leon children were absorbed into the orphanage wing and although Catherine continued to ask for her mother, David never mentioned her. Baby Hannah had been renamed Anne.

"The other children have ordinary enough names," Mother Marie-Pierre said to Sister Danielle, "and if we all call the baby Anne from now on, everyone will soon forget that she was ever called anything else."

The other orphans, Paulette, Monique and Jean-Pierre accepted the arrival of more children without question. Each of them had joined the orphan family in the convent at different times and knew that children came and went. Jean-Pierre was pleased because David was a boy and he'd been feeling a bit outnumbered. Aged eleven, he decided it was his job to show the younger boy the ropes, and Sister Danielle was pleased to see that he had sort of adopted the new boy. Paulette, nearly fourteen and due to leave the convent very soon, was delighted to be allowed to help with baby Anne, and even Monique, always something of a loner, took the young Catherine under her wing.

In the uncertain times, the children were not going to school as they had been, but were now doing lessons with Sister Marie-Joseph, and helping with chores in the kitchen and the garden.

It was in the third week after the raid that Mother Marie-Pierre's private devotions were interrupted by Sister Celestine banging with unusual vigour on the reverend mother's office door. Mother Marie-Pierre closed her missal and rang the bell for the nun to enter.

"Oh, Mother, come quickly," she cried in extreme agitation. "The Germans are here. There's a car coming up the lane. The Germans are coming here."

"Calm down, Sister," Mother Marie-Pierre instructed briskly. "I'll come and see what they want. In the meantime, send a message to Sister Danielle and tell her to keep the children in and ask Sister Clothilde to light the fire in here."

Sister Celestine drew a deep breath and murmured "Yes, Mother," before turning and running off to do as she'd been bidden.

Mother Marie-Pierre closed her eyes and breathed a prayer for wisdom and courage, and then, closing her office door behind her, went through to the hall to meet her unwelcome guests.

CHAPTER
SIX

Adelaide Anson-Gravetty paused on the steps of the hotel in London to which she had been summoned. She smoothed her uniform skirt and straightened her cap. Her shoes gleamed and the seams of her ladderless stockings, borrowed from a fellow-WAAF on the station especially for the occasion, were straight. Drawing a deep breath, she went up the steps and paused to give her name to a sentry at the door. He was in RAF uniform, and giving her an appreciative grin, he consulted a clipboard.

"Yes, you're expected," he said. "See them at the desk," he nodded back over his shoulder, "and they'll tell you which room."

Adelaide thanked him and crossed to the desk. There another WAAF checked her name and then pointed to a chair. "Wait there, please. Someone will come and fetch you when they're ready for you."

Adelaide took the indicated seat and waited. She had little idea of why she had been called in from her station near Southampton where she was a driver, all she knew was that her cousin, Andrew, had said she was wasted there with her fluent French and he'd "have a word". With whom and about what she didn't know.

Andrew was in the RAF too, but he was on special duties of some sort, not on active service, flying planes or anything like that.

When Adelaide had asked him what he did, he grinned. "Nothing very exciting, just a bod at the Air Ministry. They use my French quite a bit." That had been soon after the war had started, and she had hardly seen him since, just the one occasion when they both had forty-eight hours' leave.

When war broke out Adelaide had been anxious to join up, but her father thought she would be more use working in a job in London.

"That way you are just as useful," he pointed out, "and you release a man into the forces to do the fighting. After all what do you have to offer the services?"

Adelaide had been furious with this attitude. "Another pair of hands," she had snapped. "They train you in what they want you to do, you know."

"Of course they do," Richard Anson-Gravetty had replied soothingly, "but probably not in work that you are suited for. Surely there's plenty of voluntary work to do here in London, for the Red Cross or something? But if that doesn't appeal to you, why don't you come over to my office. We can always find you something to do there, I am sure."

Adelaide had thanked him and said she would think about it . . . which she did . . . and then took herself off to the recruitment office and joined the WAAFs.

"You're not even going to be an officer!" Her father was stupefied by what she had done, but Adelaide simply replied, "No, Father, but I am in the war."

After her basic training she was posted to an air base near Southampton where, as she could already drive competently, she was employed as a driver. Surprisingly she found she rather enjoyed life with the other girls on the station, and although it was a hard life in many ways, she never regretted joining up as opposed to taking a civilian job.

Her work was fairly routine, as she drove officers about in the course of their duties, but she met some interesting people, and on long drives got to know some of her regulars quite well. However, when she saw the work that the plotters and radio operators did, she decided that she wanted to retrain and make, what seemed to her, a more vital contribution to the war effort. She mentioned this to one of the officers she was driving to a meeting at the Air Ministry.

"I feel I could be doing something more important than just driving people about," she explained. "Anyone can learn to drive. I want to retrain as a plotter or a radio operator."

Group Captain Williamson, her passenger, sounded interested in her thoughts. "You once told me you spoke French," he said, casually.

"Yes, I do," agreed Adelaide. "But I wouldn't want to spend my time simply translating documents. I want to do my bit in a more active way."

"Then by all means put in for retraining," agreed the group captain easily, "but I shall miss you as a driver!"

It was when she'd been home on a forty-eight that she saw Andrew again. He had come to see her on the first morning.

"Andrew!" she cried in surprised delight as she greeted him with a hug.

"Heard you were home from Grand'mère," he said. "I've got a forty-eight too. Thought we might do a show, or would you rather have dinner and dance somewhere?"

"Both?" suggested Adelaide hopefully, adding as he laughed, "Well two days in London is too much of an opportunity to miss, don't you think?"

He did think, and when they came out of the theatre he took her on to the Savoy. They had a wonderful evening together and when he finally took her home again it was into the small hours of the morning. Even so, she invited him in and they sat over one last drink before he left.

"My train goes first thing," he said, nursing a glass of Richard's best cognac, "so there's no point in going home to bed."

"Won't Grand'mère wonder where you are?" teased Adelaide, knowing that he was meant to be staying at their grandmother's house.

He grinned his familiar grin. "She'll be tucked up in bed so she won't know I wasn't there, will she? Anyway, I have to go back before I leave to collect my kit, so I'll see her then."

"Where are you going?" asked Adelaide with interest. "You didn't say."

"No, I didn't," agreed Andrew. "Up north."

"Have you finished at the Air Ministry, then?"

"For now."

"And you can't tell me . . . ?"

"No."

Adelaide shrugged good-naturedly. "Fair enough. Though actually, I'm not a German spy."

"Aren't you?" grinned Andrew. "Well you never know! 'Careless talk costs lives!' " The well-worn slogan made them both laugh.

They had been talking about her life on the air base and Adelaide had told him how she felt about her driving and wanting to retrain.

"I must do something better than driving. Anyone can do that!"

"You are doing important work," Andrew said as he listened. "But, I agree, anyone trained properly could do your job. I think you're right to be looking for something else, but not a plotter or r/t operator. Don't get me wrong, I'm not belittling what you want to do," he added hastily as she began to protest, "far from it. It's just that you have other talents and skills that are not so readily available, which could be put to good use."

Adelaide looked surprised. "Like what?" she asked.

"Like speaking French like a native," he said. "Thanks to Grand'mère your French is perfect."

"And to the university. I did get my degree, you know," Adelaide pointed out.

Andrew laughed. "That's all about French lit," he said. "Being able to spout Molière is not so helpful when there's a war on and France occupied!"

"So what sort of thing?" asked Adelaide intrigued.

Andrew shrugged. "Well, translation of documents, that sort of thing," he said vaguely. "Acting as interpreter for *Free French* brass, something like that. I could have a word, if you like."

Adelaide wasn't particularly keen on this idea, but she didn't say so. She did not really think he would have any influence in such matters. For her own part she had no intention of applying for such a position. When the time came, she had decided, she would put in for r/t training.

However, Andrew must have had the ear of someone, because here she was waiting to find out what they might want her to do.

It must be using my French, she thought. I can't think of anything else.

A door opened and a man came out. He was in his early forties, tall and thin, dressed in the uniform of an army captain. He walked over to Adelaide. "Aircraftswoman Anson-Gravetty?"

Adelaide leaped to her feet and saluted. "Yes, sir. Good morning, sir."

"My name is Jenner. Please come this way." He led the way back through the door from which he had emerged and closed it carefully behind him.

The room was large and bare, furnished only with a big oak desk and some upright chairs. A second, panelled door opened into a further room, but it was closed.

Captain Jenner walked round behind the desk and waved at one of the upright chairs in front of it. "Please take a seat," he said and settled himself in his own chair.

Adelaide did so, perching awkwardly on the edge of the seat, waiting.

"I understand that you speak fluent French," said the captain, addressing her in that language.

Adelaide replied to the question in kind. "Yes, sir. My grandmother is French and she has always spoken to me in French. I spent a good deal of time with her as a child, so I speak it pretty fluently."

"I believe you also read French at university."

"Yes, sir." Remembering Andrew's comments about Molière, she did not enlarge on this.

For the next hour, Captain Jenner questioned her about her family, her friends, where she had been to school. He seemed to know a great deal about her already as he tossed in queries about her natural father, Freddie Hurst, as well as her adoptive father. He asked her why she had joined up instead of getting a civilian job. Why she had joined the ranks and not put in for officer training.

Adelaide answered him as best she could, trying to work out what he was getting at, what he wanted to know and why he wanted to know it; and the whole conversation was carried on in French. Captain Jenner's French was fluent and idiomatic, his vocabulary wide, so that on occasion he had Adelaide searching for a word that escaped her. On the whole, however, though she was surprised by the range and depth of questioning, she answered his questions as truthfully as she could, not trying to hide anything from him, though she suspected that somehow he knew all the answers already.

At last he said, "Thank you for coming to see me, Miss Anson-Gravetty. It could be that we need to send you for some special training. I assume you'd be happy about that?"

He asked this as a question, but Adelaide knew it was not, not really. She was expected to agree, and so she did.

"You should return to your present job for the time being," Captain Jenner said, standing up to indicate that the interview was over, "and report as directed when the time comes. I need hardly tell you that you should not discuss this with anyone. Careless talk costs lives."

This time the slogan did not make Adelaide laugh as she had when Andrew had trotted it out, this time she knew it was in deadly earnest.

"No, sir. I won't mention it. May I ask, sir, exactly what this training will be for?"

Captain Jenner allowed himself a faint smile. "You may ask, Aircraftswoman, but until things have been decided you won't get an answer. Good morning."

"Good morning, sir." Adelaide saluted him smartly and turning on her heel left the room.

When she had gone, the door in the corner opened and another man, in the uniform of a major, came in. He looked across at Captain Jenner. "Well, Jenner, what did you think of her? Will she do?" He took a seat in the chair that Adelaide had vacated, and Jenner returned to his place behind the desk.

"Her French is probably good enough," he said, lighting a cigarette, "with a little brushing up. Accent unexceptional. Plenty of commonsense by the sound of her. Certainly officer material, though she joined up in the ranks."

"Yes, interesting explanation for that," remarked the other man. "Did you believe it?"

"What, that she wanted to learn a trade and know how it feels to be an ordinary aircraftswoman before taking on the responsibility of telling other girls what to do?" Jenner drew on his cigarette, considering. "Yes, I think so. It seemed an honest enough answer. She's clearly intelligent."

"Ah, but can she think on her feet?"

"That we shall find out if we recommend her for training."

"She's very upper class," pointed out the major. "Will she cope with all she has to learn? It's a very tough training. Lots don't make it."

Jenner shrugged. "Can't tell for sure, obviously, but yes, on balance I think she will. She may be upper class and very well off, as I understand it in her own right, but she hasn't used that as an excuse to avoid service life as she might have done. She said her father offered her a job in his business, remember, but she turned it down. It struck me that not only is she self-reliant, but that she has a determined streak."

The major, who had listened to Adelaide's interview through a microphone, nodded. Jenner was well known as a talent-spotter and the major had great faith in his judgement.

"Who put you on to her?" the major asked.

"Two sources, which is why I had her in so quickly," replied Jenner. "One, a group captain she's been driving on a fairly regular basis, and the other, her cousin, Flight Lieutenant Driver. He's one of ours. Both spotted her potential."

"Right," said the major. "She's worth a try. We'll call her up for preliminary training and see how she gets on. If she measures up she could be extremely useful with that fluent French."

It was only a week later when Adelaide received orders to report to a manor house near Guildford, and on arrival there her life changed out of all recognition. The training was intensive. With four other girls, Adelaide worked from dawn till dusk and sometimes on into the night. Every minute of their day was filled. There was hard physical training, leaving them so exhausted that when they finally fell into their beds they sank into immediate oblivion, only to be woken, it seemed to Adelaide, minutes later to be sent on a five-mile run before breakfast. One army sergeant taught them to handle various weapons; another, unarmed combat. A third drilled them in map reading, while a fourth introduced them to signalling. There seemed so much for them to learn and the pressure on all of them was relentless. After ten days, two of the girls disappeared and did not rejoin Adelaide and the fourth girl, Cora.

"Where do you think they've gone?" Adelaide asked Cora wearily as they climbed into bed that night.

"Don't know," shrugged Cora, too tired to care. "Probably flunked it."

"And got chucked out?"

"That, or they asked to leave." She sighed. "Perhaps they didn't like what we're being trained for."

"But we haven't been told much about that yet," pointed out Adelaide as she pulled the blankets up round her chin. "Gosh, it's cold in here."

"No, not spelled out," Cora agreed, "but it's pretty clear, don't you think?"

"Undercover work of some sort?" suggested Adelaide.

"I'd put money on it," Cora said and with a sigh was instantly asleep.

Although she was tired, Adelaide did not immediately follow her friend's example. She lay in her bed thinking about the things with which they had been bombarded. It didn't take a genius to work out that they were being prepared for something really special. Their instructors were tough, tolerating no sloppiness or laziness.

"If you don't get this right first time," bellowed Sergeant Garner, spinning round on her when Adelaide had fumbled a silent approach, "you're dead meat, right? No second chances in this game. So, stop thundering about like a bleedin' elephant and try again!"

"Use your brain!" snapped Sergeant Allen. "You've got to out-think your enemy, and you've got to do it fast. If circumstances change, you've got to be ready to switch course, OK?"

102

Cora and Adelaide struggled with all that was thrust at them with determination, though there were times when Adelaide felt close to tears with frustration and exhaustion. Their fitness increased a hundred-fold, their brains remained in overdrive as they gradually became more competent. Reactions speeded up, weapons were handled more instinctively. They learned how to use explosives and practised using the wireless, spending hours transmitting to each other in Morse code.

At the end of three weeks they were called up individually to see Major Harper, the officer they had met on arrival, but had hardly seen since.

"Aircraftswoman Anson-Gravetty," he said when she was sent for. "Come in and sit down."

Adelaide did as she was told, waiting anxiously on the edge of the chair, wondering if she was going to be told she hadn't made whatever grade had been expected of her.

"Your time with us is over," Major Harper said. "This was only preliminary training, just to assess your potential use to us in the field."

"The field?"

"We are in great need of agents who can be dropped into France," he explained. "People who can pass for French, so that they can move about with comparative safety, despite the checkpoints and controls set up by the Germans. But that's just the start. Once someone is there we need them to liaise with any resistance movement that there is in the area. We need to organise escape routes for pilots who have been shot down or prisoners who may escape. We need to sabotage German installations, make life as difficult for the occupying power as we can. There are some strong resistance groups already; we need to find out what they need, give them all the help we can to stiffen that resistance. We need someone to send back all the information they possibly can about troop movements, fuel dumps, weapons stores, factories and what they are manufacturing. We need ears and eyes on the ground to keep us up-to-date on what is going on in every area. Details we can get from nowhere else. We need to boost the morale of the ordinary people, we need to let them know that they have not been forgotten or abandoned."

Major Harper paused, his eyes had drilled into Adelaide all the time he had been speaking, now he waited. When she made no comment he went on, "We think you have the makings of an agent such as this. Your French is fluent; you could pass for French, and you have done well in all the training so far, but what we are asking you to do takes courage and a cool head in danger. You will be in constant danger yourself, the danger of discovery. Discovery not only from any mistake you might make yourself, but also from those wishing to curry favour with the Germans. We have to face facts that there are all too many French who feel defeated and have decided to throw in their lot with the Germans. If they guess who you are and what you are doing, they will inform on you and you will be caught. Set against that the importance of what you may discover yourself, of what you can do in the areas I have mentioned and you will see that it is not unreasonable to ask you to go. However," the major paused again to ensure that he had her attention, "we only take volunteers for missions such as these. No one is sent unwillingly, such a person would be doomed to fail." He fell silent for a moment and Adelaide waited, not sure what to say, or indeed if she should speak at all.

"In the morning you will leave here. If you agree to further training, knowing what that training is to prepare you to do, then we shall be sending you elsewhere. If not, you will have several weeks at a particular establishment, before being posted to a new station to continue the work you were doing before you came here. In either case you will be bound by a pledge of secrecy, is that understood?"

"Yes, sir." Adelaide just managed to get the words out; her mouth felt dry and her heart was thumping.

"Right, well, I'll see you in the morning for your answer."

Adelaide returned to her billet and flung herself down on her bed.

A spy! she thought. They want me to be a spy.

Her heart turned over at the thought. Had she the courage to accept such a mission, to carry it through to the end whatever the consequences? Was this the sort of work Andrew had been thinking of when he said she had special talents? That she should be asked to use her French like this? "Is that what you're doing yourself?" she murmured to her absent cousin. "I bet it is! I bet that's where you've disappeared to!"

Cora did not reappear that evening, her bed was not slept in, though her kitbag was still stowed in the locker at the end of the room. She must have been sent somewhere else to make up her mind, Adelaide thought, so that we couldn't discuss things between ourselves.

Adelaide did not sleep that night. She lay tossing and turning, Major Harper's words churning round her brain. The very idea of being dropped into enemy occupied country terrified her. How could she possibly get away with what they were asking her to do? She remembered the bellowing sergeant. "Get it right first time or you're dead meat!" Supposing she didn't get it right? Supposing because of her other people were put at risk? Supposing she were to be captured, how would she cope? Would she be strong enough not to give away any information . . . under torture? A cold sweat broke out all over her and she lay shivering under the mound of blankets. I can't do it! she thought in panic. I'm not brave enough! I'd be terrified all the time! I'd be useless.

She remembered what Andrew had once said, that everyone was afraid at times, but it was how they dealt with their fear that mattered. How would I deal with it? Adelaide wondered now. The major said I would need a cool head. Have I got a cool head? If I go how will I get there? Major Harper said something about being dropped behind enemy lines. Dropped? By parachute? Good God, I could never jump out of a plane!

"We need to boost the morale of the ordinary French people," the major had said. Adelaide thought about her last trip to France, to visit her aunt, Sarah, in her convent. She wondered now how would the nuns be faring under the occupation? What about the children, the orphans living in their care? Where was Andrew? Had he really gone over there too?

The turmoil of her thoughts kept her from sleep and in the end she gave up. Switching off the light, she went to the window and pulled back the blackout. It was still dark outside, but she sat on a chair staring out into the night until the grey fingers of dawn crept across the sky. She watched a startling ray of sunshine, bursting from a sun as yet unseen, but piercing the greyness of the sky like a shining sword. Even as she watched, another joined it and the clouds were painted a brilliant orange, edged with gold. A new day dawning, a new beginning burgeoning with fresh hope. As the sun climbed upward from the horizon, first a half disc of burnished gold, then a full sovereign gleaming in the sky, Adelaide realised that to keep hope alive in a world at war, people had to do things they would never have considered doing before. They had to test their courage as they fought against the evil that threatened to engulf them all. Her eyes drank in the sunrise, and burned it into her brain. It would be a talisman to be conjured up in the future when her heart was low and here courage was failing. The dawn of hope, and she, Adelaide, must be part of it.

Three hours later both she and Cora were on a train to Scotland to begin their real training.

CHAPTER
SEVEN

The black car had pulled to a halt in front of the convent door. The driver jumped out and going round to the passenger door, opened it smartly. A German officer stepped out. He was about thirty-five, tall and darkly good-looking, his uniform immaculate. He stood for a moment beside the car, his hand resting on the door, surveying the countryside spread below him before turning round to look up at the convent building. Mother Marie-Pierre watched him from a window, wondering what he was going to want and how she would deal with him. She saw him look at the door as if he expected it to open, but when it did not, he spoke to the driver, who still hovered at his side, and the man ran up the steps to pull heavily on the iron bell. The bell clanged loudly in the hall, and Sister Celestine, now back at her usual place in the portress's office by the front door, looked up anxiously at Mother Marie-Pierre who still stood, concealed, beside the window. Reverend Mother could see the fear in the little nun's eyes as they flickered back to the door.

"Go ahead, Sister," Mother Marie-Pierre said, trying to quell the stab of fear she herself felt as she descended the stairs. "Let them in and show them into the parlour. Then come and fetch me. I'll be in my office." As she turned and went back along the corridor, she heard Sister Celestine open the grille in the great front door.

It was only moments later that there was a quiet knock on the office door. Mother Marie-Pierre rose from her prie-dieu and settled herself behind her desk before ringing the bell in answer to the knock. When the door opened, not only was Sister Celestine outside, but also the tall German officer.

"Mother . . ." began the little nun nervously, but the German swept past her and interrupted, in passable French.

"Good morning, Reverend Mother. I am Major Horst Thielen, Commanding Officer of the occupying force in St Croix."

Mother Marie-Pierre got to her feet, and still standing behind her desk replied coolly, "Good morning, Major. If you had cared to wait, I would have come to meet you in the parlour."

"I did not care to wait," the major said, crossing the room uninvited and staring down into the little garden below.

Mother Marie-Pierre smiled reassuringly at Sister Celestine, who stood white-faced behind the major. "Thank you, Sister. Please would you ask Sister Clothilde to bring some coffee to us here." She turned her attention back to the major as Sister Celestine scuttled away. "You will have a cup of coffee, Major?"

"Thank you." The major did not smile but looked round the room, taking in its sparse furnishings; the desk, the prie-dieu with the crucifix above it. The only signs of comfort were the two armchairs that flanked the fireplace.

"Please, do sit down and tell me how I can help you." Mother Marie-Pierre pointed to one of the chairs. She had decided that calm politeness was the best approach, as if this visitor were no more or less important than any other she might receive. She did not know why he had come, and she felt she must proceed with caution. She resented the cool assurance with which he had come striding into her office, but she had no intention of antagonising a man who might well have the power of life and death over them all. Neither would she show fear, however. She would revert to her earliest training as Miss Sarah Hurst and treat him with the cool civility one accorded to those to whom one would rather not have been introduced.

"We have just arrived in the village, Reverend Mother," he said. "I am making myself acquainted with the surrounding area." As he spoke, she looked at him. Good-looking, she supposed, with dark eyes, and a straight nose above a rather thin-lipped mouth; a cruel mouth she decided, and then gave herself a mental shake. How could she possibly know if he were cruel or not, simply from his mouth? Or was it his eyes, not the warm velvety brown of a generous man, but the cold, coal-black eyes of a hunter.

He was still speaking. "I understand that you run a hospital here."

Mother Marie-Pierre jerked her mind back to what he was saying and managed a nod. "Yes, Major, we have a small hospital here for the local people. Just two wards."

"And that you have an orphanage."

He obviously did his homework before coming here, Mother Marie-Pierre thought. "Not really an orphanage, not as it used to be . . ." She almost added "after the war . . ." but bit the words back just in time. "Yes, we do still look after some children," she agreed, "but only six at present." She called, "Come in," with some relief in response to a knock at the door.

Sister Clothilde, one of the novices, came into the room carrying a tray with a pot of coffee on it, and a tiny jug of milk. She set it down on the table and, with a nervous bob of her head, left the room.

Mother Marie-Pierre took time pouring the coffee, and then handed the major a cup. "I'm afraid we have no sugar, and only a little milk. We do have a cow, but we keep her milk for the children."

The major accepted his coffee, but turned down the milk. He took a sip and regretted having any at all. It was bitter and there were certainly no coffee beans in its make-up. He put the cup down beside him. "Does the convent have a home farm?" he asked.

Mother Marie-Pierre shook her head. "No, not really. We grow our own vegetables as best we can, and we have a cow that is kept with Monsieur Danot's herd. He sends over our milk each day, but there is little enough of it." Mother Marie-Pierre decided not to mention the few hens that scratched about in the yard behind the kitchen and were Sister Marie-Marc's pride and joy. She had no illusions as to what would happen

111

to them if the Germans decided they needed eggs or a bird for the pot. The cow would have to take her chance with the rest of Monsieur Danot's herd.

"I should like to see your convent and your hospital," Major Thielen said, abandoning the coffee after a second cautious mouthful. It was not a request, but a demand, and he set down his cup and got to his feet. "Perhaps you'd be kind enough to show me round."

Mother Marie-Pierre put down her own cup and stood up. "Of course, Major, but you do realise that though this is a religious community, it is a working one."

She took him first to the hospital. All the beds were full, for despite the passage of time since the raid on the refugees, several of the badly injured were still being cared for and there were always patients from the surrounding area. She introduced him to Sister Eloise, who greeted him briskly and then excused herself, apparently entirely unimpressed by the German uniform.

"Yes, please carry on with what you're doing, Sister," said Mother Marie-Pierre, glad that the elderly but efficient sister had shown no fear of their unwanted visitor. "I will show the major round."

They walked into the first ward, where ten beds were lined up, five on each side. It was clear that many of the patients were recovering from wounds rather than illnesses. Several were still heavily bandaged, and there had been more than one amputation. Major Thielen looked round the room. Two nuns were busy preparing to change the dressing for an old man whose right arm ended at the elbow, one sister bustling up the ward with a trolley of bandages, ointments and creams and a bowl of warm water, the other drawing a screen round the patient's bed.

"What happened to these?" demanded the major.

"These?" Mother Marie-Pierre also looked round the room, as if seeing the patients for the first time. "Oh, these were refugees. They were bombed on the road."

"They must have been in a military column," the major said stiffly.

"If they were, we found no one in uniform," Mother Marie-Pierre said calmly. There was no accusation in her voice, but the major turned abruptly on his heel and stalked out of the ward.

Mother Marie-Pierre paused a moment to speak with Sister Eloise. "Where is Marthe?" she asked softly.

"I sent her up to the children's rooms, like you said."

Mother Marie-Pierre nodded and followed the major outside.

He was staring out across the kitchen garden, where three nuns, their sleeves tucked up to their shoulders, were labouring on a vegetable patch.

"Do you sell your produce in the village?" he asked waving at the rows of potatoes the nuns were digging.

"No, certainly not," Mother Marie-Pierre replied. "We have barely enough to feed ourselves and those in the hospital."

The major nodded and continued to watch for a moment or two, as if estimating the yield of the garden, before turning back to the waiting nun. "So, we will go on."

"The operating theatre and the women's ward are the other end of the building," she volunteered, anxious to move away from any area that might encourage the major to return and load his supply lorries. "Would you like to see those?"

"No, I would like to see inside the main building."

"That is where the sisters live," Mother Marie-Pierre said quietly.

"And I would like to see their quarters." Major Thielen had been wrong-footed by the sight of the patients in the ward and their reason for being there. He was determined to wrest the initiative back from this cool-eyed nun.

Mother Marie-Pierre shrugged, as if it were of no great consequence and led the way back indoors. She showed him the kitchen and scullery where Sister Elisabeth and Sister Marie-Marc were preparing the midday meal. She led him through to the refectory where the long tables were already laid up. A single glance was enough for him there and they went on, up the stairs to the dormitory corridor where each sister had her cell.

Without invitation he opened the door of one of these and peered inside. His eyes took in the narrow bed, the locker at its side and the prie-dieu and the crucifix that were its sole furnishings.

"They are all the same," remarked Reverend Mother quietly. "None of us has more than any other." She rested her hand on the door of the next room as if to open it, but the major shook his head. These rooms, cold and bleak even in the heat of summer, were not

114

what he was looking for. He stared down the corridor for a moment. Mother Marie-Pierre thought of her aunt, old Sister St Bruno, bedridden in the room at the end and hoped that he had seen enough. It would upset the elderly nun if a man came striding into her room where she was propped up in bed dressed only in a nightgown and shawl. But he appeared to have lost interest in the rest of the rooms on this passage.

"And the chapel?" he asked abruptly. "Where is that?"

"Please, come this way." Mother Marie-Pierre guided him back through the convent to the chapel. There was no service at this time of day, but she opened the great west door softly and then stood aside. The major stepped in and then came to an abrupt halt, staring in surprise.

The chapel was warm and quiet, the scent of incense lingering heavily in the air, the sanctuary light glowing red in its hanging lamp-holder. The sun shone in through the stained glass in the south wall, casting patterns on the stone floor and striking fire from the ornate gold reredos. It was not this, however, that made the man halt in his tracks, but the sight of a nun, lying prone before the altar, cruciform; her arms outstretched, her legs arrow-straight, her forehead on the stone floor, her face concealed by her hood. He stared at her at length, and then crossing himself backed out of the door.

"What is she doing?" he asked awkwardly, as the reverend mother closed the door behind them.

"Penance," replied the nun.

He looked startled. "Penance? Penance for what?"

"I have no idea," answered Mother Marie-Pierre. "That would be between her, her confessor and God."

"And do you all do that?" The major's questions had changed character. Now he was asking because he was intrigued.

"There is always someone watching in the chapel," Mother Marie-Pierre explained. "Our Lord is never alone. The penance is not always the same." She smiled at him. "You understand, Major. You're a Catholic yourself." She had seen him bless himself and knew that it was true. His action had been instinctive and belonged to a man who had learned to cross himself as a child.

The major made no answer to this but said sharply, "Where is your orphanage?"

Mother Marie-Pierre sighed. She had hoped to get away without bringing the major face-to-face with the children, but she knew it would be pointless to refuse and probably dangerous to show reluctance. Reasonable as this German officer seemed to be, he was just that, a German officer.

"They are in the far wing," she said, "so that they don't disturb the sisters at their prayers." She led the way back through the main part of the building and then along yet another passage to a stout door set in the stone wall.

As she opened this, they were greeted by the wails of a baby and the sound of children's voices. Sister Danielle was sitting at the table encouraging a small girl to eat her lunch, while a young girl of about eighteen

116

was walking up and down the room trying to pacify the crying baby.

Sister Danielle looked up and at once came to her feet. "Mother," she said, her eyes wide at the sight of the German. "Can we help you?"

"Not at all, Sister," replied Reverend Mother. "Major Thielen was interested to see the work we do with the orphaned children." She turned to the major. "We have four other children at present, but they are at their lessons with Sister Marie-Joseph, in the next room."

At that moment the baby gave a great burp and was sick all over the shoulder of the girl who carried her.

"Marthe, take Anne to the nursery and change her," ordered Sister Danielle, "put her down for her nap and then get cleaned up yourself."

The young girl ducked her head, and muttering "Yes, Sister," hurried from the room, still clutching the baby.

"Who is that?" asked the major as the door closed behind her.

"The girl?" Mother Marie-Pierre smiled. "That is Marthe. She comes in every day from the village. We are trying to train her as a nursery nurse."

"I would like to see the other children," the major announced suddenly. "Have them brought in here."

"They are working with Sister Marie-Joseph . . ." began Mother Marie-Pierre, but he cut her short with a wave of his hand.

"I will see them now." He indicated Catherine watching him wide-eyed from the table where Sister Danielle was still trying to get her to finish a bowl of stew. "It must be time for their lunch. They will be glad to finish their lessons early."

Sister Danielle half got to her feet, but Reverend Mother waved her back. "You finish giving Catherine her lunch, Sister," she said. "I'll go and fetch the others." She opened the door at the far side of the room and disappeared for a few moments.

While he waited Major Thielen looked across at Catherine. "How old is she?" he asked Sister Danielle.

"We think she's five," replied the nun, continuing to offer the child a spoonful of stew without looking up at him.

"You don't know? Where did she come from? What happened to her parents?"

Before Sister Danielle could answer, Mother Marie-Pierre came back into the room with the four children. Paulette came first holding David tightly by the hand, followed by Jean-Pierre and Monique.

"Children," Mother Marie-Pierre said softly, "this is Major Thielen. Say bonjour."

In the brief moment outside the room, Reverend Mother had warned the children that there was a German soldier who wanted to meet them. "Just say bonjour to him, and answer politely if he asks you anything." One look at David told her that he was petrified, all colour had drained from his face and his mouth was open as if in a silent scream. "Paulette, take David's hand," instructed the nun. "Be a good boy, David, and hold Paulette's hand." She dared not leave David in the other room. The major already knew that there were four more children and she did not want him to wonder why he was only meeting three.

There was a muttered chorus of "Bonjour, Monsieur" from the three other children, but David said nothing, his eyes fixed in obvious terror on the German soldier standing in front of him, then with a wail, he ripped his hand free from Paulette's grasp and dashed screaming from the room. The three older children stared after him and Catherine, still sitting at the table, began to cry. Sister Marie-Joseph, who had been coming in through the door as David thrust past her, turned at once and followed him out.

Mother Marie-Pierre stepped forward and closed the door firmly behind them and turning said to the startled major, "I'm sorry, Major, but he has just lost his father in this war and is afraid." She turned back to the three children who were standing rooted to the spot. "Go and wash your hands for lunch," she directed, "and then Paulette, you can take Catherine out after her nap."

Sister Danielle, taking this as her cue, gathered up the still weeping Catherine in her arms and swept her out of the room, shooing the older children out ahead of her.

Reverend Mother opened the door that led back into the main part of the convent and stood aside to let the major precede her. He seemed anxious enough to leave the schoolrooms and marched out in front of her. He made no comment about David's outburst, and Mother Marie-Pierre found herself sending up a heartfelt prayer of thanks that he had not done so. She wanted no awkward questions about David. She had a prepared story of course, but she was not sure it would stand up to real scrutiny.

However, as they left the children's wing and headed back to the main hall, he asked, "Why are the children not in school?"

"School is over for the summer," Mother Marie-Pierre replied easily. "They will go back in the autumn, but in the meantime they practise their reading and numbers with Sister Marie-Joseph each day. She was a teacher before she joined us, and it does her good to keep her hand in." She looked across at her unwelcome visitor and asked, "Is there anything else you wish to see, Major?"

"No, I have seen enough. I must tell you, Reverend Mother, that I am looking for a suitable billet for myself. The men are well accommodated in the village for now, and most of my officers will live at The Manor, but I want something separate."

"Here?" Mother Marie-Pierre looked at him in undisguised amazement. "In the convent?"

"I was considering it," he admitted, "but having seen the place I do not think it will suit me. I shall take over the mayor's house as my headquarters and live there."

"But the mayor . . ." began Mother Marie-Pierre, startled at the man's casual appropriation of someone else's home.

"Will live somewhere else," cut in the major. "I understand his son has a farm not far away. He can go there."

Having made his decision, Major Thielen said, "And now, Reverend Mother, I have taken up too much of your time already. If you will kindly lead me through this rabbit warren back to the front door and my car, I shall leave you for today. I have, as you can imagine, much to do in such a place."

"I'm sure you have," murmured Mother Marie-Pierre, adding a little louder, "certainly, Major, if you'll just follow me."

The car pulled away and Reverend Mother stared out long after it had disappeared round the corner of the lane. She had found the major's visit very disturbing and she needed to talk to someone, but her position as Reverend Mother was such that it made it almost impossible to confide in any of the sisters. There was one exception, however, and that was Sister St Bruno, her Aunt Anne. The old nun might be bedridden, but she was still mentally alert, making her physical reliance on others even more of a cross to bear than it would have been for someone less aware. Mother Marie-Pierre made a point of visiting her aunt at some point every day, usually in the recreation hour before compline, but the German major's visit was too worrying for her to wait for evening. She wanted to discuss things with Aunt Anne now. She slipped into the kitchen to find Sister Elisabeth.

"I will take my meal with Sister St Bruno today," she told her. "If you will put it all together on a tray I'll take it up." Sister Elisabeth did as she was asked and as Mother Marie-Pierre carried the tray to the door, she turned back. "Please ask Sister Marie-Paul if she will preside at lunch for me today."

Sister St Bruno was sitting up in bed, her Bible lying open on her knees. She looked old and frail, propped up against the pillows, but when she saw who her visitor was her face cracked into a smile and her eyes glowed with pleasure.

"Mother!" she said. "How lovely!"

"I've brought up our lunch," Mother Marie-Pierre said, setting the tray down on the locker by the bed, and plumping up the pillows so that the old lady could sit more comfortably to eat her food. "I thought we could eat together. Sister Marie-Paul will be only too happy to preside in the refectory."

Sister St Bruno gave a wry smile and set her Bible aside so that she could take the plate that her niece was offering her. As they ate their meal Mother Marie-Pierre told her about Major Thielen's visit.

"He was perfectly polite ... correct, you know. But I felt the whole time that he was weighing up what we had here that he might use. He certainly took in what we're growing in the vegetable garden," she went on ruefully. "We don't grow much to help feed the children and the patients, but I have a feeling his men will soon be up here, taking what little there is."

"Privilege of an occupying power, Sarah," Sister St Bruno replied with a sigh. As usual when the two of them were alone together, they ceased for the duration of their privacy to be Reverend Mother and Sister St Bruno, a senior member of the community, and

122

reverted to being Aunt Anne and Sarah. It was Sarah who had insisted on this easy relationship; she loved her mother's sister and would only allow her to treat her as Mother Superior in the public life of the community. Mother Marie-Pierre had no feelings of guilt about their two relationships; none of the nuns was cut off entirely from her family, the order was not an enclosed one, and Sister St Bruno and Mother Marie-Pierre were the only family that either of them had. Alone, they became Sarah and Aunt Anne, and both enjoyed the ease that was between them.

"The thing is, I need your advice, Aunt Anne. I am concerned about the children."

"What about them?" asked her aunt when Sarah paused and did not go on. "They're safe enough, aren't they?"

Sarah told Aunt Anne about the major's visit to the schoolroom. "David took one look at him and started to scream. He ran out of the room and I had to leave Sister Marie-Joseph to look after him while I dealt with the other children . . . and the major of course. I gave some quick explanation that David's father had been killed in the war and that David was afraid."

"And did the German accept it?"

Sarah shrugged. "He seemed to. I sent the other children off to get ready for lunch and brought him out of the children's wing."

"And he didn't ask any more about David?"

"No, I thank the Lord," Sarah said fervently.

"Then the children should be safe enough, wouldn't you say?"

"I don't know," Sarah sounded anxious. "I'm not so worried about Paulette, Monique and Jean-Pierre, but David and his sisters could be at risk because they're Jews. There's no reason for the Germans to know that of course, except that there are other people who know it and secrets like that don't stay secrets for long."

"No, I agree with you there," said her aunt. "But what use has he for any children, Jewish or otherwise? They aren't old enough to be sent off to these labour camps, are they? They couldn't work in the German factories, they're far too young."

"No, of course they couldn't." Sarah looked slightly happier. "But even so I shall keep them out of the way as much as I can, until people have forgotten where they came from. We may see nothing of the Germans up here anyway, but we don't know how this occupation is going to be, do we? I mean how much the Germans are going to demand things." She told her aunt about the major's decision to turn the mayor out of his house so that he could use it himself. "He's billeted his men around the village, but he is going to have to provide for them somehow."

"You say he was considering using the convent himself?" asked her aunt.

"So he said, but thank God he realised how impossible that would be. I think if we keep a low profile he probably won't interfere with us too much ... except for allowing his men to forage in our

124

garden." She smiled ruefully. "I just wanted to discuss it with you really, just to see what you thought."

"I think we are in the hands of the Lord as always," replied her aunt with a serene smile. "All you can do, Sarah, is keep faith. You take your problems to Him in prayer and He will help you to make the right decisions if and when the time comes." She reached for Sarah's hand and said in a rallying tone, "Come on now, Sarah. At present the children are safe enough, all of them. I think you're right, too. Our work in the village may change somewhat with the arrival of the German soldiers, but I doubt if they will trouble us much actually in the convent." She looked across at her niece, adding with a twinkle in her faded eyes, "But it might be wiser if they didn't find out that you and I are English, don't you think?"

Sarah stared at her in surprise. "You won't believe this," she said slowly, "but that thought hadn't even crossed my mind! I suppose we are enemy aliens or something." She shook her head in disbelief. "I've been here so long I never even think about being English anymore."

"Nor do I," agreed her aunt, "but there are several people who are well aware that we are, and not just the sisters."

"Well, we don't have to worry about them," laughed Sarah, "not the sisters. But I suppose there are people in the village who know that I'm English. I doubt if many remember that you are. You've been here for over forty years!"

"Maybe," agreed the old lady placidly, "but we have to face the fact that there are people who are going to want to be on the winning side round here. Little snippets of information may find their way into German intelligence. So, keep your counsel."

CHAPTER
EIGHT

As the anniversary of the occupation came and went, the convent was largely ignored by the Germans. Occasionally soldiers arrived and relieved them of some sacks of potatoes or strings of onions, but Major Thielen seemed to have taken on board the fact that the nuns needed their produce to help feed the patients in the hospital, and the requisition was not, at first, excessive. The sisters went about their daily routine of prayer and service within its walls; the hospital was busy as always, and the nuns who nursed the elderly inhabitants of St Croix and the surrounding area in their own homes, travelled about the countryside unhindered. The children continued to be cared for in the orphanage and attend the local school. No one seemed interested in any of them, and Mother Marie-Pierre allowed herself to relax a little.

"It is amazing how little our lives have changed under this occupation," Mother Marie-Pierre said to Sister St Bruno as they sat together one evening before compline, "except for the shortages, of course, and they affect everyone. Rations have been cut again. Poor Sister Danielle spent five hours at the food office in Albert today, getting the children's ration cards properly stamped, and someone will have to go again next week to deal with all our cards."

"I think we'll find things get worse before they get better," her aunt said. "Remember how scarce everything was by the end of the of last war?"

Mother Marie-Pierre did remember and she sighed. "You're probably right," she said, "but it doesn't look as if we're going to win this one."

"Come on, Sarah!" Her aunt spoke bracingly. "Of course we're going to win! Where's your faith?"

St Croix gradually got used to seeing the men in German uniforms who had taken up residence there. Being the largest village in the area, it was used as a hub from which the spokes of the local occupation extended. From the town hall, now the German HQ, soldiers patrolled the surrounding country. Lists were made of the local residents and their families, to make a record of everyone in the area. French soldiers, returning, defeated and demoralised, to tend the land or the businesses that their wives had kept running during their absence, found themselves being noted, listed. If the work they had come home to do was not considered vital, able-bodied men were liable to be sent as forced labour to Germany to work in the factories. As this happened more frequently, such men began disappearing again; sons of local families slipping away before the efficient machinery of the German occupation gathered them into is jaws.

Sullen faces still greeted the German soldiers who carried out spot checks on papers, who travelled on the trains, who searched houses and barns for shot-down airmen, weapons caches and other works of a quietly growing resistance movement, but the cold loathing was reserved for those Frenchmen who collaborated with the Germans; opportunists who offered their services, passing on their local knowledge to the occupying power. Determined to be on the winning side when the war finally ended, they cheerfully gave information about local families, passed on anything they considered suspicious, betraying their countrymen without compunction.

Alain Fernand was one such. He lived in a house in the lane that ran behind the town hall, a house belonging to an elderly spinster called Mademoiselle Martine Reynaud. She had been forced to take in a boarder to make ends meet before the war, and once Fernand was ensconced she had been unable to get him out. He terrified her with threats to tell the Germans that her grandmother had been Jewish.

"But she wasn't!" protested poor Mademoiselle Reynaud.

"Wasn't she?" asked Fernand innocently. "Well, the Germans won't know that, will they?" He smiled wolfishly. "If they took you away, I could have the whole house, now couldn't I? Better not to upset me, eh?"

So he had stayed, and, confining Mademoiselle Reynaud to the room he had originally rented from her, he took over the rest of the house for himself. He was a plumber by trade, and this meant that he would not be called up for Service du Travail Obligatoire. As a skilled tradesman his work was too important for him to be sent off to Germany, and, while plying his trade in the surrounding area, he started to gather information about his customers, which he used to his own advantage.

Fernand had already informed on one young lad whom he found hiding in the barn of an outlying farm. The boy had finally returned from the war, only to hear that he was to be sent to Germany to work in a factory.

Tipping the Germans off as to the boy's whereabouts had earned Fernand a cash reward; he'd been on the German payroll ever since.

"Keep your eyes and ears open," Major Thielen had said. "We'll always pay for good information."

So, as he went about his business, Fernand had begun gathering information about his customers; who was hoarding food, undeclared in their barns, who was selling produce on the black market, which shops were saving goods for favoured customers, naming the children who had thrown cow dung over Major Thielen's car. All pretty low-grade information, but it made him a little extra money and kept him in with the Germans. And that was what Fernand wanted most. Before long, he reckoned, the war would be over, and those who had been helpful to the victors would do very well for themselves.

He also ran a small blackmail business. When Fernand hinted at what he'd discovered about them, local people were prepared to pay him not to pass that information on. He would take their money for a few months, and then shop them anyway. He knew he was hated in the village, but he didn't care. He had been rejected all his life. Unpopular at school, taunted for his lack of a father, bullied because he was too small to retaliate, beaten by his mother's succession of lovers, Fernand became a survivor. He learnt early to look after number one, because if he didn't, no one else would.

The hatred for such *collabos* smouldered beneath the surface of the entire community, liable to erupt without warning like a dormant volcano. Flashes such as these did little good, retaliation and retribution could be swift and cruel, but memories would be long and revenge was promised when the time was right.

Accommodation was requisitioned for the occupying soldiers. Madame Berniers, an old lady of ninety, was banished to the servants' quarters of her own manor house. Her maid, Ninette, almost as old as her mistress, was told to look after her, while seven German officers took over the house and made free with the wine Madame's husband had laid down in the cellar some forty years earlier. Major Thielen was satisfactorily established in the mayor's house and the other ranks were billeted comfortably enough in the barns of two farms at either end of the village.

It was not only accommodation; cars and horses were casually requisitioned by the German authorities; their troops also augmented their rations by helping themselves from local farms, at times officially, at others by stealth.

Sister Marie-Marc's precious chickens survived until they were noticed by Sergeant Franz Schultz when he was carrying the bags of potatoes he and his mates had been sent to collect from the convent garden by the quartermaster in the town. That evening when darkness was falling and the nuns, following their own idiosyncratic timetable, had retired for the night, Sergeant Schultz crept back up the path from the village and with a leg-up from his friends, scaled the courtyard wall. He opened the gate to admit his accomplices and together they made their way to the hencoop. He reached for the wooden bolt that secured its door and dragging it free, knelt down and peered into the henhouse. The birds were roosting peacefully, but as soon as he made a grab, catching the first unsuspecting hen round her neck and passing her hastily back out for one of his friends to stuff into the sack they had brought, the squawking began. He worked as quickly as he could, snatching birds from the safety of their roost and passing them back to his mates. The squawks and squooks of alarm increased in volume and the soldier posted as lookout heard the sounds coming from the convent as the back door was dragged open and someone came out with a lantern.

"That's it," he hissed as the light wobbled towards them across the yard. "Come on, let's go!"

With a mixture of muffled laughter and swearing, the hencoop raiders ran out of the gate and disappeared into the night, and poor Sister Marie-Marc was left peering round in the darkness of the courtyard, looking for her beloved hens. She found only five still inside the henhouse and another, which must have been dropped as the thieves ran away, pecking its way peacefully

132

among the clumps of weeds just outside the convent gate.

The wails of Sister Marie-Marc were even louder than the squawks of the hens had been, and when Mother Marie-Pierre appeared in the courtyard wearing a dressing gown, with only a shawl to cover her head, it took her some time to calm the irate nun.

"Don't worry, Sister," she said soothingly leading her back in through the kitchen door, "I will go and see Major Thielen in the morning."

"That will be too late, Mother," moaned Sister Marie-Marc. "*Les sales Boches* will have wrung their necks!"

"Sister!" exclaimed her superior, even as the little nun clapped a hand over her mouth in horror at her own words.

"Oh, Mother!" she cried in dismay. "May God forgive me for such words. I'm sorry, I'm so sorry."

"So I should think, Sister," reproved the reverend mother, struggling to keep a straight face. "Now, back to your bed. There is nothing more we can do this evening."

Next morning, however, Mother Marie-Pierre went down to the town hall where Major Thielen had his office, to complain.

When she arrived she was asked to wait and it was nearly half an hour later that she was finally taken in to see the major. He came to his feet as she was announced and extended a hand. "Reverend Mother, what an unexpected pleasure. How can I help you? I hope you weren't kept waiting."

"Only about half an hour," Mother Marie-Pierre replied dryly, seating herself on the chair he had set for her. "I am sure you're busy, so I won't take up much of your time."

"I am indeed," he agreed. "Now, how can I help?"

"Last night, all but six of our hens were stolen from the henhouse," Mother Marie-Pierre said coming straight to the point. "I think it was some of your men. They climbed in over the wall and escaped out through the back gate."

The major's welcoming smile faded as she spoke and the hard look she had seen before slid into his eyes. "What makes you think they were my men, Reverend Mother?" he asked coolly. "Far more likely it was your own countrymen. Several have already been caught by my men, thieving from the German army."

Mother Marie-Pierre managed to hold his gaze as she replied. "The sister who was woken by the noise the hens made, came down to the courtyard and heard them; heard them speaking German. Major," she continued, "we need those chickens to provide the extra food our patients in the hospital need to get well. We have three of your men in there at present, as you know, all of them could do with good food to help them to make a swift recovery. You've taken much of our potato crop, what's left of our carrots and the last of the onions we stored last year."

"You will be paid for those," cut in the major sharply.

"Be that as it may," Mother Marie-Pierre, who was pretty sure they would never see a cent, went on firmly, "we need our hens to provide eggs for the hospital, and

134

those you did not requisition. Is there any way you can find out who the thieves are and perhaps get the hens back?"

The major gave a short bark of laughter. "I very much doubt it, Mother. I imagine that whoever has taken your hens has already disposed of them."

"And there is nothing you can do about it," Mother Marie-Pierre stated flatly.

"There is not." The major got to his feet to indicate that the interview was over. "I have a great many important things to deal with at present, and your hens are not among them."

Mother Marie-Pierre also got to her feet and said quietly, "I am sorry your soldiers in the hospital will not receive the nourishing food they need, Major."

"Are you daring to threaten me, Reverend Mother?" Major Thielen asked. Before, he had been cool, now he was icy.

"No, Major," Mother Marie-Pierre replied calmly, "just stating a fact. The rations we receive for our patients are insufficient for their needs. With no hens and only a small part of our vegetable crop, we can no longer adequately supplement them."

As she turned to leave, the door was flung wide and another officer strode into the room. To her surprise Major Thielen snapped to attention and saluted.

"Heil Hitler!"

The newcomer returned the salute and looking across at Mother Marie-Pierre asked in German, "And who is this?"

With chill realisation, Mother Marie-Pierre saw that the uniform this man was wearing was different from the major's, and carried the now famous death's insignia on the collar. Even in the convent, word of Himmler's Waffen SS and its activities had been whispered; rumours that became increasingly frightening as they circulated. Until now the reverend mother had dismissed most of these, but now, seeing this man looking her over, as if deciding what she might fetch at market, she sensed an emanation of evil. Instinctively she drew herself up, levelly returning his gaze. The man was tall, his close-cropped hair displaying the elongated shape of his head. His eyes, grey and cold, looked out on the world from beneath pale eyebrows with hauteur and arrogance.

And I thought Major Thielen looked cruel! thought Mother Marie-Pierre.

"This is the reverend mother from the convent above the village, Colonel," the major replied, and then turning to Mother Marie-Pierre he introduced her to the newcomer, in French. "Mother Marie-Pierre, this is Colonel Hoch, of the SS."

Hoch looked at the nun standing so straight and upright before him and gave a curt nod, and speaking with a guttural accent, said in French, "Good morning. I am afraid I must ask you to leave. I have business with Major Thielen."

"We had already finished our discussion," Mother Marie-Pierre said. "I will bid you good day, gentlemen."

136

Swiftly she left the building. If only half of what she had heard of the SS and the Gestapo was true, then Colonel Hoch was a man to be feared. She hoped he would not be staying in St Croix for long.

In this she was disappointed. It was only days later that Sister Henriette returned from visiting an old woman, bedridden in the village, with the news that Major Thielen had moved to The Manor where his officers were already billeted. Colonel Hoch had taken over the mayor's house.

Mother Marie-Pierre smiled bitterly when she heard the news. Serve him right, she thought uncharitably, as she recalled the way he had evicted Monsieur Dubois. She actually said as much to Sister St Bruno when she visited her that evening.

"He had no compunction in turning out Monsieur Dubois," she said, "and now the same thing has happened to him."

"Shows how important this Colonel Hoch is, Sarah," remarked her aunt.

"There is a difference in rank," agreed Sarah. "Hoch is the senior officer."

"More than that, I think," replied the old nun. "Your major is simply in the army. An SS officer, or Gestapo or whatever he is, is much more important."

"What have you heard about them?" asked Sarah. It never failed to amaze her how well her bedridden aunt was informed about things, even though she had not left her room for more than a year.

"Oh, just snippets, you know." She smiled. "Young Marthe is quite chatty when she comes in the mornings. She tells me what is going on in the village, who says what, who does what. She's a real gossip, and I suppose I should discourage her, but when one's shut away up here, well, the child's like a breath of fresh air."

Sarah smiled too. Marthe was a cheerful girl, and was good, both with the children and with the patients in the hospital. "I'm glad she cheers you up," she said, "and you can keep me posted on the things that are going on that I otherwise wouldn't hear about!"

It was not Sister St Bruno, however, who told Mother Marie-Pierre what had happened several weeks later, but Marthe herself. Sister Danielle brought her to the office, white-faced with terror, almost unable to speak.

"I'm sorry to disturb you, Mother," Sister Danielle said, "but Marthe is here and she's in a dreadful state. I think you should listen to what she told me."

"Come in, Marthe," Mother Marie-Pierre said. "Come in and sit down. Please stay, Sister Danielle, in case I need you."

They settled Marthe down in one of the chairs, but she couldn't stay seated. Almost immediately she was on her feet again, pacing the tiny room.

"Marthe, try and calm down," Sister Danielle said, "and tell Mother what you told me."

"They're taking them!" Marthe cried. "My family. They're taking them away. Maman, Papa, François, Étienne, Jeanne, even little Margot. They're putting them in lorries!"

"Who?" demanded Mother Marie-Pierre. "Who is taking them?"

138

"The Germans," wailed Marthe. "The Germans. They came to the house this morning and made them all get up. Pushed them outside. They're in the square, Mother, a whole crowd, and there are lorries coming to take them away." The girl's voice rose on a note of panic, and she cried out. "I must go to them, Mother, I must, but Sister Danielle says I can't." She turned towards the door, but Sister Danielle was standing in front of it, as if ready to block her escape.

"Try to be calm for a moment, Marthe," Mother Marie-Pierre said quietly, "and we will think what to do. Now tell me, how do you know all this?"

"Francine, who lives next door to us; Maman managed to whisper to her, to tell me to stay away. I stayed here last night because Sister Eloise wanted me to help with the night duty. I was just going to have my breakfast with the children when Francine came to find me, but Sister Danielle wouldn't let me go!"

"And she was quite right," Mother Marie-Pierre said firmly. "Your mother didn't send you that message to get you to go to the square, did she? No, she wanted you to stay here, where you would be safe."

"But I don't want to be safe," wailed Marthe. "I want to be with my family. Where are they taking them? Francine says it isn't just them, there's a whole crowd gathered in the square."

"Marthe, listen." Mother Marie-Pierre took the hysterical girl by the shoulders and gave her a shake. "You must not go to the square. You will do no one any good if you are rounded up too. Your mother knows that, that's why she sent you the message. She wants

139

you to stay here where you will be safe." She turned to Sister Danielle. "I'll leave Marthe with you, Sister. Take her over to the children's wing. I'll go now, at once, to the village and find out what is going on. I've met Major Thielen several times, so I'll try and find out from him what's happening. I am sure there is some mistake." She smiled at Marthe to reassure her. "I know they have been taking able-bodied men to work in the factories in Germany, but there can be no reason to take your mother or the younger children. Your papa and François, maybe, but not the rest." She passed the young girl into Sister Danielle's care. "You are to stay with Sister Danielle until I come back. You understand? You are to stay here in the convent till I get back. We shall know more then."

Sister Danielle took the weeping Marthe in her arms and led her to the children's wing. Mother Marie-Pierre gathered up her cloak and leaving instructions with Sister Celestine to tell Sister Marie-Paul that she had had to go to the village on an extremely urgent matter, she hurried down the footpath that led through the copse to the village.

When she reached the village square her heart was pounding both from the exertion and with fear at what she might find. The square was deserted except for about twenty-five people, who stood pale and frightened under the watchful eyes of three armed soldiers. Most of them were adults, their faces pale and drawn, but there were children there too. Mother Marie-Pierre could see Marthe's family huddled together, a group within a group. They had one suitcase with them set down at Claude Lenoir's feet. Marthe's mother, Rochelle, was clutching a bag of what appeared to be food and the younger children clustered round her like chicks to a mother hen. François, the eldest boy, stood with his father, his face bleak, his eyes staring at the soldiers with their rifles. Apart from this forlorn little group there was no one in sight. The windows round the square were shuttered and blank, the pavements empty, the doors closed and probably bolted. The tables outside Le Chat Noir were still set out, but there were no customers and the blind was drawn down over the window. The people of St Croix had seen what was going on and were keeping well clear. Who knew who would be next? Best not to be seen. Best hide away behind shutters and blinds until the danger had passed.

Mother Marie-Pierre crossed over to one of the guards. "Please can you tell me what's happening? What have these people done?"

The man shrugged at her. "*Parle pas Français.*" But when she moved to speak to Marthe's family, he barred her way with his outstretched rifle.

"*Verboten!*" he growled, and Mother Marie-Pierre, needing no translation, backed away. Glancing again at Marthe's family she saw the almost imperceptible shake of Madame Lenoir's head. Don't speak to us, her eyes warned, don't draw attention to us or to the fact that Marthe isn't here.

Mother Marie-Pierre gave a curt little nod as if to the soldier, but in fact to the Lenoirs, and turned away.

"Where is Major Thielen?" she asked the guard.

Recognising the name of his commanding officer, the man jerked his head backwards towards the town hall.

Mother Marie-Pierre crossed the square to the building that housed the German headquarters. Again her way was barred by a sentry, but this time when she asked for Major Thielen the sentry replied in fractured French that the Herr Major was inside and too busy to see anyone; he continued to block the doorway.

Undeterred by this, Mother Marie-Pierre treated him to a smile and said quite calmly and matter-of-factly that the Herr Major would see her when he knew that the mother superior from the convent was waiting to speak with him. The man looked uncertain, and then saying, "Wait here," disappeared inside. He returned almost at once. "You will wait in here."

Wait she did, for more than an hour in a small anteroom off the main hall. Through the window she could see the desolate cluster of people still waiting amid their guard in the middle of the square. The square itself remained otherwise deserted. No one else came near, it was as if it were a group of lepers gathered there, and fearful of infection all those in the vicinity had withdrawn, clutching their clothes about them and scurried away to the safety of their homes. Even as she watched, Mother Marie-Pierre saw little Margot Lenoir whispering to her mother. Madame Lenoir looked anxiously at one of the guards and then, plucking up courage, edged her way towards him. Immediately the man raised his rifle, pointing it at her menacingly. She stopped, but called out something to him. The man, keeping his gun pointed at her, replied with a shake of his head, and when she spoke again he simply turned his back on her.

With a shrug she returned to the little girl, who was now hopping from one foot to the other. Mother Marie-Pierre watched as the family drew round her, shielding her as best they could from other eyes, and then within their tiny circle, the mother helped the five-year old lift her dress and squat down to relieve herself. The youth and innocence of the child made the act unimportant, but when, still within the protective circle of the family, all the girls and Madame Lenoir did the same thing, Mother Marie-Pierre found her heart reaching out to them . . . such a small thing, but destroying their dignity.

She got to her feet and crossed the hall to the major's closed office door. Drawing a deep breath, she raised her hand and knocked. There was no reply, and having knocked again, she cautiously turned the handle and eased the door open. The room was flooded with sunlight through windows that also looked out onto the square. Major Thielen was sitting at his desk, and he looked up angrily at being disturbed. When he saw who it was he rose to his feet, his expression still dark. "Yes, Reverend Mother, what is it? Why are you here?"

"Good morning, Major," said Mother Marie-Pierre with a calm she was far from feeling. "I came to find out what is happening in the square."

The major flicked his eyes towards the window and then returned them to her face. "That is our business," he replied stiffly. "I hardly see how it can concern you."

"I came through the square on my way to visit the sick in the village," Mother Marie-Pierre said equably, "and I saw these people standing there, surrounded by soldiers who were pointing guns at them. They are clearly under arrest for some reason, and I wondered what they were supposed to have done."

"As I said," returned the major, "I scarcely think it concerns you. Kindly do not interfere in what you don't understand."

"But I am asking, so that I do understand," said the nun. "I know these people. Why are they standing here for hours on end with an armed guard?"

"They are awaiting transport," replied the major. "Now if you don't mind . . ."

"Transport? Transport to where? Where are they going, Major?"

"To work in Germany," he answered. "They are going to work in the factories to help the war effort. Now if that is all, Reverend Mother, I'll bid you good day." He sat down abruptly and picking up a sheaf of papers from his desk, began to read.

"To work in the factories?" Mother Marie-Pierre did not accept her dismissal. "Major Thielen, there are children of only five years old out there. What use will they be in your factories?"

"Their parents will work for the benefit of the Fatherland," a smooth voice spoke from behind her, "and surely you would not wish to split up a family, Reverend Mother? Of course the children go too."

Mother Marie-Pierre spun round to find herself face-to-face with Colonel Hoch. He had come into the room silently behind her, and now he stood within inches of her, the supercilious lift of his eyebrows and the curl of his lip both designed to show his contempt for her.

"And now if you have quite finished wasting the major's time," Hoch went on, "he and I have some business to finish."

He moved a little, but not out of her way, so that she had to brush past him to reach the door. When she did so, Mother Marie-Pierre turned back and said in a soft voice, "May I speak with them, those out there?"

"No, you may not," Hoch said, and turned his back on her.

Shaking with fear and anger, Mother Marie-Pierre paused in the hallway before leaving the town hall. As she collected her thoughts and decided what, if anything, she could do, she heard the colonel speak to the major again, his voice harsh and authoritarian.

"There is still another family, the Auclons, to be rounded up," he said, "but the trucks will be here within the hour. If your men haven't found them by then they'll have to go with the next lot."

Mother Marie-Pierre did not understand all he said, but her schoolgirl German gave her the gist of his remarks and made her blood run cold. The Auclons were another Jewish family who had lived in St Croix ever since she could remember. Joseph Auclon was a barber, and his wife, Janine, helped out occasionally at The Manor where she had been in service before she married. Their two boys, Jacques and Julien, were identical twins and only about three years old.

She wondered where the Auclons were. Had they got wind of the round-up and gone into hiding? Why had these families been chosen to go to Germany? Was it because they were Jews? Probably, she conceded. Jews would be chosen first for forced labour. But what about the children? Why take the children as well as the able-bodied adults? What use would they be in a labour camp? What use would their mother be with them to look after?

Mother Marie-Pierre walked out into the sunshine again and looked across at the waiting prisoners, for that is what they were, trying to see who else had been taken. Most were young men who had returned from the war, but there were several older men there too, and three women. The women stood together, staring round them with large frightened eyes. When they saw Mother Marie-Pierre watching them, one of them ran towards her, her arms outstretched as if in supplication. At once the guard nearest to her fired into the ground at her feet, causing her to reel backwards with a shriek of fear, and to retreat sobbing into the arms of one of her friends. The gunfire brought the colonel and the major running out of the town hall, and when he saw that Mother Marie-Pierre was still standing just outside, the colonel snarled. "Nun, unless you want to go and work for the Reich as well, I suggest you go back to your convent where you belong."

Realising she could do no more here, Mother Marie-Pierre turned away and walked quietly out of the square and up the adjoining lane past the church towards the curé's house.

146

The wooden shutters of Father Michel's house were closed, as if the house were deserted. Undeterred, Mother Marie-Pierre strode up to the front door and raised the big brass knocker, but before she could let it fall, the door swung open and Mademoiselle Picarde peered out. The curé's housekeeper was a tiny, wizened woman with eyes like a snake's, harsh and unflickering, but now those eyes showed fear as they glanced anxiously over the nun's shoulder.

"Reverend Mother," she hissed, "what do you want?"

Mother Marie-Pierre was somewhat surprised at this reception. "I've come to see Father Michel."

A voice from inside the house called out. "Who is it, Rose?"

"You'd better come in," the housekeeper said ungraciously, and standing aside, allowed Mother Marie-Pierre to enter the house.

The priest appeared from a door further down the narrow corridor that ran the length of the house. "Ah, Reverend Mother," he said a little nervously when he saw who his visitor was. "Good morning to you."

"Good morning, Father," she replied. "I need your help."

"You do?" The priest looked worried and gestured her to follow him back into the room from which he had emerged. Mother Marie-Pierre had never called on the priest before, and, following him into the room, found herself in his study. The room was lit with candles, the windows darkened by their shutters.

Mother Marie-Pierre came directly to the point. "The Germans are taking some of the local people away," she said. "They've got them gathered in the square and are only waiting for transport to collect them."

Father Michel nodded. "So I heard," he said. "Rose went to buy bread this morning and told me. I suppose they will take any of our young men that they need," he added resignedly.

"But it's whole families, Father," Mother Marie-Pierre said softly, "not just able-bodied adults, there are children there as well. Little Margot Lenoir is only five. Why are they taking her? She's no use to them."

The curé shrugged. "That I can't say, Mother."

"It's because they're Jews," stated Mother Marie-Pierre flatly.

"You could be right," Father Michel replied uneasily. "But if it is, there's nothing we can do about it, is there? I mean, if they chose the Jews to work in their factories, that may save some of our own boys from having to go."

Mother Marie-Pierre stared at him for a moment. "Some of our own boys? Father, these people are as French as you are. They've lived in this country, this village, all their lives."

"Even so, if the Germans have decided to move them, then there is nothing we can do about it," replied the priest. "And surely it's better for the Lenoir family, and others like them, to stay together, don't you think?"

"Others like them?" Reverend Mother's eyes skewered him. "Which others?"

His eyes slid away before her gaze. "Well, I don't know . . ." he began to bluster. "I mean there are others

148

aren't there? The Auclons for instance." He raised his eyes to her again, adding slyly, "After all you've Jewish children in the convent, haven't you?"

Dismay registered on Mother Marie-Pierre's face before she could control her features and he continued. "I shouldn't want to draw attention to myself if I were sheltering Jews from the Germans. Far better to let them take those they've found already and hope they don't find yours."

Mother Marie-Pierre tilted her head in the candlelight the better to see him. She spoke quietly. "Thank you for your advice, Father. I knew you'd be able to help me." Swiftly she pulled wide the door, which had been standing ajar, and Mademoiselle Rose Picarde almost fell into the room.

"I just came to see if I could get you or the reverend mother anything, Father," she said virtuously, steadying herself with one hand on the door frame.

Mother Marie-Pierre answered before the priest was able to, with chilly politeness. "No thank you, Mademoiselle, I am not staying. I have things to do. I'll bid you both good morning."

Opening the front door, Mother Marie-Pierre stepped out into the fresh summer air, the relief of being out of the house an almost physical thing.

CHAPTER
NINE

Mother Marie-Pierre turned her steps back towards the
convent. As she was emerging from the lane into the
square, she heard the rumble of engines and saw two
lorries come to a halt outside the town hall.
Instinctively, she stepped back into the shelter of the
café wall, and was glad she had, for Hoch and Thielen
both came out from the German headquarters onto the
square. At an order from the colonel, the guards herded
the waiting families towards the canvas-covered trucks.
As the tailgates were let down, Mother Marie-Pierre
could see that the lorries were already crammed with
people.

Surely, she thought, there isn't room for anyone else
in there.

Even as she watched four young men and a woman
sprang from one of the lorries, sprinting away from the
truck in search of escape, of a place to hide. Each ran in
a different direction, zigzagging as they ran, making
for the illusory safety of the alleyways that gave onto
the square. Immediately chaos broke loose as both the
guards riding on the lorries and those covering the
people in the square opened fire on the fugitives. One
man was killed outright as a bullet powered into his

back, flinging him into the air before he crumpled like a ragdoll to the ground in a pool of blood. Those still in the trucks began to shout as gunfire rattled round the square, the soldiers shooting, indiscriminately, in the directions that the fugitives had taken. Those gathered to be loaded onto the lorries screamed and shrieked with fear, flinging themselves flat on the ground as bullets ripped through the air about their heads.

There was a bellow of rage from Colonel Hoch, and shouting a mixture of orders — "After them! Shoot to kill! Guard the rest!" — the officer disappeared down one of the alleyways, his pistol in his hand.

There was confusion among the soldiers. Some followed the colonel, rushing from the square in hot pursuit, their rifles at the ready; others turned their guns on the prisoners in the lorries, to deter any other would-be escapees. Major Thielen hurried back into the town hall, shouting orders to someone inside. The group who had been waiting in the square were still flat on the ground, while a German private barked orders at them, waving his rifle threateningly. There was a rattle of gunfire from further away and another scream.

From her place behind the café wall, Mother Marie-Pierre saw that several of those who had dived for cover had actually rolled underneath one of the lorries, seeking shelter from the spitting bullets. Madame Lenoir was one, her body shielding Margot, her youngest child. For a moment their eyes met, desperate appeal in Madame Lenoir's, compassion in the nun's. She held out her arms and the woman under the lorry murmured something to her daughter and then pushed her out from the shelter of the lorry, across the two metres of open space and into Mother Marie-Pierre's open arms. The nun gathered the child to her and stepped back into the shelter of the lane down which she had come. Even as she drew the little girl back behind the wall, obscuring her from the sight of the guard, the soldier saw the mother underneath the truck and roared an order at her, prodding her with the barrel of his rifle. Madame Lenoir crawled out from the other side of the lorry, her back firmly to Mother Marie-Pierre and Margot in the lane, and rejoined the rest of her family who were now on their feet again and being herded once more towards the waiting transports. She kept her eyes steadfastly away from the direction her daughter and Mother Marie-Pierre had taken, fighting with every fibre of her being the compulsion to turn for one final glimpse of her baby.

The reverend mother gathered the small girl into her arms and doubled back behind the café. She could hear the soldiers still shouting to each other as they searched for the escaping prisoners. There was another burst of gunfire close enough to make her shake, and she clutched the child to her ever more tightly.

"In here, Sister," hissed a voice, and a door in the wall beside her opened just wide enough to admit her. She squeezed through and the door was immediately closed and bolted behind her. An old woman grabbed her hand and pulled them both in through the back entrance of the café.

"Down here!" she instructed, and Mother Marie-Pierre saw that there was a trapdoor open in the stone floor of the kitchen, from which a flight of steps led down. Margot, terrified into silence until now, began to wail.

"Ssh, *ma petite*," soothed the old lady. "You're safe now. Down you go, Sister, till they've gone." She smiled up encouragingly. "Sorry, Mother. I didn't see it was you. Best keep both of you out of sight until they've driven off, at least."

Mother Marie-Pierre nodded and with Margot still in her arms sat on the edge of the hole in the floor, feeling for the steps with her feet. The trapdoor was closed over her head, and they were left in the gloom of a cellar only lit by the grey light that filtered through a narrow window set high up in the wall.

Margot was still crying. "I want Maman," she wailed. "Where's Maman? I want her."

"I know you do, *chérie*," soothed Mother Marie-Pierre, sitting down on a box with the child on her knee and getting out a handkerchief to mop her tears. "But Maman can't come just now. She wants you to stay with me for a little while. Then I'll take you to see Marthe. You'd like that, wouldn't you?" She sat rocking the little girl in her arms until she gradually calmed down, and with her thumb set comfortably in her mouth, began to doze. Mother Marie-Pierre longed to go to the tiny window to see if she could see or hear anything from outside, but she didn't want to disturb the now sleeping child. Better to wait, she decided, until her hostess and saviour came to give her the all-clear, and then, somehow, she'd have to get Margot back to the relative safety of the convent.

153

It was well over an hour later that she heard the scrape of the trapdoor above her and light flooded into the subterranean room.

"You can come up now, Mother," said the old woman.

Gently Mother Marie-Pierre lifted the sleeping child up to the waiting arms above and then followed her out into the kitchen.

"Madame Juliette," she said softly, "that was a very brave thing to do."

The old woman peered at her and then smiled. "Ah, Mother," she said, "there is little enough that we can do in these sad times. What can the Boche want with little children, *hein*?"

"I don't know, Madame." Mother Marie-Pierre looked across at the old lady, a woman she had met all those years ago when she had first come to the convent to nurse the wounded in the last war. "What finally happened out there?" She nodded her head towards the square.

"The lorries have gone," Madame Juliette said flatly. "They loaded in those waiting in the square and drove away."

"And those that ran?"

"One they killed, two they brought back, both wounded and bleeding and two ..." she shrugged eloquently. "I suppose they are still searching for them."

"And the child?" Mother Marie-Pierre looked at Margot now nestled against Madame Juliette's ample bosom. "Did they realise that she'd gone?"

Madame Juliette shrugged again. "Who can tell?" she said. "Probably not. There was such a fracas when those tried to escape. I was watching from upstairs and I don't think they counted the prisoners into the truck. The rest of the family were just pushed onto one of the lorries and then the back was secured. The last one they caught was shot in the leg and bleeding badly. They just tossed him in on top of the others." She sighed. "I think he will die."

Mother Marie-Pierre crossed herself and murmured. "May the Lord take his soul."

"Amen to that," said the old lady. Then she suddenly pulled herself together. "Now, we have to decide what to do with you and Margot."

"Well, I can come and go about the village as I always do, so I'm in no danger," began Mother Marie-Pierre.

"Until someone remembers that you are English," interrupted Madame Juliette. It was the first indication she had given that she remembered that the nun in front of her was one of the English girls who had frequented her café to eat *pain d'épice* when they had first arrived from England in 1915. "You must not trust anyone, Mother. There are too many round here who would sell their own grandmothers if they thought it would be to their advantage."

"Surely not, Madame," began Mother Marie-Pierre.

"Believe me, Mother. I remember where you came from . . . so will others. Be very careful."

"So, what do you suggest?" asked the nun.

"For the moment you should be safe enough, that major probably doesn't pose much of a threat. He's just a soldier." Madame Juliette spoke dismissively. "No, the dangerous one is that Colonel Hoch. Try not to draw his attention. He is an evil man."

"Well, I have met him a couple of times, and I think I agree with you," Mother Marie-Pierre said. "I shall certainly steer clear of him if I can. Still, for the moment, I think it should be safe enough for me to walk back to the convent, taking Margot with me. The Germans won't know that she should have been put in the lorry. They'll just think she's one of the village children."

"Better you go openly," agreed Madame Juliette. "If they thought you were trying to hide from them, that would be really dangerous. You must go in the daylight, but go with caution, they will still be looking for those two who got away. Your habit should protect you and if a patrol stops you, you must tell them you are taking the child to the hospital."

Mother Marie-Pierre nodded. "Then I think we'd better be off, before we bring any trouble to you and your family."

The old woman nodded at this and gently roused the child from her sleep. "Wake up, Margot," she said, "you're going with Mother Marie-Pierre, now. So, be a good girl and hold her hand all the way. I'll let you out the back way, Mother," she added. "If you walk down the lane to the end you'll be on the towpath and can cut back to the convent from there."

Mother Marie-Pierre smiled. "Yes," she said, "I know the way. Come along, Margot." She held out her hand to the little girl who took it obediently.

"Are we going to find Maman and Papa now?" Margot asked.

Before the nun could answer Madame Juliette said, "In a little while. Don't you worry about them, Margot. They'll be back soon. You go with Mother Marie-Pierre for now like a good girl, and in a day or two I'll bring you a little cake, just for yourself, all right?"

The child nodded and the two adults exchanged glances over her head. The lies had to be told, for Margot had to be inconspicuous as she was got to safety. A crying child would draw unwelcome attention to them. She could be told about her parents when she was out of danger.

"Is Marthe still at the convent?" murmured Madame Juliette softly.

"Yes, at least I hope she is," replied the nun. "I left her with Sister Danielle and told her to stay there until I got back."

"Let's hope she did," replied the old lady as she led the way to the back gate. She eased it open and looked out into the lane beyond. "No one in sight," she said, "but don't forget they'll still be looking for the two who got away."

Mother Marie-Pierre slipped out through the gate, still holding Margot firmly by the hand. "God bless you, Madame," she said.

"And you, Mother. It's you taking the risks now." With that she closed the gate and Mother Marie-Pierre heard the bolts being drawn across again.

"Come along, Margot," she said turning down the lane towards the river, "let's get home to the convent and have something to eat."

The lane led to the towpath that ran along the riverbank. The river itself wound its way lazily round the edge of the village before widening into a pool from which it emerged to continue its leisurely way to join the Somme. The towpath was a well-used track to some of the outlying cottages, a shortcut to the centre of the village, or to the road that led eastward beyond. Today, however, it was deserted. The river flowed slowly here, its brown water sluggish as it slid under the willows that lined its bank.

Mother Marie-Pierre hurried along the path, her eyes scanning the fields on the further bank, flicking anxiously towards the backs of the houses that sprawled untidily at the edge of the village. Keeping a firm hold on Margot's hand, she almost dragged the child in her wake.

"Halt!" The word rang out and Mother Marie-Pierre stopped abruptly as a burly soldier carrying a rifle stepped out from the end of another of the lanes that led into the centre of the village. He looked across at her and the little girl clutching the skirt of her habit, and said in execrable French, "Where do you go?"

"To the hospital," replied Mother Marie-Pierre simply. "This child needs to see a doctor."

The man, looking at them suspiciously, took a step towards them, still covering them with his rifle. Margot gave a scream of fear and buried her face in the habit. Immediately Mother Marie-Pierre scooped the child up into her arms and said sternly to the man, "Put your gun aside. Can't you see you are terrifying the little one?" She gestured at the rifle to make her meaning clear and then gathered Margot closer into her arms. The little girl was sobbing, her face hidden against Mother Marie-Pierre's shoulder.

The man lowered his weapon and looked round. "A woman. I look for a woman. Maybe shot. You have seen?"

Mother Marie-Pierre shook her head. "I've seen no one," she said and took a step forward along the path. For a moment the soldier continued to bar her way, then he stepped aside, and turning away set off along the path in the direction from which they had come.

"No," murmured Mother Marie-Pierre to his departing back, "I've seen no one, man or woman, but would I have told you if I had?" It was no time to be considering the rights and wrongs of lying to save a life, she still had a life to save here and now. Margot must be got to safety and the sooner the better. Still carrying the child, she hurried to the path that led across the fields and up through the copse to the convent. She could see the tall, grey walls above the trees, and never had she longed to be there so much as now. As she finally reached the copse, Margot heavy in her arms, she looked back across the field and saw two more men in field grey searching among the willows along the riverbank. Clearly they had not yet found all those who had made a break for freedom.

As soon as she reached the convent gate, she was greeted by an almost hysterical Sister Celestine, who rushed out to greet her.

"Oh Mother," she cried. "Thank God you are safe! We heard shots from the village and when you didn't come back, Sister Marie-Paul sent Sister Henriette down to find out what had happened, and she hasn't come back yet. And there've been soldiers on motorbikes on the road, roaring up and down and . . ." Her words came tumbling in a torrent of anguish and relief, but her superior cut her off.

"Well, as you see, Sister, I am quite safe. Please go to the kitchen and get some bread and milk and bring it up to the children's wing. I shall be with Sister Danielle. Please also tell Sister Marie-Paul that I am back and ask her to call all the sisters who can be spared from their work to the recreation room in half an hour." Even as she was speaking, Mother Marie-Pierre was striding through the hallway and along the passage to the children's rooms.

"Yes, Mother, of course, Mother, straight away." Sister Celestine scurried away to find the novice mistress, Sister Marie-Paul.

When Reverend Mother entered the children's dayroom she was greeted with a shriek from Marthe, who rocketed from her chair at the sight of her little sister. Margot, set down on the floor at last, was gathered into her sister's arms and hugged so tightly that after a minute she wriggled to be free. Sister

160

Danielle appeared from the next room and looking over the heads of the two girls raised her eyebrows questioningly. Mother Marie-Pierre shook her head slightly and the younger nun went pale.

"Now then, Marthe," Mother Marie-Pierre said briskly, "let's get Margot comfortable. Sister Danielle will take her to the bathroom before Sister Celestine gets here with her food. I want you to come with me for a moment or two."

Marthe, still cradling Margot in her arms, looked up and saw the compassion in the reverend mother's face. Gently putting Margot away from her she stood up. There was a bleak control in her voice. "Go with Sister Danielle, Margot. I'll be back in a minute to give you your tea."

The little girl reached for her sister's hand, her bottom lip quivering, but Marthe placed the reaching hand into Sister Danielle's. "Be a good girl now, Margot," she said. "I'll be back in a minute, I promise." Then turning her back resolutely on the tears that were beginning to course down Margot's cheeks, she followed Mother Marie-Pierre out of the room.

"We'll go to my office," said the nun, leading the way, and with a leaden heart, Marthe followed.

Once in the privacy of the office, Mother Marie-Pierre turned to the white-faced girl. It was heartbreaking to have to tell this girl, little more than a child herself, of the events down in the village square. For a short moment she looked at her, wondering what words to use to break the news, but Marthe didn't wait to be told.

"They've gone, haven't they?" she asked quietly. "Are they dead?"

"No, of course not . . ." began Mother Marie-Pierre, but Marthe continued almost as if she hadn't heard. "We heard the guns, you see. Shooting. Lots of shooting. I thought . . ."

Mother Marie-Pierre took the girl's hands in her own. They were icy cold and the nun chafed them gently as she spoke.

"There was shooting," she agreed, "but not at your family. They were put on a lorry to go to Germany to work in a factory there." No need to describe the dreadful conditions that they must be facing in that overcrowded lorry, no need to tell this brave girl that they were being treated worse than cattle on the way to the abattoir.

"Your mother gave Margot to me to look after until they come home again," she went on. "She knows you are safely here with us and that you'll look after Margot for her." No need to explain how her mother had put her own life at risk to save young Margot's. Let Marthe think that the Germans had had no use for such a young child and had allowed the nun to take her. "She sent you her love. They all did." Not aloud, Mother Marie-Pierre thought as she stretched the truth for the third time that day, but she had no trouble with that, she had no doubt that the love had been sent.

Marthe's face was rigid with her determination not to cry. Mother Marie-Pierre could see the tears brimming in her eyes, but the young girl would not let them fall. It was as if, before her eyes, Mother

162

Marie-Pierre saw the girl's childhood fall away, sloughed off like a snakeskin, and the cloak of adulthood envelop her.

"They've gone," she said flatly. "Margot and I have only each other now."

"Certainly for now you must look after each other," Reverend Mother agreed gently, "but there is no reason to think that your family won't return at the end of the war."

"Isn't there?" Marthe looked pityingly at the nun. "You don't understand, do you, Mother? We are Jews. There will be no Jews left at the end of this war. Jews in Germany have been disappearing for years. Now it is our turn." She gave a sharp and bitter laugh. "You think we shall be safe here in the convent? Margot and I will be safe nowhere round here where it is known that we are Jews. Before long someone will send the Germans here, you'll see. They'll come for me and for Margot and probably for those Leon children as well, and you won't be able to stop them. We shall be loaded onto a lorry, just like Maman, Papa and the others . . . and we shall disappear. There will be no end to the war for us." She had spoken with steely control, but as she uttered these last words her voice broke in a sob.

Mother Marie-Pierre moved to gather her into her arms, but Marthe pulled away and spoke, almost fiercely. "No, Mother, I'm not a child like Margot, to be comforted with a hug and soothing words. I know what we are facing, and I know that you won't be able to protect us when the time comes." She wiped the tears away with the back of her hand and went on, "I must go back to Margot, now. She'll be frightened here with no one she knows. Thank you for bringing her to me." Her voice was so unemotional and polite she might have been thanking the reverend mother for having her to tea.

Mother Marie-Pierre stood aside. "Yes, go back and find her. I will consider what we do next. You're safe for the time being, I think, but it may not be for long and we must make plans." She smiled at the young girl. "May God give you courage, Marthe."

Marthe, who had reached the door, turned back and looked the reverend mother in the eye. "There is no God, Mother. Not yours, not mine." And with that she left the room, closing the door softly behind her.

Some minutes later Mother Marie-Pierre joined the rest of her community in the recreation room. There was a buzz of conversation, but it died away as she entered, and the nuns all turned their eyes expectantly on their superior.

"Sisters," Mother Marie-Pierre began, "today the Germans have started rounding up people from the village and shipping them off to Germany. They say they are to work for the German war effort in their factories, and maybe they are. However, they are taking whole families including young children, who can be of little use in the factories. The families they are taking are those of Jewish extraction. We have all heard rumours of camps where the Jews are being held, and whether we believe these or not, the fact remains that Marthe Lenoir's family have all been loaded into a lorry today and taken away. Her mother managed to get

164

the youngest daughter, Margot, to my care before they left, but from what I have heard in the village" — she did not mention the attitude of the curé as most of the nuns would bow to his authority and accept his line of thinking — "it will only be a matter of time before someone tells the Germans they are here."

Sister Marie-Paul raised a hand and Mother Marie-Pierre nodded to her to speak. "Mother, surely their presence here will endanger the whole convent community."

There were murmurs of assent to this, but Mother Marie-Pierre cut through them. "So, what do you suggest we do, Sister? Simply hand two innocent young girls over to Colonel Hoch?" she asked sharply.

"No, Mother, of course not," Sister Marie-Paul said hastily. "I was merely going to suggest that we should find a family to take care of them until their own people return from Germany."

"Will that not put the foster family at the same risk you are saying we shouldn't take?" the reverend mother asked evenly. There was no accusation in her voice, but the other nun flushed. "We run an orphanage, Sister, and to all intents and purposes these children are orphans. They are our responsibility and we must not shirk it.

"Please, sisters, discuss this among yourselves, and if anyone can come up with a way to protect the children that have been confided to our care, then come to me so that we can consider it. In the meantime, please carry on as normal, and remember the families who

165

have been carried off in your prayers, particularly Marthe and Margot's."

As she left the room, there was another buzz of excited conversation. Never before could the nuns remember having been asked to discuss something among themselves. Usually decisions were taken by the senior members of the community, Reverend Mother, Sister Marie-Paul as Novice Mistress, Sister Eloise as Matron, and handed down from on high to be implemented without argument. This new reverend mother ruled the convent in a very different way from her predecessors, and that in itself was worth discussion.

Mother Marie-Pierre left them to their amazement and went upstairs to talk things through with Sister St Bruno. She had the germ of an idea, but needed to consider it carefully with someone whom she could trust implicitly.

CHAPTER
TEN

Sister St Bruno was dozing in her bed, her missal open upside down on her lap, her head tilted sideways on the pillow and her spectacles askew on her nose, but at the sound of the door opening she jerked awake.

Mother Marie-Pierre smiled across at her apologetically. "Sorry to wake you, Aunt Anne," she said as she came into the room, "but I need to talk to you urgently."

"I wasn't asleep, Sarah," replied her aunt, "just resting my eyes."

Sarah laughed. "Good, then I haven't disturbed you." She drew the little, upright visitor's chair to the bedside and sat down, her face instantly serious. "Aunt, we've got a problem and I need to talk it through with you."

Her aunt settled her glasses more comfortably on her nose and looked gravely at her niece. "What has happened?"

"The Germans have started taking people from the village," replied Sarah. "Ostensibly to work in their factories in Germany, but they have taken whole families, not just the able-bodied who would be of use to their workforce. The families they have taken are Jews, and among them are Marthe's family."

Her aunt stared at her in horror. "All of them?" she queried in disbelief. "Even the children?"

"All except Marthe, who was here overnight in the hospital, and little Margot, the youngest." Sarah described how Marthe had been brought to her in great distress that morning, and then went on to tell what had happened when she had gone down to the village to investigate. Aunt Anne listened without interruption as Sarah described the events of the day, finally telling of the meeting she had called in the recreation room.

"I don't know what to do," she said. "Several of our sisters think we shouldn't keep the children because we endanger the whole convent."

"Sister Marie-Paul spoke for them?" It was hardly a question, more of a statement.

Sarah shrugged. "She certainly spoke out," she agreed. "No one else did, but I had the feeling that there were others who think as she does. Our primary work is the hospital and they think that we shouldn't get involved in anything that might bring German wrath down on our heads."

"It makes sense, I suppose," sighed Aunt Anne.

Sarah stared at her in horror. "But what about the children?" she exploded. "Aunt, I can't believe you said that!"

Her aunt reached out a hand to her. "Sarah, I said it made sense, I didn't say it was right! Of course we must find some way of looking after the children, but you have to face the ugly truth. It won't be long before the

Germans know that we have them here and that they are Jews. There will be people ready enough to inform if they think it will be to their advantage . . . and those same people will probably also tell their new masters that you are English. That is something else to be considered."

"That doesn't put the convent at risk," pointed out Sarah briskly, "only me."

Her aunt inclined her head in acquiescence. "And me," she added softly.

Sarah was immediately contrite. "Oh, Aunt Anne, of course, I'm sorry."

"Don't be," soothed her aunt. "I am of no consequence. I'm over seventy and bedridden with arthritis. There is little more I can do in the Lord's service, I am more than ready when my time comes. Much more important is what we are going to do about these children. I assume we have to consider the three Leon children as well as Marthe and Margot."

"Certainly we do," Sarah agreed, "and I have asked all the sisters to try and think of something that we can do to ensure their safety."

"Was it wise to make it a topic for discussion?" wondered the old lady. "Who knows who may be listening?"

"I haven't ever revealed to the community at large that the Leon children are Jews," Sarah said. "Only those who are concerned with their day-to-day care know the truth, but in a community such as ours I am sure there are whispers about them. However, my instruction referred to Marthe and Margot." She closed her eyes, massaging her forehead as if to ease away her cares. "I have *got* an idea," she said, "but it will need careful planning and should be kept as secret as possible."

"Go on."

"Well, if Marthe was right and they are rounding up all the Jews, the children won't be safe anywhere where it is known that they *are* Jews."

Aunt Anne nodded her agreement. "So?"

"So, we need to move them to somewhere where no one knows who or what they are. It's no good fostering them out to local families as Sister Marie-Paul is suggesting, we have to get them right away from here."

"So where will you send them?"

"I shan't send them, I shall take them myself. I shall take them to Mother Magdalene. No one in the Paris house need know why they've come. We can say we needed extra room to expand the hospital. No one need know how they came to be with us in the first place, they can simply be cared for there as orphans of the war. Let's face it there are going to be enough of those."

"But how will you get them to Paris?" asked her aunt.

"I shall take them on the train," replied Sarah. "If we are stopped I shall say that we are devoting ourselves to hospital work now and that the orphans are being moved to the mother house where there is more room for them."

"It might work," conceded the old nun, "but what about Marthe? She is clearly too old to be an orphan in need of care."

170

"I've thought about her," Sarah said, "and I think that if we put her in a novice's habit she could travel with us to help look after the children. I doubt if anyone will question a young nun who is travelling with her reverend mother."

Sister St Bruno considered for a moment. "What about papers? You will have none for the children . . . or for Marthe for that matter. She can't use her own."

"Well," Sarah said, "it's only Margot that we haven't got papers for. Our own children have them of course and I managed to get new ones for the Leon children as they were orphaned in the air strike and any papers they had were never found. Of course they aren't registered as Jews now, even if they were before."

"And Margot?"

Sarah shrugged. "I hope if I'm stopped that I should be able to talk my way out of any trouble by saying she has been so recently orphaned that we haven't had a chance to replace her papers. Mother Magdalene will have to sort those out when we get to Paris. I certainly can't risk applying for those here!"

"Marthe?"

"Marthe will have to take her chances. She will have to travel without any, but I think it is most unlikely that they will bother to ask for them from a nun travelling with her superior. I will have my own, of course." She paused. "What do you think?"

Her aunt shook her head. "It's very risky," she answered. "It could work if you are bold enough to carry it out, but if you are caught . . ." Her voice trailed away.

"I know, then we shall all be lost. But I can think of no other way of protecting those children. We have to get them away from here, and the quicker the better."

"Then I suggest that the fewer people who know of this plan the better," said Aunt Anne. "If you are going through with this, you have to minimise the risks. Do you need a permit from the Germans to travel to Paris on the train?"

"I don't think so," replied Sarah. "People seem to be travelling freely enough, but I believe there are spot checks on the trains, at the stations, even in the streets. We shan't be able to avoid these controls, not moving with a group of children. We shall have to put our trust in the Lord."

As Sister St Bruno started to speak again there was a knock on the door and Sister Marie-Marc put her head into the room.

"Oh, Mother, you're here," she said with relief in her voice.

"Sister, what is it?" asked Mother Marie-Pierre. Sister Marie-Marc was clearly agitated. "What's the matter?"

"I think you should come, Mother," replied the nun. "There's somebody . . . I've found somebody . . . I mean . . . when I went to the henhouse . . ."

"Start again, Sister," Mother Marie-Pierre said calmly, "and tell me from the beginning."

"I went to the henhouse to shut the birds in for the night, and I found a woman in there. In the henhouse. Hiding."

172

Mother Marie-Pierre looked at her sharply. "Where is she now, Sister? What have you done with her?"

"I didn't know what to do, Mother. She was bleeding, you see."

"So, where is she?" Mother Marie-Pierre fought to keep the impatience out of her voice.

"I've brought her into the kitchen, Mother, and I've locked her in the pantry."

The reverend mother was at once on her feet and heading to the door. "I'll come back later, Sister," she said over her shoulder to her aunt, and hustled Sister Marie-Marc out of the door and down to the kitchen.

"Have you told anyone else?" she asked as they hurried down the stairs.

"No, Mother. All I did was to ask Sister Celestine if she knew where you were, and she said you were with Sister St Bruno."

"Good." Better to discover what this is all about before alarming the other sisters.

They came into the kitchen and Sister Marie-Marc drew back the bolt on the pantry door. She eased the door open and they both looked in. The woman, whoever she was, was lying on the floor, her face ashen, blood seeping from a wound in her shoulder, her clothes dark with the oozing blood. Her eyes opened and she scrabbled against the stone-flagged floor in an effort to get up, but the effort was too great and she sank back down and closed her eyes again.

"It's all right," Mother Marie-Pierre said gently, "we've come to help you."

The woman gave a faint moan and Mother Marie-Pierre knelt down beside her to look at the wound.

"Sister, please would you fetch Sister Eloise? I know she's busy in the hospital, but if you would just say I need her here straight away." She glanced up at the waiting nun. "There's no need to say why, just ask her to hurry."

Within minutes Sister Eloise was at her side, looking down at the wounded woman.

"What have we here, Mother?" she asked softly.

"I think this is one of those who escaped from the German lorries in the square this morning," replied Mother Marie-Pierre. "I think she's been shot."

Sister Eloise knelt down and very gently probed the wound. The woman let out a cry of pain.

"Towels, please," said Sister Eloise, and Sister Marie-Marc passed over a towel from the kitchen rack. Sister Eloise drew her scissors from her pocket and with the utmost care cut away the woman's clothes, exposing the wound, which began pulsing blood again. Quickly she ripped the towel in half and placed one piece underneath the shoulder before gently pressing the second half against the gaping wound.

"We need to get her somewhere where I can work on her," Sister Eloise said briskly. "Can we move her to the hospital now?"

"No, Sister, I don't think so," Mother Marie-Pierre replied. "Too public. The fewer people who know about her the better." She thought for a moment and then spoke to Sister Marie-Marc. "Sister, please fetch Sister Henriette . . . but as quietly as you can."

As Sister Marie-Marc disappeared Mother Marie-Pierre turned back to Sister Eloise. "We'll take her up to my cell. Sister Henriette and I should be able to carry her between us."

"She would be better in the hospital, Mother," ventured Sister Eloise, "where I have everything I need to tend her."

"I know that, Sister," replied the reverend mother, "but the Germans are probably still looking for her. She must be hidden away in case they come here." She knelt down by the injured woman again. "We are going to take you somewhere safe to see to your wound. If two of us support you, will you be able to walk at all?"

"Yes." The single word was forced out through gritted teeth, and Mother Marie-Pierre saw that the eyes that looked up at her were full of determination.

Sister Eloise sighed. "If that is really best," she said, and ripping up another towel, she tied the makeshift pads into place.

Sister Henriette and Sister Marie-Marc came into the kitchen then, and between them all they managed to get the fugitive onto her feet and support her slowly across the room.

"Clean the pantry floor, Sister," Mother Marie-Pierre instructed Sister Marie-Marc as they manoeuvred the injured woman out of the door. "Make sure there is nothing to show what went on here."

Before they emerged from the corridor into the hall, Sister Eloise went ahead and found Sister Celestine at her usual post beside the front door. She sent her to the ward kitchen with instructions to fetch some bandages and to bring them to the reverend mother's cell.

"Don't alarm anyone," she said, "it's nothing much."

With the portress safely out of sight they moved as quickly as they could up the stairs to the main landing where the nuns had their individual sleeping cells. Within moments they had negotiated their way along the corridor to that of the reverend mother, and the woman was lowered gently onto the bed. Sister Eloise set about cleaning the wound, sending Sister Henriette for hot water while Mother Marie-Pierre found more towels from the linen cupboard at the end of the passage.

As she carried these back along the landing she glanced out of the window and saw, to her horror, Major Thielen's car crawling up the lane towards the convent gate, followed by a truck full of soldiers.

"The Germans are coming," she hissed as she placed the towels on the chair by the bed. "Major Thielen's car is coming up the lane."

Sister Eloise looked up. "You've blood on the front of your habit, Mother," she said quietly. "Put on a nursing apron before you greet the major. Go now," she added as Mother Marie-Pierre hesitated, "I can manage here. Tell Sister Henriette to hurry with the water." She spoke with the ease of one used to command, and Mother Marie-Pierre nodded and hurried away, pausing momentarily at the linen cupboard to seize one of the huge white aprons the nursing sisters wore in the hospital. It was voluminous enough to cover most of her habit including the bloodstains on the front, where the woman had leaned against her. As she descended the stairs she met both Sister Henriette returning with a jug of hot water from the kitchen and Sister Celestine coming back with the bandages from the hospital.

"Give the bandages to Sister Henriette," she said to Sister Celestine. The little nun had handed them over and the reverend mother issued swift orders to Sister Henriette. "Take all that up to Sister Eloise as quickly as you can, and then go at once to the children's wing and warn Sister Danielle that the Germans are here. Tell her to take all the children up to the chapel and to lead them in prayers, aloud. If they search the convent they must find all the children kneeling at prayer in the chapel. Marthe too. Do you understand?"

Sister Henriette did. "Yes, Mother." She hurried up the stairs with the water. Even as she disappeared Mother Marie-Pierre heard the slam of a car door.

"When they ring the bell," she said to Sister Celestine, "answer the door as usual and bring the major to me in my office."

The portress looked frightened, but she nodded. "Yes, Mother."

Drawing a deep breath and firing a prayer heavenwards, the reverend mother turned away from the front door and walked towards her office ready to deal with Major Thielen when he was brought in. She came to an abrupt halt, however, when she heard Sister Celestine give a shrill cry, a cry that was abruptly cut off. Spinning on her heel, Mother Marie-Pierre hurried back to the hall where she found Sister Celestine standing, terrified, at the wrong end of a German rifle, as Major Thielen and a group of soldiers crowded in through the door.

"Major Thielen!" ejaculated Mother Marie-Pierre. "What is the meaning of this intrusion? What are these men doing in the convent?" Without pausing for him to answer she turned to the petrified nun. "It's all right, Sister, please go and ask Sister Marie-Paul to join us here."

"Stand exactly where you are!" barked the major, at which the soldier raised his rifle more threateningly and the portress, who had started to move, froze once more.

"Major," began Mother Marie-Pierre, "I really don't understand what is going on here. Why have you come and why are you threatening my sisters with your guns? If you wish to come into the convent you have only to ask, as you have done before."

Ignoring her completely, the major issued an order to his men. "Search the place," he snapped. "Look in every room, including the hospital . . . especially the hospital. Taube, Hesse, stay with me."

"Major, please," Mother Marie-Pierre tried again. "If you could just tell me what you are looking for, perhaps I can help."

The men streamed out of the hall, spreading out along the corridors towards the refectory, the kitchen and the recreation room as they began their search. Two men only remained, the one covering Sister Celestine with his rifle and another who had turned his on the mother superior. Now at last the major gave her his attention.

178

"Prisoners have escaped from the village," he said shortly. "They may be hiding here . . . even without your knowledge, Mother."

"Please ask your men to lower their rifles," Mother Marie-Pierre said. Her voice sounded calm enough, but her heart was pounding. "They are terrifying Sister Celestine, and there is really no need to do so. Neither of us is going to run away."

The major waved a dismissive hand at the soldiers and they lowered their rifles. "You," he said, jerking his head to one of them, "you come with me. We will search upstairs." He looked back at the two nuns. "You will wait for us here."

"I shall accompany you," said Mother Marie-Pierre. She fought to sound calm, but all the time her mind was racing. Had Sister Marie-Marc had time to get the pantry floor scrubbed before the Germans reached the kitchen? Any bloodstains on the floor would alert the soldiers, and they might bully information out of the elderly nun. Convent normality must be the order of the day.

Reverend Mother glanced across at Sister Celestine who was now leaning, pale-faced, against the wall. "Go and help Sister Marie-Marc in the kitchen. Tell her to prepare some coffee and bring it to my office for the major's refreshment when he has finished his search." The little nun looked anxiously at the rifle, but before she could move, Major Thielen barked out an order. "No! She stays here." The rifle immediately swung up again, and she cowered back against the wall. "You," he turned his attention back to the reverend mother, "may come with us if you insist."

"I do insist," Mother Marie-Pierre replied quietly. "It is my convent you are searching; I have responsibility for it and the community that lives within it. If there is anything or anyone to be found, who should not be here, then I wish to know of it too."

She had hoped to delay him long enough for the children to reach the comparative safety of the chapel, but with the soldiers fanning out through the convent she was now anxious that it should be the major himself who found them on their knees in prayer. She had seen the reverence with which he had entered the chapel on his first visit and could only pray that he would feel as constrained this time and not interrupt the children at their prayers. His men might have no such restraint. She hoped that Sister Henriette had taken the message as swiftly as possible to Sister Danielle and that she had acted immediately.

"And is there anyone here who should not be?" demanded the major, his eyes fixed on her face.

Mother Marie-Pierre held his gaze. "No."

Without another word he turned on his heel and started up the stairs followed by the soldier and the reverend mother. At the top he spoke to the man. "Every door, Taube."

Taube went to the first door and raising his boot, kicked it open, bursting in, rifle at the ready. It was one of the sister's sleeping cells, the very one Major Thielen had looked into before. There was nowhere to conceal anything in the room and after a quick glance round the soldier gave his report. "Nothing in here, sir."

"The doors do have handles," pointed out Mother Marie-Pierre mildly, "and none of them is locked."

The major spoke to the man again and he opened the next door in a more restrained manner, but again found nothing. As they made their way along the corridor towards her own sleeping cell, Mother Marie-Pierre wondered how she was going to keep them from searching that. As they reached the door before hers, her own door opened and Sister Eloise came out carrying an armful of bedding.

She spoke immediately to her superior apparently unaware of what was going on. "Oh, Mother," she said, "I'm afraid poor Sister St Bruno has had another accident in her bed. I've changed the sheets and put her in a clean nightdress, so she's comfortable again now." She sighed. "I'm afraid she's rather distressed, but I'm hoping she'll have a little sleep now."

"Don't worry, Sister, I'll look in on her," Mother Marie-Pierre replied, wondering just who she was going to find in the little room when they opened the door. "Just take the sheets down to Sister St Jacques in the laundry."

"Please go into this room quietly," Mother Marie-Pierre murmured to the major as she stood between him and the door. "A bedridden sister is in here. She is old and frail and will be very scared if you burst in." She then whispered confidentially, in case the major had not already picked up on her conversation with Sister Eloise. "I'm afraid she's . . . well, as you see we've had to change her sheets. She can't always control herself, poor dear."

The major's lip curled in distaste and when Taube opened the door Mother Marie-Pierre swept in past him cheerfully. "Hallo, Sister, how are you feeling today?"

Sister St Bruno was propped up in the bed, her hands plucking at the wide blanket draped across her thin body. There was a strong smell of disinfectant in the room, at which Major Thielen, coming into the room behind the reverend mother, sniffed fastidiously.

"Not at all well, Mother," replied the old nun in a petulant voice. "Sister Eloise says I had another accident." She broke off as she noticed the German officer for the first time. She gave a little cry. "Mother, there's a man in my room." She pulled her shawl down over her face as if to hide from the major. "Make him go away, Mother," she quavered. "I don't want a man in my room. Make him go away. Oh, oh, the shame!"

"Hush now, Sister," soothed Mother Marie-Pierre. "He's only looked in to see how you are."

"Is he a doctor?" asked the nun. "Are you a doctor, young man?" Sister St Bruno peered out at Major Thielen from under her shawl."

"No," he replied, and with another sniff of disgust he stalked out of the room and waited for Taube to open the next door.

"Now you settle down and have a nice little sleep, Sister," the reverend mother said in a clear voice. "Sister Clothilde will be up with your supper later and I'll come and see you before I go to bed." As she spoke

182

she raised her eyebrows in query, and Sister St Bruno pointed down with her forefinger. Not daring to check, Mother Marie-Pierre could only assume that the injured woman was stretched out on the floor beneath the iron bedstead, concealed only by the blanket that trailed to the floor on either side.

The search continued along the landing, and included the linen cupboard, which Taube emptied out into the passage in three swift movements, tumbling sheets and towels, pillow cases and aprons into a heap on the floor, but finding no one hiding in its depths. The bathrooms were empty, the lavatory doors open. Major Thielen did not seem to be expecting to find anyone concealed here and when every door had been opened and the bare rooms scrutinised he had already thought of what was coming next. "Now the chapel, Reverend Mother."

Mother Marie-Pierre raised her eyes as if in surprise, but acquiesced readily enough. "Certainly, Major. Come this way." As she had done before she led him through the convent to the door of the chapel.

Surely, she thought, after the time we've spent searching the nuns' sleeping cells there's been time to get the children safely in here.

She paused outside the door, barring the way as she spoke firmly. "I would prefer your man to leave his gun outside. This is, after all, the house of God."

The major spoke to Taube and the man stepped back, taking up a watchful position in the corridor, his rifle at the ready.

"Thank you, Major." Mother Marie-Pierre opened the door and stepping aside allowed the German to precede her. The warmth of the chapel, with its rich scent of incense, enfolded them as they entered. Candles flickered in front of the statue of the Virgin Mary and the sanctuary light, in its brass holder, gleamed red before the altar. The major paused on the threshold as he saw that the chapel was in use. There, kneeling in front of the statue of the Virgin was a line of children with one of the sisters on the end. She was leading them in prayer and as he listened he heard the familiar words. "Holy Mary, Mother of God, pray for us sinners now and in the hour of our death."

Mother Marie-Pierre touched his arm and spoke quietly. "Sister Danielle always brings the children in for their evening prayers before they have their supper."

The children continued to chant the prayer. "Hail Mary, full of grace, blessed art thou among women and blessed is the fruit of thy womb, Jesus . . ."

Major Thielen nodded, but he did not back out of the chapel this time, he moved swiftly towards the altar, and then behind it. The chanting faltered as the children became aware of him and watched what he was doing. Returning to the front of the altar he lifted the corner of the embroidered frontal and peered beneath it. Letting the cloth fall back into place he moved to the side chapel where the children were kneeling in front of the statue, but to Mother Marie-Pierre's relief his eyes were on the little curtained recess to one side. He lifted the curtain and saw the shelves where the votive candles and a pile of prayer books were stored. Again he let the curtain drop and paying no attention to the row of children, who were still kneeling just feet away, he moved on to the vestry on the further side of the high altar.

At a gesture from Mother Marie-Pierre, Sister Danielle began the prayer again, her voice clear and firm, and gradually the children joined in, so that the chorus of "Hail Mary" was well under way when the major re-emerged from the vestry. He took one more look round the chapel as if to ensure that he had not missed a possible hiding place and then returned to the door where the reverend mother waited. Pausing only to dip his hand into the stoup of holy water and bless himself, he walked past her, out into the corridor where Taube waited, his rifle trained on the chapel door.

At that minute there was a commotion at the end of the passageway and the sound of boots on the flagged floor. Mother Marie-Pierre closed the door on the children and, standing in front of it, watched as a sergeant marched up to the major and saluted with an echoing "Heil Hitler". He made his report, and it was clear that neither he nor his men had discovered anyone hiding within the convent building.

Major Thielen turned to Mother Marie-Pierre. "My men have searched the convent and the hospital and have found no trace of the prisoners. We will disturb you no longer."

"I see," Mother Marie-Pierre said. "Well, I'm glad. Will your men be leaving the convent now, Major? It is nearly time for vespers and our evening meal, and we should like to carry on with our normal routine. Of course if you would care to join me for a cup of coffee in my office before you leave, you would be most welcome."

Major Thielen, having clear memories of the coffee he had been served on his first visit to the convent, refused, saying that he must get back to headquarters and supervise the search for the escaped prisoners elsewhere. "Colonel Hoch and his men are searching the outlying farms and houses, I must return and see if he has made a capture."

They turned their steps back to the main hall, where the rest of the men were waiting. Major Thielen dismissed them, thus releasing Sister Celestine at last from the threat of Hesse's rifle, and as they trooped out Mother Marie-Pierre sent up a prayer of thanks for their departure and the convent's deliverance. She was only too aware that if it had been Colonel Hoch who had searched the convent, he would not have been fooled by an apparently incontinent old lady, and a row of children saying their prayers.

As soon as she was sure that the lorry-load of soldiers and the major in his car really had driven away, she locked the front door and hurried back up the stairs to her sleeping cell. Sister St Bruno was sitting in a chair while Sister Eloise attended to the wounded woman who was once again lying on Mother Marie-Pierre's bed.

"Sister, you were wonderful," Mother Marie-Pierre said as she came back into the room. "How did you manage to get everything arranged in such a short time?"

186

Sister Eloise didn't look up from her work. "Sister Henriette helped me. Now, Mother, if you could get Sister St Bruno back into her own bed, I would be grateful. Then I need a hand here."

Mother Marie-Pierre had no hesitation in following the instructions given by her hospital matron. All through the Great War, Sister Eloise had issued Sarah Hurst, as she had been then, with instructions and orders that she had obeyed without question. Now, although their roles were reversed, with Mother Marie-Pierre the more senior in the community, she knew that it was Sister Eloise who knew best in situations such as these.

"Come, Sister," she said to her aunt, formal as always in front of another sister, "let's get you back to bed." She needed a word with Aunt Anne in private anyway. With great care she raised the elderly nun from the chair and taking almost all her fragile weight, she supported her from the room and along the passage back to her own cell.

Sister St Bruno eased herself back onto her bed and sighed. "Are the children safe?" she asked.

"Yes, for now," replied her niece, "but if the raid had been carried out by Colonel Hoch I think it would have been a different story. I don't think the major's heart was in it. I mean —" She paused to consider exactly what it was she did mean. "I mean, he was not happy about searching the convent. He left most of it to his men, only taking charge in the rooms where he was pretty sure he would find nothing." She grinned across at her aunt. "You were amazing," she said. "Talk about

187

fractious old lady!" Then she was serious. "But it was a grave risk you took, you know."

"Nonsense," replied her aunt, "no more than you or Sister Eloise. What else could we do? Turn the poor child over to your major?"

"No, of course not," agreed Sarah, "and he's not my major."

"Maybe not," returned Aunt Anne, "but he seems to trust you and it could be useful to have him on our side in the future."

"I doubt if he'll ever be that," Sarah replied seriously, "but he may be less of a threat than Colonel Hoch."

CHAPTER
ELEVEN

The visit from the Germans persuaded Mother Marie-Pierre that she must put her plan to move the children to Paris into action at once. While Sister Eloise continued to minister to their patient laid out on the reverend mother's bed, Reverend Mother herself was hurrying back to the chapel. Sister Danielle was still there with the children, though she now had them sitting on chairs listening while she read them a Bible story. Marthe had Margot on her knee and was rocking her gently as the child's head drooped against her shoulder in sleep.

"I think it's time for the children to go back and have their supper now, Sister," Mother Marie-Pierre said, "and while they are having it, perhaps you'd come to my office. I need a word with you."

"Yes, Mother, of course," replied the nun. "I'll be there directly." She led her charges out of the chapel and closed the door behind them. Mother Marie-Pierre slipped onto her knees in front of the altar.

"Oh Lord," she prayed, "help me to get these children to safety, away from the horrors and dangers of this war." She stayed in the chapel for another five minutes, allowing the peaceful silence to have its familiar, calming effect, and when she rose to return to her office to speak to Sister Danielle, she knew that she had drawn strength from her five minutes alone with her God.

"We have to get these children away from here," she said, coming straight to the point when Sister Danielle had come to her. "The SS are in the village. It isn't just the German army now. Major Thielen carried out the search of the convent today, and he still has some respect for our calling and our cloth, but Colonel Hoch of the SS is a different man altogether. He's looking for Jews. If he discovered the Leon children and Marthe and Margot were Jews, they would be rounded up and taken away as the rest of Marthe's family were today."

"But where shall we send them, Mother?" asked Sister Danielle anxiously. "Where will they be safe from such a man?"

"We must take them to Paris," Mother Marie-Pierre replied briskly. "To Mother Magdalene. No one there need know their origins, just children orphaned by the war."

"But how will we get them to Paris?" asked Sister Danielle.

"I shall take them myself," said her superior. "I shall simply take them on the train. All we have to do is get them to the station in Albert and take the train to Amiens and then Paris."

"Am I to come with you?" asked Sister Danielle.

"I shall need someone," replied Reverend Mother. "I think it should be you as the children know and love you best. But there may be danger. Will you come?"

190

"Yes, Mother, of course," answered Sister Danielle. "They are my children."

"In that case I will tell you the plan I have and see what you think of it."

Reverend Mother outlined the plan she had discussed with Sister St Bruno earlier.

"I think the safest way is to travel openly, not try to hide our journey," she said. "It will look far more suspicious if we try to hide what we are doing. The only one I am worried about really is Marthe. She is clearly not a child and she does have a Jewish cast to her features. I have decided to put her into a novice's habit and let her travel as if she were one of the sisters going to visit the community in Paris."

"And you will leave her there, as a novice?" Sister Danielle sounded doubtful.

"I shall leave her in Mother Magdalene's care," answered Mother Marie-Pierre. "She must decide what is best for the girl once we get her clear of here. That Colonel Hoch is not going to be satisfied when he hears that there were other Jews in the area who were missed in this last round-up. And have no doubt about it," she added bitterly, "he will hear."

She did not mention the wounded woman lying on her bed upstairs. The fewer people who knew about her the better. It wasn't that she didn't trust Sister Danielle, or any of the sisters for that matter, but mistakes could be made, a careless word could endanger not only the woman herself, but the nuns who had sheltered her.

"We shall leave as soon as it can be arranged," said the reverend mother, "so please make sure the children are packed and ready to go at short notice."

As Sister Danielle stood to return to her charges, Mother Marie-Pierre went on, "Please ask Sister Marie-Marc to come and see me." She paused, gravely. "And Sister, these children are truly at risk, the less we discuss this the better."

Sister Danielle smiled. "I shall say nothing, Mother," she promised. "Do you want me to get a novice's habit for Marthe?"

Reverend Mother shook her head. "No, I will speak to Sister Marie-Paul myself."

As she waited for Sister Marie-Marc to come, Mother Marie-Pierre stared down into the little walled garden below her window and considered how much to say to the old nun. When she had come to the convent as plain Sarah Hurst during the Great War, it was Sister Marie-Marc who had been in charge of the kitchen. Now such work was too much for her and she simply helped Sister Elisabeth with light tasks when necessary, and looked after her beloved hens.

Sister Marie-Marc may be old with creaking joints, Reverend Mother thought now, but she's in no way senile. When she found the wounded woman, she kept her head, locking her safely in the pantry and then coming to find me. She must have cleaned the blood from the floor, too, before Major Thielen's search party had arrived in the kitchen, as they didn't find anything. Pray God we can get the children away before another search, and also find some way of protecting that poor woman upstairs; though what we're going to do with her is yet another problem.

A tap on her door heralded the arrival of Sister Marie-Marc.

"Come in, Sister," Mother Marie-Pierre said and pulled a chair round so that they could sit comfortably across from each other as they talked. "Now tell me, was there any problem when the soldiers came searching through the kitchen?"

The elderly nun gave a cackle of laughter. "No, Mother," she replied. "I had cleaned the floor, but when *les sales Boches* came in I hadn't had time to empty the bucket. I heard them coming, so I tipped the bucket into a pan and I put it on the stove. Then I stirred it, as if it were soup."

In spite of herself, Mother Marie-Pierre laughed. "Soup?"

"Oh yes, Mother. And if they'd asked for a taste I'd have given it to them."

"Then I can only thank God that they didn't ask," replied her superior, trying to control her quivering lip. "Now, Sister, we have a problem. The woman you found is badly wounded, but she is also wanted by the Germans. We have to keep her hidden and safe until she is well enough to move on."

Sister Marie-Marc nodded.

"So the fewer people in the convent who know she was actually here," went on Mother Marie-Pierre, "the better."

"So you're not going to tell our sisters."

193

"No, Sister," Mother Marie-Pierre replied gently. "I think it is safest for all of us if as few as possible are in on the secret. You know, of course, and Sister Eloise. So does Sister Henriette, who has been helping Sister Eloise. There is no need for anyone else to know that we are sheltering an escaped prisoner."

"In the Great War," Sister Marie-Marc said slowly, "we were fighting the Germans, our army fighting theirs, but they weren't here, in France. They weren't living in our village, taking people's homes, sending people away to Germany. Shooting people. It can't be right, Mother, for them to do what they are doing to the ordinary people of France."

"There is always cruelty in war," Mother Marie-Pierre said, "we saw enough last time. But I agree this is different, and we must respond differently." She smiled across at Sister Marie-Marc. "Now, we shall have to find a way of looking after the woman you found, but I know I can rely on you if I need you."

Mother Marie-Pierre and the children set out for Paris the following day. Jean Danot, the farmer, had agreed to take them to Albert in his farm wagon and they had piled all the children and their luggage into it. The children were both excited and fearful. The older ones were leaving the only home they had ever known, but with a growing excitement at the thought of Paris. The Leon children kept close to Sister Danielle, the new rock in their swirling sea of change and anxiety. Marthe, dressed in the flowing habit and small headdress of a novice of the community, held on tightly to Margot's hand, each the last link with her lost family.

When Mother Marie-Pierre had approached Sister Marie-Paul to give her a novice's habit, Sister Marie-Paul had been horrified.

"It is a blasphemy for a Jew to wear the habit of a Christian sister," she cried. "I cannot believe you'll sully these holy garments in such a way."

Mother Marie-Pierre fought down her anger. "The garments are not holy, Sister," she said. "They are simply clothes. But, with God's help, they will protect Marthe from the Germans."

When Sister Marie-Paul said nothing, simply tightening her expression, Mother Marie-Pierre went on. "The sooner she is safely in Paris the better, Sister. Mother Magdalene can take responsibility for her then."

"We should not become involved in what is happening beyond the convent walls, Mother," replied Sister Marie-Paul. "Our place is to nurse the sick in the hospital and to follow a life of prayer."

"Certainly, Sister," said Mother Marie-Pierre equably, "and to fight against evil wherever it rears its head. It cannot be right to send children like Margot to a camp somewhere in Germany."

"She should have gone with her mother," Sister Marie-Paul said. "Stayed with her family. There was no need to bring her here."

Faced with Sister Marie-Paul's intransigent attitude, Mother Marie-Pierre could only feel relieved that her novice mistress did not realise that three of the other children were also Jews. She sighed inwardly. "Well, they won't be here for much longer, Sister, and you can relax again."

"It's very difficult when someone senior, like your novice mistress, is not in tune with your thinking," Sarah confided to Aunt Anne later that evening. "I wonder how Mother Magdalene would have handled the situation."

"Maybe more forcefully than you," conceded her aunt, "but not necessarily better."

"I've borrowed Sister Marie-Joseph's papers for Marthe," Sarah told her. "They might do at a pinch, one nun looks like another to the layman, but they won't bear close scrutiny. I've nothing for little Margot. We'll just have to pray we aren't stopped."

"You will all be constantly in my prayers," her aunt assured her, as she clasped Sarah's hands in farewell.

The farm cart lumbered away from the convent gate, pulled by a huge carthorse. There was no fuel for the farm truck, and even if there had been, Monsieur Danot would not have wasted it on taking a group of nuns and children to the station in Albert.

To reach the main road to Albert they had to pass through the village square. This was the part of the journey that Mother Marie-Pierre felt posed the most danger. Once they were clear of St Croix, there would probably be little interest in a group of nuns and children travelling from one convent to another, but should they be seen by Colonel Hoch, or even Major Thielen, questions would surely be asked. However, the risk had to be taken, there was no other practicable way to reach the Albert road.

196

Mother Marie-Pierre sat up beside Monsieur Danot and the rest of the party were crammed into the back. As they entered the square, Colonel Hoch emerged from the German headquarters. It was almost, Mother Marie-Pierre thought later, as if he had been lying in wait for them.

A sharp order from him had them halted and covered by the rifles of three of his men. The SS officer strode over and addressed her.

"What is this?" demanded Hoch. "Where are you going?"

Mother Marie-Pierre's heart was pounding, her fear realised, but she managed to answer smoothly. "I am taking the children to our mother house in Paris, Colonel," she replied. "The hospital is overflowing and so we are moving the children out to make more space."

The colonel peered at the children and the two other nuns crowded into the back of the wagon. "Out!" he ordered. "All of you!"

There was no hesitation, Mother Marie-Pierre climbed down from the front and everyone else scrambled out of the back. Marthe, uncomfortable in her unaccustomed clothes, tripped and would have fallen if Sister Danielle hadn't caught hold of her.

The colonel stared at her for a moment and she lowered her eyes, as Mother Marie-Pierre had told her to do if she were addressed by a German soldier, but the reverend mother could see that her hands were shaking as she clasped them together within the wide sleeves of her habit. Margot ran to her immediately and

Marthe bent down to her, putting her arm round her, drawing her against her protectively. Colonel Hoch's gaze moved across the other children as they stood grouped around Sister Danielle, who was carrying baby Anne Leon in her arms.

"And who are these?" he demanded.

Mother Marie-Pierre answered for them. "They are our orphans, Colonel. Our convent runs an orphanage as well as a hospital. They've lived with us ever since their parents died. I have their papers here if you wish to see them." She made as if to produce papers for everyone, but the colonel ignored her; it was as if she hadn't spoken.

"You," he pointed. "What is your name?"

Jean-Pierre stared at him, wide-eyed with fear.

"Come on, boy." Hoch took a step towards him. "What is your name?"

"Jean-Pierre," muttered the boy, cowering back.

"Jean-Pierre what?"

"Jean-Pierre Malpas."

"Well, Jean-Pierre Malpas, learn to speak when you're spoken to." Hoch turned and, with a jerk of his head, summoned one of his men. "Search this cart."

The man climbed up into the back of the cart and heaved out all the luggage. "No one here, sir," he said when all the baggage was strewn on the ground and the wagon was clearly empty.

"Look underneath," ordered Hoch, and the soldier dutifully crept in underneath the cart.

"Nothing here, sir," he said as he emerged.

198

Hoch glowered at them all before turning on his heel and going back into the town hall. The soldier slouched off after him.

"All right, children, let's get our things back into the cart," Mother Marie-Pierre said bracingly. "We don't want to miss the train, do we?"

Everything was gathered up and put back into the wagon, and the children and the sisters climbed back on board.

"They're looking for someone," Mother Marie-Pierre said quietly to Jean Danot when he had whipped up the horse again and they were lumbering out of the village.

"Still haven't found the two who escaped from the trucks," grunted Jean. "They've been over my farm three times. Sticking bayonets into the hay bales weren't enough. They pulled the whole lot out into the yard last time. It took me all day to get it safely back under cover again."

"They searched the convent too," said Reverend Mother. Only once though, she thought, so they might be back, and what would happen then? She had left the woman — her name was Simone — in the charge of Sister Eloise, and for the time being there was nothing more that Mother Marie-Pierre could do for her. Now she had to concentrate on getting the children safely to Paris.

Silence rested between them. Jean Danot was a man of few words at the best of times, he had no time for idle gossip . . . dangerous gossip, he thought it. You couldn't trust anyone, nowadays, not even nuns.

The train for Amiens belched its way into the station and Mother Marie-Pierre and Sister Danielle got their small flock on board. Marthe, still moving awkwardly in her habit, had been given charge of Margot. It would give her something to concentrate on during the journey, Mother Marie-Pierre thought. It was Marthe and Margot who were at the greatest risk. They were the only ones without valid papers.

The train was crowded and the little group crammed themselves into a compartment, the smaller children sitting on the nuns' knees.

The train was slow and stopped several times, so that when they finally drew into Amiens it was late and they had missed their connection.

"What shall we do now, Mother?" asked Sister Danielle anxiously, Anne still held in her arms, and Catherine clutching the skirt of her habit.

Reverend Mother looked round the bustling station, and then took them into the waiting room. "Wait here," she said, "and I will find out if there is another train today."

There wasn't, and when she asked the stationmaster if they might all stay in the waiting room for the night, his reply was not encouraging. "Sorry, Sister, you'd be breaking curfew."

Mother Marie-Pierre had forgotten about the curfews imposed by the Germans. They had little relevance to the convent as none of the nuns were ever out at night. "What time is that?" she asked and he told her it was eleven o'clock at present.

200

"I see," she said. "Then we'll have to find somewhere else to stay. Is there a pension, or hotel which might have room for us all?"

"You could try the Lion d'Or," the man suggested doubtfully, "they might have room." He gave the reverend mother directions and, with her little brood in tow, she set off through the streets. The Lion d'Or had no room. The proprietor had taken one look at the group on his doorstep and raised his shoulders in an exaggerated shrug. He regretted he had no room for such a party.

"Then perhaps you could suggest somewhere else." Mother Marie-Pierre fought to keep her voice polite. The man shrugged again and she turned away in frustration. As she did so, she noticed a church on the corner of the next street. Surely they would be able to seek shelter there.

"Come along," she said briskly, and led the way to the church. Once inside she sat them all down. "You are all to wait here," she told them. "I will go to the priest and tell him of our plight."

The priest's house was not difficult to find, and when she knocked on the door she was welcomed by the housekeeper.

"Why, Sister, come on in," she said when Mother Marie-Pierre had told her that she needed to speak to the priest. "Father Bernard is in his study. I'll find him for you." She showed the nun into a sitting room and leaving her there went in search of Father Bernard. When he arrived, Mother Marie-Pierre explained that she was taking a party of orphans to the mother house in Paris, but that their train had been delayed and they were now stranded in Amiens. She passed lightly over the reason for their journey. The less information she gave the better for all.

The priest took in the situation at once. "You must all come here," he said. "It will be a bit of a squash, but we shall manage. Do go and fetch them while I warn Madame Papritz that we have guests."

With great relief, Mother Marie-Pierre collected her charges from the church and brought them across to the priest's house.

Madame Papritz was as welcoming as Father Bernard, and she soon had the children sitting round her kitchen table. While she fed them bread and honey, Father Bernard took the three nuns upstairs to a bedroom at the front of the house, which offered a sagging double bed.

"The children can sleep in here," he said. "It's a bit small, I'm afraid, and there aren't any more beds, but I've plenty of blankets. You sisters can sleep in the room next door." He opened another bedroom door. This contained only a narrow single bed. Father Bernard sighed. "There used to be two of us in the parish, but Father Gilbert went into the army as a chaplain. He didn't come back, God rest his soul."

"If you don't mind, Father," Mother Marie-Pierre said, "I think it would be better if we split up and had some children in each room. Then if they wake in the night, they'll be with someone they know."

"Arrange it entirely as you wish, Mother," the priest said cheerfully. "I'll find you some blankets and then when the children are settled, perhaps you would join me for the evening meal."

How different from Father Michel in St Croix, thought Mother Marie-Pierre later, as she lay on a blanket on the floor with Jean-Pierre and David sleeping top-to-tail in the single bed beside her. He would never have put himself out in this way.

Madame Papritz found breakfast for them all before they set off once more to catch the train to Paris, so that the children were all well fed and comfortable for the rest of their journey.

Father Bernard said brief prayers with them and then gave them a blessing, but as they passed out into the street, he held Mother Marie-Pierre back for a moment.

"Mother," he said quietly. "You must remind the young sister, Sister Marie-Joseph, is it? You must remind her to answer to her name . . . and teach her the Lord's Prayer, if nothing else. Otherwise, she will give you all away."

Mother Marie-Pierre held his eyes for a moment. "Thank you, Father. I will speak to her."

"Go with God, Mother, and may He keep you all safe." He raised his hand. "If ever you find yourself in need of somewhere to stay in Amiens," he added in a soft voice, "please remember that you will always be welcome here, you and whoever is travelling with you."

Mother Marie-Pierre took his hand. "Thank you, Father. I'll remember."

The nuns shepherded the children onto the Paris train and settled them into a compartment. It had been empty and as they filled it, no one else tried to get in with them. Several peered in through the door, but passed on down the corridor when they saw nuns and children packed into the small space.

At last the train started and Mother Marie-Pierre felt herself relax. They were on the last leg of their journey. When they reached the Gare du Nord they would be only a short walk away from the convent, safety and the commonsense of Mother Magdalene. Sister Danielle was singing rhymes with Monique, Catherine and Margot; Anne was sitting comfortably on Marthe's knee playing with the cross she wore round her neck, and the boys were peering out of the window at the countryside rushing past. Mother Marie-Pierre closed her eyes, soothed by the rhythm of the train.

She awoke with a jolt as the door was hauled open with a loud rattle and two men came in. They were not in uniform, but there was no doubt that they were German and official.

"Papers," growled the first one and held out his hand towards Mother Marie-Pierre. The singing stopped abruptly and the three little girls stared fearfully at the two men. Paulette looked anxiously at Marthe and then Mother Marie-Pierre, and the boys turned from the window, the colour draining from David's face. Marthe ducked her head and began rocking baby Anne in her arms. The child crowed with delight at the sight of the men and held out a chubby hand to them.

Mother Marie-Pierre calmly took the papers she carried for all of them and handed them over. Please God, she prayed silently as they began to look at them, let me think of the right words to say when they ask about Marthe and Margot.

She saw them glance at her own papers first, then Sister Danielle's, then Sister Marie-Joseph's. His interest seemed only cursory at first, then he turned to Mother Marie-Pierre. "You're the reverend mother, right?"

Mother Marie-Pierre agreed that she was.

"And where are you all going then?"

"I'm taking these children home, to the order's mother house in Paris," she replied.

"Why's that?" he demanded.

"They are orphans, Monsieur. We run an orphanage there."

The man grunted. "Which of you is Sister Danielle?" he asked, looking over to the other two nuns.

"I am." Sister Danielle raised her hand.

"So you're Sister Marie-Joseph," he said to Marthe.

Marthe kept her face close to the baby squirming in her arms. "Yes, Monsieur," she whispered.

"Just a minute." The second man had been scrutinising the children's papers. Mother Marie-Pierre felt her heart give a jolt as he went on. "We're one set of papers short here." He looked at the children. "Answer your names," he said gruffly.

Mother Marie-Pierre decided it was time to speak. "You are quite right, Monsieur, we have no papers for little Margot Lenoir." She indicated the child who was huddled against Sister Danielle. "She has only just come to us. Her father died last year in the retreat to Dunkerque, her mother last week in a fire. Her papers burned with the house. We have no replacements for her yet. We shall apply for those when she is living in the convent."

"You should not have travelled without them," said the man eyeing her suspiciously. "A fire? Sounds rather convenient. How do I know it's the truth?"

Mother Marie-Pierre looked him in the eye. "Because I have told you it is."

At that moment there was a noise from further down the corridor, some shouting, the sound of a shot and the train began screeching to a halt. Although it had not been travelling particularly fast, the carriages swayed violently as the brakes locked and the two boys, standing by the window, were thrown across the compartment, knocking Margot off Sister Danielle's knee. The little girl began to cry, but her distress was forgotten as another shot rang out from further up the train.

The two men spun round and out into the corridor where a thin man, with blood streaming down his face, tried to force his way past them. There were more cries from behind him and with a terrified glance over his shoulder, he gave the men a violent shove and tried to open the door of the still moving train. The two men staggered against each other for a moment and then went after him, one grabbing at him to stop him from jumping from the train, the other drawing a gun from his pocket.

The fugitive forced the door open and without a second glance behind him flung himself out as the man raised his pistol and fired. The train finally ground to a halt, its wheels screeching against the track in protestation and immediately the two men — Gestapo, as Mother Marie-Pierre had recognised them to be — leapt out after the fleeing man. More men shoved their way along the corridor, and jumping down onto the line fanned out in search of the fugitive. There was the sound of more shooting before Mother Marie-Pierre slid the compartment door closed, and turned to her white-faced companions.

"Whoever that poor soul was, he saved us from the Gestapo," she murmured.

"Were they Gestapo, Mother?" Sister Danielle asked softly.

"Almost certainly, Sister." She smiled at the children. "Now then, guess what kind Madame Papritz gave me before we left."

Paulette, old enough to realise the danger they had been in, tried to sound interested. "I don't know, Mother. What?"

"Some *pain d'épice*!" She produced the gingerbread from her bag and as the children watched in delight, broke it into five pieces. The children took it hungrily and were happily munching when the train jolted and began to move forward again. An hour later than scheduled, it steamed into the Gare du Nord.

When they arrived at last at the mother house, they were taken at once to see Mother Magdalene. One look at Mother Marie-Pierre's face was enough to tell her things were seriously wrong. She sent Sister Danielle and Marthe, whom she still assumed to be a novice, off to settle the children in the guest quarters and then sat

Mother Marie-Pierre down to hear why she had come. She was a good listener and she heard Mother Marie-Pierre out without interruption.

"You did right to bring them to me," she said at last. "They will be safe here. I will get papers for little Margot, and they can live with us here as long as is necessary. We have ten other children here in the orphanage with us already. They will soon fit in and feel at home."

"What about Marthe?" asked Mother Marie-Pierre. "She cannot go on disguised as a novice. Father Bernard, in Amiens, saw at once that she was not a nun, and she herself is not at all happy with the deception. I had great difficulty getting her to wear the habit, even as a disguise."

"You say she used to work in the hospital as a lay worker?" Mother Magdalene asked.

"Yes. Sister Eloise says she has the makings of a good nurse."

"Then there is no problem," Mother Magdalene said serenely. "She can work with us as a lay sister, and I will try and get her trained properly as a nurse so that she can support herself outside the convent."

Mother Marie-Pierre joined the sisters in their chapel that evening and again in the morning for Mass, and then she set off for the station and the journey home.

"Won't you stay a few days?" suggested Mother Magdalene. "Just till the children settle in?"

"No, Mother, I can't. The sisters in St Croix need me. But if you'll keep Sister Danielle for a week or two, that will make the transition for the younger ones a little easier."

It was agreed, though Sister Danielle was anxious about Mother Marie-Pierre travelling back to St Croix on her own.

"Don't be silly, Sister," Mother Marie-Pierre said briskly. "If the trains run on time, I shall be home before dark."

She was lucky, there were no delays and she managed to hitch a lift from Albert to the village on a carrier's cart, so she didn't even have the long walk back to St Croix. She was back at the convent by late afternoon.

She was greeted by Sister Celestine, who, on opening the door, cried out in relief to see her.

"Oh Mother, thank God you are home."

Mother Marie-Pierre looked startled at her tone. "Why, Sister, whatever is the matter?"

Sister Celestine seemed about to tell her something but then hesitated and replied rather lamely. "Nothing, Mother. I mean, Sister Marie-Paul asked me to say that she needs to speak to you as soon as you get home."

"I see." Mother Marie-Pierre raised an eyebrow. "Then you'd better run and tell her I'm back. I shall be in my office."

CHAPTER
TWELVE

As the reverend mother and the children trundled out of the village square in Jean Danot's farm cart, Colonel Hoch strode back into the Gestapo headquarters calling to his aide, Lieutenant Weber.

"I don't trust that nun," he snapped as the man came into the office to join him. "She's up to something."

Weber knew his officer well enough not to question this statement, though privately he doubted that the reverend mother was up to anything. After all, what could a nun do?

"Find Major Thielen," Hoch said, "and then come back here."

Major Thielen entered the room to find the colonel pacing the floor.

"That nun, the one who came here about the Jews the other day," Hoch said. "I don't trust her. She's just set off to Paris with a cartload of children."

"But surely, Colonel, you searched the cart before they left the village," Thielen said tentatively. He had watched the whole thing from his window and had been very relieved when there proved to be nothing concealed in the cart. He disliked Colonel Hoch and he disliked his tactics. Everything Hoch did antagonised the local population. Occupation was not easy and Major Thielen, although authoritarian himself, had tried, to some extent, to work with the local people. Co-operation backed up with information from whoever was prepared to provide it was his preferred method. He was aware that there were pockets of resistance in the area, and information encouraged and bought was far more useful than Hoch's arrogant approach. That was more likely to harden that resistance than to defeat it.

Hoch was, Thielen thought bitterly, as he'd watched him search the cart, the worst type of upstart; a bully, not a true army officer, but one of what Thielen privately called Himmler's gang. He found now, as they stood face-to-face, that he had to school his features well to hide his loathing of the man.

"I don't trust her," repeated the colonel. "Who searched the convent?"

"I did, sir. I had ten men with me and we searched the place from top to bottom."

"And what did you find?" demanded Hoch.

"Nothing, sir. There was nothing out of the ordinary. We searched the hospital, the chapel, the cellars, everywhere."

"And this nun, this reverend mother? How did she behave?"

"Some of the sisters were afraid when we arrived, but she calmed them down and then led me round the convent."

"Did she indeed?" Hoch considered for a moment and then spoke to Weber. "Franz, I think we should pay another visit to this convent, a surprise one while the reverend mother is away. Bring twenty men and then fetch my car." He turned back to Major Thielen. "You, Thielen, give me the geography of the place. How many entrances? What's the place like at the back?"

Major Thielen considered. "There's a courtyard behind the main building, which has a high wall round it," he said. "The hospital has been built on there. In the courtyard there are some outbuildings, a shed, a henhouse, that sort of thing, and there is a door into the kitchen. There is also a little walled garden."

Hoch nodded. "I assume your men searched these outbuildings."

Thielen stared woodenly ahead of him. "Of course, sir."

"Right, well, we'll search them again. They won't be expecting us back again so soon, and without that reverend mother there things may be easier. You, Thielen, will stay here to receive the reports from those still searching the outlying farms."

Hoch strode out of the building into the square, leaving Major Thielen fuming in his office.

The men Hoch had sent for were formed up, waiting.

"We are going to search the convent again," he snapped. "I shall arrive at the front door, and as soon as it is open, ten of you will go straight in and search the main building. You know the drill, look for any possible hiding places, pay particular attention to the cellars.

The rest of you will have approached the place from the back. When you get the signal, you go in that way. There is a door in the courtyard wall. Break it down if you have to. Search the outhouses — they are just the sort of place a Jew might hide. Go into the hospital, check every patient.

"Remember, this convent is an old building, there may well be secret places where someone could be hidden. Those two Jews are still at large and I want them found. I'll have no escaped Jews on my patch." He looked at the men standing in front of him. "You" — he pointed to the group on the left — "will go in from the back with Lieutenant Weber. Remember, surprise is vital. We don't want them to have time to hide anyone. And also remember that if they learn to be afraid of us now, we shall have less trouble with them later. Heil Hitler!" He turned to the lieutenant. "I'll give you twenty minutes to get your men into position, Weber, and then I shall drive up to the front door with mine. I will fire my pistol into the air, that is your signal to go in." Then, almost as an afterthought, he added, "If the nuns are scared of us, so much the better. You understand, Franz?"

Weber nodded and then saluted.

"Twenty minutes, Franz, and wait for my signal."

Weber led his men off, through the square and up the track through the copse leading to the back of the convent. Hoch sent one of the waiting men to fetch a lorry, and the rest of the search party scrambled into it. It would be difficult for a group of men to approach the front of the convent unnoticed on foot, so Hoch decided that they should all arrive at once, giving as little warning as possible. He needed this raid to be a success.

He had been working in Berlin on the personal staff of Heinrich Himmler when he had received the unexpected and unwelcome posting to this rural part of occupied France. His great fear was that someone, back there in Berlin, had discovered his darkest secret — that his paternal grandmother had been a Jew. She was safely dead now of course, but that didn't mean that someone jealous of his swift rise through the ranks of the SS had not murmured the fact into the ears of those high in the Nazi party, even to Himmler himself. Hoch's promotions had come fast, but this sudden, downward move told him that he was regarded with suspicion. Why else would such a potential high-flyer be sent to such a backwater? Hoch knew, with deadly certainty, that he must prove himself a merciless predator, his prey the Jews. There had been some trouble with resistance groups in the area, as well, and those he was also determined to root out and destroy, but his main prey were the Jews, for failure to destroy them might lead to his own destruction.

Hoch climbed into the black Citroën he had requisitioned from the mayor, and his driver pulled away, the lorry lumbering in his wake. When they drew up outside the convent front door, Hoch jumped down, and running up the steps hammered on the great front door while the lorry disgorged its load behind him. When the grille in the door was drawn aside and Sister

Celestine peered out, she found herself looking down the barrel of a pistol.

"Open the door," Hoch snarled at her, and had the satisfaction of hearing the bolts being drawn on the inside. He raised his pistol and fired it once in the air, and as the door swung open he stepped inside pushing roughly past the frightened nun who had opened it.

"Carry on," he barked at the men who swarmed in behind him. They fanned out through the convent, several rushing up the staircase, others disappearing down the corridors leading to the kitchens and the children's wing, their boots echoing on the stone floors.

"Please . . ." began Sister Celestine bravely, but fell silent as Hoch raised his pistol and pointed it at her again.

"Who is in charge here?" he demanded.

"Reverend Mother is away," said Sister Celestine, pale-faced and shaken.

"I'm well aware of that," said Hoch. "So, who is in charge now?"

"Sister Marie-Paul?" Sister Celestine sounded doubtful.

"Then you'd better take me to her."

He replaced the pistol in its holster and followed the frightened nun along a corridor to the small room that served the novice mistress as an office. On reaching the door, Hoch barged past Sister Celestine and flung the door open. Sister Marie-Paul was kneeling at her prie-dieu and looked up startled at the intrusion. When she saw the large SS officer standing on the threshold she leapt to her feet and shrank back against the wall.

This show of fear gave Hoch another jolt of satisfaction. He knew he had been right to come to the convent when the reverend mother was not there. Clearly this woman, second in command as she might be, had not the strength of personality to demand things of him as the other one had done.

"Good day, Sister," Hoch said. "I am Colonel Hoch of the SS. My men are searching for two escaped prisoners. You will have nothing against them searching the convent, I am sure."

With the shock of seeing him standing over her absorbed a little, Sister Marie-Paul straightened her back. "Of course not, though I am afraid the reverend mother is not here to escort you."

"That doesn't matter," he replied equably. "I don't need an escort. My men will search and then I wish to speak to you again. This," he glanced over his shoulder to where Sister Celestine still cowered behind him, "this sister tells me you are in charge of the convent while your mother superior is away."

"I and one other," said Sister Marie-Paul, her courage trickling back and her face loosing its pallor of fear. "Sister Eloise, the sister in charge of the hospital."

"Then I suggest we find this Sister Eloise. I wish to speak to you both. Please send for her . . . at once."

"Certainly I will tell her you would like to speak with her," said Sister Marie-Paul. "Perhaps we should go to the guest parlour, where we can be more comfortable." She turned to Sister Celestine, still hovering in the background. "Please ask Sister Eloise to come to the parlour, Sister."

216

The little nun ducked her head and disappeared down the passage almost at the run, followed at a more leisurely pace by Colonel Hoch and Sister Marie-Paul. She led him to the parlour beside the front door. The parlour door already stood open, and it was clear that the room had been searched. The small cupboard doors stood open, the chairs had been tipped over and the picture of Christ displaying His Sacred Heart had been taken from the wall as if someone had been looking behind it.

For a moment Sister Marie-Paul surveyed the scene, and Hoch watched her reaction. She said nothing, simply righted the chairs and replaced the picture on its hook above the prie-dieu.

"I am sure that none of your community is stupid enough to get involved in affairs which don't concern them," Hoch remarked as he went to the window and looked out. As instructed, one man was stationed outside, his rifle trained on the front door in case anyone eluding the search made a break for it. There would be another man posted in the courtyard.

He turned back to Sister Marie-Paul. "So," he said, "and where has your reverend mother gone?"

"To Paris," she replied. "We have so many coming into the hospital now that we will have to extend it into the children's wing. Mother has taken the children to our convent in Paris. It also runs an orphanage and there is room for them there."

"I see." It was the same story that the reverend mother had told, but Hoch was not surprised at that.

Clearly that was the story that had been agreed. "How many children were there?" he asked casually.

"Six, no, seven," Sister Marie-Paul corrected herself hastily.

"You don't know?" Hoch was immediately suspicious.

"Seven," repeated Sister Marie-Paul more firmly.

He was about to ask who the children were and how they came to be living in the convent when there was a commotion in the hall and one of his men came clattering down the stairs into the hall.

Hoch strode out of the parlour to find out what was going on. "Well, Schwarz?"

"Better come upstairs, sir," said Schwarz, and turned back to the stairs. Hoch pushed past him and took the stairs two at a time. Schwarz followed and so did Sister Marie-Paul.

When they reached the landing they found two other men standing outside one of the cell bedrooms. One had his rifle pointed at Sister Eloise, who was backed against the wall of the corridor, the other was aiming his rifle into the room.

"Well?" barked Hoch. "What have you found?"

"Found a woman, sir. In the bed here . . . all bandaged up," replied the man covering Sister Eloise. "Looks like gunshot wounds."

Hoch elbowed him aside and striding into the cell stared down at the figure on the bed. His lip curled as he took in the wan face of the woman who lay on the bed, and there was a flash of triumph in his eyes.

"Name?" he barked at the terrified woman.

"Simone," came the whispered reply.

"Simone? And your surname, *Mademoiselle*?" The sarcastic emphasis on the title made the woman flinch.

"Simone who?" His tone brooked no argument and Simone, having no energy for one, murmured, "Isaacs!"

"As I thought. A Jew." He turned away as if disgusted by the sight of her. "Hartmann, take her away," he said dismissively. "I'll talk to her at headquarters."

The two men lowered their rifles and one hauled the injured Simone from the bed. Her legs folded underneath her as he tried to make her stand up, and without more ado he hoisted her up over his shoulder in a fireman's lift. As he did so, she gave a shriek of pain. Sister Eloise moved forward, her hands held out as if to halt them, but the second man pushed her violently against the wall, out of the way.

"Stay back," he ordered, raising his rifle again.

Hartmann carried Simone along the corridor to the stairs without slackening his pace. Her nightgown was bunched up above her knees and as they disappeared down the stairs, the pale curve of her buttocks was displayed to them all.

"Take the nun as well," Hoch ordered the other man. "She was harbouring a criminal."

"I was tending an injured woman," Sister Eloise said mildly. "It is my calling."

"The woman is an enemy of the Reich," replied Hoch smoothly. "Harbouring her makes you an enemy of the Reich. Take her away, Schmidt."

Schmidt took Sister Eloise roughly by the arm and made as if to march her along the passage in the wake of his comrade, but the nun shook off his hand. "There is no need for that. I will come with you." She glanced across at Hoch. "Simone will need my care again when you have finished questioning her."

Hoch raised his hand and dealt her a stinging blow across her face. Her head jerked back and the marks of his fingers flowered red upon her cheek, but she made no sound as she turned her back on him. With quiet dignity she walked along the landing, pausing only to speak to Sister Marie-Paul, who was standing, stupefied, at the top of the stairs. "Don't worry, Sister. Everything is in the hands of Our Lord. Tell Reverend Mother what has happened when she gets back." Then with Schmidt behind her, his rifle still raised in case she ran, she descended the stairs.

Hoch, white-faced with anger, spoke softly to Sister Marie-Paul. "You! Nun! Gather all your nuns together somewhere. I wish to speak to them."

Sister Marie-Paul controlled her mounting anger. "I'll call them to the recreation room."

"Do it now," ordered Hoch. He turned to the last soldier, still standing on the landing. "You and I, Schwarz, will finish the search up here." He strode to the next cell and kicked the door open. Sister St Bruno was sitting up in her bed staring vacantly at the wall. She had heard the commotion on the landing and had prepared herself for the intrusion.

Hoch glanced round the tiny room, and this time did take the trouble to pull aside the blanket that draped the bed. The space beneath the bed was empty. He glowered at the apparently senile nun in the bed, who

220

gave him a happy smile and spoke in a quavering voice. "Hallo, young man. Have you come to visit?"

Hoch turned on his heel and slammed the door behind him. Inside the cell, Sister St Bruno relaxed against her pillows, and picking up her rosary began to pray for Sister Eloise and the unfortunate Simone.

Sister Marie-Paul gathered the community from wherever they were in the convent. She was boiling with anger, not at the violent intrusion of the Gestapo officer and his men, but at the knowledge that there had been someone hidden in the convent without her knowledge. She had been kept in the dark about the Jew.

As one of the three most senior sisters, I should have been told, she fumed. I should have been told that we were sheltering yet another escaped Jew within the convent walls. It was bad enough that we were putting the convent at risk of reprisal by sheltering the Lenoir children, but to hide one of the escaped Jewish prisoners . . .

What made it worse was that it was clear Reverend Mother had trusted Sister Eloise with the secret, and who knew whom else? Other sisters must have known.

Sister Marie-Paul's whole being flooded with anger at these thoughts. The entire community had been put at risk by the reverend mother, and now she wasn't even here to deal with the consequences. Sister Marie-Paul had been glad when Reverend Mother had decided to take the two Jewish children off to Paris. She wished them no ill, but felt that they had no place in the orphanage here; and after all Marthe was not even a child.

Well, she decided, since Reverend Mother wasn't here, and Sister Eloise had been arrested as a direct consequence of sheltering escaped prisoners, it was now up to her, Sister Marie-Paul, to do what she could to retrieve the situation.

"Is everyone here?" demanded Hoch when she led him into the crowded recreation room.

"Everyone except Sister St Bruno, who is bedridden," replied Sister Marie-Paul. "And there is one sister left in each of the hospital wards."

Hoch nodded. He remembered the gaga old nun he had seen upstairs; she was not important. The nuns left in the hospital could be told what he had said by their sisters.

"My name is Colonel Hoch," he said, looking round at the assembled women. "I am in charge of security in this area. I root out spies and traitors and Jews. All the enemies of the Reich. I do this with or without the co-operation of the people who live here. If it is without their co-operation, and anyone is found harbouring such filth, well, it will be the worse for them." His eyes roved round the room and he picked out a white-faced novice and pointed a finger at her. It was a tactic he had used on other occasions, and he knew it instilled fear into the whole company, not just the one singled out.

"You," he said coldly, "what is your name?"

"Sister Clothilde," came the whispered reply.

"Well, Sister Clothilde, remember this." His eyes roved the room again to ensure he had their full attention. "*All* of you remember this, I shall be watching you. We have already found one escaped Jewish prisoner in hiding here. I have removed her and the nun who was with her. From now on, I shall take a sister for every fugitive I find here . . . in the hospital . . . in the convent."

There was an audible gasp, and Hoch smiled grimly. "Exactly," he said. "One nun for every one I find. This, *sisters*," he stressed the word, "is no idle threat. I mean every word of it. People who work against the Reich do so at their peril." He smiled again into the stunned silence that greeted his words. "So, we shall leave you now. Please remember what I have said." Turning on his heel, he strode out of the door.

An outburst of talk followed his departure, but Sister Marie-Paul did not quell it as she would usually have done. She, too, hurried from the room. She was horrified at what the colonel had said and she wanted to speak with him before he drove away.

Hearing her footsteps behind him, Hoch paused in the hall. "Well?"

"I just wanted to assure you, Colonel, that I had no idea we were harbouring any escaped prisoners in the convent."

He gave her a long cool look and she hurried on. "It is not for us to become involved with the world outside our door. This is a house of prayer. This is where we serve God by healing the sick and praying for their souls." Hoch still said nothing, and anxious to get her point across, Sister Marie-Paul continued. "You can be sure that such a thing will never happen again."

Hoch's lip curled. "Can I, Sister? And what happens when your reverend mother returns from her trip to Paris? Will she agree with you, I wonder?"

"Of course she will," Sister Marie-Paul said stoutly. "She will have only the best interests of the community at heart."

"And if she does not? Will I hear about it, I wonder?" His eyes bored into her face. "From someone who *does* have the community's interests at heart? I should certainly take note of anyone who was helpful in such a way."

Sister Marie-Paul did not reply, but a look of understanding passed between them before he turned away again and she ventured just one more question.

"And Sister Eloise?"

"I shall be speaking with Sister Eloise," he replied brusquely, and without another word strode out to his waiting car.

Sister Marie-Paul watched him go. Standing in the empty hallway she looked out over the countryside spread below. She had lived here, in this convent, since she had entered at the age of eighteen. Her family had encouraged her, knowing that it was unlikely that such a plain girl with no dowry would find a man to marry her, and she had never returned to her father's house. The convent had become her home and her life; now thanks to the new reverend mother, it was all under threat. But Colonel Hoch had made Sister Marie-Paul an offer; the safety of the convent in return for information. As she considered this, she realised he had offered her more than a chance to keep the community safe from further German attentions, he had given her a lever with which to remove the upstart English woman who had leapfrogged her in seniority to become Reverend Mother, leaving Sister Marie-Paul with responsibility only for the novices. She had resented it at the time, and her resentment had grown as she saw the way that the new reverend mother exercised her authority with the least dictatorial and confrontational attitude that had ever been seen in the convent. Governing by consent was not the way Sister Marie-Paul would have set about the job. She would have stamped her authority onto the community in no uncertain manner, and no one would have dared to query any of her decisions. There would have been no general discussions, like the one to decide the fate of Margot and Marthe Lenoir. Sister Marie-Paul would have handed them over to the German authorities and kept the convent safe. Now, with threats from the SS hanging over them, would be the perfect time to undermine the reverend mother's casual attitude, and oust her from her position.

Her chance to save the convent and to become its superior was approaching, and Sister Marie-Paul was determined not to miss the opportunity. She got to her feet and returned to the recreation room where all the nuns, undismissed, awaited her.

"Sisters," she said, "this has been a frightening afternoon for all of us. The Germans have gone now, but have taken Sister Eloise with them. I have, of course, spoken to the colonel who was here, but he says he will deal only with Reverend Mother. So, there is nothing more we can do until she comes home to us. In the meantime, we must all go about our duties in the normal way. When Reverend Mother does return, it will be I who will tell her what has happened here. I will explain, so please ensure, Sister," Sister Marie-Paul turned her gaze on Sister Celestine, "that she is told I need to see her the moment she gets home. You will not tell her why. Is that understood?"

"Yes, Sister." Sister Celestine sounded nervous as she gave her assurance. "Quite understood."

Sister Marie-Paul gave her a tight smile. Sister Celestine had acted as her eyes and ears in the convent before and could be relied upon. "Good." Sister Marie-Paul rose to her feet, dismissing them all. "Then back to work, all of you. We have a hospital to run."

CHAPTER
THIRTEEN

Mother Marie-Pierre seemed unruffled as she went to her office, but she sensed that something serious had happened in her absence, something that had clearly shaken the white-faced Sister Celestine, and she wondered what on earth it could be. She wished she had time to go up to see Aunt Anne and discover more before she had to face Sister Marie-Paul, but she knew that really would enrage the novice mistress. She wondered, too, if something had happened, why it was Sister Marie-Paul who was asking to see her, and not Sister Eloise, her official deputy. It was not long before she found out.

"Arrested! Sister Eloise?"

"Yes, Mother," replied Sister Marie-Paul, looking grim. "The Germans came and took her away, with a Jew who was hidden in the convent, hidden in your cell, Mother." Her voice was accusing. "You must have known she was there."

"Of course I knew," snapped Mother Marie-Pierre. She had got to her feet and was pacing the room, her palms pressed together as if in prayer. "But that doesn't matter now. Start from the beginning," she instructed, as Sister Marie-Paul seemed about to interrupt. "Tell me exactly what happened."

Sister Marie-Paul described the arrival of the Germans, their simultaneous approach from back and front of the convent, the ruthlessness of their search, the harshness of their officer.

"Not Major Thielen?"

"No, a Colonel Hoch. When they found the escaped Jew with Sister Eloise, he had them both taken to his headquarters in the village. Then he called us all together and threatened us with what would happen if we sheltered any more runaways." Sister Marie-Paul repeated the threats Hoch had made. "The whole convent was put at risk by sheltering this fugitive. She could have been a criminal for all we knew about her. I gave the colonel an undertaking that it would not happen again." She stared defiantly at her superior, as if challenging her to disagree, but Mother Marie-Pierre did not take up the challenge. "Sister Eloise?" she asked, simply.

"I asked about her, of course," replied Sister Marie-Paul, "and the colonel said that he would be interviewing her at his headquarters."

"And this all happened the day before yesterday?"

Sister Marie-Paul nodded.

"And you've heard nothing since?" Mother Marie-Pierre tried to keep the incredulity out of her voice. "You've done nothing since?"

Colour crept up Sister Marie-Paul's neck into her cheeks. "What could I do?" she demanded fiercely. "What can anyone do?"

"I'll go and see Colonel Hoch," said Mother Marie-Pierre tightly, her anger at the novice mistress's complacency almost exploding. How could this woman have simply left her sister to her fate? "I'll see him and find out where she is."

"What about the sisters here?" asked Sister Marie-Paul. "Shouldn't you speak to them first? They were all very afraid when the Germans searched the convent. They need your reassurance that it won't happen again."

"The sisters are quite safe for the present," Mother Marie-Pierre replied, "they will understand that I must go and find Sister Eloise straight away."

"If only I had known that she was nursing an escaped prisoner, I might have been able to save her," Sister Marie-Paul said pointedly. "How did the woman get into the convent? Why weren't we told she was there?"

"I found her in the yard and brought her in," replied Reverend Mother evenly. "Sister Eloise came to look after her when I asked her to. It was unnecessary to involve anyone else." She made no mention of the part played by Sister Marie-Marc or Sister Henriette, there was no need to arouse Sister Marie-Paul's anger further.

"If I may say so, Mother," Sister Marie-Paul's eyes glowed with righteous indignation, "Sister Eloise is now in danger because you chose to interfere in matters that do not concern us here. The Germans being here have nothing to do with us."

"You may say so," replied her superior more calmly than she felt, "but I would remind you, Sister, that we are called to heal the sick and help the afflicted, and the woman I found was clearly both." She opened the door to show that the interview was now over. "I shall go down to the village straight away to see what is happening. In the meantime, please carry on as usual. At supper you can reassure our sisters, and tell them where I am and what I am doing. I will speak to them all when I get back, if it is not too late, or in the morning if it is."

As she hurried down the path to the village, Mother Marie-Pierre considered what had happened in her absence. She had no illusions about the raid. Once Hoch had seen she was safely out of the way, he had searched the convent again, not, she thought, because he expected to find anyone there, but to demonstrate his power. Finding the hidden woman must have been an added bonus and he used it to ensure that the nuns were afraid, afraid enough not to offer shelter again to anyone in hiding. With Sister Marie-Paul at least he had succeeded. She said she had given him an undertaking that they would not help fugitives in the future. Mother Marie-Pierre did not consider herself bound by that undertaking, but she knew now that she could no longer trust Sister Marie-Paul. The earlier divisions among the sisters about the fate of the Lenoir girls would be deepened now and those who considered Sister Marie-Paul was right would form a faction. There had always been factions within the community, it was inevitable, but Mother Marie-Pierre had sought to reduce the friction between them by her open discussion of issues that affected them all, and she had felt that she was beginning to make progress. Now all that would be at risk again. However, such problems were secondary at present, the most important thing now was to try and get Sister Eloise released. She thought about the injured Simone and sighed. She knew that there would be no saving her from the clutches of the Gestapo.

Dusk was falling when she reached the village, but she went straight to the German headquarters where a few chinks of light escaped from badly blacked-out windows. One of the sentries outside demanded her business and when she asked to see Colonel Hoch, he left her waiting in the square while he went in to enquire.

Hoch had heard that she passed through the village to the convent and was expecting her visit. However, he was in no hurry to deal with her; he decided to let her wait and wonder. It was another of his favourite tactics, a way to increase fear and anxiety so that when the time came for interview he already had the upper hand. "Tell her to wait," he snapped. "I'm too busy to see her now."

The message was relayed to Mother Marie-Pierre and she was shown once again into the tiny room that had once been the office of some minor clerk in the Mairie. She sat patiently, her rosary comforting in her fingers as she prayed for Sister Eloise and for herself, that she might find the right words to say when she finally got to see Colonel Hoch. She understood only too well why she was being left there and was determined that the tactic should not succeed. The familiar ritual of the rosary soothed her as she waited.

It was another two hours before she was shown into Hoch's office, by which time she was cold and stiff and in need of a bathroom.

Hoch did not offer her a seat, he simply regarded her from behind his desk with cold eyes. Mother Marie-Pierre stood perfectly still and did not speak. At last Hoch spoke. "Well?"

"I have come to find Sister Eloise."

"So I assumed. She is in a cell at the gendarmerie ... being interrogated." Hoch's face was almost expressionless. "She was harbouring an enemy of the Reich."

"She was nursing an injured woman," Mother Marie-Pierre said quietly. "It is her calling."

"Then she will be carrying out her calling elsewhere in future," Hoch said coldly. "As she wishes to look after such people, it has been arranged. She will accompany her patient to an internment camp."

Mother Marie-Pierre stared at him in horror, and he saw that he had finally pierced her calm façade. "To an internment camp? But Colonel, have you no respect for her cloth?"

"It is because I respect her cloth, as you put it, that I am not having her shot," he replied coolly.

"Shot? For nursing an injured woman?"

"An enemy of the Reich," he repeated. "And, as I am sure you have already spoken to the nun you left in charge at the convent, you know that I have warned her, warned all of you, what will happen if such

232

incidents occur again. You are the reverend mother, it is your choice." He stood to show that the interview was over, but Mother Marie-Pierre, her mind racing, stood her ground.

"May I see her?" she asked quietly.

Hoch shrugged. "If you wish. She will be leaving in the truck that's coming through in the morning. Schwarz! In here!" He barked the order through the open door and the guard outside came rushing in.

"Take this nun over to the gendarmerie and let her see the other one. She may have ten minutes." He turned back to Mother Marie-Pierre. "I do not expect to see you here again, Reverend Mother, for any reason whatsoever. This country is still at war, and I will do whatever I consider necessary to protect its people from saboteurs, spies . . . and anyone else who becomes the enemy of the Reich. Do you understand?"

His eyes drilled into her, and she lowered her own, murmuring, "Certainly, Colonel. I do understand."

"Take her to see the other one," he snapped again, and she was dismissed.

Schwarz led her to the gendarmerie, where two local gendarmes were sitting, smoking. He jerked his head at Mother Marie-Pierre, and was brusque. "She's to see the other nun. Ten minutes."

Captain Gregoire got to his feet, his cigarette still hanging from his lip, and picked up a ring of keys from the desk in front of him. "In here," he growled, and Mother Marie-Pierre followed him through a door into a passage beyond. Several doors led off this and Gregoire paused outside one. He raised the flap on a spy hole and peered in, then he turned a key in the lock and let Mother Marie-Pierre pass him into the cell. It contained nothing but a low stone platform to serve as a bed, and an open drain in the corner.

Sister Eloise was sitting on the bed, but as Mother Marie-Pierre came into the room, she stood up shakily. Her habit was torn and dirty, her hood gone, so that her hair, grey and short-cropped, was exposed as it had not been since she had been professed. Her face was bruised, her lip split and one eye nearly closed. Without the dignity of her wimple she might have seemed diminished, to have dwindled into a little old lady, but the light in her eyes was undimmed.

"Mother!" she cried as she saw who was there. "I knew you would come!" She held out her hands, but Mother Marie-Pierre gathered her into her arms.

"My poor sister," cried Mother Marie-Pierre. "Eloise, what have they done to you?"

Sister Eloise managed a smile as she rested her bruised cheek against the reverend mother's for a moment. "Nothing that won't mend, Mother." She withdrew from Mother Marie-Pierre's arms and sank back down onto the stone bed.

Reverend Mother sat beside her and took her hands. "Tell me what happened."

Sister Eloise told her about the Gestapo search and Simone being found. "We thought it was safe to keep her in your bed while you were away," she explained. "We didn't think the Germans would come back, and when she was better, Sister St Bruno had suggested that we could keep her as a lay worker instead of

234

Marthe. We thought she'd be safe in the convent." She sighed. "But they came without warning, swarming over the whole convent. I was in the middle of changing the dressing on Simone's shoulder. It was impossible to hide her."

"Where is she now?" asked Mother Marie-Pierre quietly.

"I don't know," replied Sister Eloise. "I haven't seen her since we were brought here. That Gestapo colonel thought I could tell him about the other missing prisoners, you know, the ones that escaped from that lorry. He seemed to think we were hiding them at the convent too. I told him we had only seen Simone, I think he has finally decided to believe me. He says I'm to be sent to some camp or other, to keep me out of trouble."

"I know, he told me." Mother Marie-Pierre sighed. "Oh, Sister, I'm so sorry. It's my fault that you're in this place, I should never have . . ."

"Oh yes, you should," cut in Sister Eloise swiftly with much of her old determination and energy. "What the Gestapo are doing is the work of the devil, and we should fight evil wherever we find it." She gripped her superior's hand. "Mother . . . you have always been a woman of great courage and determination. From the moment you arrived at the convent as Sarah, a green girl keen to do your bit, you have devoted yourself to what you thought was right; what God was calling you to do. No, let me finish," she said as Mother Marie-Pierre tried to interrupt. "You were an unusual choice as Reverend Mother, being so young and comparatively junior in the community, but I have no doubt that you were God's choice, and He had His reasons for choosing you. I shall be moving on tomorrow . . . somewhere . . . but wherever it is He will have work for me there."

"Sister, you have such faith," whispered Mother Marie-Pierre, feeling humble in the face of it.

"So do you," replied Sister Eloise. "So do you. If it pleases God that I return to the convent at the end of this war, I know I shall find it standing firm, safe in your care. If not, we shall meet again in God's own good time."

The key scraped in the door behind them, and Sister Eloise drew Mother Marie-Pierre to her once more, murmuring urgently into her ear. "Fight this evil, Mother, from wherever it comes."

"Time's up," growled Gregoire as the two sisters embraced for the last time.

"God bless you, Mother," Sister Eloise said as she let her go.

"And you, Sister. You will be in our prayers, night and day."

"Out!" barked Gregoire, moving to push them apart. "Out! Your time's up."

Mother Marie-Pierre left the cell and heard the door clank closed behind her, separating Sister Eloise from her community for the last time.

Gregoire almost pushed Mother Marie-Pierre out of the gendarmerie, and she found herself outside in the darkness of the street, but the chill in the autumn air was nothing compared with the bleakness in her heart.

236

She stood for a moment, about to walk back to the convent, but with sudden resolution she turned towards the church and the curé's house. Perhaps Father Michel could speak to Colonel Hoch and get him to reconsider his decision to send Sister Eloise to the internment camp.

No lights showed from the windows, but she knocked and waited just the same. At first there was no reply, but as she went to raise the knocker again she heard the scrape of bolts being drawn back, and the door opened a fraction. Mademoiselle Picarde peered round it, and saw who was outside. "Reverend Mother, what do you want at this time of night?"

"I wish to speak with Father Michel," replied Mother Marie-Pierre. She kept the anger she felt out of her voice and stepped towards the half-closed door.

"He's very busy," said Mademoiselle Picarde, but encountering the look of determination on her visitor's face she took a step back and allowed Mother Marie-Pierre to push the door open and enter the dimly lit hall.

"Wait here, please," the housekeeper said. Opening a door and switching on a light she showed Mother Marie-Pierre into a parlour. "I will tell Father Michel you are here."

The elderly priest came out at once and led the nun into his study at the back of the house. Here a small fire burned in the grate, and it was clear that this was where Father Michel spent most of his time.

"Thank you, Rose," he said to his housekeeper, and the woman backed out of the room closing the door behind her. Indicating she should take the chair in front of his desk, the curé took his own seat behind it. "Now, Mother, what can I do for you?"

Mother Marie-Pierre explained about Sister Eloise. "She was simply nursing an injured woman, Father," she said. "That is no reason for the Gestapo to deport her to a camp in Germany."

"The trouble is," Father Michel looked at her over his steepled fingers, "the trouble is that she became involved in secular matters, matters that shouldn't concern you in the convent. You are not to know who is a criminal and who is not. People who come to the hospital with gunshot wounds should be reported to the authorities."

Sister Marie-Paul's words echoed in Mother Marie-Pierre's head, and she realised where they had originated. "Did Sister Marie-Paul come to you for advice, Father?" she asked though she already knew the answer.

"She did, Mother. In your absence she had nowhere else to turn."

"I understand, of course." Mother Marie-Pierre was conciliatory, though anger burned inside her. It was better to let the priest think she agreed with what he said, to keep him safe in his authority so that he would not question hers. She smiled sadly. "I just thought you might have some influence with the colonel, that he'd respect your cloth and perhaps release Sister Eloise."

"I'm afraid not, Mother. I really feel it would be wrong to involve myself in such secular affairs. 'Render unto Caesar', Mother. Remember Our Lord's teaching,

238

and at the present time 'Caesar' is the German authorities."

Mother Marie-Pierre got to her feet and ducked her head as if in submission. "I quite understand, Father. Thank you for seeing me. I must go now or I won't be in before curfew." She turned and walked to the front door followed by the priest. He raised his hand in blessing and then closed the door quickly behind her, shutting her out into the night.

CHAPTER
FOURTEEN

The convent was in darkness when Mother Marie-Pierre let herself in fifteen minutes later. The sisters had all retired for the night, and the Great Silence had settled on the house, but even so she had half expected Sister Marie-Paul to be lying in wait for her and it was with immense relief that she made her way up to the chapel without meeting anyone. As always, one of the sisters was in the chapel keeping watch, kneeling in prayer before the altar, but she was alone and did not turn when Reverend Mother came in and knelt quietly at the back. In the sweet-smelling silence that enfolded her, Mother Marie-Pierre laid out all her troubles before her Lord, and when she rose from her knees some forty minutes later, she felt stronger and knew a measure of peace. She left the chapel as silently as she had come and went to her own cell. She longed to discuss everything with her aunt, but the Great Silence prohibited that and she must wait until morning.

She had just begun to remove her hood when there came a scratching at her door. Throwing a shawl round her head, she opened it to find Sister Marie-Marc outside. She was fully dressed, and despite the Silence, it was clear that she needed to speak. Constrained by

240

the Silence, Sister Marie-Marc simply stared at her, her eyes intense and urgent. Obviously there was some emergency and Reverend Mother broke the Silence.

"Sister! What has happened now?"

Sister Marie-Marc put her finger to her lips and stepped a little closer. Mother Marie-Pierre stood aside and let the nun enter, closing the door softly behind her.

"Sister. You may break the Silence, Sister."

"Mother, thank God you are home."

"Sister, what on earth has happened now?" Mother Marie-Pierre asked in alarm.

"I have found someone," whispered Sister Marie-Marc dramatically. "In the shed."

"Who? Who have you found, Sister?" Mother Marie-Pierre's thoughts ran immediately to the other Jew who had escaped from the lorry.

Sister Marie-Marc looked a little guilty and murmured. "It is a man, Mother."

"A man? What man? Who is he?"

"He is an airman, Mother, an English airman, shot down. His plane crashed and he jumped with a parachute." Sister Marie-Marc's eyes were round with the wonder of it.

Mother Marie-Pierre sank onto her bed and looked up at her expectant sister. Drawing a long breath, she asked, "Where is he?"

"In the cellar, Mother."

Mother Marie-Pierre sighed. "You'd better tell me," she said, and reaching for her hood she began to replace it on her head.

Sister Marie-Marc drew a breath and began. "I was collecting the eggs this evening, when I heard a noise in the shed behind me. I thought it was a rat. They've been getting into the chicken feed. I ran in and grabbed the pitchfork to kill it with. It was getting dark and I couldn't see much but I stabbed the fork into the heap of straw Jean Danot had left there for me."

"A whirlwind with a pitchfork," was how Flight Sergeant Terry Ham described it to Mother Marie-Pierre later, as she sat with him in the darkness of the convent cellar.

Once he discovered that she could speak English, he launched into his tale. "I reckoned I'd found somewhere to hide for the night at least, and then she come in, jabbing away. I was lucky not to get stabbed, and that's a fact. I didn't want to make no noise, but I had to stop her from jabbing." He grinned ruefully. "She says I didn't hurt her when I took the pitchfork off her . . . least, I think that's what she said. I don't know the lingo, but she didn't scream nor nothing, and when she saw my uniform she pushed me down under the straw again and pulled the door shut." He looked across at Sister Marie-Marc who was hovering by the cellar door. "She's a game old bird, begging your pardon, ma'am. She brought me some bread and water to keep me going, and then when it got dark she brought me in here," he waved his hand round the cellar, "and give me some soup."

He went on to tell them how his plane had been hit as it was returning to England after a raid. "Skipper said bail out, so out I bailed. Not sure if the rest of

242

them made it. I saw other chutes open, but it was windy and we was blown apart. So I've been trying to find them, the others. See if we can get ourselves back to England."

Mother Marie-Pierre listened carefully to his story, her mind running through what they might or might not be able to do for this man. She looked across at him, small and wiry, with light curly hair and a boyish face. It was the sort of face she remembered so well from the last war, the face of a young man who was afraid, but determined to hide it with a show of bravado.

"Not sure how to set about it," he admitted when Mother Marie-Pierre asked him if he had any real plans for escaping. "Suppose I should try and get to the sea, find a boat or something. Perhaps go to Spain. I heard of other blokes getting home that way."

"Well, the first thing to do is get you hidden safely here," said Mother Marie-Pierre. "It wouldn't be a good idea for it to be known in the convent that you were here. Sister," she turned to the little nun still waiting in the background, "where else can we hide him?"

"Nowhere," replied Sister Marie-Marc. "The cellar is the best place. Only Sister Elisabeth and I come down here for the vegetables. It's big. No one goes into the places beyond the coal cellar."

Mother Marie-Pierre had only inspected the cellars once, when she had become Reverend Mother. She knew they extended under the main part of the convent, left over from the days when the nuns kept their winter stores in its coolness; some areas were as small as cells, others spacious and lined with shelves and racks. Little of their capacity was used these days. There were a few old garden tools, some discarded items of furniture and some empty packing cases, but there was little food to store and almost no coal. Sister Marie-Marc was right. Few of the sisters would have any cause to come down the old stone steps at all, and if they did they would be unlikely to venture into the darkness beyond the first cellar.

"But the Germans certainly will," Mother Marie-Pierre pointed out. "The cellars will be the first place they search if they raid again." She shook her head at the young man. "I'm sorry," she said, "but you won't be able to stay here very long. If you were caught here, the whole convent would suffer."

"I understand," he said. "I'd better move on then, while it's still dark."

Sister Marie-Marc watched their faces as they spoke, unable to follow the conversation in English, but when she saw the airman get to his feet she made as if to push him down again. She turned to her superior. "Surely you are not letting him go, Mother? We must help him get away."

Reverend Mother repeated what she had said about the Germans searching and the little nun nodded. "But the Boche will not come again," she asserted. "That Gestapo man, he thinks he has frightened us, so we will not help anyone else."

"I hope you're right, Sister," said the reverend mother, "but we can't rely on that."

"This boy will be safe for a few days while we think of a plan," said Sister Marie-Marc stoutly. "If they find him, Mother, they will shoot him."

"If they find him here, they may shoot us all," returned her superior dryly. "There are several sisters who would be most unhappy to know he was here."

"Then we will not tell them," replied Sister Marie-Marc with a shrug.

"Let's have a look at the rest of the cellar," said Mother Marie-Pierre, and picking up the oil lamp they had brought down with them, she led the way. Together they explored the underground space. It was dark and musty, smelling of damp. Some parts were little more than caves hewn from the rock, others, with old wooden doors, were more like walk-in cupboards. At the far end of the cellar they came to one of these. The lamp showed stone walls and a flagged floor; there were some slatted shelves where apples might once have been stored, otherwise the room was empty, but it did have a stout door to close it off.

"This might do," suggested Sister Marie-Marc hopefully.

"It's the furthest from the door," remarked the airman, peering into the dark corner, "but it don't smell as musty, somehow."

Reverend Mother sniffed the air. There was a coolness to it and it certainly smelt fresher. She held the lamp higher to cast the light further and the flame flickered within its chimney.

"There's a draught," exclaimed the airman. "Here, give me the lamp."

He took it from her and held it up above his head. The flame continued to flicker, but by its light they saw there was an iron grating set into the ceiling.

"Must be to let air circulate in the cellar," said Terry Ham as he peered up at it. It was clearly overgrown, choked with vegetation, no light penetrated, but fresh air seeped through, dispelling the mustiness of the air below. "I reckon I could loosen that if I had a crowbar, then if anyone comes poking about down here, I can nip up and out sharpish."

"That depends on where it comes out," pointed out Mother Marie-Pierre. "You could climb straight into the arms of whoever is waiting above."

Sister Marie-Marc thought for a moment, trying to orientate herself. "It must extend beyond the walls of the building as it is open to the outside air," she said. "Maybe it comes up in the courtyard."

"Well, we can't go and look now," said Reverend Mother. "Tomorrow you can search, Sister, while you are seeing to the hens. In the meantime," she turned back to the airman, "you must stay down here, in this furthest corner of the cellar." She looked the young man in the eye. "Under no circumstances are you to come out of this part of the cellar, is that understood?"

His eyes held hers as he replied. "Yes, I understand."

"Sister Marie-Marc will bring you food and water and a bucket for . . . your needs." Reverend Mother looked away in some embarrassment as she said this, as did the young man.

"All right," he mumbled. "Thanks."

246

"I will come down again tomorrow night and we'll decide what, if anything, we can do for you." She turned briskly to Sister Marie-Marc and explained what was needed. "Make sure you are not seen, Sister. The fewer people who know about Flight Sergeant Ham the better."

"My name's Terry," he said.

Mother Marie-Pierre smiled. "Well, Terry. We'll do our best for you."

When she had regained the privacy of her own cell Mother Marie-Pierre lay on her bed and considered what she could do. Clearly Terry Ham could not stay in the convent for more than a day, it was too dangerous for everybody, but where could he go? How was he going to get home to England? Wouldn't it be better if he gave himself up to the Germans? He'd be a prisoner of war, after all, not a spy. They wouldn't shoot a prisoner of war, they'd just send him to a prison camp. Wouldn't they? If he surrendered to Major Thielen he'd be all right, wouldn't he? Then she thought of Colonel Hoch and shivered. *He* might do anything.

If only I had someone to discuss it with, she thought, as her mind churned with worry and indecision. Aunt Anne maybe, but she was an old lady and would probably tell her to do what she thought best. She needed someone outside the convent, but there was no one, no one she could trust anyway. If only Father Michel were a stronger man, she could go to him, but after this evening's visit she knew that was hopeless; she already knew what his advice would be.

If only he were more like Father Bernard in Amiens, she thought. Now there was someone you could trust. Mother Marie-Pierre felt her spirits lift a little. If I could only get Terry to Father Bernard, she thought, he'd know what to do.

For the next hour she lay in bed, considering and rejecting plans for Terry Ham's escape, and only slipped into a fitful sleep as the rising bell rang out through the convent, calling the sisters to matins.

"I would like to speak to everyone after breakfast," she told Sister Marie-Paul to pre-empt any comment. "Please take the meal, and I will see you in the recreation room when you have all finished."

Sister Marie-Paul inclined her head. "Yes, Mother, of course."

Leaving the sisters to go into the refectory, Mother Marie-Pierre went to the kitchen, and, collecting Sister St Bruno's tray, carried it up to her. As the old lady ate her bread and honey her niece told her everything that had happened since she had left the convent three days earlier with the Jewish children. Then she reached the discovery of the English airman in the cellar. "Of course Sister Marie-Marc did right to hide him, at least I think she did, but what am I to do with him now? I wish I had somewhere to send him, as I did with the children."

"Well, I think you may have," her aunt said. "Why not send him to this Father Bernard in Amiens? He helped you before, and clearly he knew what you were doing then. Maybe he will help again."

"He might, I suppose." Sarah sounded doubtful. "I did think of him, but how on earth do I get Terry to him? How can he travel without papers? He will be picked up at once. And supposing Father Bernard turns him away?"

"Do you think he will?"

Sarah considered for a moment. "No. No, I don't think so, but it will put Father Bernard in danger as well. I don't know if that is justified simply because he didn't give me and the children away last time. Anyway, I still don't know how to get him there."

"As you did with Marthe," replied her aunt.

"Marthe?" Sarah stared at her. "But Marthe went disguised as one of us."

"So she did; so could he."

"But he's a man."

"Indeed he is," replied Aunt Anne patiently, "but put him in a nun's habit and who is to know it? How big is he? Does he have a moustache? A beard?"

That drew an unwilling laugh from Sarah. "No, he doesn't have either."

"Is he tall?"

"No, quite small actually." Sarah thought for a moment and saw there might be a possibility here. "But where will I get a habit from? Sister Marie-Paul isn't going to give me another. It was bad enough last time, when it was for a girl, and someone we knew. She would consider it sacrilege for a man to wear it. Anyway," Sarah looked a little guiltily at her aunt, "you know, I don't really trust her. She says we shouldn't get involved with secular things. I don't think I can rely on her to keep the secret anymore."

"There's mine," suggested Aunt Anne.

Sarah stared at her. "What did you say?"

"There's my habit. I don't get up much these days, so I don't need it for a while. I'll just stay in bed, or in my room anyway."

Sarah's eyes flicked to the habit hanging on the back of the cell door. Sister St Bruno had been tall and though she had shrunk since she'd had to take to her bed, the habit was quite long. As Terry Ham was not in any way a big man, he might fit into it.

"He couldn't go by himself," Sarah said musingly. "Someone would have to go with him to do the talking. He doesn't speak any French. And he'd need papers."

"What did you do about papers for Marthe?"

"I used Sister Marie-Joseph's."

"Then use them again."

"He doesn't look anything like Sister Marie-Joseph," Sarah laughed.

"Very little of him will show," pointed out her aunt. "And, with luck, all people will see is a nun."

Sarah considered the idea. It was on the face of it quite outlandish, disguising a grown man as a young nun, and yet the very absurdity of it meant that there was an outside chance that it would work. People saw what they expected to see. Even so.

"I'll think about it," she said at length, getting to her feet. "We can't do anything until I can speak with him again tonight." She sighed. "In the meantime I must go and talk to the sisters. I have to tell them about Sister Eloise."

"Remember what she said to you when you left her," said her aunt quietly. "You must fight evil wherever you find it."

"Are you suggesting Sister Marie-Paul is evil?" Sarah was startled.

"No," replied her aunt sadly, "just misguided, but the results may be the same."

Throughout the day Mother Marie-Pierre considered Sister St Bruno's suggestion. Sometimes it seemed almost feasible and at others quite impossible. She had an opportunity to speak to Sister Marie-Marc, privately, before the midday meal, and was assured that their visitor had been supplied with all he would need for the day.

"I'll come down and see him again when everyone has gone to bed," Reverend Mother promised. "Then we'll discuss his escape."

By the time the convent was quiet, Mother Marie-Pierre had come to some sort of decision. She took Sister St Bruno's habit, and, rolling it up under her arm, slipped quietly down the stairs to meet Sister Marie-Marc in the kitchen. Together they went into the cellar, carrying the oil lamp and a dish of stew for their guest.

"I am sorry you've been in the dark all day," Mother Marie-Pierre said as she set the lamp on the floor and Sister Marie-Marc handed him the stew. "We simply couldn't risk anyone seeing the light either from the outside, or if they came down into the cellar for something."

"That's all right, Sister," Terry said, and turned his attention to the food. When he had finished, he wiped his mouth on the back of his hand. "So, what next?"

"I have an idea for getting you away from here," replied Mother Marie-Pierre, "but it depends on several things if it is going to work."

"OK. Shoot!"

So, Mother Marie-Pierre explained her plan. "One of the sisters will go with you, as you don't speak French. The story will be that you are going to the mother house in Paris."

"On a train?" Terry looked doubtful. "What about papers and that?"

"You'll have the ones that belong to one of our sisters," Mother Marie-Pierre told him. "But none of this will work if you don't fit into this." She held out the folded habit.

Terry stared open-mouthed. "Me? Wear that?"

"Try it on now," instructed Mother Marie-Pierre. "Sister Marie-Marc and I will give you time to change, then we will come back and arrange your hood." And before he could protest any further, Reverend Mother drew Sister Marie-Marc out of the little room and into the main part of the cellar.

"Did you discover where the grating is, Sister?" she asked as they waited for their guest to struggle into his disguise.

"Not in the courtyard, Mother. Nowhere in the courtyard is that overgrown. I think it must be outside the wall. I haven't been able to find it yet, but I will keep looking."

"You can come back now," Terry said in a strangled whisper, and the two nuns returned to his cellar. He stood awkwardly in the lamplight, his face red with embarrassment. Mother Marie-Pierre fought down the urge to laugh, but Sister Marie-Marc had no such inhibitions and laughed aloud, making Terry's young face crack into a grin. She was immediately hushed by her superior, and together they set about dressing the young airman in the wimple and hood, which would do more for his disguise than the habit itself.

When they had finished they stepped back to survey their handiwork and Sister Marie-Marc gasped. "It will work, Mother," she breathed, and Mother Marie-Pierre, looking critically at the young nun before them, actually began to believe that it might. Terry Ham was young and his face, if they could get him a razor, would be smooth. The wimple covered his hair, his forehead and his ears, fitting snugly under his chin, the shape accentuating the roundness of his boyish face. The hood, with its starched peaks, stood away from his head, and the whole presented a rather coltish nun, but at a glance a nun, nevertheless.

"I'll bring you a razor from the hospital," Mother Marie-Pierre said, "and then I think you'll do." She smiled at the look of dismay that still played on his face. "Don't worry, we'll get you out of here and safely to Amiens. It will be a start."

Terry looked down at his feet. "What about my boots?"

Reverend Mother looked at them, emerging from under the habit. That could be a problem. The nuns all wore black-laced shoes, but they were nothing like as heavy as the flying boots Terry was wearing.

"We've no ordinary shoes big enough for you," she said. "You'll just have to pull the habit down as far as you can, and try not to let them show. Keep your hands in your sleeves, too. They don't look like a woman's hands."

Terry dutifully tucked his hands into the wide sleeves and tried walking across the room without letting more than the toes of his boots show. Sister Marie-Marc giggled, and he treated her to another grin.

"Who's going with me?" he asked anxiously. "I'll be putting them into danger."

Reverend Mother had been considering this. She wanted as few people as possible to know that he had been staying in the convent. The plan was that he, and whoever she sent with him, should set out at dawn and walk into Albert, from where they could take the train to Amiens. She wanted them well away from the village before people were about. She was praying that they would not be stopped, at least until they had reached the town, but she had to send someone who could deal with any problems on the way. She wished Sister Danielle was back. She looked across at Sister Marie-Marc but dismissed the idea at once. She was too old to make such a journey, and she spoke no English, so she wouldn't be able to communicate with her charge. In any case she could not think of a reason why she might send Sister Marie-Marc to Paris.

"I'm not sure yet," she admitted.

"Can it be her?" he asked nodding in the direction of Sister Marie-Marc. "I know her."

"I don't think so," she began, but was surprised when Sister Marie-Marc spoke at the same time.

"Who will go with him, Mother?" she asked. "Will you send me?"

"No, Sister, not you." The nun started to protest. "You could not walk all the way to Albert, and you do not speak any English, and," she added firmly to prevent further argument, "I shall need you here to be my eyes and ears while I am gone."

"You're going?" Sister Marie-Marc sounded incredulous.

"It is the only answer," replied Reverend Mother. And indeed, she had recognised in that instant, it was. "I shall take Terry on the train to Amiens and leave him in Father Bernard's care. We don't want anyone else to know that he's been here. Then if the Germans do come back, well, the sisters will all be as innocent as they seem."

"All except me," remarked Sister Marie-Marc.

"I know I can rely on you to be the picture of innocence," smiled her superior. She turned back to Terry and spoke in English. "I will be going with you as far as Amiens. But we will have to wait another day so that I can organise the trip without it looking suspicious to anyone here.

"I shall tell Sister Marie-Paul that I am going back to Paris to fetch Sister Danielle," she explained to Sister Marie-Marc, "that I don't want her to travel alone in such uncertain times . . . which indeed I do not. I will set out very early in the morning, alone. You and Terry will leave before it gets light and wait for me on the other side of the village. Then we shall go on and you will come back."

"But Mother . . ."

"It is decided, Sister." Mother Marie-Pierre spoke in a tone that brooked no argument. "I have lost Sister Eloise, I will not put anyone else at risk." Turning back to Terry Ham, she went on: "We'll get you a razor and some hot water to shave." She gave him a brief smile. "Make sure it is a close shave, *hein*, your life may depend on it."

Thirty-six hours later, Sister Celestine let Reverend Mother out of the front door into the cold grey of a November dawn. In her pocket she carried her own papers and those of Sister Marie-Joseph, which she had neglected to return to the young nun.

"God go with you," murmured Sister Celestine as Mother Marie-Pierre paused on the threshold. "Bring Sister Danielle back safely to us."

"Thank you, Sister, I will." Sister Marie-Paul had accepted the story that she was going to fetch Sister Danielle as she did not want her to travel alone.

"But you will be travelling alone, Mother," she pointed out.

"That is my risk," replied Mother Marie-Pierre, "I do not want Sister Danielle to take that risk unnecessarily."

"I understand," said Sister Marie-Paul, thinking even as she smiled that Reverend Mother was clearly feeling guilty about the fate of Sister Eloise. And so she should, she thought. "I will see to things here while you are away, Mother."

Now, with her cloak drawn round her shoulders, Mother Marie-Pierre hurried along the path through the copse, and then, taking the track by the river, skirted the village and joined the road beyond. As she passed behind the outlying houses, their shutters still closed against the night, her eyes searched the lanes and gardens for any sign of an early German patrol. She saw no one and could only pray no one saw her.

Where the path met the road, she found Sister Marie-Marc and Terry, carefully attired in habit and hood, waiting in the shelter of a hedge. From a distance Mother Marie-Pierre certainly could not tell that the taller of the two nuns was a man, and even when she drew near it was not immediately apparent.

As she came up with them she spoke in a low voice. "Everything all right?"

"Easy," replied Sister Marie-Marc, her eyes alight with the excitement of it all. "We slipped out of the back gate. No one saw us go, it was still dark and there were no lights on in the house."

"And you saw no one on the path?"

"No, Mother. No one."

"Good," replied Reverend Mother. "Now you must go back quickly and try not to be seen coming in at the gate."

Sister Marie-Marc shrugged. "I will collect eggs," she said. "My naughty hens often lay outside the gate at the edge of the field."

"Have a care," her superior warned, resting a hand on her arm. "This is not a game we are playing, Sister."

Sister Marie-Marc bowed her head slightly. "No, Mother. I'll be careful," she promised.

Reverend Mother gave her a brief smile. "I know you will, Sister. God willing, I'll be back in two days with Sister Danielle."

As Sister Marie-Marc turned away, Terry caught her hand. "Mercy, Sister, mercy for everything." Before she could pull away, he planted a kiss on her hand. She snatched her hand away, but she smiled at him before she turned back along the footpath.

"I'd have kissed her proper, on the cheek, if it hadn't been for this hat thing," Terry said as he watched her go.

"It's a good thing that you didn't," remarked Mother Marie-Pierre tartly. "Nuns don't kiss each other, and you could have been seen. Now, Sister, ground rules. Don't speak from now on. For any reason. You never know who will overhear. If we meet anyone, let me do the talking. Keep your eyes down, don't make eye contact, and when we are standing still anywhere, keep your hands in your sleeves. It'll be all too easy for you to give yourself away, so concentrate on being a nun all the time, whether there is anyone there or not. And do not speak. Understood?"

Terry Ham gave her an impish grin. "Yes, Mother," he said in a demure voice.

"Good," replied Mother Marie-Pierre with asperity, "for our lives may depend on it." Then she added, "If by any chance I address you as *ma soeur*, you simply nod, as if in obedience, all right?"

"Masseur?" Terry grinned at the word.

"It means I'm calling you 'Sister'. All right?"

"Masseur," repeated Terry obediently. "I'll remember."

It took them two hours to reach Albert, following the twisting lanes and taking footpaths wherever possible. At the station Mother Marie-Pierre bought two tickets for Paris, but then they had to wait for a train. No one could tell them when it would come, so they joined the crowd on the platform. The station was crowded, and there were plenty of German uniforms among the civilians. Terry did as he'd been told and stood in silence, head bowed, eyes on the ground, with his hands tucked into his sleeves.

"Excuse me, Sister," came a man's voice from behind them. Mother Marie-Pierre turned sharply to find herself face-to-face with a German officer. "Please, do take my seat on the bench." The German, who had spoken in fluent if accented French, indicated the wooden bench where he had been sitting.

Although her heart was pounding, Mother Marie-Pierre managed to keep her voice steady. "Why thank you, sir. We'd be most grateful." She touched Terry on the arm and edged him towards the bench. "Come, Sister, let's take the weight off our feet while we can." As she had spoken in French, Terry had no idea what she had said, but hearing the word he had been waiting for, he nodded, and following her example sat down on the bench beside her.

259

The German major seemed disposed to make conversation, and asked where they were going. Mother Marie-Pierre produced the story she had rehearsed; that they were going to the mother house in Paris, as Sister Marie-Joseph had been asked to help with the nursing there. The German turned politely to Sister Marie-Joseph, but found that she had her head bowed, her rosary beads in her fingers, and was murmuring prayers under her breath. Embarrassed, the major looked away, peering along the platform to see if there was any sign of the train coming. Even as he looked there was a puff of smoke in the distance, and the crowd on the platform surged forward. Mother Marie-Pierre placed a warning hand on her companion's arm, waiting for the major to move away. She had no wish to share a compartment with him all the way to Amiens.

She need not have worried. The major had felt a fool when he found one of the nuns was actually saying her prayers, in public, on a station. He did not want to share a compartment either. Far too embarrassing if she started to pray again.

The two nuns clambered up into the train, but, as they had held back for a moment or two, there were no seats, and they had to stand in the corridor. Wedged between a large woman with a basket and a fat man in a shiny suit, they rocked with the train as it trundled slowly out of the station. The journey was slow, but uneventful. There were no spot checks, for which Mother Marie-Pierre gave thanks, as at such close quarters it was likely that even the most short-sighted inspector would notice that there was little similarity between the picture on the second nun's papers and the person it purported to represent. It was with great relief that they climbed down from the train when it finally reached Amiens. Here too the station was busy, as the train disgorged its passengers to add to the crowd waiting not so patiently to board the train.

"Keep close to me," murmured Mother Marie-Pierre as she edged her way through the crush towards the exit. Terry nodded, and shuffled along behind her, trying to keep his boots hidden below his habit. There was a long queue at the gate, where two German officers were checking documents. Mother Marie-Pierre paused, allowing several people to pass in front of her. Terry waited at her side. The people in front filtered through the checkpoint and the two nuns moved forward. As they reached the gate and Mother Marie-Pierre presented the two sets of papers, Terry stood demurely behind her, eyes lowered, hands in sleeves.

"I thought you were on your way to Paris, Sister," said a loud voice behind them. Mother Marie-Pierre turned round to find the German major at her elbow.

"We are, Major, but I have an errand to run for Reverend Mother in Amiens on the way." Mother Marie-Pierre's thoughts were racing. Her excuse sounded lame even to herself, but something at the back of her mind warned her to say as little as possible.

"Oh, you have a convent here in Amiens?" asked the major.

"No, but we have links with some of the parishes here." Mother Marie-Pierre summoned a smile to her lips and turned back to the soldier scrutinising their papers. He was now holding them out impatiently to the two nuns, who were clearly known to the major and thus hardly a threat to security. Reverend Mother took the papers with a quiet "Thank you", and pushing them into the pocket of her habit gave the major another, more spontaneous, smile, then turned to Terry. "Come along, *ma soeur.*"

Masseur! Again, Terry heard the word he'd been waiting for and nodded dutifully, before tripping along behind her as she strode out into the street.

Knowing how conspicuous they would be even on the crowded streets in the centre of the town, Mother Marie-Pierre turned into a side street as soon as she could, so that the German major, who had come out of the station behind them, should not follow their progress.

Twenty minutes later they were standing outside the Church of the Holy Cross. The street was quiet and no one paid any attention to the two nuns as they pushed open the door to the empty church. The faded light of the winter's day hardly penetrated the ornate windows, and in the gloom the red sanctuary light glowed before the altar. In the Lady Chapel several votive candles flickered in the draught from the door, but there was no sign of anyone else in the church.

Mother Marie-Pierre led the way into a pew at the back and knelt in silence for a moment or two. Terry did the same. She sat back. "You did very well, Terry," she said softly. "Especially when the German came up to us on the platform. Pretending to say the rosary was a clever move."

Terry laughed. "I wasn't pretending, Mother, I was praying like hell!"

Mother Marie-Pierre couldn't repress a smile at his forthright answer. "I should continue to do so," she said. "You wait here. Stay on your knees with your head bowed and then even if someone comes in, they won't bother you. I'm going to find Father Bernard. We're in his hands now. If he won't help, I don't know where we go from here."

"You'll go to Paris and fetch your Sister Danielle," Terry replied promptly. "And I'll disappear into the woodwork."

"I'll be back as soon as I can. All right?"

Terry nodded and remained on his knees as she left the church and crossed the road to the priest's house.

Madame Papritz opened the door as before, and immediately recognising her visitor led her straight through to Father Bernard, who was working in his study.

"Mother Marie-Pierre!" he exclaimed as she was ushered in. "What a lovely surprise!"

Mother Marie-Pierre smiled. "Thank you, Father. I hope you'll think so when you've heard why I'm here."

The priest's smile faded. "I see, well you'd better tell me."

Mother Marie-Pierre knew that having come here she had to trust Father Bernard implicitly. He could do one of three things, he could inform the German authorities about them, he could remain silent, but send them away, or he could offer his help in some way. Mother Marie-Pierre had gambled on the last, but if her trust were misplaced, then she and Terry were in trouble.

"It's like this, Father," she began, and told him the whole story, from Sister Marie-Marc's discovery of Terry Ham hiding in the shed to their arrival in Amiens.

He listened without interruption until she had finished. "And this young man is waiting in my church now?"

Mother Marie-Pierre replied that he was.

"Then I think you'd better go and fetch him straight away."

When Terry was safely installed before the tiny coal fire in Father Bernard's study, his host looked at him with interest before turning to Mother Marie-Pierre. He spoke with a smile. "I see how you got away with it . . . this time. You were lucky he is not a big man. Still, I think the first thing should be to turn him back into a man again . . . he won't bear close scrutiny, you know."

Mother Marie-Pierre gave Terry a quick translation and the young man looked very relieved. "He's right," he said with fervour. "I can't wait to get out of this hat thing."

Father Bernard took Terry upstairs, returning moments later without him. "I've given him some of Father Gilbert's clothes."

"Won't Madame Papritz wonder . . . ?" began Mother Marie-Pierre, but Father Bernard shook his head. "Madame Papritz sees everything and says nothing. She is the perfect priest's housekeeper. I trust her completely."

"What are we going to do with Terry now, Father?" Mother Marie-Pierre at last asked the all-important question.

"Don't worry about him," Father Bernard said calmly. "He'll be all right. I have connections. Better you know no more than that. Is the little Jewish girl safe?"

"Yes, she is." Mother Marie-Pierre smiled at him. "You weren't fooled then either, were you?"

"No," he agreed, "but I had ample opportunity to study her. Anyone meeting her in the street might well have accepted her as what she seemed."

"It was because of her that I came to you," Mother Marie-Pierre said. "I had nowhere else to turn."

The door opened and Terry came in. He was wearing the collar and cassock of a Catholic priest. "It's a relief to get out of that hood," he said. "But I'm still wearing a bloody frock!"

CHAPTER
FIFTEEN

The light above Adelaide's head changed from red to green. "Go!" bellowed the voice over the roar of the aircraft, and Adelaide, closing her eyes, went through the hole in the fuselage and into the night air, free-falling for a second before her parachute opened above her head with a reassuring crack. She was aware of other parachutes opening above her in fast succession as her suitcase and other containers followed her out of the plane, then she had no time to think of anything else as the ground rushed up to meet her. The instructions that had been drummed into her during her brief training at Ringway came to her aid and she rolled as she hit the ground, trying not to absorb the impact with her legs. For a moment she lay winded, and then she was struggling to her feet, pulling at the release of the parachute harness.

A young man ran over to her and spoke in French. "You OK?"

"Yes, give me a hand with this."

Together they bundled up the parachute and dragged it to the edge of the field. "We'll hide it here," the man said, and began stuffing the unwieldy silk bundle in a hollow under some bushes."

Adelaide grabbed his arm. "No, we were told to bury them."

"Not now. It'll be dealt with. Now we have to gather everything up and get clear before the Germans realise there's been a drop. Come on . . . move."

The reception party who had signalled to the plane were already busy at work. Shadows moved in the darkness as they collected the packages and containers that had dropped from the aircraft as it made its pass over the dropping zone, before roaring away into the sky. As it disappeared, the moon rode out from behind a cloud and the field was bathed in clear, pale light.

"Hurry." A tall man who seemed to be directing operations spoke to Adelaide. "All OK? No injuries?"

"Fine. You Marcel?"

"Yes."

"Antoinette," she returned briefly, and looked round for her suitcase.

The reception party had gathered up the equipment and were loading it into a farm cart, working quickly in the shifting moonlight. Adelaide spotted her own small case and picked it up.

"Right, get going," Marcel said to his men as the last container went onto the cart. "Tomorrow, at six."

The cart began to move away and Marcel turned back to Adelaide. "Welcome to France," he said. "Follow me."

He set a tough pace, leading her across fields and through a wood before skirting a village that lay silent and still in the moonlight. Adelaide had no trouble in keeping up, though her suitcase was a nuisance. Marcel did not offer to carry it for her and for that she was glad. She wanted to prove herself and she wanted no favours.

Though, she thought, as she manoeuvred it over a stone wall, perhaps I should have let it go on the wagon.

In the distance a dog barked, and Marcel put out a warning hand to halt her. There was no other sound and at last he moved on, keeping to the shelter of the hedgerows as far as possible, straining his ears before hurrying her across an open road and down behind a stone wall on the far side. There was a dirt track along the edge of another open field and then they were through a gate and approaching the dark bulk of a farmhouse, surrounded by outbuildings.

Marcel led the way confidently through the farmyard to the back door. It opened and they slipped inside. Once the door was closed again a light was switched on and Adelaide found herself in a warm, stone-flagged kitchen. Marcel waved to a chair at the big kitchen table.

"Sit down," he said, and, as Adelaide sank gratefully into the chair, he put his head round the inner door. "Maman!"

An elderly woman appeared from the depths of the house, and greeting Adelaide with a smile she poured coffee into mugs from a pot on the range. Adelaide took hers gratefully, warming her hands round the mug. It had been freezing cold in the plane despite having a blanket wrapped round her. She had been dressed for her landing in France, all her clothes made by French tailors in London, cut in the French style, and despite the flying suit on top, they did not keep out the cold at the high altitudes of the plane's flight.

Maman then asked Adelaide if she were hungry. By now it was the early hours of the morning and Adelaide shook her head. "No thank you, Madame," she said. "The coffee is all I need."

"Anything from Rousseau?" Marcel asked the old woman.

She shook her head. "Nothing. No movement." She smiled at Adelaide, said goodnight and left the room.

"Now we can talk," Marcel said. "And you can tell me what orders you bring from London."

"London wants to set up an escape route for airmen who are shot down over Germany," Adelaide replied. "They know what your group is doing, of course, through Bertrand" — she used the codename of the wireless operator who had been sent in some weeks earlier to make contact with the resistance — "and they were very interested in one of your reports. They've sent me to follow it up."

"The convent," Marcel said.

Adelaide nodded. "Yes. I have to find out exactly what is going on."

Marcel scowled. "I can't see why they had to send someone over from England just for that. We could have infiltrated the convent ourselves."

"They sent me because I already have a contact inside the convent," Adelaide said tersely. "They sent me from England so that if something went wrong your entire network would not be jeopardised." She smiled at him. "They sent me to help," she added more gently. "My grandmother is French, I have come to help France."

There was a silence between them for a moment, and then Marcel spoke. "And your cover story?"

"I am Adèle Durant and I have come to help my uncle Gerard Launay on his farm. My parents are dead. He is elderly and he and his wife can no longer manage on their own . . . since their son was killed during the German invasion." She looked at him questioningly. "London believes you to have made this arrangement already. My papers support it."

Marcel nodded. "I just wanted to be sure we both had the same cover for you," he said. "Tonight you stay here, and in a few days, when I have made the proper arrangements, I will take you to the station in Albert. From there your uncle will come and collect you from the train and take you home to the farm." Marcel got to his feet. "Now I suggest you go to bed. You should be safe enough here. My people have cleared the dropping zone, and it seems that the drop went undetected, by the local Boche, anyway. We have someone keeping watch so we should have warning if there is any sign of them. In the morning I will start the arrangements for you to join your uncle. Bertrand will let London know that you are safe and send any other messages that you may have for them."

The old woman led Adelaide upstairs to a room over the kitchen, furnished with a large bed and little else. Left alone, Adelaide got ready for bed, and then snuggled under the feather comforter. Although she was dog-tired, her nerves were strung taut as piano wire and sleep eluded her. As she lay in the darkness, her mind churning, she thought back over the last few days.

She had at last finished her special training and then been sent to a small flat in London for what she had thought would be her final briefing. In the past eight months she had had a thorough training in a great many skills that would have been inconceivable for a woman in the earlier days of the war. Relentless physical training had ensured that Adelaide was now superbly fit. In Scotland she had learned how to live off the land, and survive in open countryside in all winds and weathers. She learned signals and codes, she learnt how to use explosives, trained in unarmed combat, became familiar with a variety of weapons. She had learned to kill silently, to fade into the background. She had learned to listen, she had trained her memory and her rudimentary German had improved so that she could at least follow a conversation. She had spoken French most of the time, immersed herself in the language, so that her instinctive response would be to cry out in French, to answer in French, to challenge in French.

There had been times when she had almost given up, when it had all seemed too much and she couldn't cope with the ruthlessness needed, the perpetual fear, the concentration of living a lie. Then she thought of Andrew, and her resolution hardened with bitter determination and she applied herself again. Andrew, her beloved cousin, more brother than cousin, was dead. Grand'mère had written to tell her, and Adelaide had been numb with the pain of it. Every fibre of her being cried out against it. Andrew? Why Andrew? There were no details of his death, the family had simply been told he'd been killed in action. Adelaide herself did not actually know any more than they did, but having guessed that he was involved in some sort of clandestine work, she also guessed that he had been dropped into occupied territory somewhere, probably in France as his French was as fluent as her own, and he had not returned. He had risked himself in the war behind the lines and Adelaide knew that she must do the same.

So, her training went on. She had spent two days at Ringway near Manchester, learning to parachute, something that had filled her with almost more dread than the thought of living on her wits in occupied France. How could she fling herself out of an aeroplane? The very thought of it brought her close to blind panic. Cora, who had been with her for much of the training, seemed to have no problem with the jump, and it was she who gave Adelaide the strength to go through with it. Almost paralysed with terror, Adelaide had done it, and now she was ready . . . or as ready as she'd ever be.

She and Cora had grown close during their training, each helping the other in areas where they felt insecure, but at the end of their training, Cora had disappeared, sent on some mission of her own. Adelaide did not know where or what that might be. No one knew anything that was not absolutely essential; even the most courageous would eventually talk if caught and questioned by the Gestapo. Knowledge of another agent put that agent at even greater risk. Now Cora had gone, Adelaide was on her own, to live and die by her own wits . . . and the silence of others.

"You'll be dropped near the town of Albert in north-east France." It was Captain Jenner, the officer who had first recruited her who was briefing her now, sitting across the table in the tiny flat, as if they were normal people sharing a pot of tea. "Your accent will pass in that area and we need someone to carry out some special work there." He looked at her and smiled. "The reports that have come through about your training are very good, and we think that you are the right person."

"Thank you, sir," was all Adelaide said, wondering what was coming next.

"Your codename will be Antoinette," Jenner told her. "You are going to join up with a resistance circuit being built in the Somme area. We have already dropped in a wireless operator who has linked up with the local resistance to gather information. We need information about anything and everything that might be of use to us, both now and in the future. We need to know exactly what the Germans are up to. What they are building, what they are manufacturing, where their troops are and why. Airfields, anti-aircraft guns, roads and railways, any troop movement. All that is vital and the local circuit is beginning to gather such information for us. However, though you'll have a link with them, we have a special job we want you to do. Marcel, the local resistance leader, will be told why you are there and will give you any help that doesn't put the circuit at risk. Marcel, that's a codename too of course, will be your cut-out. He, and only he, will liaise with you. You will know no one else in the circuit unless he feels that it is essential, and then only by codename. That way if anyone is arrested, neither you nor they will jeopardise the whole network. Do you understand?"

Adelaide nodded. "Yes, sir, but . . ."

Major Jenner went on as if she had not spoken. "Marcel is arranging his end of the cover story you will be given. I'll give you that to work on before I leave today."

"Am I responsible to him?" asked Adelaide. "This Marcel?"

"No," replied Jenner, "but you will need him and you should be guided by him. He's the man on the ground, the man with the knowledge of exactly how things stand in the area." Jenner looked at Adelaide sharply. "Why, is that a problem?"

"No, sir," she answered, "I just wanted to be sure of my status."

"Your status, as you put it, is that you work for us. You are responsible to us, but to have any hope of completing the task you will have to have a good working relationship with the local *réseau*."

"I'm sorry, sir," Adelaide persisted, "but if the resistance already have a network, and I'm not to be part of it, what am I going to be doing?"

"The farm you are going to is near a village called St Croix in the Somme area," the major told her.

Adelaide's surprise was clear on her face.

274

"Yes, I know you are familiar with the area. I know you visited it for a few days before the war. That's why we're considering you. It adds to the risk in some ways, but we think the advantages of using you will outweigh that."

"I see," said Adelaide lamely.

"No, you don't," replied Jenner cheerfully, "but you will. Now what we want you to do is this . . ."

He outlined the plan, not dwelling on the added risk he was asking her to take, but not ignoring it either. He went into no detail of what would be required of her. That would come later . . . when he was sure. Now he spoke only in generalities.

"We need you to get work in the convent, as a maid, or a cleaner or some such, so that you can come and go without causing comment. They employ girls from the village, I believe." Jenner looked across at her, watching her face, gauging her reaction to his words. If he was not completely sure about her, there was still time to pull her out, to try and find someone else. He didn't want to do that. In most ways she was perfect for the job he had in mind, and training someone else for it would take time he could ill afford. He had said the advantage she offered outweighed the risk, but did it?

"Will there be anyone who might recognise you?" he asked.

Adelaide thought for a moment. Apart from her aunt and great-aunt, she doubted that any of the nuns would recognise her as the reverend mother's niece. It had been almost five years ago and she had only stayed at the convent for three days. Now if she turned up there, she would be completely out of context, completely unexpected. With a different hairstyle, with no make-up, wearing the clothes of a French working girl, she would bear little resemblance to the chic young lady who had visited the reverend mother all those years ago, but Adelaide knew that she must not jeopardise any potential operation by being too confident about this.

"I doubt it, sir," she replied, "apart from my aunts. But I suppose the possibility is there."

"I understood an aunt of yours is the reverend mother," Jenner said, "but you said aunts, plural."

Adelaide explained about her Great-Aunt Anne. "But she's virtually bedridden. In fact I don't even know for sure that she's still alive. Obviously I've had no news of them since France fell."

"Hmm." Jenner was thoughtful. A thorough check had been made on Adelaide's background before she had been cleared, finally, for training. It had not turned up the information about her connection with the convent at St Croix. It was purely by chance that he had learned of that from her cousin, Andrew Driver, before he had returned to France for the last time. Together, they had been debriefing an airman who had been shot down over France and somehow managed to get home. When the man had gone, Driver had made his observation. "This convent Ham mentioned, I think it may be the one where Adelaide's aunt is the Reverend Mum. You know my cousin Adelaide Anson-Gravetty? You've got her in training now."

From this snippet of information, an idea had been sown in Jenner's mind, had germinated, taken root and grown. At first he had considered sending Driver and Adelaide in together, but Driver had been captured by the Gestapo, and had disappeared, so that plan had to be discarded.

Now, after another mention of the convent had appeared in a report from the local resistance leader, they were considering resurrecting it, but sending Adelaide in on her own? Jenner had come to have another look at her, to sound her out, perhaps to prepare the ground. "Tell me about these aunts," he said. "How do two English women come to be nuns in a French convent?"

"They nursed in the convent hospital during the Great War," Adelaide explained. "My great-aunt was already a nun there, I'm not sure how she came to be there, but Aunt Sarah went out to St Croix with her maid to help nurse the wounded in the hospital. After the war, she stayed on." She smiled ruefully at Captain Jenner. "I only heard about them in 1937, when I was twenty-one. They were related to my natural father who was killed on the Somme. My father, the man I thought of as my father, was actually my stepfather. That's when I went to see them. I wanted to find out more about my blood father, Freddie Hurst. Sarah, Mother Marie-Pierre, is his sister."

Jenner nodded, encouraging her to go on.

"I went to visit them that year, but I only stayed for three days. I haven't seen them since, and I doubt if either of them would recognise me immediately. As to the other nuns, though I was staying there, they paid little attention to me. They have a small guest wing at the convent where people can go and stay for retreats . . . quiet weekends . . . so they have people coming to stay quite often. I doubt if they would remember me particularly." She looked across at Jenner. "If I'm not actually to live in the convent it is most unlikely that anyone would think of me as anything but a local village girl. I would have thought that any risk of being recognised would be minimal."

"Fair enough," Jenner said, and got to his feet. "I'll have to get the final all-clear, but then I'll be back to brief you fully, probably in a few days' time. You'll stay here, in this flat, and I'll come back to you. Please don't leave the building, I may need to talk to you again. In the meantime," he handed her a sheaf of papers, "get stuck into these . . . and make sure you're word perfect when I get back."

Adelaide waited anxiously through the whole of the next day. She had thought she was definitely on her way, and now it was all up in the air. There were only a few days on either side of the full moon when a drop was feasible. If she missed her slot she would not be able to go for another month, and the thought of delay filled her with dread. Now that her training was complete, she wanted to go and get on with what she had been trained to do. Idling her time here in the tiny London flat, she felt claustrophobic; her anxieties grew, expanding, feasting on each other, and the coiled spring of her nerves became ever more tightly wound.

278

She was allowed to see no one except Monica, the woman who looked after her in the flat. Monica had done her best. She spent hours taking Adelaide through the cover story Jenner had left with her, rehearsing it over and over, answering questions that might be put by a nosy gendarme or a curious agent of the Gestapo. Her papers named her as Adèle Durant. "Better to keep as close to your own name as possible," they had told her when working on her new life history, "and birthday too, so that you really don't have to think about that." She was the niece of Gerard Launay, an elderly farmer who lived with his wife, Marie, on a farm outside the village of St Croix. Their son, Victor, had been killed in the early days of the war and she, also on her own, had come to live with them and to give a hand on the farm, perhaps to find work locally too. Speaking only in French, Monica questioned her over and over again. Where was she born? Who were her parents? When did they die? Why had she come to St Croix? Where had she lived before? Had she other relations? How old was she? Always speaking in French.

"You'll do," Monica said eventually, but as they spent the evening playing backgammon or chess, she would toss in a question in English, trying to catch Adelaide off her guard. This drilling on her story gave Adelaide some confidence, but even so, long before Major Jenner returned, two days later, she was pacing the flat like a caged lion.

When he did finally come back, they sat together once more in the small living room overlooking the park.

"We have been discussing the information you gave me," he said coming straight to the point, but not saying who "we" were. "And we've decided that although there is extra risk in your going to an area where you were known before the war, we are going to send you. Now, what I tell you from now on is for you alone to know. You may not discuss it with anyone, except your reverend mother aunt."

"With Aunt Sarah?" Adelaide was amazed. "What has this got to do with her? Surely you're not going to embroil her in the resistance."

Jenner smiled at her outrage. "She is already embroiled, as you term it. She is already helping Jews, and our airmen who have been shot down, to escape from the occupied territory."

Adelaide listened in amazement as she heard how her Aunt Sarah had helped a flight sergeant called Terry Ham to escape from the Germans by disguising him as a nun.

"He isn't the only one. We have heard through our contacts in the area that she has also assisted a Jewish family to escape from the Germans. What we want you to do is try and establish a permanent escape route, using the convent as a base. Clearly your aunt is prepared to help our airmen, but we need to get in on the ground there and build up a secure escape route, so that the men can be moved on quickly across the country to safety. Your job will be to organise the section in the Somme, and the convent seems to be excellent cover. You'll persuade your aunt to give you a job there, so that you can come and go without question. The Germans will be unlikely to suspect the place is a safe house. We learned from Terry Ham that there are cellars under the convent, which sound as if they could be adapted to suit our purposes. I like the sound of this convent." Jenner nodded to himself. "Yes, I do. It has possibilities. What we need you to do is convince your aunt. If you're there, she'll have no need to take any more risks herself. If she'll just give you a job in the convent, so that you can come and go without looking suspicious, you can work out how to hide these men while they are in your area. You can plan a way to move them on, to provide them with what they need . . . papers, clothing, money."

"But where . . . ?" began Adelaide, but Jenner cut her off.

"That is why you will need to liaise with Marcel. He will help to procure the necessaries, papers, clothes. Find out from your aunt how she managed to sneak the Jews out from under the nose of the Germans. Once you have considered what you need to put this scheme into operation, messages can be sent back through Bertrand."

"When do I leave?"

"Tomorrow night, if the weather holds," replied Jenner getting up. "Monica will make sure you're ready to go."

Monica had driven them both to Bedfordshire the next day, where they had arrived at a country house outside the village of Sandy. They'd eaten a meal together in an elegant dining room, and when they had drunk their coffee, the best coffee Adelaide had tasted since the beginning of the war, they had gone up to the room set aside for them.

"Now we must sort out your clothes," Monica said. "You'll have to change from the skin out. Everything you wear must be French-made. There are some things here for you to try on."

Adelaide stripped to the skin, her own underwear and clothes set aside to be packed into a suitcase to await her return. In their place she pulled on the chemise and cotton drawers which Monica handed her, followed by a navy blue coat and skirt, and a white blouse, all cut in the French style. Thick stockings and a pair of scuffed black leather shoes completed her outfit. The shoes had the name of the French *cordonnier* inside them, the coat and skirt a label from a store in the Rue de Ste Anne in Paris. When she was satisfied with how Adelaide looked in these clothes, Monica gave her some more underwear, a flannel nightgown, two more blouses, another skirt, a handmade cardigan. "And for when you are helping your Uncle Gerard on the farm," she said with a smile, "some dungarees and *sabots*." Lastly, she gave Adelaide a grey felt hat and an old grey raincoat that reached nearly to her heels and was belted at the waist. It had once been good quality, and although it had seen better days, it would still keep out the cold and rain. "It used to belong to your mother," remarked Monica casually when Adelaide tried it on, "that's why it is a little too large."

Adelaide looked at the clothes, wondering where they had come from. Who had worn them before? Who had pulled that grey felt hat onto her head or cinched the belt tightly about the waist of the raincoat? Had they been worn here, in England, or on some other, previous mission in France? It was hardly a large wardrobe, but adequate for the poor country girl that she was purporting to be, and each garment carried a French label. She packed them into the small cardboard suitcase Monica had provided, along with some toiletries . . . all of French make.

"Now your hair," said Monica and led her to the dressing table. "I think we need a change of style here." She picked up a pair of scissors, and started snipping at Adelaide's hair, reshaping it with such speed and dexterity that within ten minutes the whole shape of her head seemed to have changed. Gone was the smooth thick pleat of hair that Adelaide had worn up under her cap as a WAAF, and tied back out of the way during her training. In its place was a rather ragged bob, hair framing her face and straggling to her collar. It looked, Adelaide decided as she studied herself in the mirror, as if she had hacked it off herself with a pair of blunt garden shears. When she said as much to Monica, Monica laughed. "I've no doubt you will have to cut your own hair from now on if you want it cut at all. Adèle Durant won't be able to afford to go to a hairdresser." She looked at her critically in the mirror for a moment. "Here, these might help," she said, and picking up a pair of combs slid them into Adelaide's hair, scooping it up above her ears.

"There," she said. "That's better. Not hair that's been styled, but clearly this girl has made an effort to look chic!"

Adelaide exploded into laughter. "That's chic?"

She had been given another meal before she left, a good hot meal of beef and roast potatoes with thick savoury gravy.

"I couldn't," she murmured, as she looked at the food heaped on her plate.

"You must try," encouraged Monica. "You may not get anything else for some time now, and you need to keep alert . . . more difficult when you're hungry."

Adelaide did as she was told and as she began to eat she found that she was much hungrier than she had thought. Surprisingly the food seemed to quell the butterflies which had been flapping so violently in her stomach, and when at last she was driven to the nearby Tempsford Airfield to board the Hudson that was to take her to France, she found it was yet again the thought of the actual jump from the plane that terrified her, not the thought of what awaited her when she landed.

The jump had been all right, she thought as she lay curled up in the feather bed at the farmhouse. There had been no time to hesitate as she had been almost pushed out of the aircraft. Now, she had to meet up with Uncle Gerard and Aunt Marie, and get herself established and accepted in the village. From now her every thought and word must be conducted in the manner of Adèle Durant, a young girl, displaced by the cruelties of the war.

Gradually, at last, the warmth of the bed overcame her and she relaxed into sleep, and so conditioned was her mind that even her dreams that accompanied that sleep were in French.

CHAPTER
SIXTEEN

"Over there, coming in now," murmured Marcel as he and Adelaide mingled with the crowd who had just got off the train from Amiens. "The one in the black cap."

Adelaide glanced at the elderly man who had just walked into the station. He paused, as if looking round for someone. She turned back to confirm the identification with Marcel, only to find that he had already disappeared, melted into the press of people the train had disgorged.

Well, Adèle, she thought, this is it.

Crossing to where the old man stood, she called out in a cheerful voice. "Uncle Gerard, Uncle Gerard, here I am!"

The man peered at her and then a smile lit his face. "Little Adèle," he cried. "It's been so long. I'd hardly have known you if you hadn't looked so like your mother." They embraced, and then the old man held her away from him, studying her face. "So like your dear mother," he murmured. Then, more businesslike, he took her suitcase from her. "I've the horse and cart outside. Do you remember dear old Sunshine? She's still going strong, thank God. Without her I don't know what we'd do. There's almost no fuel for the tractor or my old car. It's Sunshine and the cart these days."

Anyone overhearing would have no doubt that the old man was delighted to see his niece . . . anyone listening. Adelaide fought the urge to look around her to see if anyone was paying them any attention, and joined in the conversation.

"How is Aunt Marie? Is her back any better? Does she still get a lot of pain?"

"She's not too bad," replied the old man. "Of course she has pain, but don't we all when we reach our age? It'll be a great help to have you there to do some of the heavy work. She's really looking forward to seeing you again. How long is it? Ten years? Eleven?"

As he chatted on about his wife, he led the way to the station entrance. At the gate was a checkpoint. Police were checking everyone's papers as they came out of the station and Adelaide felt her pulse quicken as they joined the queue. This would be the first test of the papers that had been prepared for her in London.

When they reached the gate, Gerard handed his papers over first. The policeman gave them a cursory glance before handing them back. Then it was Adelaide's turn. The papers gave her place of birth as Vire, in Normandy.

"You're a long way from home, Mademoiselle," the man said, looking at her quizzically.

"Yes, Monsieur," she replied, keeping her voice even despite her inner tension. "I have come to stay with my uncle." She indicated Gerard. Never give more than the minimum information, they had taught her in England. Try to avoid statements that can be easily checked.

"How long are you staying?" asked the man. His eyes slid over her, taking in her face, pretty despite the lack of make-up, her trim figure undisguised by the old raincoat she wore; regarding her not with suspicion, but with obvious lust.

"As long as he needs me," Adelaide said.

"Hmm, lucky man." The man licked his lips suggestively, but handed back her papers and allowed her to pass on.

"Animal!" muttered Gerard when they were out of hearing, but the innuendo and the lustful glances had not worried Adelaide at all. She was simply relieved that her documents had survived their first scrutiny. From now on she would present them with more confidence.

"Papers change," London had warned her. "Check them with Marcel when you arrive and if there have been any recent changes made make sure we know about them." Marcel had looked at them and pronounced them up-to-date but, even so, Adelaide realised there could always be something that might arouse suspicion.

Gerard led the way to where his horse and cart were standing, waiting patiently in the sunshine not far from the station. He heaved Adelaide's suitcase into the back, then climbed up onto the driver's seat and with a flick of the reins they set off on the journey back to St Croix.

They spoke little as they drove, and Adelaide had a chance to study the man who, at the risk of his own life and that of his wife, was providing her cover. He was probably in his early fifties, but looked older with grizzled hair and grey stubble on his face. He had the weathered look of someone used to working outdoors, and although he was a tall, spare man, his shoulders seemed to have sagged, and he had, she noticed, walked with a limp.

Adelaide didn't know quite what Gerard and his wife knew of her mission. She hoped very little. All she needed from them was the cover of somewhere to live and a reason for being there. That would be risky enough for them, without them knowing exactly what she was up to.

For the last mile or so, they drove along the wide track that constituted the towpath beside the river. Beside an old stone barn, a right fork led them onto another, narrower track. Adelaide could see farm buildings ahead, low and squat, crouching behind a stand of sheltering trees. When they finally reached the farm, Gerard pulled into its yard. "Aunt Marie" emerged from the back door into the yard and stood watching as Adelaide climbed down from the cart. She was a small woman, dressed in an overall, her hair tied up in a scarf. Her face looked worn and tired, but her eyes were still bright as she looked at Adelaide.

"Here she is at last, Marie," Gerard called as he moved to Sunshine's head. "The train wasn't too late."

"Adèle," Marie said. "How lovely to see you! I'm so glad you've come to us." She reached up and gave her niece a brief hug. "I was so sorry to hear about your poor mother."

To be safe they had to live the life they had been given, and Adelaide was relieved to see that her "aunt" and "uncle" were intending to do just that. It was impossible to know who might be watching or listening; a collaborator collecting information to use to his own advantage.

"Always assume you are being watched," Monica had impressed upon her when they had been studying her legend. "Always assume that there is an informer sitting at the next table, or waiting beside you in the queue. Never drop your guard. These people are your aunt and uncle, it is vital that all three of you remember it *all* the time."

"It's lovely to be back, Aunt Marie," Adelaide said now. "It's been so long since I was here." She looked round the farmyard, taking in the cowshed, the half-empty barn, where some chickens were scratching among the hay on the dusty floor. "It hasn't changed," she said with a smile. "It's just as I remember it."

For the next few days, she learnt her way about and worked extremely hard. Marie taught her to milk, and though it took her a while to get the hang of it, she was soon able to help Gerard with his cows. She carried fodder and mucked out the cowshed. She dug potatoes from the field and heaved them to the house. She collected wood and mended fences. She brought the cattle in and sent them out again. She swept the yard and shovelled dirt. She went with her aunt into the village on market day, to the village bakery to queue for

290

the bread ration, to Mass on Sunday in the parish church. Gradually she became recognised as the Launays' niece come from Normandy. At the end of each day she almost fell into bed, completely exhausted. But at least she was well fed. There were fresh eggs and milk, and Aunt Marie made cheese and butter. Adelaide's days were so filled that she began to wonder if she would have any time to do anything else. It was, however, time well employed, as Marie Launay's neighbours began to say how lucky she was to have her niece staying and helping out.

She found an old bicycle in the barn, its tyres flat, its frame rusty, but with a serviceable saddle, a basket on the front and a child's seat on the back. Pulling it out into the yard she asked Marie if she could use it to get about.

Marie shrugged. "It's very old," she said doubtfully. "It's the one I used to ride when Victor was little, but if you want to try and mend it." She shrugged again, considering it a pointless task.

Adelaide worked on the bike, cleaning it, oiling it, trying to mend the punctures. The outer tyres were not too bad, but the inner tubes were in a bad state. Gerard had produced a repair kit, and between them they managed to patch the holes well enough for the tyres to stay up if pumped frequently. It was not long before Adelaide was a regular sight in the neighbourhood, riding the lanes, picking up firewood and carrying it home in the bicycle basket and wedged into the child seat. The errands she ran for her aunt took her to the village and the market as she delivered their surplus butter and eggs. She was often seen at the side of the road, pumping up the slowly leaking tyres, but the bicycle got her about, and no one questioned her exploration of the countryside.

At length Adelaide decided the time had come to make a move. When they were sitting over their evening meal at the end of the day some two weeks after she'd arrived, she made her announcement. "It's time I went to the convent to see if I can get a job."

She had had to confide this as her purpose in coming to the area, but she was no longer worried about telling the Launays that much. Over the weeks she had been with them she had come to know them well and knew their history. Gerard had been at Verdun in the last war and had been lucky to escape with only a shattered leg. Most of his unit had been wiped out in the valiant defence of the Bois de Caures, and Gerard had received his crippling wound in the subsequent retreat. When he had returned, wounded, to his father's farm in 1916 he had almost died; but for the nursing he received from his beloved Marie, he would surely have lost his leg. They had married as soon as he was well enough, and their son, Victor, was born ten months later.

"He was killed on the retreat to Dunkerque," Marie confided to Adelaide one day when they were working together in the dairy. "Machine-gunned from a dive-bomber." Her eyes hardened. "A column of men and refugees simply slaughtered from the air, not just soldiers like our Victor, but women and children too." She turned bleak eyes on Adelaide and now spoke coldly. "Machine-gunned and left dying in the road.

Such people are not human. There is not much we can do against them, but what little we can, we will." Twice the Germans had shattered the Launays' lives, and now they were prepared to take risks to fight back.

"When Victor died, I thought my life was over," Marie said. "Now it has another purpose. We're getting old, but we can still fight in our own way. Just let us know what we can do to help you."

Understanding their motive for offering her shelter and cover made Adelaide feel a little more secure. Revenge drove them, and their revenge had added strength, because although they knew the risks, they no longer cared for their own safety. They were protecting her cover as their niece, and her arrival in the local community had been greeted with little more than indifference.

"If we're asked, we will say that we cannot afford to keep you, that you must do something to bring money into the house." Marie gave a tight smile. "I have a reputation for being careful with my money."

Since her arrival at the farm, Adelaide had made no attempt to contact Marcel. Indeed she didn't know where he lived, but assumed it was Albert. She was fairly sure that it wasn't at the farmhouse he had taken her to originally; that, she thought, was another safe house. It was also unlikely that "Maman" was actually his mother.

All she knew was that if she needed Marcel she had to go to the café, Le Chat Noir, in the *place* in St Croix, wearing a red scarf round her hair. Whoever it was who saw the signal would alert Marcel and he would meet her in the woodland beyond the Launays' farm the next evening.

The next time she went to the market with Aunt Marie, her hair was caught up in a red scarf. Having made their few purchases they sat at a table outside the café in the spring sunshine and drank a cup of ersatz coffee. Marie chatted easily to the waitress, and Adelaide let her eyes wander round the square, wondering who would be reporting back to Marcel. On the other side of the *place* was the town hall, now the German HQ, its façade draped with a huge swastika. German soldiers were coming and going, but none of them paid any attention to the two women taking the weight off their feet after their marketing. Even so, Adelaide was ever conscious of their presence. It was one thing to practise living a clandestine life while safely home in England, it was quite another to do it for real. Every time there was a demand for her papers, or she heard German being spoken, or she had to step aside to make way for a German soldier hurrying about his business, Adelaide felt her heartbeat quicken. Despite truly living her legend, it would be so easy to make a mistake and give herself away . . . herself and the Launays.

Marcel was waiting in the woods when she arrived the next evening. They sat down on the grass, their backs against a fallen tree trunk, for all the world like a courting couple looking for a little privacy.

"Settled in?" he asked.

"Yes, thanks," Adelaide replied. "I've been gradually finding my way around, and as far as I know there

294

haven't been any queries as to why I've come. The Launays haven't heard anything either. Have you?"

"Nothing, except that you've come from Normandy to help out on the farm."

"Then I shall make my approach to the convent tomorrow," Adelaide said. "I'm hoping to find out how they moved our airman out of the area. When I have any more news for you, I'll signal again."

"Don't signal unless you've something important to tell me," Marcel said. "We should meet as little as possible. Every time we do we're at risk."

Adelaide made no comment on this, and changed the subject. "Please ask Bertrand to report my progress to London."

"Will do," Marcel promised.

"There is one other thing," Adelaide said, as he was about to get to his feet. "Are you able to get me some inner tubes for my bike? We've done our best with the ones we've got, but they aren't going to last much longer."

Marcel nodded. "I'll see what I can do."

"Thanks," Adelaide said and made to get up, but as she was about to get to her feet, he suddenly pulled her into his arms and began to kiss her. Adelaide's body went rigid and she tried to pull away. But Marcel was too strong for her and held her tightly against him, pressing her down on the grass with the full weight of his body. Keeping her pinned beneath him he moved his mouth to her ear and muttered. "Kiss me back! We're being watched." Immediately his mouth found hers again, and she felt his hands roving over her body.

She no longer struggled to get free, but relaxed beneath him. She could feel her skirt rucked up above her knees, and her blouse pulled free from its waistband. She did not open her mouth to him, but she did put her arms round him so that if they were indeed being watched she would appear to be a willing participant.

After a moment or two Marcel raised his head, and she gave him a slight push so that he rolled away. As she looked past him she saw a figure standing at the edge of the clearing, staring across at them. Adelaide gave a little scream, pulling her skirt down round her legs again and straightening her blouse. Marcel spun round, as if surprised by her scream, to see a man standing at the edge of the clearing, grinning as he watched Adelaide's obvious discomfort.

"Had a good look, have you?" sneered Marcel, getting to his feet and reaching down a hand to help Adelaide to hers. "That how you get your kicks, then?"

The man walked towards them. "I heard voices," he said. "In the woods, late at night . . ."

"Hardly late!" snapped Marcel, but the man went on as if he had not spoken.

"Could have been someone suspicious, up to no good." His eyes gleamed malevolently. "You never know what people are up to these days." His lip curled. "But I might have guessed it'd be some couple rutting like rabbits."

Adelaide felt Marcel tense beside her. The man was setting out to provoke him and she was afraid Marcel would indeed snap and do something they would both

296

regret. She burst into tears, sobbing onto Marcel's shoulder.

"It's all right, *chérie*," he soothed, putting his arms round her again and stroking her hair. "It's all right, I'll take you home now." He turned his back on the man, who was still standing there, enjoying their discomfort.

"Yes, you do that," the man mocked. "Don't want to be out after curfew, do you?"

Marcel kept his arm round Adelaide's waist. "Don't worry. We're going. Just wanted a bit of privacy, that's all." Keeping her firmly within the circle of his arm, he led her across the clearing and out onto the track that led back towards the village. Adelaide could feel the man's eyes on her back as they walked, and she found she was truly grateful for Marcel's supporting arm.

"I wonder what *he* was doing, skulking in the woods," Marcel said thoughtfully when they were well clear.

"Do you know him?" she asked.

"Yes, a piece of scum called Alain Fernand. Petty criminal turned snout. Happy to do the Germans' dirty work for a few privileges. Thinks he's on the winning side."

"Does he know you?" Adelaide asked anxiously.

"Not yet," Marcel said, "but he will . . . one day. When this war is over I will skin him alive and then stick his head on a pike in the village square . . . and even that will be too good for him."

Adelaide heard the barely controlled hatred in Marcel's voice and shuddered. She had no doubt that if he were alive at the end of the war Marcel would do exactly what he promised.

"In the meantime," Marcel said, "keep your eyes open for him and those like him. They'll sell you to their German masters whether they know anything about you or not. Evidence can be manufactured, and men like him are past masters at it."

They reached the gate of the Launays' farm and Marcel turned her to face him.

"You did well back there," he said. "Kept your head."

"I was afraid you were going to lose yours," she retorted.

Marcel smiled ruefully. "Yes, well, if I had we'd have had one less *collabo* to worry about . . . but probably a lot of trouble too."

He reached for her again, and taking her face in his hands spoke with a grin. "Just in case he's followed us and is still watching!" He kissed Adelaide again, and as he recognised a response in her, took his time over it.

When they finally broke free Adelaide cautioned, a little breathlessly. "We should change our rendezvous."

Marcel shook his head. "No, now he thinks he knows why we go there, we have the perfect reason to go again." He raised her hand to his lips. "Be very careful. Adèle," he said. "Fernand will know you again."

Next morning, Adelaide pedalled up the hill to the Convent of Our Lady of Mercy, and, leaning her bike against the wall, tugged on the old bell pull. Almost immediately the grille in the door opened and a nun peered out at her.

298

"Good morning," she said through the grille, "may I help you?"

Adelaide drew a deep breath. This was it. "I'd like to see Reverend Mother, please," she said.

"What would that be about?" asked the nun, not opening the door.

"I'm looking for work," Adelaide began, but the nun cut her off.

"I'm sorry, Mademoiselle, but I'm afraid there are no jobs here." The grille began to close, and Adelaide put her hand up to stop it.

"Wait," she cried. "I just want to see Reverend Mother."

"Mother is busy," replied the nun. "She hasn't time to see any passing vagrant looking for work. I've told you there isn't any."

"I am not a passing vagrant," Adelaide said hotly. "I am the niece of Monsieur and Madame Launay. They know the reverend mother and have sent me to see her."

The grille opened properly again. "What did you say your name was?"

Adelaide hadn't given her name, but she did so now. "Adèle Durant," she said. "Monsieur Launay's niece."

There was a rattling of bolts, the heavy door was eased open and the portress peered round it. It was the same Sister Celestine who had greeted Adelaide when she had arrived before. The little nun surveyed the visitor, taking in her working clothes, her scrubbed face and hands, but there was no flicker of recognition in her eyes. "You'd better come in."

Adelaide stepped inside the door and was left to wait in the hall while Sister Celestine scurried off to find out if Reverend Mother would see this person.

She was back within a few moments. "Mother says she will see you," she said in a voice indicating that she was surprised by this decision. "Please come this way."

Adelaide followed her along the passage to Mother Marie-Pierre's office and waited outside while she was announced.

"Mademoiselle Durant, Mother."

Adelaide stepped inside the room to be faced by not only her aunt, but another sister, who was standing beside the desk.

"I'm sorry, Mother," began Adelaide. "You have someone with you. I can wait until you are not busy."

"It is not a problem, Mademoiselle," replied the reverend mother. "Sister Marie-Paul and I have finished our discussion." She turned to the nun at her side. "Thank you, Sister, I'll leave that to you then." Sister Marie-Paul inclined her head and, with an uninterested glance at Adelaide as she passed, left the room.

As the door closed behind her Mother Marie-Pierre looked at Adelaide. "Now, Mademoiselle, how can I help you? I understand from Sister Celestine that the Launays sent you."

It was clear to Adelaide that neither her aunt, nor Sister Marie-Paul, whom she had encountered on several occasions during her last visit, had recognised her, and that was good. Very good. But how long would it be before her aunt did recognise her, she wondered?

It would be a good test. She continued to speak as Adèle Durant.

"Yes, Mother," she answered. "I am their niece. I have come to help them on their farm. It is too much for them these days, but I also need to earn some money to help with my keep."

Mother Marie-Pierre raised an eyebrow. "I would have thought," she said, "that your work on the farm would have covered your keep."

"It does, Mother," the girl agreed, "but I need some cash, you know, for a few personal things. My uncle and aunt feed me, of course, but there are always things one needs, even in this war." She smiled, and it was her smile, her father Freddie's smile, that revealed her to her astonished aunt.

"Adelaide?" she whispered.

Adelaide nodded and laid a finger to her lips. For a moment Mother Marie-Pierre stared at her and then she was round the desk and gathering her into a hug.

"My dear girl," she said, holding her away from her, much as Gerard Launay had done on the station, to get a better look at her. "My dear girl, is it really you? What on earth are you doing here? What's this nonsense about being the Launays' niece?"

Adelaide went to the door and checked to see that it was properly closed before she gave her reply. "I'm here because of you," she said.

"Because of me?" Her aunt looked startled. "Here, come and sit down, so we can talk properly." As before they sat on the chairs that flanked the tiny fireplace, but this time there was no fire to warm the room. "Now,

Adelaide, tell me everything. What *is* this about being the Launays' niece?"

"Sarah —" Adelaide began and paused. Now that she was here she wasn't quite sure where to begin, how much to say.

"Yes?" Mother Marie-Pierre said encouragingly.

If I can't trust Sarah with at least part of the story, there's no point in being here, Adelaide thought. "I've been sent from England to work undercover," she said, "and my cover story is that I am the Launays' niece. I live with them on the farm and help out. I do much of the heavy stuff that they're finding more difficult." She gave a laugh. "I've even learned to help with the milking. Anyway, I've been sent here because of what you've been doing."

"What I've been doing?" Mother Marie-Pierre looked at her in disbelief. "What do you mean?"

"Flight Sergeant Terry Ham made it home," Adelaide said, "and he told us how you'd helped him."

Mother Marie-Pierre's face broke into a smile. "Terry? Oh, that's wonderful. I'm delighted he made it," she said. "I heard nothing after I'd left him with Father Bernard."

"We've also heard that you have been helping Jewish refugees," Adelaide went on quietly.

Mother Marie-Pierre looked at her sharply. "Where did you hear that?"

"We're in touch with the local resistance," replied Adelaide. "There was something about it in one of their reports."

"I see," sighed her aunt. "Well, I suppose it was bound to get about. The whole village knows what happened to Sister Eloise."

"Sister Eloise? What did happen to her?"

Reverend Mother told the story of the escaped Jew, Simone, the raid by the Germans and Sister Eloise's arrest. Adelaide listened in silence.

"She's been sent to Germany, to a camp somewhere, where according to Colonel Hoch they send the enemies of the Reich." Sarah looked across at her niece. "I feel so guilty, because it was I who asked Sister Eloise to look after the woman. It's my fault she's in some dreadful camp."

"But surely, Sister Eloise and the other sisters would have nursed the woman whoever she was. Isn't that what your community does? Nurse the sick?"

"She wasn't in the hospital. We knew she was a Jew, so we were nursing her in secret." Mother Marie-Pierre sighed. "The convent is split down the middle," she explained. "Some of the sisters think it was right to shelter the poor woman, others think that we ought not to involve ourselves with the politics of the war; that we should continue to nurse the sick in our hospital and maintain our life of prayer, not shelter 'enemies of the Reich'."

"I see." Adelaide looked thoughtful. "What did they think about Terry Ham?" she asked. "Wasn't he an enemy of the Reich?"

Her aunt gave a rueful laugh. "They didn't know. Only two of us were involved with that." She reached out and took Adelaide's hand in hers. "I still don't understand why you are here, Adelaide."

"Adèle, Sarah. My name is Adèle, even to you."

Sarah smiled ruefully. "Adèle, then. So, why are you here?"

"I've come to set up a proper escape route for people like Terry Ham," Adelaide replied. "So many of our planes are being shot down over enemy territory, the crews bail out and then find themselves stuck behind enemy lines. We are trying to find a way to help as many as possible get back to England. I'm to find safe houses in this area, where they can be hidden until they can be moved on along the line."

She smiled at her aunt who suddenly realised what she was going to be asked.

"You can't use the convent," Mother Marie-Pierre said quietly. "Too many people could suffer if things went wrong. After what happened to Sister Eloise, I can't put any more of the sisters' lives at risk."

"I see that is a danger," said Adelaide, "but if we can implement the plan I have worked out, none of the other sisters need know anything about it."

"No, Adelaide, I'm sorry. I don't even want to hear it." Mother Marie-Pierre was firm. She told her niece about the threats Colonel Hoch had made. "He will carry them out, you know. He is an evil man. He enjoys what he does." She reached out and took Adelaide's hand. "If it were myself alone, there would be no problem, but I am responsible for the safety of everyone in this community."

"I understand, Sarah. It is a heavy responsibility. I'll try looking elsewhere. It's just that it seemed to London that a convent would be the last place the Germans would suspect of resistance work."

"Well, they're wrong. Since they found Simone here, they treat us with great suspicion, me in particular. Colonel Hoch organises spot checks. Searches the place without warning. We were lucky he didn't do so when Terry Ham was here. There have been three raids since then. I am sorry, my dear, but I really don't think I can help you."

"Terry mentioned the convent cellars." Adelaide wasn't quite ready to give up yet. "He said there was an outside entrance to them, a metal grille or grating somewhere."

"Yes, we saw the grille from the inside and Sister Marie-Marc has since found it from the outside."

"Sister Marie-Marc?"

"She was the sister who found Terry Ham hiding in the shed. When he'd gone she went looking for the grating."

"Why did she do that?" asked Adelaide. "Where was it?"

"I think she had much the same idea as you," replied Mother Marie-Pierre. "I think she thought we might hide people from the Germans in our cellars, but I'm afraid it is out of the question . . . and so I've told her." She looked across at Adelaide, her face serious. "Every time the Germans have come the cellars have been thoroughly searched. Anyone hiding in them would be found."

"Suppose we managed to wall off that section of the cellar?" suggested Adelaide. "The room with the grating."

"Wall it off?" Mother Marie-Pierre gave a brief laugh. "Adelaide, how on earth would we do that without anyone knowing? The whole convent would know, and the Germans soon after. It would be discovered at once."

Realising that for the present she would have to concede defeat here, Adelaide changed tack.

"Tell me about this Father Bernard," she said. "Where does he fit into the picture?"

"He's the priest at the Church of the Holy Cross in Amiens," replied Sarah. "I found him quite by accident when I was taking the children to our mother house in Paris." She explained how Father Bernard had helped with the children. "He was the only one I could think of to turn to when we were trying to get Terry Ham away." Sarah paused. "There is one other person who might be prepared to help you with what you are trying to do. Madame Juliette, who runs the café in the square. At least she did . . . in the last war. Her daughter has it now, I believe. Anyway, when I rescued Margot, one of the Jewish children, she hid us both for a while. I don't know if she is involved with your resistance group, but I do know she is a good-hearted woman who was prepared to risk her life to save a little girl. You might find her ready to —"

They were interrupted by a knock at the door. They looked at each other in alarm for a moment before Mother Marie-Pierre crossed the room and sat behind her desk. Adelaide stood in front of her, and then the reverend mother rang her bell. The door opened and Sister Marie-Paul came into the room. Entirely ignoring Adelaide, she spoke to her superior.

"Colonel Hoch's car is at the door, Mother. I thought I should let you know."

Mother Marie-Pierre rose to her feet. "Thank you, Sister, I'll come at once." She turned to Adelaide and addressed her in a tired voice. "It's time you went, Mademoiselle. As I said, I'm afraid there are no jobs in the convent at present. Should the position change I will contact you at your aunt's."

Adelaide lowered her eyes. "Thank you, Mother," she muttered. She followed the two nuns out of the office and back into the hall. Colonel Hoch was already standing in the hallway, admitted by a clearly terrified Sister Celestine.

"Ah, Reverend Mother," he began, and then caught sight of Adelaide. "Who is this?"

Reverend Mother shrugged. "A girl from the village looking for work."

"You, girl." Hoch looked Adelaide up and down as if she were a horse he might buy. "What's your name?"

"Adèle Durant, sir."

"What are you doing here? Papers!" He held out his hand and Adelaide took her papers from her coat pocket and passed them to him. He glanced at them. "Why are you here?"

"I came to ask Reverend Mother for work," Adelaide answered. She kept her eyes lowered, not challenging him in anyway. She knew that this might be the end of her mission before it had really started.

"I might find you work in the Kommandatur," he said, his eyes resting appreciatively on her neat figure, incompletely hidden by the old grey raincoat.

"I'm sorry, Colonel," interjected Mother Marie-Pierre, before Adelaide had time to speak, "but I have just given Mademoiselle Durant a job in our kitchens." Quelling Sister Marie-Paul, who had overheard her refuse the girl any work, with a frown, she went on. "There is too much for Sister Elisabeth to do on her own and Sister Marie-Marc is getting too old to be of much help." She smiled at Adelaide. "Another pair of hands for a few hours each day will be most welcome. Please present yourself to Sister Elisabeth on Monday morning at 7.30, Adèle, and she will tell you what you are to do. Off you go now."

It was a definite dismissal and Adelaide gave a little bob and spoke demurely. "Yes, Mother. Thank you, Mother."

CHAPTER
SEVENTEEN

When Alain Fernand discovered where the Auclon family was hiding, he was elated. There had been a big search for them when the other Jews from the village were rounded up, but they'd never been found. Finally it had been assumed that they had somehow managed to get out of the area.

Fernand found them by accident. One evening he was collecting firewood in a stand of woodland beyond the village, when he thought he'd heard voices. Always alert for anything unusual, he put down his sack of sticks and made his way stealthily between the trees, trying to follow the sound. Before he found anyone, the voices had died away, but he had found the cottage. It was deserted and derelict, its doors locked and barred. When he pressed his nose against its dirty windowpanes Fernand could see no sign of life. Disappointed for the moment, he collected his firewood and went home, but his curiosity was not satisfied.

He'd heard voices again a few days later and crept forward to spy. He found a courting couple lying on the ground, the girl with her skirt hiked up about her hips, the man almost on top of her as they kissed. Fernand watched them for several moments before they noticed him. It excited him to watch; he'd like a girl like that. Suddenly the couple realised he was there and they broke apart. The girl burst into tears, and the man looked about to explode, but after a sharp exchange, they had gone off, leaving Fernand alone in the twilight to wonder if they had been the people whose voices he had heard before.

It was the third time he heard voices that he struck gold. He stole silently between the trees and there they were, a man and a woman, with two little boys, sitting outside the cottage. They were very thin and pale, their clothes almost rags, but they sat on an old bench, their faces held up to the last rays of the sun. The two little boys were playing with some sticks in the dust at their feet. Even as he watched, the parents gathered up the children and disappeared round behind the house. Fernand waited for several minutes and then crept stealthily from his hiding place and darted across to the cottage. There were no voices now; and the eerie silence of dusk enveloped the place. He edged to a window, and peering in found himself looking into a gloomy kitchen. It seemed empty, except for a large old kitchen table, a stove and a stone sink. He moved quietly round the corner of the house to look in through the next window. This showed him a bedroom, but there was still no sign of the family. He went on to the back of the house where there was a lean-to shed.

They must be in here, he thought, but when he pushed the door, it opened easily and revealed only a few logs stacked against one wall, some sacks in a heap in the corner and an old canvas bag hanging on the back of the door. His eyes rested greedily on the logs. Fuel was at a premium and he could sell these for a tidy amount. Leaving them for the moment, he returned to the cottage. He circled it again, trying each door, and peering in through all the windows, but with no luck. The family seemed to have vanished.

Fernand knew well who they were. He had immediately recognised Joseph Auclon, the barber, and his wife Janine. Jews. He remembered the round-up of Jews last summer. These must have escaped somehow. Well, they wouldn't escape this time. Fernand hated Jews. Everyone knew that they always ganged up together against real Frenchmen. Everyone said so. Fernand had, himself, been thrown out of Joseph's little shop off the village square because he had complained that Joseph had cheated him. Everyone knew that Jews charged more to their non-Jewish customers, and when Fernand had accused Joseph of this, the barber had told him to get out and not to come back. Fernand left the shop, angry. But he'd had the last laugh, he realised. He hadn't paid at all! Let the money-grubbing Jew put that in his pipe and smoke it.

He went back into the shed, filled a sack with some of the logs and set off home with his loot. He'd come back for more logs, he promised himself, and when he did, he'd bring a crowbar to break into the cottage and see what he could find.

He was back the next evening, and hearing nothing, he crept up to the cottage and again peered in the windows. All looked as it had the evening before. He examined the front door. It was still locked and there was no way he could break it open without a good deal of noise. If the Jews were hiding inside he didn't want to alert them, so he went round to the back door. This was closed with a heavy wooden bar, locked in place with a stout padlock. Fernand was about to try and lever the padlock away from the bar when he noticed something. He put the crowbar on the ground and ran his hands along and behind the wooden bar. A gleam of understanding showed in his eyes and he smiled. The bar was separate, not attached to the door at all. From a distance it looked as if bar and padlock kept the door firmly locked, but on closer inspection he saw that the door could be opened with the bar still in place. He lifted the latch and pushed. The door didn't move. It must be locked on the inside. He went back to the window to have a look, but it was at the wrong angle and it was impossible to see. He tried the door again, but it wouldn't budge.

But the Jews must be in there somewhere, he thought, excitedly. All I have to do is wait for them to come out again.

He made his way back to the shelter of the trees, and finding a sturdy oak at the edge of the clearing climbed into its branches. From this vantage point he had an uninterrupted view of the back door, and he settled down to keep watch. He waited until it was full darkness before he gave up.

Perhaps they don't dare come out every night, he thought. I'll just have to keep coming back until they do. I must be sure they really are here before I go to Thielen, or better still, Hoch. Yes, Colonel Hoch was the one who hunted Jews. Fernand's eyes glittered at the thought of the bounty there might be on a whole family of them.

It was four nights later that he struck lucky. Ensconced in his tree Fernand heard a soft creak and saw that the back door was being opened from the inside. Joseph Auclon's head appeared, and, having decided that it was safe, he emerged, followed by his wife and the two boys. Once outside, Joseph crossed to the shed and moments later returned carrying a heavy bag. He went straight back into the cottage, only to re-emerge moments later. He still carried the bag, but this time it was empty and he returned it to the shed.

Fernand was exultant. Not only were the family hidden somewhere in the house, they were being supplied with food by someone. He remembered seeing the empty bag in the shed when he had looked in the first time, but it hadn't dawned on him that it had any significance. He remained in the tree for the twenty minutes or so the family allowed themselves in the fresh air, but as soon as they went back into the cottage and he'd heard the bolt on the inside of the door scrape home, he scrambled down and hurried back to the village.

He was just coming out of the woods when he met a local farmer, Étienne Charbonnier, walking his fields, his dog at his heels.

"Evening, Charbonnier." Fernand tried to sound casual, and kept walking.

"Hey, Fernand, what are you doing on my land?" demanded Charbonnier, suspiciously eyeing the sack

Fernand carried. The dog, hearing the tone of his master's voice, flattened his ears against his head and growled.

Hearing the growl, Fernand stopped and looked back at the dog nervously. He had never liked dogs. "Keep that dog under control, Charbonnier," he snarled.

"What are you doing on my land?" asked Charbonnier again, making no move to quieten his dog.

"Just walking," replied Fernand, his eyes fixed on the dog, whose lips were curled back menacingly. "Collecting firewood." He indicated the empty sack over his arm.

"Any firewood on my land is mine," snarled Charbonnier. "Clear off. You've no right to be here."

"I'm going, I'm going," muttered Fernand, and turning his back on the farmer and his dog, hurried off down the track that led back to the village.

Étienne Charbonnier watched him until he had reached the road before turning back to his own house.

Fernand had returned to the village and by the time he'd reached the German HQ he'd decided his information was definitely too important for Major Thielen and asked for Colonel Hoch. He was made to wait, but at last he was summoned into the colonel's office.

Hoch was working at his desk when he was told that Fernand wanted to see him, and was surprised. Thielen usually dealt with the likes of him. He wondered what information Fernand was bringing him. He despised him, a snivelling weasel of a man, but useful. He had eyes and ears where Hoch's men could never go, and the information he had brought in so far had been reliable, if not particularly important. Now he was demanding to see the colonel, saying that he had something very important to tell him. Hoch had kept him cooling his heels for nearly an hour; he had no intention of letting the little collaborator get ideas that he could simply demand the colonel's time, but he was intrigued all the same.

There was a knock at the door and Hoch picked up a paper from his desk before bellowing, "Come." The door opened and Fernand came in. Hoch continued to read the paper without looking up, and Fernand was forced to stand in front of the desk, his cap in his hand, waiting for the colonel's attention. When at last Hoch did look up, he ran his eyes over the man standing before him with distaste.

Fernand was small, with a narrow face, his watery blue eyes set close together over his sharply pointed nose, his hair wispy and thin, combed over a balding pate. He shuffled now, his eyes not quite meeting the colonel's.

"Well?"

"I think I've found some more Jews," Fernand said. "The Auclons. They slipped the net in the round-up last year."

"I see, and where are these Jews?" Hoch spoke without any apparent interest, but he remembered that the Auclons had never been found and his eyes sharpened.

"I've found their hiding place," Fernand said. "I've been watching them for some time."

"Have you now? And why didn't you report this immediately?"

"I wanted to be sure, Colonel. Didn't want you to come on a wild goose chase."

"I see. And now you are sure?"

"Yes, sir. Quite sure."

"So, I ask you again, where are these Jews? How many of them?"

"Four, sir. Parents and two kids. Twins."

Hoch smiled. "The whole family, then."

"Yes, sir."

"Where?"

"There's a derelict cottage over in the woods, beyond Étienne Charbonnier's farm. There used to be a farmhand lived there, but he didn't come back from the last war."

"Show me!" Hoch crossed to the large map of the district that hung on the wall. "Point out where this cottage is."

Fernand looked at the map for a moment before placing a grubby finger on the woods beyond Charbonnier's farm. "About there, sir," he said. "There's a clearing, and the cottage is there. The trees have grown up round it over the years. You don't see it until you reach the clearing."

"And this family . . ."

"The Auclons, sir."

"The Auclons . . . are living in this cottage?"

"Yes, sir. Well, not in the cottage itself. I think there must be a cellar."

"And you've seen them?"

"I've seen them go in and out of the cottage."

"So why haven't they been found before?"

"There must be a hiding place inside the cottage, sir."

"And you think it's a cellar?"

"Yes, sir." Fernand nervously ran a finger round the inside of his grubby collar. "They sometimes come out in the evening, for a bit of fresh air, like."

"And how have they survived, four of them in this cellar, for so long?" Hoch wondered.

"Don't know, sir. Someone must have been bringing them food and stuff."

"Who?" asked Hoch.

"Don't know, sir. But I saw Joseph Auclon fetch a bag from the shed. It must have had food in it. Don't know who left it, sir."

"Then you'd better go and find out," snapped the colonel. "I want to know who's been helping them. We'll have them as well. Go and find out. I want to know who's been sheltering them. Understand?"

"Yes, sir." Fernand nodded vigorously.

"In the meantime," Hoch said thoughtfully, "we'll pick up the Jews tomorrow. A dawn raid." He glowered at the little man in front of him. "Report back to me as soon as you know who it is." When Fernand hesitated the colonel growled. "Well, get on with it."

"Yes, sir." Fernand beat a hasty retreat out of the office and onto the square. Once outside he drew a deep breath and allowed himself a moment for his heart rate to slow, then with a satisfied smile he set off through the village. He had a shrewd idea who had been feeding the Auclons, and he was sure it wouldn't take long to confirm his suspicions.

Even better, he thought. The bounty for a whole family of Jews should be worth having, *and* something for the fools who'd been giving them shelter.

Hoch thought it was important too, and called in Lieutenant Weber.

"A sighting of that missing Jew Auclon and his family," he said. "We'll pick them up tomorrow." He pointed to the map. "I've information that they're here, in this wood." He explained about the derelict cottage. "Organise a raiding party to move up there before dawn. Get the place surrounded and then break the door down. They may be hiding in a cellar. Bring them all back here."

Weber saluted. "I assume you want them alive, sir?"

"Certainly I do," snapped the colonel. "I need to find out who's been sheltering them. The parents'll talk soon enough if we've got their children."

Fernand went home and collected a torch, which he slipped into the pocket of his jacket, along with his sheath knife. He wanted to be there when the Germans captured the Auclons. He wanted to see the fear on their faces. He wanted Joseph Auclon to know who it was who had found him. He wanted the barber to know that he couldn't cheat decent, real Frenchmen with impunity.

It was beyond midnight as Fernand crept from his house and headed to the wood once more. The village, under curfew, lay silent in the darkness as he threaded his way between the houses and onto the track across the fields. It was pitch black in the woods and several times he had to risk shining the pinprick of light from his masked torch. He was certain no one would see it out here, but even so he only flicked it on and off for a moment each time, just long enough to show him the path. Once he thought he heard something. A footfall? The crack of a twig? He ducked quickly into the shadows. He waited for several minutes, crouching in the shelter of some bushes, but no one passed his hiding-place and he heard nothing more. Must have been an animal of some sort, he thought, and, straightening up, he continued his stealthy approach to the cottage.

As Fernand emerged from the trees into the clearing the starlight provided faint light, enough for him to make out the shape of the building, its roof and tumbled chimney dark against the night sky. He went across to the barred door, and, as he always did, lifted the latch to make sure it was still locked from the inside. This time it wasn't. To Fernand's amazement the door opened with a creak, the bar and padlock still barring the way in. Flicking on his torch, he ducked down beneath the bar, and pushing the door gently went into the kitchen. He paused on the threshold, listening. The silence was absolute. The thin beam of his torch revealed nothing except the table and the stove he had seen through the window, a deep stone

319

sink and an old range, which had not been visible from the outside. Cobwebs curtained the ceiling above the door that led from the kitchen to the rest of the house. There was no sign of anyone. There was nowhere for anyone to hide. Flummoxed, Fernand crossed to the other door, and lifting the latch went through. Cobwebs clung to his face and he swatted them angrily, dashing them from his eyes, and even as he did so he realised that no one could have used this door for ages, or there would have been no cobwebs. Still, he went on through to the other part of the house. There was a tiny hallway, which smelt damp, and another door also draped with thick grey spiders' webs. Fernand swung his torch through these to clear a path and opened the door. Beyond it was the cottage's only bedroom, and this too seemed exactly as he had seen it from the outside, an old iron bedstead, a single chair, a cupboard built into the corner and a fireplace full of cold, black soot. Fernand wrenched open the cupboard door. Empty. No one here. No sign of anyone ever having been here.

Fernand felt a cold finger of fear down his spine. He had told Hoch the Auclons were definitely here and now not only were they not here, there was no sign that they ever had been. He shone his torch into the fireplace and up the chimney, more in desperation than in the hope of finding anything. Nothing. Colonel Hoch was sending an arresting party here at dawn, and there was no one for them to arrest. The colonel would be furious at being made to look a fool, and Fernand shuddered at the thought of his rage. He shone the torch round the floor. Stone flags with no covering to soften them. Close to despair, Fernand returned to the kitchen. Again his torch revealed nothing, there was nowhere to hide. The floor in here was also stone flagged. He shone the torch under the sink. It had been fed by a pump and emptied into a pipe, which drained to the outside. He crawled under the table, running his fingers over the stones in the hope of finding some sort of trapdoor. Nothing.

He sat back on his heels, his mind racing feverishly. He had seen the family come into the house only a few hours ago. He had heard the door being bolted on the inside, but now there was no one there.

Damned, bloody Jews! The thoughts raged through his head. Where the hell had they gone? He turned on his torch again, and pulling the masking tape from the front shone the full beam round the room, yet again.

It was then that he saw it. A footprint. On the table. Someone had stood on the table and left a scuffmark in the dust. Fernand pointed his torch up at the ceiling. The rafters ran the width of the kitchen, blackened beams supporting the roof above, and between the two that passed over the middle of the big old table was . . . ? Fernand was not sure what he could see. He scrambled up onto the table, and shining the torch directly upward peered at the ceiling. There, he found what he was looking for. Carefully contrived, between the rafters, was a trapdoor. Fernand reached up. He could touch the ceiling but he was not tall enough to raise the trapdoor. He jumped down from the table and fetched the old chair from the bedroom. Placing this on the table he climbed gingerly onto it and lifted the trapdoor. It was hinged and once it was upright crashed open. Fernand stuck his head through the gap and stared in amazement at what he saw. There was a loft in the roof space that covered the whole area of the house. Its floor was boarded and though there was no furniture as such, the space had been kitted out with a few things to make life possible there. Blankets and pillows were piled against the chimney breast, a mug and a couple of plates stacked in a tin bowl. There was a candle end on a saucer, and a box was upended to serve as a table. A galvanised bucket stood in a corner. Someone had been living here, and, from the smell emanating from the bucket, had been there very recently.

Fernand felt relief wash through him. The Auclons weren't here, but they had been. When Hoch's men arrived in the morning they wouldn't find the family, but they would find where they had been hiding, and it would be only a matter of time before they ran them to earth. Hoch would be angry that they'd given him the slip once more, but if Fernand worked fast he could probably find them again before the Germans did, and turn them in as planned. However, he was not keen that the arrest party should find him at the cottage when they arrived. It was time to go. He left the trapdoor open and the chair on the table so that the soldiers would find what he had found, and then pulling the door to behind him beat a hasty retreat into the woods.

There were two families who Fernand thought might have been sheltering the Jews; the Launays and the Charbonniers. Both families had more than a normal

322

grievance against the Germans. Both had lost a son during the invasion, and Fernand had been wondering about them for some time. He'd had no occasion to visit either farm, but his encounter with Étienne Charbonnier earlier this evening made him very suspicious. Had Charbonnier been on his way to the cottage with more supplies? Fernand tried to think back as to whether the man had been carrying anything with him. He thought not, but he couldn't be sure. Had Charbonnier suspected him, Fernand, of anything? He might have and come to warn the Auclons, to get them away to another safe place. But where? To his own farm? Unlikely. It was the nearest and the first place that would be searched.

What would I do if I were him, wondered Fernand — where would I take them? To friends? They'd have to be very good friends to take that risk, very good friends . . . or family. Family. Isn't Étienne Charbonnier related to Marie Launay? Cousins or something? Worth going to both farms and having a snoop round, he decided, and wondered which to visit first. He was about to set off in the direction of the Charbonniers when he remembered the sounds he'd heard on his way to the wood. Could that have been the Auclons actually making their escape? If so, they weren't going towards the Charbonniers. Changing his mind, Fernand set off along a different path, heading for the Launay farm.

There was already the grey light of a false dawn creeping into the sky when he reached the farm and crept into the farmyard. To his surprise there was a thread of light at one edge of the blackout over the kitchen window. He crossed the yard and put his eye to the crack. Marie Launay was sitting at the kitchen table, her head resting on her arms, apparently asleep. Fernand stared at her for a moment, then turned and went to the yard door. Taking his knife from his pocket, he eased the door open and went inside.

CHAPTER
EIGHTEEN

"Adèle, wake up! You must come, quickly."

Adelaide sat up with a jolt as Marie Launay shook her awake. The room was still in darkness, but she could hear the urgency in Marie's voice.

"Aunt Marie! What is it? What's happened?" She reached for the bedside light, but Marie caught her hand.

"No lights," she hissed. "Come downstairs, Adèle, we need you." Marie was already out of the door and on the stairs. "You must get dressed."

"I'm coming." Adelaide swung her legs out of bed and threw on some clothes. However, before she followed Marie downstairs, she slipped the garter, on which she carried her razor-sharp knife, up above her left knee, where it nestled hidden by her skirt. It was the first time she had taken the knife with her, but as she had no idea what the problem downstairs was, she wanted to be prepared.

In the kitchen she found not only the Launays, but five other people, two of them children. A couple were seated, pale faced, at the table and the children were standing beside them. The little family turned fearfully as Adèle came into the room, and she saw to her surprise that the children were identical twins, young boys, their faces pinched and pale, their eyes wide and dark, one clinging to his father's hand, the other within the circle of his mother's arm.

A second man, standing by the window, was speaking. "Albertine will clear up as best she can," he said. "I must get back to help her now. Anyway, if I'm seen near here, it's the end for all of us."

Gerard nodded and shook the man's hand. "You're right, Étienne. Be careful . . . and good luck."

The woman at the table caught at Étienne's hand as he moved to the door. "God bless you, Étienne," her voice cracked with emotion, "you and Albertine. We shall never forget you."

Étienne patted her hand awkwardly. "Sorry we can't help any more," he said gruffly. Gerard turned off the light and Étienne slipped through the scullery and out into the darkness, the back door closing softly behind him.

Gerard switched the light on again and the woman turned to him. There were tears in her eyes. "And now we put you in danger."

"Don't worry," Marie Launay said quietly. "We'll do our best to get you all away." She turned to Adelaide and went on. "This is the Auclon family. Joseph and Janine and their sons, Jacques and Julien. They're Jews, but their family has lived round here as long as I can remember. They managed to escape the Gestapo roundup last year, and Étienne, my cousin, and his wife Albertine, have been hiding them in a derelict cottage on their farm ever since. But today Étienne saw that

326

scum, Alain Fernand, sniffing about in the woods nearby. He thinks that Fernand has somehow got wind of the hiding place. If he has, it won't be long before he reports it to his German masters. Étienne had no choice but to move them, for everyone's sake."

"Where shall we hide them?" asked Adelaide, though she thought she already knew the answer. "There's nowhere here."

"In your safe room," answered Gerard. "It is the only chance they've got. If Étienne's right about Fernand, the Germans will be swarming everywhere tomorrow. We've nowhere to hide four people here."

"I don't know how safe the room really is," warned Adelaide. "It's not been tested yet. There hasn't been a German raid since it was finished."

Gerard shrugged. "It's the best we can do for now. They must be hidden before morning. Then we can try and work out some long-term plans." He gestured. "This is Antoinette." He used her resistance code name, though she doubted that it was of much protection in the circumstances. "We'll try and get you to a safe place, but you'll have to stay hidden there until we can make some plan to move you further away."

He turned to Marie. "Can you put up some food and water for them to bring?" he said. "We may not be able to get back to them for several days."

Marie nodded, and went into her pantry to see what she could find.

"You'll have to make sure the children stay quiet," Adelaide warned the mother. "We've got to move round the village, and there may be patrols."

Madame Auclon smiled wearily. "It has become their life, to be quiet," she said. "They won't make a sound."

Marie returned with two baskets of food, and having filled two bottles of water from the tap, handed them to Monsieur Auclon.

"Ready?" said Gerard. "Let's go." He smiled reassuringly at the Auclons. "Don't worry, we'll get you safely hidden."

They collected a length of rope from the barn, which Adelaide coiled round her waist, and Gerard tucked a short crowbar under his jacket. Thus equipped, Gerard led the little group out of the farmyard and along the river path towards the convent. Monsieur Auclon carried the baskets of food, with Madame holding each child firmly by the hand, following behind. Adelaide brought up the rear. There was no moon, but the sky was clear and faint starlight lit their way. As their eyes adjusted to the night, they made steady progress and Gerard found his way to the copse below the convent without any difficulty. There had been no sound in the darkness as they had edged round the village, their ears strained for the slightest noise that might warn them of approaching danger. The night remained still as they followed the path up through the trees to the convent wall.

"Wait here," Gerard whispered, as they reached the edge of the copse. "Stay back in the trees, and don't move. We'll come back for you in a minute or two, all right?" He didn't warn them again to be quiet; there was no need.

Leaving the little family deep in the shadows, Adelaide and Gerard moved out into the open ground beside the convent wall.

"How far along?" Gerard murmured as they reached the wall.

"At the edge of the field," whispered Adelaide. "Ten paces beyond the courtyard gate." They reached the gate and then counted their steps until they found the stunted bush, its roots thrust through the iron bars of the grille, which both marked and masked the grating.

"Here," murmured Adelaide, and they set to work with the crowbar.

When Adelaide had presented herself at the convent kitchen door that first morning at exactly 7.30, Sister Elisabeth, large and red-faced with the sleeves of her habit tucked up to her shoulders, was expecting her.

"So, Adèle," she greeted her briskly. "Mother says I'm to use you to relieve Sister Marie-Marc from some of the heavier work." She surveyed Adelaide for a moment and sniffed, as if she found her wanting.

"I'm stronger than I look, Sister," Adelaide ventured. "Just tell me what you want me to do."

"Well, first thing, you can get to work on those dishes," Sister Elisabeth said, waving her hand at a stack of plates on a trolley being wheeled through the kitchen into the scullery beyond by another, older sister.

"Sister Marie-Marc, this is Adèle," Sister Elisabeth announced in the sort of voice reserved for the hard of hearing or the stupid. "She's come to help with the work here in the kitchen. When you've finished the dishes between you, she can bring up potatoes and onions from the cellar and you can prepare them for lunch."

"Yes, Sister," Sister Marie-Marc replied mildly. She smiled at Adelaide, her eyes bright amidst the wrinkles of her face, and piled the plates into the deep stone sink. "Hello, Adèle. We're very glad to have you helping out." She pointed to the huge black range, which occupied one wall of the kitchen. "There's a pot of hot water on the stove, will you bring that through here? Then you can wash and I'll dry."

Adelaide fetched the heavy pot and poured hot water into the sink while Sister Marie-Marc turned on the single tap, to add the cold.

When the dishes were done, Sister Marie-Marc nodded to a door behind them. "That's the way down to the cellar. You'll find a sack of potatoes down there, and some onions."

Adelaide had spent some time the previous evening wondering how she was going to be able to get into the cellar and assess its possibilities as a hiding place. Despite Reverend Mother refusing her permission to use the convent, or its cellar, as a safe house, Adelaide had not yet given up the idea. If she could find a way of using a part of the cellar without putting the nuns at risk, she could either go back to Sarah and put it to her again, or, and this was an option she was loath to take but was probably the more likely, she could make use of it without her aunt's knowledge.

Now was her chance to have a quick look. She opened the door and peered down into the darkness below.

"Be careful," Sister Marie-Marc warned her, handing her a pot for the potatoes. "Those steps are steep."

"I'll be careful," Adelaide promised, and with a tight grip on the single handrail descended the stone stairs into the cellar. By the light that filtered down from the open door, she could see the racks of stored vegetables in the first cellar. A slatted table held apples, spread in neat rows, above which were several shelves lined with preserving jars, all labelled with their contents, soft fruits, jams and honey. Several rounds of cheese wrapped in cotton cloth were standing on a marble slab, and there were stone butter jars just like those in Marie Launay's pantry. Below the apple table were bulging sacks, which, when she investigated them, Adelaide found to contain carrots, turnips and the potatoes. Strings of onions hung from hooks in the ceiling and there were more large stone jars standing on the floor, marked flour and rice. As her eyes grew accustomed to the darkness, she could see that there were other cellars beyond, rooms opening off each other. She looked into the first and saw a heap of coal, but beyond that there was no light.

I'll have to come down with a lamp or a candle or something, she thought as she peered into the darkness. I must look at the place properly.

Afraid she would occasion comment if she were too long fetching the vegetables, she filled her pot with

331

potatoes from an open sack, took a string of onions from one of the hooks and scurried back up the steps. Later she was determined to find a way to explore the cellars beyond.

When she emerged back into the kitchen, Sister Elisabeth was nowhere to be seen, and Sister Marie-Marc was standing at the range stirring a stockpot with a huge iron spoon.

"You found them? Good. I'll get on with those." She took the vegetables from Adelaide and laid them on the table. "Sister Elisabeth has been called away, but she says you're to bring up some coal from the cellar, to fill those." She indicated three iron containers set in a recess beside the range. "That really *is* a job for a younger back."

"Yes, Sister," Adelaide replied, moving to pick up one of the huge buckets.

"I doubt if even a youngster like you will be able to carry one of those full," said Sister Marie-Marc. "We usually bring the coal up in a smaller bucket which is in the cellar, and fill the big ones where they stand. Come with me, I'll show you." Giving the stew a good swirl with the spoon before she left it, the old nun led the way back down into the cellar.

"There's no electric light down here," she said cheerfully, as she picked up an oil lamp Adelaide hadn't noticed before. "So, look where you're going." She lit the lamp and led the way into the first side cellar. "The coal, what's left of it, is over here, and there's the small bucket for carrying."

"Fine, Sister, I'll bring some up for you." Adelaide smiled. "Don't forget your stew," she added, as the little nun seemed inclined to linger.

With a cry of dismay, Sister Marie-Marc disappeared up the stairs, and Adelaide was left in the cellar, with the lamp.

Quickly she shovelled coal into the first bucket, and then leaving it ready to bring up to the kitchen took the lamp and began to explore. She held the light high as she walked through the musty rooms that made up the cellars. One had garden implements stored in it, two spades, a garden fork, a hoe and a rake; another was stacked with old furniture, a third had some empty packing cases, an old ladder with several rungs missing and a bicycle without a front wheel. Finally she reached the last, and saw the faint daylight filtering through the grille in its ceiling.

This must be the one, Adelaide thought, where they hid Terry Ham.

She considered it for a moment. It had distinct possibilities. It had a sturdy door to close it off. There was no lock, but that could be rectified. The grille above was just about big enough for a man to squeeze through . . . if he could climb up to it. The only things in the cellar were some old shelves and a heap of rags in the corner.

Yes, Adelaide decided, it does have possibilities. But first I must find out where that grating comes out.

She had no more time now, Sister Marie-Marc would wonder why she was taking so long with the coal, so she hurried back to the coal cellar, picked up the waiting bucket and carried it up to the kitchen. When she'd emptied it into one of the large scuttles at the side of the range, she returned to the cellar for more. On each journey she took a few moments to learn the geography of the cellars, to try and work out where the grille might emerge. Before she carried the last bucket up the stairs, Adelaide held the lamp to her ceiling of the coal cellar, and there sure enough was what she had half-expected to see; a coal chute which must open into the yard above.

If I can find that, she thought excitedly, I can probably work out roughly where the grating must be.

When Adelaide carried the final bucket up to the kitchen, she found Sister Elisabeth was back. The nun looked at the full coalscuttles with approval.

"Very good, Adèle," she said. "That should be enough to last us right through until tomorrow."

"And tomorrow I'll fill them again," Adelaide promised.

Adelaide went to the convent each morning for four hours, and gradually fell into a routine. She knew what was expected of her, and, once the nuns realised it, they let her get on with it.

On her second day she had found the grating from the outside. It had been easy to see the coal chute in a corner of the courtyard and from there to guess where the grating might be. Almost buried in a patch of scrub at the edge of the field, it was just outside the convent wall. Clearly it had not been lifted for years. Thickly covered with weeds, it lay concealed and forgotten. Adelaide knelt down and pretended to do up her

334

shoelace while she inspected the grille more carefully. Was it the one, or simply some sort of drain? She picked up a twig and pushed it through the iron bars. Next time she visited the cellar, her twig was on the floor.

Each day Adelaide collected coal for the kitchen range, and each day she worked on the end cellar, Terry's cellar. Under her skirt, she smuggled in a bradawl, a screwdriver and metal bolt, all provided by Gerard Launay, and while she was supposed to be shovelling coal, she gradually equipped the door with a bolt on its inside, so that anyone hiding there might lock himself in, perhaps buying enough time to make a break for it through the ceiling grille.

It was when she had just finished this job she turned round to find Sister Marie-Marc standing watching her.

"Sister!" Adelaide held the screwdriver in the fold of her skirt, hoping the nun hadn't actually seen what she'd been doing. "Did you want me? Is there something I can do?"

Sister Marie-Marc smiled. "No, I just wanted to see what you were up to down here."

"Up to? I'm not up to anything," Adelaide smiled. "Though I have to admit to curiosity. I was just exploring the cellar, that's all."

"No it isn't," replied Sister Marie-Marc conversationally. "Over the last few days you've loosened the grating, you've brought a chair in from the other cellar and now you've put a bolt on the door . . . on the inside." The nun's bright eyes studied her. "So, who are you, Adèle, and what are you doing here? Does Mother know?"

Adelaide thought fast. How much, if anything, should she admit to this elderly nun? Sister Marie-Marc had already helped a British airman to escape from the Germans, but was she really prepared to risk her life and the lives of her sisters to go on helping men to escape? Whatever happened, they couldn't spend any more time down in the cellar now, without causing comment or suspicion.

"Sister, we must go back upstairs. Sister Elisabeth will be wondering where we are." She moved towards the main cellar, but Sister Marie-Marc put out her hand to stop her.

"No, she won't. She's been called over to the hospital to discuss something with Sister Marie-Paul."

"But we must finish making the pastry for lunch," pointed out Adelaide.

"Indeed we must," Sister Marie-Marc agreed, "and while we do it, you can tell me why I shouldn't tell Sister Elisabeth what you've been doing down here when you're supposed to be bringing up the coal." She turned back towards the cellar steps, speaking over her shoulder as she did so. "I should leave your tools down here, they'd be hard to explain to Sister Elisabeth."

Sister Marie-Marc had turned out to be a born conspirator. Adelaide decided she had to trust her with at least part of the truth.

"I've come from England," she said. "Your friend Terry made it back."

Sister Marie-Marc's face lit up. "Terry is safe?"

"Yes." Adelaide smiled at the nun's obvious delight at the news. "And he told us how you and Mother Marie-Pierre had helped him escape. I've been sent to try and arrange an escape route for other airmen who are shot down."

"Does Mother know?" asked Sister Marie-Marc.

"She knows why I'm here." Adelaide paused, not quite sure how to explain.

"But not what you are doing." Sister Marie-Marc nodded her understanding. "It's better she shouldn't know. I will not tell her."

"Thank you," murmured Adelaide, slightly amused at this.

"Because if I do," Sister Marie-Marc went on cheerfully, "she might not let me help you."

"Help me?"

"Of course, you need someone on the 'inside' *hein*?" The eyes were bright with excitement.

"I thought you were bound by a vow of obedience," remarked Adelaide.

"Of course. But I am not disobedient. Mother has not told me I should not help you."

They continued work on "Terry's room", equipping it with a few necessities, most of which Sister Marie-Marc produced from other parts of the convent. There were some candles and matches, a couple of old blankets, two jars for water and the bucket Sister Marie-Marc had provided for Terry Ham's use. Together they carried in the broken ladder, which was tall enough to enable anyone hiding there to reach the grating in the roof. As they propped it against the wall,

Adelaide looked round the room. "Well, I think that's the best we can do. Let's see if we really can hide the door."

They closed the door, and between them dragged an old bookcase in front of it. This hid the door from any casual glance, and in front of this they gradually stacked all the other disused and broken furniture. Each time one of them came down to the cellar for something, she put another piece of the old furniture in front of the bookcase, until it was almost impossible to see anything beyond the stack. They had spread some of the other rubbish into the cellar where the furniture had been, sweeping smooth the scuffmarks they had made while dragging the heavier pieces into place, and to the unsuspicious eye the cellar still looked very much as it always had, a succession of rooms filled with an accumulation of junk.

"If the Boche do see the door, they'll have to move all this stuff before they can get inside," Sister Marie-Marc remarked with satisfaction, looking at the old furniture. "That should give time to escape."

"So it should," Adelaide agreed, "but once they have broken in that will be an end to it. It will put the whole convent at risk, so I shan't use it except in an emergency."

And this, thought Adelaide, as she and Gerard bent in the darkness to prise up the grating, is an emergency. The clink of iron on iron sounded incredibly loud to her but, with their combined strength, the grating lifted easily enough, and was laid aside.

Wedging the crowbar across the opening, Gerard knotted the rope to it and dropped the other end down into the hidden room below.

"I'll keep watch here," murmured Gerard. "You go and fetch them."

"All right," whispered Adelaide, and, leaving him beside the hole, hurried back to the family. She found them waiting patiently where they had left them, crouched in the deep shadow of a tree. Even as she reached them, Monsieur Auclon grabbed her hand and dragged her deeper into the shadows. He put his mouth to her ear. "Someone is coming!"

Adelaide strained her ears and then she, too, heard something. The sound of a twig cracking, followed by a stifled oath, made her freeze, her back pressed against the tree so that she was lost against the darkness of the trunk. Standing perfectly still, Adelaide strained her eyes into the night to see who was coming so stealthily up the track through the copse. The Auclons were as stone, the little boys pressed against their mother, their faces buried in her skirt, the father standing protectively in front of them. Adelaide could feel that they were poised for flight, and knew that it would be fatal to them all if their nerve failed now. She heard another sound, a foot against a stone, and the murmur of a voice. Adelaide felt a cold chill run down her spine as she realised that there were at least two of them and that they were speaking German. She gripped Monsieur Auclon's arm, and, pressing her lips to his ear, murmured. "Don't move unless I say!" Her hand slid under her skirt and grasped the handle of the little knife. The feel of it in her fingers was reassuring; despite its size its honed blade would slit a man's throat. She waited, poised, in the darkness. At least she had the element of surprise, but the last thing she wanted to do was to kill German soldiers here, where there was nowhere to hide their bodies, where they would be immediately missed. She held her breath . . . and waited.

The Germans passed within four feet of them, unaware of the trembling group, and continued up the path until they reached the convent wall.

"Stay back," Adelaide murmured, and moving silently between the trees, her senses straining, she crept after the Germans. Her mind whipped into action. How could she warn Gerard of the men's approach? At once she dismissed the idea. She couldn't warn him without giving them all away. She'd have to hope he was on the alert and had heard them coming. Surely he would take cover.

The sky was beginning to lighten now, and, as she reached the edge of the trees, Adelaide could make out the men standing beside the convent wall, two darker shapes against the grey stone. They were edging along to the gate. It was clear they did not want to be heard, so they were not a regular patrol.

So what the hell are they doing? Adelaide's mind was racing. And what shall I do? If they go much further they'll not only find the hole, they'll fall into it! If that happens it's all over.

Make a noise and run? I should be able to lose them in the dark of the copse, and, if they're following me,

Gerard should be able to get the Auclons safely into the hidden room.

She was about to reveal herself, to draw them off, when they stopped. They had reached the closed wooden gate that led into the convent courtyard. Even as she watched, Adelaide saw one cup his hands as a step and hoist his mate up and over the gate. The man waited for a moment and then the small side gate was opened and he disappeared inside.

The sound of an angry squawk from the henhouse told Adelaide what they were up to; stealing chickens. Moments later the gate opened again and the two men came out, stifling laughter, and each with a hen under his arm. With no attempt at stealth now, the two of them set off down the hill at speed, and Adelaide could hear them crashing through the bushes as they made their escape with their prizes.

Poor Sister Marie-Marc, thought Adelaide as she heard them go. That's the third raid on her henhouse.

The men's noisy flight told them they were safe for a moment, and Adelaide collected her charges from their hiding place and led them out across the open ground to where Gerard was coming to meet them.

"What was all that about?" he hissed as they reached him.

"German soldiers stealing chickens," she replied briefly. "Too busy thieving to notice us."

"Thank God for that!" Gerard turned to the Auclons. "Come on, nearly there!" He led the way along the wall, past the wooden gate, to the open entrance to the hidden cellar. "You first, Madame." He held out his hand to Madame Auclon. "Sit on the ground, hold onto the rope and lower yourself down." Madame Auclon did as she was told, and the children, one after the other, followed her into the comparative safety of the cellar. Adelaide hauled up the rope and lowered each of the baskets of food Monsieur Auclon had been carrying. She leaned down and placing her face through the opening spoke softly. "The sisters won't know you are here. You must keep the children as quiet as you can, your lives may depend on it. Any sound in that room could well be heard from out here. We'll get back to you as soon as we can. Good luck."

"God bless you, Mademoiselle," came the whisper from below.

Adelaide moved away from the opening so that Monsieur Auclon could slip down into the cellar, but he paused on the edge. "Thank you, Monsieur Launay, Mademoiselle Antoinette."

"You shouldn't be too uncomfortable if it's only for a few days," Adelaide said softly, taking his extended hand. "When one of us comes to you, we'll push two twigs down through the grating so you'll know it's us. You may hear noises in the cellar, but don't panic, just keep the children quiet. You can bolt the door on the inside and you should be safe. If someone tries to break in through the door, get out this way. The grating should move fairly easily if you push hard enough. Remember, at most you'll have three or four minutes to escape."

Jean Auclon nodded, and taking a grip on the rope slid down into the cellar below. Gerard and Adelaide replaced the iron grille, its marker bush still protruding through its bars. A few dead branches completed the camouflage, and leaving the little family concealed there, they crept away, stealing through the grey light of dawn back to the farm.

Gerard hurried into the house to reassure Marie that they were safely back, while Adelaide put the crowbar and the rope back into the barn. As she reached the back door, left ajar for her, she heard raised voices. Gerard was shouting.

"What the hell's going on? What are you doing here? Marie?"

Adelaide edged round the back door and paused in the scullery, out of sight of anyone in the kitchen. Another man spoke, a voice that Adelaide did not know.

"All I want is some information," the voice said. "Then no one will get hurt. Your wife here refused to tell me what I need to know, so I waited for you. I'm sure you don't want me to take her eyes out, do you? Life's difficult enough just now without having a blind woman to look after." The voice was soft, almost cooing as it spoke, and was all the more sinister for its lack of emotion.

"All you have to tell me is where the Auclon family is hidden. No skin off your nose. They're Jews after all . . . scum."

"You're the scum," exploded Gerard, "collaborating with the Germans."

There was a muffled cry of pain and Gerard cried out. "No, no!"

Adelaide moved softly to the scullery door, putting her eye to the crack of the hinge so that she could see part of the kitchen without being seen. Marie was sitting on a chair, her back to the window; a rope lashed her firmly in place, her mouth was stuffed with a handkerchief. Her eyes wide with fear, she strained away from the man who stood behind her. Adelaide recognised him at once as Alain Fernand, the man she and Marcel had seen in the wood; the man snooping round Étienne's farm. He held a knife to Marie's face, the blade caressing her skin. His threats were clearly not idle, she already had a stark red line across the pallor of her cheek, from which blood oozed and trickled down her neck.

"Just tell me where you've hidden the Jews and you'll hear no more about it. I won't tell the Germans that you helped to hide them." His voice hardened and he went on. "Don't make me have to cut your wife any more, Launay. You'll tell me in the end . . . why put her through the pain first? And don't even think of rushing me, or my knife goes straight through her eye . . . and into her brain."

Adelaide couldn't see Gerard, but she guessed he must be just inside the door. There was no way he could reach Marie in time if Fernand was prepared to carry out his threat, and from the sound of his voice Adelaide knew Fernand was enjoying himself; enjoying the fear he induced, enjoying the power he wielded.

"I know that fool Étienne must have been hiding them all this time." Fernand's voice returned to the conversational. "How he managed it for so long I can't imagine! Still, I sniffed them out and here we are. Now, don't waste any more of my time, Launay, or your wife will suffer." Even as he spoke he flicked the blade carelessly across Marie's other cheek.

Adelaide's thoughts were racing. A diversion! She must cause a diversion. She couldn't reach Marie either, but she could perhaps cause a diversion so that Gerard had some chance to attack Fernand. Grabbing one of the stone jars Marie kept butter in, Adelaide stepped out into the yard and hurled it with all her strength at the kitchen window, which shattered with a crashing explosion of flying glass. Even as the window disintegrated, Adelaide was back through the scullery and into the kitchen. There was glass everywhere. Fernand had spun round as the window exploded behind him and Gerard had launched himself across the room, knocking Marie and her chair to the floor. He was grappling with Fernand, trying to grab the knife. But Fernand was younger and stronger; his grip tight on the knife, he forced Gerard down to the floor, the blade thrusting ever closer to the older man's head. Adelaide was across the room in a flash, her own knife already in her hand. With a swift and merciless blow, she drove it hard between Fernand's shoulder blades. Fernand gave a grunt, stumbling forward and Adelaide jerked the knife free, only to drive it once more into the collaborator's back. Fernand collapsed onto the floor, a dark stain spreading across his jacket; the knife he had been grasping skittering away across the flagstones. Gerard took one look at him and then catching up the dropped knife rushed over to Marie, still lashed to the overturned chair. Swiftly he cut her bonds and pulled the grubby handkerchief out of her mouth, gathering her into his arms as she began to sob.

Rocking her gently back and forth, Gerard looked over his wife's head. "Is he dead?"

Adelaide had pulled her knife free and was standing with it in her hand, looking down at the body on the floor. "I think so," she whispered. She stared at the crumpled heap of humanity lying at her feet and felt cold. She had killed a man. She had been trained to kill with a knife, but she had never imagined that she would actually have to do so.

"If it's him or you," Sergeant Grant had impressed upon her as he taught her to handle a knife, "don't hesitate. If it's kill or be killed, you do the killing!"

Not him or me, thought Adelaide as she stared down at Fernand, but him or Marie, Gerard and the entire Auclon family.

"Yes," she said abruptly. "So now we must deal with his body. He probably hasn't been to the Germans yet, but we can't rely on that. Come on, Gerard, we have to get him out of here, and fast."

"But Marie . . ." Gerard began.

"Marie is fine," said his wife bravely, pulling away from him. "Adèle is right. We must move the pig out of here and get rid of him." She got unsteadily to her feet and Gerard stood up beside her.

"Will people be looking for him?" asked Adelaide, as she ran the blade of her knife under the kitchen tap. "Family? Friends?"

346

Gerard shrugged. "Perhaps," he said, "I don't know. He probably won't have told anyone else about the Auclons yet. He'd want the credit for finding them himself."

"Let's hope so," said Adelaide. "Come on, there's no time to waste. We must make sure that there is no sign that he was ever anywhere near here. We'll have to bury him. Where do you suggest? We can't move him far." She looked from one to the other. "Where can we bury him?"

Marie, calm now, had a suggestion. "In the old well. It's very deep and unless someone climbed down to the bottom, they would never find him there."

"Right." Adelaide took charge. "Let's get to it. Gerard, you take his legs." But now the immediate danger was over, Gerard's strength seemed to have deserted him, and he shook his head.

"Come *on*, Gerard," Adelaide urged, "we've got to move him now. Where's the well?"

"In the yard, I'll show you." Marie led her out into the yard and pointed to the corner where there was a large, flat stone, with a ring set into it. "When we stopped using it, we had it capped. We'll have to lift that stone."

"Then we need the crowbar again," Adelaide said and went to fetch it from the barn. "Call Gerard to help."

The ring was stiff to lift, but Adelaide worked on it with the crowbar and at last managed to get it upright so that they could use it to manoeuvre the stone. The stone itself was very heavy, but between them, using the crowbar and a garden fork, they were able to lever it up and slide it clear of the top of the well. Adelaide peered down into the shaft that had opened at her feet. Marie was right, it was unlikely that anyone could see to the bottom of the well even with a powerful torch.

"Let's do it," she said tersely, and went back into the kitchen. Fernand was heavy, but they rolled him onto the hearthrug, which was already stained with his blood, and dragged him out into the yard and over to the gaping well shaft.

"Head first," instructed Adelaide, and they swivelled him round so that his head was over the edge of the shaft, then she lifted his feet and with surprising ease slid him into its darkness. With a slither he was gone, and moments later the faintest splash announced his arrival at the bottom of the well. Adelaide rolled up the bloodstained hearthrug and dropped it in after him.

"Let's get the stone back." Adelaide reached for the crowbar and together they edged the capstone back over the shaft. When it was in place, Adelaide knelt on the ground and pushed the ring back into place.

"We need a broom," she said, and Marie scurried off to find the yard brush. Adelaide took it from her. "You start on the kitchen floor," she said, "I'll finish up here."

Gerard and Marie disappeared indoors and Adelaide swept away the telltale marks left by the dragged hearth rug. She brushed the dust back over the capstone, treading it down into the cracks, pressing it round the ring with her fingers so that there was no sign that the stone had been moved. Once the cattle came into the

348

yard for the morning milking, all traces should be obliterated.

When she returned to the kitchen she found Marie on her hands and knees scrubbing the floor. Fernand had fallen forward, and though his wound had bled, a little of his blood had pooled on the floor, and she was managing to remove the stains. Gerard was collecting up the glass from the shattered window. The force with which Adelaide had hurled the butter jar had sprayed glass all over the kitchen. Adelaide helped him pick up the larger pieces and then they swept up the remaining shards and carried them outside.

It was full daylight before they had cleared away all signs of their night's work, and when they had finally finished, they all three of them slumped into chairs round the kitchen table.

Gerard buried his head in his hands, the last vestiges of his strength ebbing away. Marie, surprisingly the stronger of the two, looked across at Adelaide and gave a weak smile.

"Adèle," she said, "you saved our lives. If that pig had got what he wanted, he would have turned us into the Gestapo, and if he hadn't, he would have killed us both. Thank you. You're very brave."

Adelaide smiled back at her. "You too," she said. She knew that she had been running on adrenaline and now she too felt exhausted. "Tell me what happened."

"It was not long after you'd gone. Fool that I was, I hadn't locked the back door. I heard someone in the scullery and I thought one of you must have come back for some reason." Marie grimaced. "I went to see what you wanted and" — she drew a deep breath as the fear struck her again — "and there he was, with his knife at my throat.

"I tried to scream, but he hit me across the face. I staggered against the wall and he grabbed at me, threatening to stab me if I made any more noise. Then he tied me up to the chair. He asked about the Auclons, and when I said I didn't know anything about them, he said we'd wait for Gerard." She looked across at Adelaide. "I don't think he knew you lived here too, and thank God for it."

Adelaide squeezed her hand. "We should bathe your face, Marie," she said, looking at the long gash across Marie's cheek. The bleeding had stopped, but it was a nasty cut. "It really needs stitches — you should go to the doctor."

"And how will she explain it?" demanded Gerard, suddenly looking up.

"The broken glass from the window," suggested Adelaide. "We are going to have to account for the broken window somehow. You'll have to try and get some glass to mend it."

"What will we say?" Gerard said wearily.

Adelaide thought for a moment. "If you're asked, you say you were using the axe to chop wood in the yard and the head flew off and smashed the window."

Gerard looked at her blankly as she went on. "Come on, Gerard, it could have happened like that. We have to have a story ready in case we are asked. If we aren't, fine, but if we are, we must all say the same thing." She reached across the table and took the hand of each of the Launays in hers. "You've both been so brave tonight, sheltering the Auclons and then standing up to Fernand. You were amazing, but we have to see it through. If Marie doesn't go to the doctor to have that gash stitched, it will look more suspicious than if she does. If you'd had an accident with the axe, you'd have taken her straight over." She squeezed their hands gently. "You've kept the Auclons safe, and we'll find a way to help them escape."

Marie nodded. "Adèle is right, Gerard, we must look as normal as possible. I will go to Dr Monceau in a little while. You must do the milking, and Adèle must go to the convent. All must be as normal."

All must be as normal, Adelaide thought as she pedalled her way up the hill to the convent. What is normal in these dreadful times? A family hiding in a cellar, a man threatening torture and ending up at the bottom of a well? Me killing someone, plunging a knife into his back?

The memory of the knife jarring into the man's body flooded through her and Adelaide tumbled off her bicycle and was sick in the hedge. But although her body had reacted against her action, her mind did not. Him or us, she reminded herself as she re-mounted the bike. Him or us.

CHAPTER
NINETEEN

The Germans raided the convent while the nuns were at early Mass. The thundering on the front door could be heard all over the building, and Father Michel's reedy voice faded away as the pounding continued. Sister Celestine, the portress, stumbled to her feet, her face ashen with fear, but Mother Marie-Pierre also stood. She murmured to Sister Celestine that she would deal with whoever was at the door, and quietly left the chapel. She was in no doubt as to who was demanding entrance; only the Germans knocked that way, the Germans under Colonel Hoch.

When she reached the door, she flung it wide, so that the soldier hammering with the huge knocker almost fell in. Colonel Hoch was standing on the steps, at the head of a group of men, but Mother Marie-Pierre could see soldiers already trampling the bushes along the drive, and she had no doubt that there would be other men in the courtyard, searching there.

She drew a deep breath. "Good morning, Colonel Hoch. Is there something I can do for you?"

352

"Reverend Mother," he looked her up and down, "how unusual that you should open the door yourself."

"My sisters and I were at Mass," Mother Marie-Pierre said coolly. "I came, so that they shouldn't be disturbed."

"You will all be disturbed," remarked the colonel, "if I choose to disturb you." He waved a hand at the men waiting beside him. "Carry on, Sergeant," he said. "And make it a thorough search."

The men flooded into the hallway and dispersed throughout the convent building. Mother Marie-Pierre saw several head up the staircase while others made for the kitchens.

"Perhaps you could tell me what you are looking for," she suggested to Hoch who had followed his men into the hall and now stood, his cold eyes roving in every direction.

His gaze returned to her, but he did not answer her question. "Go and tell your nuns to stay in the chapel until I say they may come out."

Mother Marie-Pierre nodded and turned to go back to the chapel. As she did so, one of the soldiers came back from the kitchen, pushing Adelaide in front of him.

"Found her in the cellar, sir. Says she's the maid."

Mother Marie-Pierre didn't understand what had been said, but she did recognise the word "keller" and guessed where Adelaide had been found.

Colonel Hoch looked at Adelaide for a moment and then spoke in French. "Name?"

"Please, sir, Adèle Durant, sir."

"I've seen you here before," Hoch said. "What were you doing in the cellar?"

Adelaide had no need to pretend she was afraid; her voice shook as she answered. "Bringing up the coal for the range, sir. It's my first job in the mornings."

Her hands were black with coal dust and the colonel seemed to accept this answer. He directed his next question to the man who had brought her. "Have you searched the cellar, Schultz?"

"Not yet, sir. I was about to when I found the girl. Thought she might be one of the ones we were looking for, sir."

"Well, go back and search. You, girl, wait in the kitchen."

Schultz took Adelaide by the arm and pushed her in front of him down the passage to the kitchen. Two men were already searching here, but Schultz ignored them. "You, girl, bring a light."

"I don't understand," Adelaide wailed, wringing her hands in agitation.

Schultz repeated his order, this time in heavily accented and ungrammatical French. "Find light. Come with me."

Ignoring the searching men, he moved straight towards the cellar door. It was clear to Adelaide that this man knew his way about, that he must have searched the place before.

Would he remember exactly how the cellar had looked last time, she wondered? Would he notice that all the furniture had been moved, that it was now stacked in a different place?

354

He flung open the cellar door and then turned round. "You," he shouted at Adelaide again, "bring lamp."

"It's at the bottom of the stairs," Adelaide told him, pointing down the steps. "An oil lamp."

Again he gestured with the rifle. "Go, make light."

Adelaide did as she was told, gripping the handrail of the cellar steps tightly as she made her way down. Her heart was pounding as she struck a match to light the lamp, but her mind was racing. You've got to stay cool, she told herself. You've got to decide what to do if he finds the hidden room.

Nothing, she decided ruefully. There was nothing she could do if he actually found the room, but she might be able to distract him in some way, before he did so.

Schultz followed her down, and, pausing at the bottom of the steps, looked about him. His eye fell on the jars of preserves standing on the shelf. Without comment he reached up and took two jars of honey, stuffing them into his pockets. He ran an eye round the cellar for anything else that he might be able to purloin, but seeing nothing easily portable, he turned his attention to the rest of the cellar.

"Bring light," he ordered. Obedient to a jerk of his head, Adelaide preceded him through the remaining cellars. He peered into each until he came at last to the pile of furniture. Adelaide found she was holding her breath and forced herself to breathe again as he gave it only a cursory glance.

"What a load of junk," he said, reaching out for an old three-legged stool. There was a scuffling sound and

355

he leapt back, jerking his hand away, as a large brown rat emerged from the heap and scuttled away across the floor. Adelaide gave a loud shriek, clutching her skirt about her.

His attention diverted from the furniture, the man gave a harsh laugh. "Stupid woman!" He pushed her ahead of him to light his way back to the stairs. As he passed the apple store he helped himself to a couple of apples, pushing them down into his pockets, his eyes daring Adelaide to comment on the theft. She lowered her own, as if afraid to meet his challenge, exulting inside that his greed should have blinded him to anything in the cellar that he could not steal.

When they returned to the kitchen, it was clear that his men had found nothing. The sergeant threw open the back door and they stalked out into the courtyard to join in the search there.

Adelaide slumped onto a chair, relief flooding through her that the safe room had so far escaped detection. If the Germans left empty-handed they would concentrate their search somewhere else, and perhaps the Auclons would be safe enough for a few days. But it worried her that the Germans were already looking for the little family. Alain Fernand must have told them about the Auclons before he came searching at the Launays'. That meant, before long, they would realise he was missing. Had he mentioned the Launays as well? Would they come searching there? Adelaide shuddered to think what would happen to them if his body was discovered in the well.

When the Germans had finally departed empty-handed, Mother Marie-Pierre went back to the chapel where the entire community was waiting. Father Michel sat in the carved oak chair to one side of the altar, his head in his hands. Soldiers had burst into the chapel, searching the Lady Chapel, disappearing behind the high altar, jabbing at the velvet hangings with rifle butts and banging about in the vestry, peering into the confessional box before slamming out again. Thoroughly shaken by this invasion, Father Michel had hastily muttered the final prayers of the Mass, and, having divested himself of his vestments, simply sat down to wait. The nuns were all in their stalls, some on their knees, others seated reading their office. No one spoke. All looked up, some expectantly, others fearfully, when the door opened again and Reverend Mother came in.

"Thank you, Sisters, for your patience," she said briskly. "The Germans have now gone, so I suggest we all get back to our normal duties as quickly as we can." The sisters began to file out of the chapel, each genuflecting as she passed in front of the altar.

Father Michel hurried down the aisle, his face pale. He did not return Reverend Mother's greeting, but simply nodded to her and hastened away, as if he couldn't wait to get out of the place.

Mother Marie-Pierre waited by the door and as Sister Marie-Marc came past her, she spoke quietly. "Sister, would you be kind enough to ask young Adèle Durant to come to my office, please."

Sister Marie-Marc bobbed her head, murmuring, "Yes, Mother, of course."

Reverend Mother waited until all but the sister on watch had left the chapel, and then she slipped into a seat near the back. She needed a few moments of silent peace to draw her thoughts together. She prayed for strength, and she prayed for wisdom, that she might know what to do. The German raid had left her both angry and afraid.

Colonel Hoch had been as cold as always, his chilly eyes completely lacking emotion, but she knew he had expected to find something . . . or someone.

The search had been thorough. Every room entered and searched, furniture moved, cupboards emptied. The chapel, the kitchens, the cellar, the sisters' cells, even her own office, each had a detail of soldiers to carry out the search. Hoch had stood in the hallway, waiting for each group to report back to him, and Reverend Mother had returned from the chapel defiantly standing with him, determined to remain unintimidated, but she almost sagged with relief when the final report came in. Nothing to be found.

"Now the hospital," he barked, and led his men out through the courtyard gate to the hospital beyond the wall. They swept into the wards, leaving Sister Marie-Paul, Sister Jeanne-Marie and Mother Marie-Pierre to watch helplessly, as the colonel and his men searched every cubicle, every cupboard, every storeroom.

"What are they looking for?" murmured Sister Marie-Paul, as one of them upended a basket of dirty linen.

"Some escaped prisoners, I think," replied Reverend Mother softly. "He seems to think they are in the convent."

Every name above a bed was checked against the ward list, medical reports scrutinised and papers inspected. At last, satisfied that all the patients were genuine and accounted for, Hoch had got back into his car and his men had disappeared to search elsewhere.

As usual, the incense-scented silence of the chapel worked its cure. Reverend Mother had always laid her problems at the feet of her Lord, and the moments of peace spent with Him now calmed and strengthened her, and when she left the sanctuary of the chapel she returned to her office with renewed resolve.

Within moments someone tapped on the door, and she knew it must be Adèle. Mother Marie-Pierre seated herself behind her desk and rang the bell to summon her into the office.

"Ah, Adèle," she said coolly as the girl came in. "Come in and shut the door."

Adelaide closed the door firmly and then turned back to face her aunt.

Mother Marie-Pierre came straight to the point. "You know the Germans were here, searching the convent this morning, Adèle. Was that anything to do with you?" Her eyes were steely as she looked at Adelaide. "Have you hidden your escaping prisoners in the convent in spite of what I said?"

Adelaide, taking in Reverend Mother's serious tone, addressed her formally. "No, Mother. Not exactly."

"What do you mean? Not exactly? Have you put the convent at risk?"

Adelaide returned her gaze levelly. "I have, yes, but . . ."

"How dare you!" The anger in Mother Marie-Pierre's voice was barely controlled. "After I expressly told you that it was out of the question?" She stared at her niece for a moment and then spoke more calmly. "You may be prepared to put the whole convent at risk, Adèle, but I am not. Where are these prisoners? Where have you hidden them? They should be handed over as prisoners of war. They'll be locked up, yes, but no harm will come to them."

"Sarah . . ."

"Mother," corrected her aunt, icily. "You will no longer presume on our relationship."

Adelaide inclined her head, accepting the rebuke, but she spoke firmly. "Mother . . . look, it's not what you think. I have hidden people in the convent, yes, but not escaped prisoners of war."

"Then who?"

"The Auclon family."

"What?" Mother Marie-Pierre stared at her in disbelief.

"The Auclon family. They're Jews and . . ."

"I know who they are," interrupted Reverend Mother, still disbelieving. "They're here? In the convent?"

"Well, they've been in hiding, hidden by some good people for months, but now that hiding place has become unsafe. They were brought to our farm last night and we were asked to hide them. We had nowhere they could be hidden, so I brought them here. Father, mother and the twin boys."

"But where did you put them?" asked her aunt faintly. "Where are they now?"

"I hid them in the cellar."

"But the Germans searched the cellar . . ."

"And they didn't find them. I put them into the room where you hid Terry Ham. The one with grating to the outside."

"But why didn't the Germans find them?"

"I pulled all the old furniture over in front of the door. You can't see it unless you move all the furniture away. The sergeant who searched the cellars insisted on searching alone because he wanted to raid your stores. His search was only cursory; he was more interested in stealing food from your store cupboard than looking for Jews he didn't expect to find."

"But when?"

"Last night. Gerard and I brought them up. We moved the outside grating and got them in that way."

"No, not that. When did you move all this furniture?"

"I did it several days ago," admitted Adelaide with a wry smile. "I'm sorry, Mother, but I had to have a safe place for people to hide in case of emergency. Last night I decided this was an emergency. I was remembering what you told me Sister Eloise had said to you, 'You have to fight evil wherever you meet it.'"

"Don't use poor Sister Eloise to justify what you did," snapped Reverend Mother.

"Why not?" Adelaide would not give ground. "It's what she said and it's what I did." The two women stared at each other for a moment before Adelaide spoke more gently. "It's what you'd have done, Mother. What was I to do with those children? They're only four years old. They've been living in a derelict cottage for the last six months and now they're underground, in a cellar. We couldn't just let the Germans ship them off to some camp. Don't worry, Mother, I promise you it's just a short-term measure. I'm going to get them away."

"How?" asked Reverend Mother. "There are four of them to move. They will be extremely noticeable, especially Monsieur Auclon. He has typical Jewish features, and he's well known around here. He'll be spotted a mile off."

"I've thought about that," Adelaide said. "I have the beginnings of a plan, but the less you know of it the better. I have to work out the details and it will take a few days to put into action, but I think we should be able to get them safely out of the area." She looked earnestly at her aunt. "I need to get this family to your friend Father Bernard. No one will be looking for them in Amiens. It's here they are known, it's here they were betrayed."

"Betrayed?" Reverend Mother was shocked. "Who by?"

"A local man. He's a known collaborator. We guessed he'd discovered their hiding place and he must have tipped off the Germans."

"He must have seen you bringing the family here, and that's why they came to search."

362

"No, I'm sure he didn't," Adelaide said firmly, knowing for certain that he hadn't. For an instant she saw Fernand's body on the kitchen floor, her knife protruding from his back, and her stomach turned somersaults but, forcing the image from her mind, she dragged her thoughts back to the present. "We were very careful. We did see two German soldiers come and raid poor Sister Marie-Marc's henhouse, but they didn't see us. They were too interested in taking the hens."

"And what about the people who gave them shelter?" asked Mother Marie-Pierre quietly. "What's happened to them?"

"I don't know," admitted Adelaide. "The Germans may have been there already. We'll try and find out later, but if they haven't, we don't want any attention drawn to them."

"It makes no sense," replied her aunt. "The Germans would have gone straight there. Why did they come here?"

"When they found the family weren't where he'd told them, I imagine they'll be searching everywhere," Adelaide said, and heard again the splash as Fernand reached the bottom of the well. She could only pray that when there was the inevitable search of the Launays' farm, he would not be found. "You sheltered Jews in the convent before, it was the obvious place to start."

Mother Marie-Pierre nodded, accepting this. "So, how will we get them away?"

Adelaide noticed the use of the word "we", and smiled. "I will arrange everything," she promised. "Do you think your mother house in Paris would give the children a home if necessary?"

"I think so, but not the parents."

"Never mind about them for the time being. Let's start with the children. I may need your help when the time comes."

"What sort of help?"

"I'll explain nearer the time. The less you know, the safer you are, really. All I need from you now is where to find Father Bernard."

"He's the parish priest at Holy Cross in Amiens. His house is opposite the church." She described how to find Father Bernard's church, and Adelaide memorised the directions carefully. "You can tell him you come from me."

Adelaide smiled. "Thank you, Mother. I'm sure that will reassure him."

"What about the Auclons in the meantime?" asked Reverend Mother. "Have they got food and water? How will you let them know what is going to happen?"

"Leave it all to me; they'll be fine." Adelaide tried to sound reassuring. "But I will have to be away for a couple of days. I'll send a message to say my Aunt Marie is sick and I can't come to work." She got to her feet. "I'd better go back to the kitchen now though," she said.

Reverend Mother stood as well. "Just one thing, Adèle, I am assuming that you, I and the Launays are the only people who know about this hidden room. Yes?"

Adelaide smiled ruefully. "And Sister Marie-Marc," she admitted. "She followed me into the cellar and found out what I was doing."

"Sister Marie-Marc," repeated her aunt. "I might have guessed. She is incorrigible. Does she know the family are in the room?"

"No," replied Adelaide. "We may need her help when the time comes, but in the meantime it would be better if she knew nothing of what's happening."

Reverend Mother could only agree. Coming round the desk she held out her hands to Adelaide and her eyes softened. "I know you felt you had to do this, Adelaide," she said, "but you have put the convent and its community in grave danger. Please get them away from here as soon as you can."

When she had finished her work at the convent, Adelaide went straight to Le Chat Noir, wearing the blue headscarf, the sign that she needed immediate help. She had no idea who would respond to the signal, all Marcel had said was that if there was an emergency she should sit in the café, wearing the blue scarf.

"Someone will come and speak to you. They will say, 'You should wear that colour more often, it suits you,' and you may trust that person implicitly."

The café was almost empty when she arrived, and she took a table outside so that she could easily be seen. The waitress came out and she ordered a cup of coffee, then she sat in the afternoon sun, reading a newspaper and sipping the bitter brew. How long would she have to wait, she wondered? After a quarter of an hour, anxious not to make herself conspicuous, she got up to leave. She would come back later and hope the contact would be made. There was little else she could do. She had no idea who Marcel really was, or where he lived. She had never seen him in the village, and so assumed he must live elsewhere. She went inside to pay for her coffee. Two old men were playing dominoes at one of the tables, and two German officers were sharing a bottle of wine at a table by the window, but none of them even glanced at her as she went up to the bar to pay. There was no sign of the girl who had brought the coffee, but an elderly woman sat at the till. She looked up and smiled. "You're Marie Launay's niece, aren't you?" she said as she took the money. Adelaide said she was and the woman went on. "You should wear that colour more often, it suits you."

Relief flooded through Adelaide. "Thank you, it's one of my favourites."

"I've got some wool for your aunt," the woman went on conversationally. "I know she's a great knitter and I can't knit anymore." She displayed fingers twisted with arthritis. "Come through to the back and I'll find it for you."

"Thank you, that's very kind." Adelaide followed the old lady through a door behind the counter and found herself in a small parlour. The old lady closed the door behind them and turned to face her.

"You've got a problem," she stated in a matter-of-fact voice.

"Yes, I have to speak to Marcel as soon as possible."

"The red scarf would have done for that," snapped the woman. "Blue is for emergency only."

"This is an emergency," Adelaide retorted. "I have to see Marcel at once." She paused, wondering how much to reveal to this old lady, but remembering Marcel saying that she could trust the contact implicitly, she went on. "I have the Auclon family in a safe house, but they can't stay there. We have to move them on and soon. I must see Marcel. If he can't come to me, I must go to him."

"He'll come." The woman relaxed a little. "They're safe, you say? The Auclons?"

"For the moment," Adelaide replied. "But there are other complications. It's vital I speak to Marcel today."

"I understand. I will get a message to him straight away. Will you meet him at the usual place?"

"No, too dangerous. The Germans are everywhere, looking for the Auclons. They've already searched the convent. Better to meet somewhere out of sight."

"Come back this evening," said the woman. "Come to the side door in the alley at eight. Marcel will be here." She picked some balls of wool out of a basket by the stove and handed them to Adelaide. "Go back through the café now," she said, and opening the door led the way.

"It really is most kind of you," Adelaide was saying as she emerged into the café. "Aunt Marie will be delighted to get her hands on some more wool. Thank you so much."

Adelaide headed straight home, anxious to pass on the good news that the Auclons had not been found when the convent was searched, but the moment she rode into the farmyard she knew there was something wrong. Gerard should have been bringing the cows in for milking, but the yard was empty. Her eyes immediately flicked to the stone that covered the well, but it was still in place, and there were no signs that it had been moved. She parked her bike against the wall and went into the kitchen.

Marie and Gerard were at the table, talking, both looking pale and anxious. The cut on Marie's face had been stitched, the sutures a dark cobbled seam against the pallor of her skin. The window behind them was boarded up, leaving the kitchen in a gloomy half-light, despite the sunshine outside.

Marie jumped to her feet. "Adèle, thank God you're back safe."

"What's happened?" Adelaide asked as she joined them. "Trouble?"

"We don't know," replied Marie. "Gerard went over to see Étienne and Albertine this afternoon, to let them know the Auclons were safe for now and . . . well, you tell her, Gerard."

Gerard took up the story. "When I reached the farm, there was no one about. I looked round the yard, but no sign of anyone. Then I noticed the back door was open so I went in, calling to them, you know. No one there either, the place was empty; but there was a meal on the table, bread and cheese and a bottle of wine. One chair was tipped over, the other pushed back as if someone had just got up. I called again and then I searched the whole house, but there was no one there.

368

Then, when I went back out to search the yard properly, I noticed heavy tyre tracks in the mud." He sighed. "Only the Boche have trucks heavy enough to make those, so I think we have to accept that Étienne and Albertine have been arrested." His voice was tight with hatred. "That scum Fernand must have told the Germans before he came here."

"He may have," Adelaide agreed, "but that doesn't really make sense. If he'd already told the Germans where to find the Auclons, why did he turn up here?"

"Because he'd lost them again." Gerard got to his feet and began to pace the room. "Don't you see? He finds out where the Auclons are hiding, and goes back to tell his masters. In the meantime, Étienne's got suspicious of him hanging about the place, so he moves the family here. Fernand goes back to watch the arrest, only to find that the birds have flown. When his friends the Germans arrive they aren't going to be pleased with him, are they? So he sets out to find them again, and, knowing Étienne's Marie's cousin, he comes here."

"It's possible, I suppose," Adelaide said doubtfully.

"It's the only thing that fits what we know," Gerard said warming to his idea.

"But why didn't the Germans act at once?"

"Dawn raids," Marie said. "They tend to raid at dawn to catch people before they're properly awake."

"That's right," Gerard agreed. "They would have crept up to the ruined cottage in the dark and surrounded it, but they wouldn't go in until it was daylight . . . to make sure no one got away under cover of darkness."

"And now they've got Étienne and Albertine," said Marie bleakly.

"And they'll be looking for Fernand," pointed out Adelaide.

"I suppose so," said Gerard.

"Of course they will," Adelaide said. "They have to find him. If there's no Fernand, and Albertine did manage to clear the cottage in time, they've no proof the Auclons were ever there."

"Since when do the Germans need proof?" asked Gerard bitterly.

"Adèle's right, Gerard," said his wife. "They may have no evidence. They may have just taken them in for questioning."

"And we all know how the Germans question people!" muttered Gerard.

"Which means they may come looking here," said Marie.

"They're already looking for the Auclons, or for somebody," Adelaide told them. "They searched the convent this morning."

"They didn't find them?" whispered Marie.

"No. The secret room held. But we do have to get them out as soon as we can. I'm seeing someone this evening to make plans." Adelaide got up. "We may need to go to the market in Albert tomorrow," she said. "Can Sunshine take us in the cart? We could all have a day out."

At exactly eight o'clock Adelaide knocked on the side door of the café, and it was opened immediately by the old lady.

370

"Come in," she said, glancing quickly up and down the alley to see if anyone had noticed Adelaide's arrival. It was not yet dark, but a damp drizzle had drifted in with the evening and there was no one about.

Marcel was sitting at the kitchen table and he got to his feet as Adelaide came in. "Antoinette, what on earth has happened?" His eyes glowed with suppressed anger. "It puts us all at risk for me to come here."

"I know," responded Adelaide as she sat down opposite him, "but we would be at even more risk if I hadn't been able to speak to you straight away." She glanced across at the old lady who had seated herself in a chair by the stove.

Marcel followed her glance. "You can talk in front of Juliette, she's with us." He picked up a bottle of wine from the table and filling a glass passed it over to her. "Here, have a drink, and then for God's sake tell us what has happened."

Adelaide took a sip of the wine and then putting down her glass began. "Well, firstly," she said, "Alain Fernand is dead."

"Dead! Christ, what happened to him?"

"I killed him," Adelaide said. "He was threatening to kill Marie to get some information out of Gerard. He didn't know I was there. I stabbed him."

"Stabbed him?" echoed Marcel.

"In the back," said Adelaide. "He had a knife to Marie's face and was threatening to blind her." Her eyes held Marcel's. "He was trying to make Gerard tell him where a Jewish family were hidden."

"The Auclons," put in Juliette.

"Yes, the Auclons. They had been brought to us in the hope we could hide them. Gerard and I managed to get them to a safe place, but when we got back Fernand had Marie tied to a chair in the kitchen." She explained what had happened when they'd come back and found Fernand in the kitchen.

Marcel listened until she had finished and then, with a look of new respect on his face, he addressed her quietly. "I wouldn't have thought you had that in you."

Adelaide gave a shaky laugh. "I wouldn't have thought so either," she admitted. "I was sick afterwards. But it wasn't just him or me, was it? It was to save a family with small children, as well as the three of us."

"You don't have to justify your actions to me," Marcel said cheerfully, "I applaud them. But it has left us with a problem. What have you done with his body?"

Adelaide explained how they had tipped it down the well. "It was the only place we could think of in a hurry."

"Well, he'll be safe enough there I should think," Marcel said, tasting his wine and pulling a face. "It's most unlikely they'll find him, unless they have some idea where to look. Do you think anyone else knows he was coming to the Launays' farm?"

Adelaide shrugged. "He may have told someone, but we doubt it, or they'd have been round already." She then explained Gerard's theory. "He could be right," she added. "The trouble is Étienne and Albertine have disappeared, so we have to assume that they've been arrested. That means we could get a visit from the Gestapo as well."

"Yes, probably," Marcel agreed. He lit a cigarette, looking thoughtful.

"But there's nothing to find," Adelaide continued with more confidence than she felt. "In the meantime, I want to get that family moved out of the area. Apart from their own safety they're endangering too many other people."

Marcel shook his head. "Almost impossible with the activity there'll be in the next few days. You'll have to wait until the heat dies down."

"To make the move, maybe, but I want to set the plans in motion, so I'm ready when the time comes."

She outlined her plan for getting the Auclon family away from the area. Marcel listened carefully and when she'd finished he pinched out his cigarette, putting the remains into a small tin to save for another time. "Well, it is the basis of a plan, but it leaves an awful lot to chance."

"I know, but provided this priest" — she was careful not to name him even to Marcel — "will take the children, I think they can be got to safety. The parents are another matter. We shall do our best, but they will find it more difficult to get through."

"The Boche will be looking for a family," pointed out Juliette, speaking for the first time. "Moving the children separately will cut down the risk for them, but double the risk for you."

"I can't move them together for two reasons," Adelaide reminded her. "One, they are identical twins and that makes them too noticeable, and two, I have only room for one on my bicycle at a time."

They continued chewing over the plan, discussing possibilities, trying to foresee the problems that might arise. But there were few preparations they could make until Adelaide had been to see Father Bernard.

"It'd be safer if I had some sort of papers for them," Adelaide said. "Difficult to get identity cards, we can't get photos, but perhaps if I had ration cards for them . . . ? They'd still be J1s. Can you help there? I'd only need one if I'm moving them separately."

Marcel shrugged. "I'll try," he promised. "Give me a day or two. Anything else? What about the parents?"

"Ration cards would help there too," Adelaide said, "but we'd have the same problem with identity cards. Just do the best you can. And Marcel, I really need those inner tubes or the whole plan could fail because of a puncture!"

"I'll get them," he promised. He looked at his watch and got to his feet. "I'd better get moving," he said. "Don't want to be caught out after curfew. I'll be in the café two nights from now. You come to the side door and if it's safe Juliette will come and fetch me." He shook hands with Juliette and then coming round the table embraced Adelaide, kissing her on both cheeks. "You're a brave girl," he said. "We'll get them away."

"And Fernand?"

"They'll be looking for him," Marcel said, "that's certain, but they won't find him, will they? Oh, they'll guess what's happened to him, but they won't know where to look."

"They might make reprisals," Adelaide said in a small voice.

"If he was a missing German they might, but not for a Frenchman, even if he was a collaborator."

Marcel had slipped out of the side door and disappeared into the darkness, and Adelaide waited another ten minutes before she followed him into the night.

Next morning Gerard put old Sunshine between the shafts of the cart and they were on the road for Albert before most of the village had opened its eyes. It was a glorious summer morning, the sun sparkling in the dew and teasing out the hidden colours of the hedgerows. Birdsong filled the air, and Adelaide was struck by the beauty around her as if seeing it for the first time. How could there be a war going on in such a stunningly beautiful world? The countryside spread away on either side of her; meadows with cattle grazing peacefully, a meandering river, way-marked with willows; fields showing the tender green of new crops.

She thought of the Auclon family, confined to the hidden cellar, as much in prison as if they had been in a dungeon. She wondered how they were coping with so little space and only the daylight filtering through the grating to see by. How long could they keep two four-year-old boys quiet? Children their age should be out playing in this glorious early summer sunshine, not entombed underground, fearful for their lives. Anger rose like bile in her throat at the evil that forced them to remain there, and the day lost its brilliance.

During the previous afternoon, she had returned to the convent kitchen to tell Sister Elizabeth that her aunt was ill and that she would not be able to come to work for the next few days. The nun had been sympathetic and had accepted her story. Sister Marie-Marc had looked at her speculatively, but Adelaide greeted the query in her eyes with a bland smile. "I hope to be back in a few days."

As she left the courtyard through the back gate, she had paused by the grating, and with the pretence of removing a pebble from her shoe she had stuffed a note down between the bars of the grille. It had told the prisoners below little more than that she would return soon, and her plans were underway, but at least they knew they were not forgotten.

Her thoughts were jolted back to the present by the sound of an engine coming up behind them. Gerard pulled Sunshine into a gateway, to allow a black Citroën, flying the swastika on its front wings, to sweep past them, and disappear in a cloud of dust. It had been impossible to see who was travelling in the car, but Adelaide recognised it as one she'd seen outside the German headquarters in St Croix. "Colonel Hoch?" she suggested.

"Maybe," Gerard said, as he shook up the reins and Sunshine lumbered out into the lane once more.

At least whoever was in the speeding car wasn't interested in a country cart on its way to market, Adelaide thought. She could only hope that no one would be interested in a woman on a bicycle with a child in the seat behind her.

When they reached the edge of town Adelaide slipped down from the cart and made her way to the station, while the Launays trundled on into the centre, with the few items of produce they had brought to sell, or exchange, at the market.

Adelaide went to the station and found that there was a train for Amiens due within the hour, so she got herself a ticket, bought a newspaper from a stand and sat down to wait. Surprisingly the train was almost on time, and along with a crowd of others she scrambled gratefully into a carriage. As the train pulled out of the station some minutes later, she found herself crammed into a compartment with seven other people. Opening her paper she hid behind it, only emerging to show her ticket to the ticket inspector. There were no spot checks of identity cards, and when they reached Amiens Adelaide was able to get off and leave the station unchallenged. Following Sarah's directions, she had little trouble in finding the Church of the Holy Cross.

The notice board outside proclaimed the parish priest to be Father Bernard Dupré. Mass was at eight o'clock every morning, and confession daily between two and four o'clock.

Adelaide had been going to knock on the door of the priest's house and ask to see Father Bernard, but now a better idea came to her. She looked at her watch. It was half-past two. He would already be in the church ready to hear confessions. How much better it would be if she approached him in the confessional. She could speak to him privately without giving rise to comment or suspicion.

She pushed the church door open and slipped inside. She could see the confessional box in one of the transepts. There was an old lady kneeling in a pew outside, but the door of the box was open to show that the priest was ready to receive his next penitent. Adelaide knelt for a moment or two, her head bowed, then she rose and went inside, pulling the door closed behind her. It was so long since she had been to confession that she had almost forgotten the words.

"Bless me, Father, for I have sinned."

She heard the murmur of a voice from the other side of the curtain and spoke softly. "Father Bernard, is that you? Mother Marie-Pierre sent me."

For a moment there was silence and then the curtain twitched aside and the priest looked through at her.

"I'm sorry, my child," he said, "but I think you must be mistaken. I don't think I know a Mother Marie-Pierre."

"I understand, Father . . . but even so she sends you this message. Sergeant Terry Ham reached home in safety. That's what she asked me to say."

The priest looked at her from under hooded brows. "I am always glad to hear that people are safe," he said cautiously.

Adelaide held his gaze, and then took the plunge. "There is a family who need your help, Father. May I bring them to you?"

"What could *I* do for them?" he asked.

"They need to get away to somewhere they aren't known," replied Adelaide. "You have contacts." When the priest didn't answer she went on. "There are two little boys, twins, only four years old. Jacques and Julien. If I don't get them away soon, they will surely be found."

"Where are their parents?" asked Father Bernard. He seemed to have come to some decision.

"With them at present, but they will be safer not moving as a family. They will travel separately."

"How would you bring the children?"

"One at a time, on the train. They're identical. They would be too conspicuous if we moved them together."

"It doubles the risk for you," pointed out the priest.

"Yes," agreed Adelaide, "but it's the only way."

"And the parents?" Father Bernard asked again.

"They will travel in disguise. Mother Marie-Pierre will provide a nun's habit for the mother, I was hoping you could give me a cassock to take back for the father. With luck, dressed like that they won't be challenged."

"And if you are stopped while bringing the boys to me, what will you say?"

"I'll have a letter from a doctor saying that the child needs to see an eye specialist at the hospital here in Amiens. I hope that will be explanation enough."

"We've talked long enough here," said the priest. "When you leave the confessional, stay kneeling in the church for a while as if doing penance, then go over to the house and tell Madame Papritz that I said you were to wait for me there. I'll come across as soon as I've finished here."

It was some time later that Father Bernard was able to join Adelaide in the priest's house. In the meantime she had been left in the parlour by Madame Papritz, who, on hearing she had had nothing to eat, brought her some bread and a teaspoonful of jam.

"I am sorry there is not more to offer you," she apologised, "but you know how things are."

Adelaide certainly did; food was scarce everywhere, but in the cities it was far worse than in the rural areas, where people could supplement their diet with home-grown produce. She thanked the housekeeper, and having eaten the bread and jam she settled back to wait for Father Bernard.

When the priest came in he took Adelaide into his study and closed the door.

"Now then, Mademoiselle."

"Antoinette."

"Antoinette. You'd better tell me the whole story, and then we'll see what I can do to help."

CHAPTER
TWENTY

Adelaide returned to Albert carrying a small cardboard suitcase. Again her train journey was trouble-free, and it was with relief that she met the Launays as arranged in a café close to the market. They did not ask her where she had been, or whom she had met. They all knew that it was safer for them to know nothing. Gerard simply put Sunshine between the shafts and they set off home together through the early twilight.

By the time she kept the appointment with Marcel at Madame Juliette's, Adelaide had her whole plan mapped out. Marcel greeted her with a kiss on either cheek, and, having poured them each a glass of wine the three of them sat round the table in Madame Juliette's kitchen. Adelaide told them how she had got on.

"The priest is prepared to take the children and has provided a cassock for Joseph Auclon's disguise. As soon as I can get the twins to him, he will move them on. As far as the parents are concerned, if they can reach him safely, he will do his best for them. He'll tell them where the children are, but they won't be reunited with them in the foreseeable future. It's too dangerous."

"Supposing the parents won't let the children go?" suggested Marcel.

"I'm sure they will when they realise that it may be the only way to save their lives," Juliette said. "They'll put their children first."

"I'm going to tell them this evening, after I leave here," Adelaide said. "And then I hope to take the first child tomorrow. How did you get on with the ration cards, Marcel? Any luck?"

"More than I'd expected," Marcel said. "If you can call it luck. A little lad called Olivier Costeau died of diphtheria a couple of weeks ago. He was only four. When I explained what we needed, his parents gave me his identity card and his ration card. The picture probably isn't very like the Auclon boys. What colour is their hair?"

"Dark," replied Adelaide.

"Good. So was Olivier's, so it may be better than nothing." Marcel held out the documents and Adelaide took them, looking carefully at the photograph. She forced from her mind that she was looking at the picture of a dead four-year-old, and concentrated on the use to which his papers could be put.

"It's a grainy picture of a little boy," she said, passing it across to Juliette. "If we part the Auclon boys' hair on the same side and make the front stand up in that little quiff, they might pass muster provided the papers are only given a cursory glance. It's worth a try anyway."

Juliette nodded. "Best we can do," she said, "and certainly better than being without any."

Marcel then produced a parcel wrapped in brown paper. "I've got these, too," he said. "Some of Olivier's clothes." He passed them over to Adelaide. "His parents said that they hoped they would be of use to some other boy now."

Adelaide unwrapped the parcel. There were two sets of good sturdy clothing and two pairs of shoes. She remembered how ragged the twins had looked as they sat in the Launays' kitchen, and her heart went out to the parents of little dead Olivier.

"Thank them for us," she said to Marcel. "And for Madame Auclon. She'll be so grateful. Those boys are dressed in rags."

"Now I have something for you," Madame Juliette said. She crossed to a little desk at the side of the room, and, opening it, produced a piece of paper. "I went to see Dr Monceau this morning," she said, "and while his receptionist was in with him I managed to get hold of a piece of his headed paper. Only one, though, so we need to do a practice run before we write on it."

Adelaide beamed at the old lady. "Madame Juliette," she said in admiration, "you are amazing!" She looked at the paper with Dr Monceau's name, address and qualifications across the top. "This is perfect."

Together they worked out the wording they would need in the doctor's letter, and then, having practised the doctor's spidery hand from a prescription Juliette had, Marcel carefully wrote the letter on the stolen paper.

Dear Doctor Aristide,

I am sending this boy, Olivier Costeau, to you because I am gravely worried about his deteriorating sight. Though his eyes seem clear enough much of the time, on occasion they cloud over and the child loses his peripheral vision. This is happening with increasing frequency and as it is not something I have come across before, I would appreciate you taking a look and recommending some treatment before this loss of sight becomes permanent.

I remain, yours faithfully,

Denis Monceau

"That should cover us if we're stopped," Adelaide said with more assurance than she felt. Would a German soldier, or a French gendarme for that matter, accept the letter at face value? She could only pray that they would.

"With the identity card, a ration card and the child in reasonable clothing, and the doctor's letter, you should get through safely enough," Marcel agreed. "Now all we have to do is to convince the Auclons to let the boys go."

"And convince the boys to leave their parents," added Madame Juliette.

This problem had been vexing Adelaide too. How would the little boys react to being taken away from their mother and father? They were only four years old after all, and for much of their short lives had been living in fear. How would they behave when she took them, one at a time, from the security of their parents? It was vital to the whole plan that they went with her without fuss, that they did nothing that would draw attention to themselves.

"We shall have to rely on the parents for that," Adelaide said now. "It's all we can do. And I'd better go and get on with it."

"I'm coming with you," Marcel announced, adding as Adelaide was about to veto the idea, "we'll be far less suspicious if we are seen as a courting couple." He gave her a grin. "It worked before!"

Adelaide gave a reluctant smile. "All right then, but I don't want to put you at risk when this really has nothing to do with you."

"Anything thwarting the Germans has to do with me," Marcel retorted. "Come on, it's time to go." He hid the parcel of clothes under his jacket, and Adelaide took charge of Olivier's papers, hiding them in her underwear.

"I have some food here for them," Madame Juliette said, passing over a packet for Adelaide to stow in her shoulder bag. "Just some bread and cheese and hard-boiled eggs. Not much I'm afraid, but it may keep them going for another few days."

She gave each of them a hug. "Be very careful, both of you," she said. "There are spies everywhere." She opened the back door and checked that the alley was empty, before Adelaide and Marcel slipped out into the night and made their way to the copse below the convent. It was full darkness, but a sliver of moon hung in a cloudless sky, allowing them to see — and be seen. It was not yet curfew and so they walked together, arm in arm, a courting couple; they met no one, but you never knew who might be watching. Once in the shelter of the copse, they moved silently between the trees up the hill towards the convent wall. Here they waited for several minutes, listening. The night around them seemed empty and still and so they ventured along the track to where the little bush marked the grating.

Adelaide pushed the two twigs through the grille and then after a moment she and Marcel levered it up, allowing Monsieur Auclon to poke his head up from below.

"We must talk to you," whispered Adelaide. "We can't risk you coming out here, we'll have to come down."

Joseph Auclon nodded and disappeared. Adelaide lowered herself through the hole, followed by Marcel, who drew the grille down over their heads once more. The atmosphere in the cellar was fetid, the smell of unwashed bodies, urine and faeces combining with the stale air to make an almost tangible miasma.

We have to get these people away, Adelaide thought even as she greeted the family. They can't stay in these conditions much longer.

Joseph lit a candle end and sheltered it in a box so that its glow was concealed from above. In the flickering light Adelaide could see the anxious faces of the parents and the wide eyes of the children, all afraid of what she was going to say.

386

"We've brought some more food," she said, handing the packet to Janine Auclon. The woman's hands shook as she opened it and passed out a piece of bread to each of her children, folding the rest back into the bag and setting it aside.

"This is Marcel," Adelaide told them. "He's going to help me get you away from here. He has some things for you, too." Marcel handed the bundle of clothes to Madame Auclon who stared in a mixture of disbelief and gratitude when she saw what they were.

"We have a plan to get you away," Adelaide continued, "but it has to be done in stages. We have only one set of documents for the boys, so they will have to travel separately."

"Oh no!" Madame Auclon gave an involuntary cry, but her husband hushed her with a hand on her arm. "Let Antoinette finish."

"I will take one of them with me this evening," Adelaide said. "He'll stay at the farm overnight and then first thing in the morning I will ride into Albert on my bike with him in the child seat on the back. Once in Albert, we shall take the train. There is a priest who will take him in and look after him until I bring his brother, transported in the same way." She went on to explain about the letter from the doctor.

"I shall only use that if I absolutely have to. They might check. Then, once both the boys are safely with the priest, he will move them on to a place of greater safety."

"Where?" asked Madame Auclon, unable to remain silent any longer. "Where will he take them?"

"I will tell you in time, Madame," Adelaide promised. "But for the moment the fewer people who know the better. It is safer for us all."

"We understand," Joseph said. "But if these people are risking their lives for us . . ."

"You will know in time," repeated Adelaide. "But their risk is greater if you know who or where they are. If you were captured —" She let the sentence hang in the air.

"And us?" asked Janine Auclon quietly. "What are you going to do with us?"

"When the boys are safe, I will come back for you, and try and get you to the same priest. After that it is out of my hands. I don't know his contacts any more than he knows mine." She took Janine's hand in hers. "I'll come back and I'll bring disguises for you both. We'll have an arranged signal for you to open the inner door. Then we'll get you out through the convent."

"What disguises?" asked Joseph suspiciously. "How will we be able to travel without papers?"

"You will be disguised as a Catholic priest," replied Adelaide calmly, "and Janine as a nun. Travelling together, as priest and nun, you may not be troubled for your papers. I might even have some for you by then, I don't know."

"Must we really split up?" asked Janine. "The boys are too young to go without us. What will happen to them? How will I bear it?"

"The Germans are still searching for you," Adelaide told her, "and they're looking for a family. If we move you all together, we shall fail. You'll all be caught. This way you all have a chance to escape and survive. Once you reach the priest you will be out of the immediate area and so, probably, out of immediate danger."

"But must you take the boys tonight?" asked Janine in a querulous voice, hugging them both to her.

"I must take one of them when I leave now," Adelaide said firmly. "It is the only way. And whichever it is, he must understand that he must be quiet and do exactly what I tell him. I know he's only four, but it is imperative that he does as he is told."

"I will talk to him," Joseph said. "They may only be four years old, but they have learnt that their lives depend on their instant obedience." He turned to one of the boys and held out his hand. "Julien, come here."

One of the boys detached himself from his mother and took his father's hand.

"This is Antoinette, Julien," Joseph said. "She has brought you some new clothes. In a minute we are going to get you out of those dirty old ones and let you put them on. Then Antoinette is going to take you to her house for the night. You will ride on her bicycle . . . won't that be exciting! Tomorrow you're going on a train and then you are going to stay with a very kind gentleman until Maman and I come and fetch you."

"Can I go, too?" came a little voice from across the room. "I don't want Julien to go by himself."

"You can go the next day, Jacques," promised his father with a smile. "Mademoiselle Antoinette only has one seat on her bicycle. Julien and the kind gentleman will be waiting for you when you get there. Then you'll be together until Maman and I can come and find you." He held out his other hand and the second boy came to him. "You must both be very brave and do exactly what Mademoiselle Antoinette tells you. She will look after you on your journey."

"We must go," Marcel said suddenly. "We've been here too long. Please get the child changed and ready to come, Madame." His voice was harsh, but Adelaide was glad he had taken control. It was breaking her heart to take these children from their parents with no guarantee that they would ever be reunited.

She, too, became businesslike, and while Janine Auclon stripped off Julien's old clothes and dressed him in Olivier's, Adelaide spoke urgently to Joseph. "If for any reason I don't come back tomorrow night at about the same time, don't panic. It could be for any number of reasons. Just have Jacques ready to go with me at the same time the night after. Once they are safe, I will come back for you." They agreed the signal for him to unlock the door that led in to the convent cellar, and there was a final failsafe. "If anything happens to me and I don't come back within a week, Marcel will try and contact you. If you hear from neither of us after ten days, then you are on your own and must do whatever you think is best."

"If that happens how will we find our children?" demanded Janine, who had been listening to this last exchange.

"Once both are safe and you are out of here and on your way I will give you your next contact."

"And if something happens to you in the meantime?"

"Madame . . . Janine." Adelaide was adamant in her reply. "This is the only way we can do this. If you want your children to stay with you that is your decision, but in that case I can't help you any more and you will have to leave here."

"Won't you even tell me just the town where they are going?" pleaded Janine. "I must know where to begin looking if we lose them."

"If I don't return at any time," Adelaide said reluctantly, "you can ask Reverend Mother. She will set you on the right road. Now, we must go." She got to her feet and held out her hand to the little boy now dressed in clean and tidy clothes. They were a little on the large side, but Adelaide decided that didn't really matter. Any prudent mother would buy a size too big to make the clothes last as long as possible, especially as clothes needed coupons.

For a moment the boy held on to his mother, clinging to her waist, his head buried against her, then gently she put him away from her and spoke softly. "Go with Antoinette, Julien. We'll be with you again very soon, I promise." She reached down and kissed him and then turned away before he could see the tears that were streaming down her cheeks. Joseph took the boy's hand. "Be a good boy for Antoinette, Julien."

Marcel already had the grating lifted away and had slithered through to the open air above. He stuck his head back down to give the all-clear. Joseph gave his son one last convulsive hug, handing him up into Marcel's waiting arms, before turning away to comfort his wife and Jacques, both of whom were sobbing.

Adelaide climbed the ladder and hauled herself out onto the grass, then together she and Marcel replaced the grating, checking the marker bush was in place and scattering the loose twigs around it.

The little boy was shivering in the darkness and Marcel scooped him up into his arms. "Now, *mon brave*," he said encouragingly, and setting the boy on his shoulders he strode off down the hill.

"It must be past curfew," Adelaide warned as they reached the edge of the copse.

"I know," Marcel agreed. "You take him now." He lowered the child to the ground. "As we go along the towpath, I'll go ahead, in case of trouble. You follow behind. If necessary, I'll cause a diversion and you get him safely back to the farm. All right?"

"All right." Adelaide took Julien's hand and crouched down beside him. "We have to be very quiet now, Julien, OK? If we meet someone just do what I do." She could just see him nod in the faint light of the moon. "Good boy. Come on then."

They walked along the river path until they reached the track that led to the Launays' farm. From there it was only a matter of moments before they were safely in the big kitchen with the door shut and bolted.

Marcel did not come in with them. "I'll see you tomorrow, when you get back."

"No," Adelaide said firmly. "Don't come. I don't need you and it's pointless to take the risk. I can go and fetch Jacques. They'll let him go now."

"You'll need help getting the parents out," he said.

"If all goes well with the boys," Adelaide said, "I'll meet you at the café in two days' time. If something goes wrong, stay clear. There'll be nothing you can do for me."

Marcel knew it was true, but he also realised that this girl, so brave and independent, had slipped into his heart without him noticing. He held her briefly in his arms. "All right, two days. Be very careful, Adèle. What you are doing is very dangerous."

Adelaide smiled up at him. "My just being here is dangerous," she said.

He kissed her then, a hard possessive kiss, before he let her go, and turning away disappeared into the night.

Marie Launay sat Julien at the table and gave him a bowl of warm soup. The little boy took the bowl in his hands and, tilting it to his lips, didn't put it down again until it was empty. Then he took the piece of bread she had put beside him and wiped the bowl round and round until it was spotless. Adelaide, watching, realised just how hungry the family must have become shut away for days in the cellar. No wonder the child was so small for his age, small and filthy. Marie filled a tin bath with warm water and sitting him in it she scrubbed his skinny body from head to toe, and when he was clean Adelaide took him into the bed beside her. To her surprise he fell instantly asleep and as she lay next to him, listening to his quiet breathing, she thought about the coming day.

Soon after dawn the next morning, Adelaide slipped Julien into the child seat of the bicycle and they set off. As Julien had devoured the egg and milk Marie gave him for breakfast, Gerard had replaced the two worn inner tubes on the bike with two slightly less patched ones Marcel had managed to find, and Adelaide had studied Olivier Costeau's papers, memorising his address and date of birth. She had parted Julien's hair on the right and combed it forward into the quiff shown in the photograph.

"There's some similarity," she said, showing the picture to Marie, "if you don't look too hard!"

She had impressed upon Julien that today he was going to be called Olivier. "I shall call you Olivier," she told him, "and if anyone asks you your name, you must tell them it's Olivier. We'll make a game of it. Every time I say, 'OK, Olivier' you must say 'Yes, Auntie'. OK, Olivier?"

He looked at her for a moment and then responded hesitantly. "Yes, Auntie."

Adelaide beamed at him. "Bravo, Olivier."

"Take something for later," Marie said, and Adelaide took two apples from the Launays' meagre store and put them in her shoulder bag.

Adelaide pedalled along the track that skirted the village. Even though he was small, Julien's weight made it hard going along the bumpy track. Adelaide was soon puffing, but she dare not stop. The further away they were before anyone saw them, the better. Once they were clear of the village and on the road to Albert the going got easier, and they began to make better time. The country was comparatively flat, and though on occasion she had to get off and walk, pushing the bike up a slope, the hills were not steep. There was no traffic at first, but as they began to get closer to Albert, they met farm carts, other bicycles and even an occasional car.

On reaching the railway station, Adelaide dismounted and lifted Julien out of his seat. She bent down to him and spoke softly. "OK, Olivier?" He looked at her for a moment, his big eyes solemn in his pale face, and then whispered back, "Yes, Auntie."

"Good boy," she said. "Come on, let's find the train." She chained her old bike to a railing and headed to the ticket office.

A train came steaming in just as they reached the platform, and Adelaide was able to lift Julien into a compartment, clambering aboard behind him. She sat in a corner and put the small boy on her lap. With her arm protectively round him, she whispered, "OK, Olivier?" and the child snuggled against her, murmuring, "Yes, Auntie."

Today the train was nothing like as full as it had been last time Adelaide had travelled to Amiens. To her dismay a German officer also got into the compartment, who, from his insignia, Adelaide knew to be a captain in the SS. It was enough to deter others from joining them and when the train finally pulled out of the station they were the only people in the compartment.

For a while they all sat in silence, and then, trying to sound natural, Adelaide began to talk to Julien, pointing out things from the window as they chugged along.

"Look, Olivier," she said, "there's a market down there. Can you see all the people? Olivier, look at the man fishing! Look, Olivier, there's a dog chasing some sheep. What a bad dog he is!"

"Would your little boy like some chocolate?"

The question jerked Adelaide's attention from the world beyond the railway carriage, back to the officer, sitting opposite.

"I'm sorry, Monsieur?" Adelaide kept her voice even and polite.

"I said, would your little boy like some chocolate? I have some here." He held out a bar of chocolate, still in its wrapping.

"You're very kind," Adelaide began, "but . . ."

"Please, Madame, take it for him." The captain smiled, still holding out the chocolate.

"Thank you," Adelaide said. "You're very generous." She took the chocolate and broke a piece off. As she handed it to the child she reminded him to be polite. "Say thank you, Olivier."

"Yes, Auntie," Julien replied dutifully, but he didn't say thank you. Adelaide popped the piece of chocolate into his mouth so that he wouldn't say anything else, before speaking herself. "I'm sorry, he's very shy."

"I know how it is," the man agreed. "I have a son of my own about the same age, Kurt. When you want him to be quiet he never stops, prattling on about anything and everything, but when you want him to speak up he goes all shy."

396

Adelaide tried to hand back the rest of the chocolate bar, but the soldier shook his head. "No, keep it. Give him some more later . . . or have some yourself."

Adelaide smiled. "Thank you. I'll keep it for him. It'll be a special treat." She settled Julien more comfortably on her lap, and turned her head again to the window.

"Are you going to Amiens?" asked the German.

"Yes." Adelaide was extremely unwilling to be drawn into conversation with the man, but neither did she want to arouse his suspicions. "Yes, we are."

"To visit family?"

Adelaide hesitated, better not to invent family and come unstuck somehow, better to stick with the cover story. After all it was perfectly feasible, and she need not show him the letter.

"No," she replied. "I am taking my nephew to the hospital. He has something wrong with his eyes."

"Oh, poor child, he does look very pale. My son Kurt is very strong, and big for his age." He reached into his pocket and brought out a creased photograph showing a woman smiling into the camera, a young boy held in her arms, reaching out towards the photographer with one hand, the other firmly round his mother's neck. "He will have a brother or sister very soon."

It was clear to Adelaide that the German was homesick for his family and she encouraged him to talk about them, thus directing the conversation away from her and Julien. When at last the train steamed into Amiens Station she felt she knew almost all there was to know about the man's family and was very relieved that they had arrived.

She got to her feet, keeping firm hold on Julien's hand. "OK, Olivier?"

"Yes, Auntie."

The officer got up as well. "I have a car waiting for me here," he said. "I will drive you to the hospital."

"Oh, no, really, please don't trouble," Adelaide began, "we'll be fine . . ."

"It's no trouble, Madame," he insisted, and getting down from the train ahead of her turned back to lift Julien down. The boy clung to Adelaide, his face buried in her skirt, and she could feel that he was rigid with fear. Very gently she reassured him. "It's all right, Olivier. It's all right." She glanced up at the captain who still stood with his arms extended to take the boy.

"Thank you, Monsieur, but I can manage."

As if he hadn't heard her, the German reached up and pulled Julien out of her grasp and then set him down on the platform, before extending his hand to help her down as well.

"My car will be waiting outside," he said. "Come along."

Adelaide was about to protest again when she saw that there was a documents check at the barrier, so she simply gathered Julien up into her arms. "You're very kind." They followed the officer to the barrier and, when it was obvious that she was with him, followed in his wake when he was waved through. As they came out into the open she saw a sleek black car, similar to the one Colonel Hoch drove around in, and a chill ran through her. The waiting driver was leaning on the bonnet, but the moment he saw the captain he leapt to attention with a smart "Heil Hitler!" and opened the door.

The captain ushered them in ahead of him, and, unable to do anything else, Adelaide slid into the back seat and drew Julien safely into her arms. She broke off another piece of the precious chocolate and put it into his mouth, the wondrous taste silencing him. Adelaide could only pray that he stayed silent until they were set down. The captain gave some instructions to the driver and then got in beside them. As they drove through the streets, people averted their eyes from the car flying swastika flags. No one wanted to see who had been picked up this time.

"You really have been most kind," Adelaide said when they reached the hospital and the car came to a halt. She opened the door and put Julien out onto the pavement. Slipping out herself, she turned back and smiled at the captain, still sitting, she thanked God, in the back of the car. "Thank you very much, Monsieur."

It was with profound relief that she shut the door and saw the car slide away to disappear round the corner. Taking Julien's hand she moved quickly away from the hospital doorway, and turned into a side street, for fear that the car could simply be turning round and might come back the same way.

"Not far, Olivier," she said brightly as they set off along the narrow street. "OK?"

"Yes, Auntie," came the dutiful reply.

And he's only four, thought Adelaide despondently.

Father Bernard greeted them warmly, and Julien was soon ensconced in Madame Papritz's kitchen.

399

"Any problems?" asked the priest quietly as they watched the little boy tuck into yet more food.

Adelaide told him about the German who had been so kind to Julien.

"They're not all monsters," Father Bernard said with a sigh. "Many of them are perfectly decent men who'd rather be at home with their families."

"Well," replied Adelaide, "I was thinking how ironic it would be, if we'd been caught because of a German officer's kindness." She thought of the dark, ruthless face of Colonel Hoch and shuddered. They were two very different men. "But he'd have changed his tune if he'd realised that he had an escaping Jew in his car."

Though she had not eaten all day, Adelaide refused food from Madame Papritz. "I'll eat when I get home again," she said, loath to take any more of the household's precious rations. "Here, you'd better have these," and she handed over the two apples and half the remaining chocolate for Julien. The rest of it she kept to give Jacques, the next day.

"I should be back again tomorrow, if all goes well," she promised the priest as she took her leave. "I can't leave you the papers I have for Julien as I need them for Jacques tomorrow, but once he is safely here you can keep them."

Father Bernard blessed her and wished her God's speed, and she set off back to the station.

She reached the Launays' farm without any problem and sat in the kitchen to eat the bean stew that Marie had made. She wished that she'd been going to see Marcel; to tell him how the journey had gone, about

400

the captain and the chocolate. She had told the Launays nothing except that Julien was safe.

They, however, had plenty to tell her. As they'd thought, Étienne and Albertine had been arrested by the Germans, but had since been released. Gerard had met Étienne in the village and heard what had happened to them.

"The Germans came and searched the farm," Étienne had said, "and then they dragged us up to the cottage. Virtually taken that apart they had, but we'd been back and cleared the loft, so there was no sign it had been used lately. They took us to their headquarters and that Major Thielen asked us some questions, whether we'd seen anyone near there, that kind of thing. We said we hadn't seen anything, and eventually he let us go."

"You can thank God it was Major Thielen who asked the questions," Gerard said. "Different matter if it had been Hoch!"

"Have they been to you?" asked Étienne.

"Not yet," replied Gerard glumly. "But no doubt they will."

When he got home Gerard found German soldiers in the process of searching his farm and outbuildings. Marie was sitting on a chair in the kitchen, watched over by a young soldier holding a rifle. She leapt to her feet as Gerard came in and the young man shouted at her to sit down again.

"It is my husband," Marie explained. The soldier motioned with the rifle to the other chair at the table, and Gerard sat down.

"How long have they been here?" Gerard asked softly.

"Not talk!" shouted the soldier, waving his rifle at them. "Not talk!"

The search of the farm revealed nothing, and with a warning that they should report any strangers they saw in the area, the soldiers departed to look elsewhere.

"But they'll be back," sighed Gerard. "And next time they'll be looking for Fernand. It won't be long before they realise he's gone missing."

As darkness fell, Adelaide was again crouched above the grating. She dropped the signal twigs through the grille and it was raised at once from below.

"He's safe," she said as Joseph Auclon's head appeared. "Is Jacques ready?"

"Yes, he's ready," replied Joseph with a sigh. He ducked down into the cellar and moments later lifted his tearful second son out of the hole. With the admonition, "Remember, do what Mademoiselle Antoinette tells you," he lowered his head again and Adelaide was able to slide the grating into place. The little boy stood beside her, shaking, as she hid the entrance again. Then she took his hand and led him quickly away. As they hurried past the convent, a pale face looked down from a window. Intent upon reaching the shelter of the trees, Adelaide didn't look up, didn't see the eyes watching her from its shadows.

"We must be very quiet, Jacques," Adelaide whispered once they were hidden among the trees. She crouched down so her face was at his level and

402

murmured to him. "Don't be scared, Jacques. Just be a good boy and hold my hand."

"I want Maman," wailed the child, his voice reedy and thin, but oh so loud in the darkness.

Adelaide put her arms round him and hugged him tightly. "I know you do, *chéri*, and you'll see her very soon, I promise. But now you have to come with me so we can go and find Julien." She reached into her pocket and found a small piece of the chocolate she had saved for him. "Here, try this." She slipped the square into his mouth and at once his crying ceased as he tasted the sweetness. "Come on, now," she whispered.

They reached the farm without meeting anyone and it was with relief that Adelaide handed the little boy over to Marie who gave him hot food, something he hadn't had for months, before they bathed him and put him to bed, where, like his twin the previous night, he fell asleep at once.

In the morning Adelaide dressed him and did his hair. She taught him the "OK Olivier?" game, and although he still had a tendency to be tearful, she put him onto the back of the bicycle and set off. When they reached the station in Albert, they found there was a check being made on all papers. Adelaide bought their tickets and then waited well clear of the barrier in the hope that the checkpoint would be closed before she needed to go through. She was out of luck. The man in the ticket office had said that a train was due very soon, and she couldn't risk missing it. Heaven only knew when there'd be another.

She knelt down and spoke to Jacques. "We're going onto the platform now, Olivier," she said gently, and when the child didn't react she paused. "What's your name?" she asked.

"Jacques," he replied.

"No, chéri, not today. Your name is Olivier, remember? Olivier."

"Olivier," the child repeated obediently. Then he looked across at the gendarmes who were checking the papers. "I don't like those men."

Adelaide felt her heart beat faster, but she soothed as calmly as she could. "They're nice men. They won't hurt you . . . but if they ask you your name what will you say?"

"Jacques," replied the boy, a note of surprise in his voice.

Adelaide was at her wits' end. They had to pass the barrier and the checkpoint, she could only hope they wouldn't speak to Jacques at all. She gave him another piece of chocolate.

She joined the queue and when at last her turn came she was faced with a bespectacled, elderly man who looked at her and addressed her gruffly. "Well, who have we got here?" He took her proffered papers and glanced at them.

"Hold my hand, Olivier," she said sharply, as she felt the little boy move behind her. "We don't want you to get lost."

The man looked up, still holding their papers. "Where are you going, Mademoiselle?"

"To Amiens, Monsieur," Adelaide answered, and when he appeared to be waiting for more knew she must explain. "Olivier has to go to the hospital there."

"Why the hospital there? Why not the one here?" The man peered at her through his thick spectacles.

"He has something wrong with his eyes," she replied. "He has to see the eye specialist there." She waited. The man still held their papers, but she could hear the train chuffing into the station behind her. When he didn't hand them back she pressed him. "Please, Monsieur, we shall miss the train."

The man grunted and handed the papers back. "Go on," he said, and removing his glasses rubbed his own red-rimmed eyes. "Get him to his eye doctor, or he'll end up with eyes like mine."

Almost weak with relief, Adelaide dragged Jacques across the platform and bundled him into a carriage already full.

"There's no room for two," someone grumbled, but Adelaide responded immediately. "That's all right, Olivier can sit on my knee."

The journey to Amiens was uneventful. Adelaide sat crammed in between an old woman with a huge basket on her lap and a young thin man, whose elbow dug into her for much of the time. People got on and off at various stations, and by the time they reached Amiens, Adelaide had managed to secure a window seat and was able to amuse Jacques as she had Julien, pointing out things through the window. When the train pulled into the station, she clambered down with Jacques in her arms and moved towards the exit. There was no checkpoint there today and she was just breathing a sigh of relief that she was on the last step of her journey when a hand touched her arm. "Good morning, Mademoiselle. Here again?"

Adelaide spun round to find herself facing the German captain she'd met the day before. She felt the colour drain from her face, but the captain was bending down to speak to Jacques. "Hello, young man. And how are you today?"

Jacques simply stared at him, and the German went on. "Still too shy to talk, I see." He turned his attention back to Adelaide, who was struggling to regain control of her features. "What did the doctor say yesterday?"

"He . . . he . . . er . . . had a look and then he put some drops into Olivier's eyes. We have to go back again today so that he can look again."

"I see, well let's hope he can discover something this time, it's a long way for you come each day." He broke off, his attention diverted to someone or something behind Adelaide's back. "Excuse me," he murmured and strode off across the platform. Adelaide took Jacques by the hand and hurried him out of the station, only glancing back as they turned into the street. The captain was greeting another SS officer who had just got off the train. It was Colonel Hoch. He didn't appear to have seen Adelaide, would probably not have recognised her at this distance anyway, but it was all she could do not to gather Jacques up into her arms and make a run for it. The same sleek black car was outside the station, the same driver leaning against it. Adelaide, walking as unhurriedly as she could, turned down the first side street she came to, fighting the urge for a backward glance, a glance that might have revealed her face to Hoch as he emerged from the station.

Once he was reunited with Julien, Jacques became a different child. He became animated, smiling and chatting in some sort of private language.

Perhaps, thought Adelaide as she watched them, they miss each other more than they do their parents. The close bond of twins. She hoped they did for she was pretty sure that they weren't going to see their parents for a very long time . . . if ever.

"I'll get them moved on to the convent in Paris as soon as I can," Father Bernard said. "I have contacts who can do that for me."

"I've only the one set of papers," Adelaide reminded him.

"I know, but they're a start and I can probably sort out another set, given time."

"And when the parents come? If they come."

"I'll get them moved to a safe house," said the priest. "We'll try and get them there right away, but really nowhere's safe for them these days."

Adelaide slipped away without saying goodbye to the boys. They were sitting up at the table, prattling away to each other and she left them to Madame Papritz.

"Here's something for them," she said to Father Bernard, and handed over the last of the precious chocolate.

CHAPTER
TWENTY-ONE

Adelaide approached the station with extreme caution. She could not afford to be seen either by the captain, without "Olivier", or by Colonel Hoch. It was early evening and the station was busy with people going home from work. There were plenty of German uniforms among the crowds on the platform, and so she slipped into a ladies-only waiting room, out of sight. She prepared a story about how Olivier had been kept in the hospital in case she had the misfortune to meet the captain yet again, but in the event she didn't need it. When the train finally steamed into the station, she hurried out, keeping among the crowds, and although she kept a sharp eye out for either of the German officers, she saw neither. She reached Albert in safety, despite a document check on the train, and collecting her bicycle pedalled slowly to St Croix. The nervous energy she had expended taking the two little boys to Amiens left her feeling exhausted, and it was all she could do to make it back to the farm.

"Safe?" asked Marie.

"Safe," replied Adelaide. "For the moment."

That evening she went to meet Marcel as planned. When she tapped on the back door of the café, it was Madame Juliette who let her in.

"He's in the bar," Madame Juliette said. "I'll let him know you're here." She disappeared through the connecting door into the café. Moments later there was another tap on the back door and Marcel was there.

"Safe?" he asked. And when Adelaide nodded, he gathered her into his arms. "Thank God. Thank God you're safe."

For a moment Adelaide allowed herself to rest against him, feeling the strength of his arms around her, and then she pulled away and dropped into a chair.

"The children are safe," she said, "but we still have to get the parents away."

"Tell me how it went," Marcel said, sitting down across the table from her. "Any problems?"

Adelaide had longed to tell Marcel the details of the two journeys, to share the relief of having succeeded, but now she held back. It was safer for them all if he didn't know exactly where the children had gone. He knew they'd been on a train, so she contented herself with telling him how she had had to share a compartment with an SS captain.

"They've been searching the village," she added. "Taken people in for questioning, but so far they haven't kept anyone." She looked across at him gravely. "They've been out to us, but they didn't find the well. Surely they'll be looking for Fernand by now. They must realise that he's disappeared."

"I shouldn't worry too much about him," said Marcel reassuringly. "They may guess what's happened to him, but I doubt if they'll pursue it. They'll soon recruit someone else to take his place."

Madame Juliette reappeared with a carafe of wine and two glasses, which she set on the table before she left them alone again. Marcel poured them a glass each, and then, tasting his, pulled a face.

Adelaide laughed at his expression of disgust, and took a sip of hers. "It's better than nothing!"

"I'm not sure it is," Marcel groaned.

"I'll go back to the convent tomorrow," Adelaide told him, "and make the arrangements to get the parents away. Reverend Mother will be glad when they've gone. She wouldn't give them up, of course, but she doesn't want them there. After Sister Eloise was arrested, Hoch threatened the convent with reprisals if he finds them hiding anyone else." Adelaide was silent for a moment, thoughtful. "Will you get a message to London? Tell them I think I've done all I can here and ask what they want me to do next. I don't mind staying if there is something else they need me to do, but we shan't be able to use the convent as a safe house as we'd hoped."

"I'll get Bertrand to send that on his next transmission," Marcel promised. "Now, tell me what you need me to do."

"I'm not sure yet," replied Adelaide. "I have all the help I need while they are in the convent, it's getting them to Albert so that they can catch the train that is the difficult bit. I know they could walk, but they'd almost certainly be picked up. We really need some sort of transport to get them out of the village."

Madame Juliette came in and they told her their problem.

"You can bring them here," she said. "If you can get them to me under cover of darkness, they can catch the weekly bus into Albert in the morning. No one will look twice at a nun and a priest on the bus."

"That'd be very dangerous," Adelaide said dubiously.

"It is better to be bold, as you were with the children," Madame Juliette asserted. "You're less suspicious if you're moving about in the daylight, with nothing to hide."

"But hiding them here overnight?"

Madame Juliette shrugged. "Who will look here?"

"It's probably the best we can do for them," Marcel said, and Adelaide reluctantly agreed.

On her way to meet Marcel, Adelaide had been to the convent. Entering by the courtyard gate she stopped by the grating, and while retying her shoe had pushed a note through the grille, telling the Auclons that their children were safe. She also warned them to wait for her signal on the inner door the following evening.

Sister Marie-Marc was in the kitchen when Adelaide arrived at the back door, and was delighted to see her.

"Are you coming back to work?" she asked. "Is your aunt better?"

Adelaide smiled at this enthusiastic reception and said that she was. "That's what I've come to say. I'll be back tomorrow morning, but Sister," Adelaide lowered her voice, "please could you tell Reverend Mother that I would like to speak to her when I get here."

Sister Marie-Marc nodded conspiratorially. "Yes, I will tell her."

Next morning Mother Marie-Pierre sent to the kitchen and summoned Adelaide to her study. When Adelaide entered the room in answer to the bell, Mother Marie-Pierre had one simple question. "Have they gone?"

"The children, yes. The parents, tonight if you'll help me."

"What do you want me to do?" asked Reverend Mother.

Adelaide outlined her plan. "When the sisters are all in bed, I will come to the back door and you must let me in. We'll go down to the cellar and move the furniture away from the door so that the Auclons can come out that way. I will bring the cassock that Father Bernard has given me, and you said you could provide a nun's habit for Madame."

Mother Marie-Pierre nodded. "Yes, I can do that. Then what?"

"Then we get them dressed and I take them out of the back door and they're gone." Adelaide smiled across at her. "Then you can relax, the convent will be safe."

"Where are you going to take them in the middle of the night? How will they get to Amiens?" asked her aunt.

"Better you don't know. We'll try and get the habit back to you later."

412

"I've still got these." Mother Marie-Pierre opened the door of her desk and produced some documents. "These are Sister Marie-Joseph's papers. Of course she is much younger than Madame Auclon, but up until now the soldiers have only looked at the habit and not the person inside it."

Their plans made as far as they were able, Adelaide returned to the kitchen and finished her morning's work. Sister Marie-Marc looked at her speculatively, but Adelaide merely smiled at her and went down to fetch the coal. They had agreed they would need someone else to help, and the obvious choice was Sister Marie-Marc.

"I'll speak to her nearer the time," promised Mother Marie-Pierre. "She can leave the back gate unlocked for you, and keep watch while we get them changed and ready to go."

Adelaide knocked gently on the back door of the convent that night and it was immediately opened by an excited-looking Sister Marie-Marc, who beckoned her in and then closed the door behind her. The kitchen was in darkness, except for a crack of light edging the cellar door.

"I'll go back to keep watch," the nun whispered. "Mother's already down in the cellar."

Adelaide nodded and went down the cellar steps. Below she found Mother Marie-Pierre carefully removing the furniture from the outside of the hidden door. She greeted Adelaide with a tired smile and a kiss on the cheek, the first sign of affection she had shown since she learnt that Adelaide was using the convent cellars for her own purposes. Together they shifted the larger pieces of furniture and then Adelaide tapped the agreed code on the door. They heard the bolt being drawn back and then the door eased open to reveal the two scarecrows that were Joseph and Janine Auclon.

Mother Marie-Pierre drew in a sharp breath when she saw them and the state to which they had been reduced. The Auclons had been in hiding too long. They were half-starved, having given most of any food they'd obtained to their children. Their eyes had sunk into faces that were gaunt and grey. They were dirty, their hair matted, their bodies malodorous and foul, their clothes in rags, and Adelaide and Sarah had to get them clean enough to pass unnoticed in broad daylight.

"Adèle, quickly, fetch hot water from the stove."

Adelaide nodded and ran back up to the kitchen and drew off some water from the large cauldron that stood, ever ready, on the back of the range. She returned to the cellar to find Mother Marie-Pierre handing out food that she brought down with her. When Adelaide returned with a second bowl of water, Joseph retired to the far corner, and, with a razor Mother Marie-Pierre had brought from the hospital, attacked the full beard that he now had, cutting it back ruthlessly with a pair of scissors before finally shaving it away. Adelaide passed over the cassock she had brought, and leaving him to get cleaned up as best he could, she and Mother Marie-Pierre set about turning Janine Auclon into a nun. It all took time. Too much time, Adelaide thought, as she fetched yet more hot water for Janine to scrub away the grime. It's taking too long, far too long.

414

Adelaide looked anxiously at her watch as she helped cut Janine's hair short enough to fit under the wimple, muttering, "We should be out of here by now."

"Is there soup in the pantry?" Mother Marie-Pierre asked softly, and Adelaide nodded. "Yes, usually."

"Then go and heat some up. We have to get something warm inside them."

Adelaide found the soup, and having heated it brought it down to the cellar in two large cups. The Auclons had made some progress, and she found Joseph now clean-shaven, his hair cut short above his ears, dressed in his cassock. It was too short for him, and his feet poked out from the bottom, displaying his bony ankles and worn leather shoes.

But at least his shoes are black, Adelaide thought as she handed him the cup.

Janine was wearing the habit, and the wimple fitted closely round her head and face. She too grasped the cup of soup in her hand and began to drink it down greedily.

Suddenly they heard footsteps coming down the cellar steps. They all froze, knowing there was nothing they could do to escape. Sister Marie-Marc appeared.

"What is it, Sister?" Mother Marie-Pierre said sharply.

"You were so long," Sister Marie-Marc said. "I was worried something had gone wrong."

"Nothing's gone wrong," snapped her superior. "Go back upstairs and keep watch."

"Yes, Mother." Sister Marie-Marc disappeared into the darkness, and Reverend Mother turned her attention to Janine's hood. She had just put it on when there were more footsteps, running this time, and Mother Marie-Marc reappeared in the cellar, her eyes wide.

"Mother," she cried, "Germans. All creeping up round the convent. I saw them from the landing window. All round the house."

Adelaide looked at Reverend Mother. "I must have been followed."

"Never mind that now," the nun replied. "Let's think."

She stood for a moment, her eyes squeezed closed and then turned to the terrified Auclons. "Come with me. You, Sister Marie-Marc, go back to bed. Adèle, out through the grating."

"Where are you going?" asked Adelaide.

"To the chapel," replied her aunt. "It's our only hope. Now go, both of you."

Sister Marie-Marc obediently scuttled up the stairs, and Adelaide watched as Mother Marie-Pierre grabbed the dazed couple by the hands and hurried them up into the convent building.

"Go," she said over her shoulder to her niece. "I'll look after them."

Adelaide scrambled up the ladder to the grating, and listening hard heard nothing from the outside. Cautiously she lifted the grille enough to see out, and immediately ducked down again. Standing only a few yards away, his rifle trained on the courtyard gate, stood a German soldier. He didn't appear to have seen the hidden grating, he was concentrating on the gate.

Adelaide lowered herself back into the cellar and looked up at her escape route, now effectively blocked. The soldier hadn't seen her, but there was no way she could get past him. If she went that way she'd have to kill him, and although she hadn't seen any others, he wouldn't be alone. No, there was no escape that way, she'd have to go back through the convent. Quietly she closed the door of the hiding place and stole back up to the kitchen, shutting the cellar door behind her. She didn't lock it. That would be pointless, a locked door wasn't going to keep them out.

As she emerged into the kitchen there was a thunderous pounding on the front door, the doorbell pealing and a loud voice shouting. "Open up! Open up!"

Four minutes, or at the most five since Mother Marie-Pierre had hurried the Auclons away from the cellar. What had she done with them? She'd said the chapel, but Adelaide knew that would be as thoroughly searched as anywhere else. She drew back from the hall, her mind racing as she considered the various places she might hide, and finally ducked into the refectory. There was nowhere to hide in the stark room, so Adelaide left the door ajar and stood behind it to watch the hall through the crack.

A minute later lights flooded on and Sister Celestine appeared at the head of the stairs, dressed in an old blue dressing gown, a shawl thrown over her head. She stumbled down the stairs to the door, and, as another tattoo commenced on the outside, began to draw back the bolts and the great chain that secured the door for the night.

The moment she slipped the chain, the door was flung open, and she was knocked backwards as Colonel Hoch strode into the hall, ordering his men to search the building.

"And bring the reverend mother to me," he roared, as the soldiers who had flooded in behind him fanned out round the building.

"Good evening, Colonel." The voice was quiet and steady. "What is it you want that you disturb us in the middle of the night?"

The colonel looked round and saw Reverend Mother, standing at the mouth of an inner passage, looking at him, unflinchingly. He strode across the hall.

"Want? I'll tell you what I want. I want whoever you are hiding here, that's what I want."

"Hiding?"

"Don't play the innocent with me, woman," snarled Hoch. He turned to the men who were at his back, and snapped at them. "Search the place, every cupboard, every corner. Get them all out of bed." He turned back to Reverend Mother. "Why aren't you in bed asleep like all the others?"

"I was in the chapel, keeping watch with Our Lord," Mother Marie-Pierre replied calmly.

"In the chapel." Hoch's eyes bored into her. "Right, I'll start there. Show me the way."

Mother Marie-Pierre inclined her head graciously, as if she had a choice. "Very well, Colonel. Please follow me." She turned back down the passage and, with the colonel hard on her heels, led the way through the convent to the chapel. When she reached it, Hoch thrust her aside and flung the door open. The chapel was in darkness except for the flickering candles on the Lady Chapel altar and the red glow of the sanctuary light above the high altar. Hoch turned abruptly. "Turn on the lights," he ordered, and stepping round him to the switches on the wall Mother Marie-Pierre switched them on. The electric light flooding the chapel seemed harsh after the softer light of the candles, and its brightness revealed one of the sisters, lying face down, cruciform on the floor in front of the altar.

"What's she doing?" demanded Hoch.

"Penance for her sins," replied Mother Marie-Pierre. "She will remain like that all night in atonement."

"She will not," retorted Hoch. He stepped forward and prodded the prone figure with the toe of his boot. "You, nun, get up."

The nun got shakily to her knees and then to her feet, and stood with downcast eyes, her hands folded into her sleeves.

"What's your name?" demanded the colonel.

The nun did not reply, and the man shouted. "Answer me! Are you deaf?"

"No, Colonel," Reverend Mother intervened. "Sister Angelique is under a vow of silence until she has finished her penance. Wait outside the door, Sister," she added. "The colonel wants to search the chapel."

Sister Angelique gave a tiny bob and went out into the corridor.

The colonel began his search, and when he reached the vestry he gave a cry of satisfaction as the opened door revealed a priest kneeling at a prie-dieu.

"And who is this, lurking in the vestry? Come out here where I can see you properly. Name?"

"Father Yves Belvoir," replied the priest.

"And what the hell are you doing in a convent chapel in the middle of the night?"

"Preparing to say Mass for the sisters first thing in the morning," stammered the priest nervously.

"Father Yves is a visiting priest," Mother Marie-Pierre said.

The colonel stared at the priest for several moments, taking in the short cassock and the worn-out shoes, then he strode to the door of the chapel and called in the two men who were waiting in the passage.

"Strip this man," he said, his voice icily calm, "and see if he is a Jew."

The men grabbed the priest and without hesitation ripped at the cassock, pulling it open to reveal the threadbare trousers and dirty shirt which were concealed beneath it.

"Wait!" Hoch's voice was a whiplash. The two men stepped back and waited. "Not very well dressed for a priest, are you?" Hoch remarked, touching the grubby shirt with a fastidious finger. "Take off your trousers."

The priest hesitated and Hoch spoke again, his voice soft and threatening. "Take off your trousers, you snivelling little Jew, and we shall all see the proof of what you are."

420

"Colonel, this is the house of God," protested Mother Marie-Pierre, and then gasped as she saw that the order was being backed up with the colonel's pistol.

"Then we'll take him out into the hall. We'll divest him of his clothing in the recreation room. Then all the sisters will see that they've been harbouring a filthy Jew." He turned to his men. "Take his trousers off and bring him to the recreation room. Let's give them all a thrill." He laughed and his men laughed with him, as they ripped off not only the tattered trousers, but the ragged underwear underneath, leaving Joseph Auclon standing clad only in his shirt, his genitals clearly visible.

Mother Marie-Pierre averted her eyes as if to preserve the man's dignity, but he had none left; his humiliation was complete. Hoch regarded him with contempt and the soldiers sniggered at the pathetic creature they had revealed.

"This is the man you were hiding," Hoch said to her. "This scum. Don't look away, Reverend Mother." Hoch emphasised the word Reverend. "It's too late for that. All you nuns shall look at this piece of shit before we take him away, so that you know what a Jew looks like. So that you won't make the same mistake again. So you won't mistake a snivelling Jew for a Catholic priest. Follow me."

Hoch strode out of the chapel, followed by the men leading Joseph Auclon, naked below the waist, his arms pulled hard behind his back. Stunned, Mother Marie-Pierre followed, unable to do anything else. She had known there was little chance that Joseph and

Janine would not be discovered, but she had done her best in the few moments that she'd had. She saw Janine, Sister Angelique, standing in the shadows, and reached for her hand, pulling her gently along behind her. The best place to hide her now was among all the other nuns. They would know she didn't belong, of course, but Mother Marie-Pierre thought she knew her sisters well enough to be sure that no one would give the woman up to the Germans.

When they reached the recreation room, they found the nuns already gathered there, rounded up by Hoch's soldiers. There was an audible gasp as Joseph was led into the room and made to stand on the dais at the front. Almost as one they turned away, covering their eyes, and Mother Marie-Pierre was able to push the terrified Janine into the room beside Sister Marie-Marc.

"Look after Sister Angelique," she hissed. Sister Marie-Marc, wide-eyed, nodded and stepped in front of her, so that she was concealed from direct view and became just another nun.

Hoch looked round the terrified gathering. "Is this all of them?" he demanded of his sergeant.

"All but one, sir. A bedridden one, who's off her trolley."

"Bring her down. I want her here." He looked across at Sister Marie-Paul. "You," he said. "You run the hospital, don't you?"

"I am in charge of it, yes," Sister Marie-Paul replied, "under Reverend Mother of course."

422

"Ah, yes, Reverend Mother. Well, she's no longer in charge of anything. She will be coming with me." His eyes roved the frightened faces in the room. "I warned you, all of you, that if I found anyone else hidden in your damned convent I would make an example of two of you. Clearly your reverend mother was well aware that this Jew was hiding in the chapel, dressed in the garb of a priest . . . a holy priest of God. Where did those clothes come from, I wonder? No doubt Reverend Mother will tell me . . . in time." He paused to allow these words to sink in. "And now we have to decide who else will pay for this . . ." — he gestured to Joseph Auclon who still stood in front of them — "this piece of foolishness. Reverend Mother, you have defied me and have sheltered enemies of the Reich. Another of these nuns must pay the price . . . so who shall it be?" He walked over to where the novices were cowering together. "One of these young ladies? My men would surely enjoy entertaining one of *them*. Or this old bag," he pointed to Sister St Bruno who at that moment arrived carried in by two burly soldiers and was dumped unceremoniously on the floor. "Or what about the one who was doing penance? She could do her penance in prison in Germany. Where is she? What was she called now? Sister Angelique?"

"But we haven't got . . ." Sister Marie-Paul's exclamation, distinctly heard, died away in the silence.

"Haven't you now?" remarked Hoch. "Well, that is interesting. We'll have a roll call. It appears to me that there are children missing as well. We understood that there was a whole family of Jews to be found. Where are those children I wonder?" He looked across at Mother Marie-Pierre again. "No doubt Reverend Mother will tell us that . . . in time . . . as well." He pointed again to Sister Marie-Paul. "You," he said, "you seem to have some commonsense. You will point out this unknown Sister Angelique to me . . . because if you don't I will send *all* your novices down to the barracks in Albert and let my men have some fun with them." The threat hung in the air, and Sister Marie-Paul's eyes slid round the room, looking at all the sisters gathered there. Sister Marie-Marc stood firmly in front of "Sister Angelique", but there was no point. Sister Marie-Paul saw her at once. "She's over there," she said softly. Hoch followed the line of her gaze, and then pushing Sister Marie-Marc roughly aside grabbed hold of Janine Auclon and dragged her forward.

"So she is," he said gently. He ran his eyes up and down her body. "No obvious way to determine if she's a Jewess," he said. "Not like with her husband, but we could perhaps have a look anyway." And he raised his hand to the neck of her habit.

There was an explosion of rage and Joseph ripped himself free of the hands that still restrained him, flinging himself at Hoch, reaching for the colonel's throat, his fingers grasping, gripping, gouging, until he was dragged away once more, his arm forced so high behind his back that he screamed in pain. Colonel Hoch, shaken by the sudden attack, quickly recovered his dignity and barked out. "Take them away. I'll deal with them later." The soldiers dragged both Auclons out of the room, and Hoch turned to face the nuns

424

once again. Several of them were openly weeping, others were white-faced with fear, no one spoke. Sister Marie-Paul stood erect a little apart from her sisters, across the room from her superior, and Sister St Bruno lay in a heap on the floor at her niece's feet. Ignoring the colonel, Sarah bent down to her aunt and whispered, "Are you all right?"

Sister St Bruno nodded. "Just a little bit bruised," she murmured. "Don't worry about me, Sarah."

Hoch summoned more men and told them to take hold of Mother Marie-Pierre. "And another," he began.

"Take me," cried out Sister St Bruno, "I'll go."

"Shut up, old woman," snapped the colonel, aiming a kick at her. "No one would take you anywhere."

"I'll go," said a voice behind him, and Sister Marie-Marc stepped forward. "If you are determined to arrest two of us, I'll go. I knew they were here."

Hoch gave a contemptuous laugh. "You'll do. Take them away."

Two soldiers grasped the two nuns by the arms and unceremoniously hustled them from the room. As she was forced out into the hall, Sarah heard her aunt cry out, "Courage, Sarah, God is with you. Evil shall not prevail!" She began to chant, " 'Yea though I walk through the valley of the shadow of death, I will fear no evil: for Thou art with me; thy rod and thy staff comfort me . . . '."

Some of the other sisters began to murmur the psalm with her, and Hoch, who was following them out of the recreation room, turned back to where Sister St Bruno still lay crumpled on the floor.

"I told you to shut up," he growled, and with great deliberation he kicked at her head. His jackboot connected with her skull with a sickening crack. The murmuring of the psalm ceased abruptly as, without even glancing down, he turned and once again strode from the room.

Hoch deposited all his prisoners in the cells at the gendarmerie, where Mother Marie-Pierre had visited Sister Eloise before she was taken away. The nuns were put in a cell together, but they had no sight of the Auclons.

"What will happen to us now?" asked Sister Marie-Marc fearfully.

"We shall be questioned, I expect. They'll want to know where the children are."

"Do you know?"

"No." Reverend Mother knew it was vital that Sister Marie-Marc should think that neither of them knew where the children had gone.

"Where is Adèle?" asked Sister Marie-Marc, a little querulously.

"I don't know, Sister. Safe, I pray. All we can do now is commend them all to the Lord's care."

Together the two nuns knelt on the floor of the cell and began to pray, their voices in unison as they, too, began chanting the psalms. A bellow for silence from the guard outside went unheeded as they continued to call on their Lord.

CHAPTER
TWENTY-TWO

Adelaide had known there was very little chance of evading capture, but she had remained behind the refectory door in the hope that she might be able to slip out through the hall if it were left empty. She almost made it. Two soldiers had pushed the door wide, striding into the refectory and switching on the lights. One began searching beneath the tables that stretched the length of the room, while the other had climbed up onto the dais and peered behind the lectern where the nun on duty would read during meals. Neither was watching the door, and Adelaide edged her way round it. She was almost into the empty hallway when the man on the dais looked up and saw her. With a shout he was after her, chasing down the length of the room, knocking chairs aside as he came, his mate right behind him. As they pelted out into the hall, Adelaide sprinted down the corridor. A soldier emerging from another door reached out to grab her, but with a short, sharp punch to his solar plexus that left him doubled up and gasping, Adelaide evaded him and dashed into the kitchen, slamming the door behind her. It gave her the few seconds' respite she needed.

The back door, left open for her earlier by Sister Marie-Marc, was still unlocked, and now she flung it wide, before darting down the cellar steps, closing that door softly behind her. She raced to the secret room, closing and bolting its door before climbing the old ladder once again. She listened intently through the grating. She heard the two soldiers storm out into the yard, heard them shout to the guards at the gate and heard an answering call. She risked raising the grille enough to peer out.

The guards outside had run towards the convent gate, calling back to the men who had chased after her and were now searching the courtyard.

It was now or never. Adelaide eased the grille aside and hoisted herself up through the hole, sliding as quietly as she could on her belly away from the gate into the sheltering darkness of the bushes beyond. She knew she had to get away quickly; it wouldn't be long before they found the hidden room; the locked doors wouldn't hold them; they would realise she was away and the search would be on.

Once round the corner of the wall she was out of immediate view, and she risked coming to her feet, running at the crouch away from the convent, and to begin with away from the village. Half a mile further on she circled back, crossed the footbridge over the river, and taking the towpath hurried to the end of the twisting lane that led to the back of Juliette's café. In the distance she heard shouting and guessed they had found her escape route. There was little moon as she crept up the lane and one knock on the door had it

428

open. Seeing Adelaide, white-faced and alone, the old lady hauled her inside.

"It's all gone wrong," Adelaide said breathlessly. "German raid on the convent. Don't know if they've caught the Auclons, but they're certainly looking for me."

"Into the cellar," Juliette said, and together they rolled back the rug to open the trapdoor. "I'll watch to see what happens," the old lady promised as Adelaide slipped down into the space below. "Remember, no light!" hissed Juliette as she looked down. "There is a small window, and the light would show. I'll be back."

Adelaide nodded, and ducked down as Juliette lowered the trapdoor over her head. The darkness in the cellar seemed complete, but as her eyes grew accustomed, she realised she could make out the slightly paler rectangle of a window high up in the wall. Hands outstretched, she edged across the small room, feeling her way around some furniture she encountered on the way. She reached the window, but it was too high. She felt for a chair and, dragging it under the window, stood up on its seat and tried to see out. The window, at ground-level outside, was coated in grime, and, she realised, faced out into the alley at the side of the house, giving her a view of absolutely nothing. Frustrated, Adelaide sat down on the chair and waited. It was all she could do. As she sat alone in the darkness wondering what was going on at the convent, whether the Auclons had been found, whether Sarah was safe, she realised a fraction of the living hell that must have been the Auclons' life for the past year, and more extremely, for the past few days. Not knowing what was happening. Not knowing if loved ones were safe. The silence was deep and unbroken. She could hear nothing from the outside world, and had no clue as to what was going on.

How could they have lived weeks and months in this sort of limbo, she wondered? Not knowing. Did they get used to it? Would *I* get used to it?

She felt exhausted, and she tried to relax back into the chair, but she was too strung-up to sleep. The events of the night played over and over in her mind. Could they have got the Auclons clean away if they had been able to take them straight from the cellar? Should they have brought them here before trying to get them cleaned up? Why had the Germans come? Had she been followed to the convent? Was it she who had triggered the raid? The more she thought about the evening, the more she was sure that she had not been followed. So what had made Hoch raid the convent on that particular night? Had he found the Auclons? She was sure that he must have done, and if he had, what had happened to Sarah and the other nuns? She thought of Sister Eloise and shuddered. Surely Hoch wouldn't take a reverend mother from her convent? But she knew, of course, that he would if he wanted to; and he *would* want to, to make an example, to keep people in line. If the local populace defied him in any way, Hoch would make reprisals, and the local populace knew it. It was what made them, despite their grumbling, tolerate the German occupation with comparatively little resistance.

430

Adelaide gave some thought then to her own position. What was she going to do next? She couldn't stay here, that would put Madame Juliette at risk. Did Sarah need her help? Could she, in fact, help Sarah, or would she simply put her in yet more danger? Should she go back to the farm? Would any of the soldiers who had chased her be able to recognise her again? If so, not only would her cover be blown, but it would bring the Launays into more danger, too. Could Marcel get her away, out of the area?

Everything churned round in her mind as she sat entombed in the silent cellar, and she came to no conclusions. "If you're in a tight spot, stay calm and think" had been drummed into her during her training. Well, she was in a tight spot now . . . so, stay calm and think. It all depended, she decided, on what Juliette had discovered. When she knew exactly what had happened, she could begin to make plans.

It was more than an hour before she heard the trapdoor opening and light seeped into the little underground room.

"Adèle, you can come up now," whispered Madame Juliette, and Adelaide gratefully climbed the steps out of the darkness. Blinking in the dim light Juliette had on in the kitchen, Adelaide rubbed her eyes.

"They've taken prisoners to the German HQ," Madame Juliette told her. "Four of them. Almost certainly the two Auclons, and two sisters. I think it was Reverend Mother with another sister. I watched from the upstairs window with the binoculars, but it was very dark and I'm not sure. Poor Joseph, he was stripped naked from the waist down. Janine was wearing a nun's habit, but her head was bare."

"You're sure it was Reverend Mother?"

"Almost," replied Madame Juliette. "But the other sister . . . well, I don't know. Poor Reverend Mother, once they discover she is English, it will be even worse!"

Adelaide stared at the old lady. "How did you know she was English?" she asked.

Madame Juliette shrugged. "I have always known. She came here during the war . . . the last war . . . to nurse with her maid. They came to my café for cakes and tea."

"But who'd tell the Germans that she is English?" demanded Adelaide.

Madame Juliette smiled sadly. "Almost anyone in St Croix," she replied, "if they think it is worth their while. People here want a quiet life. They know there will be reprisals if the Germans are attacked in any way. Few will resist, because they want no bloodshed."

"It doesn't mean that they will inform."

"That is naïve, Adèle. In war everyone looks out for number one. It is human nature. If someone thinks Reverend Mother will cause more trouble, they will tell. The Germans take her away and pouf! The problem has gone."

The two women discussed what Adelaide should do next.

"You must stay here for the rest of the night," asserted Madame Juliette. "They will still be searching for you out there. Did they get a good look at you?"

"I don't know," answered Adelaide. "The corridor isn't well lit and I was running."

Madame Juliette ran her eye over Adelaide's black slacks and jersey. "A change of clothes would help, something bright, and a scarf to cover your hair." She disappeared for a moment or two and then reappeared with a cotton dress, pale blue spattered with daisies, a white cardigan and a white cotton headscarf.

"My daughter's," she said briefly. "In the morning, you will look nothing like the girl in black trousers who ran away. But now," she said firmly, "you must go to bed and sleep. If they come here before morning, we will say you were helping me, were too late for curfew and stayed over. Give me your clothes and I will deal with them. Get up in Rose's dress in the morning."

To her surprise, Adelaide did fall asleep in the little room above the café. Its one tiny window looked out onto the square, and before she slept, Adelaide turned off the light, pulled back the blackout curtains and looked out. Across the square she could see the dark shape of the town hall, but there was no activity there now. Where had they put the prisoners, she wondered? Were they still in the German HQ, or had they been locked up in the police cells for the night, like Sister Eloise had been?

She woke early as the rising sun forced a ray between her curtains to dance on her pillow and finger her face. Once again she peeped between the curtains and looked across the square. The town hall stood silent, its once proud façade draped with two swastika flags, and beneath these, one either side of the door, stood two sentries, rifles in hand, on guard.

Adelaide and Madame Juliette had decided that the first thing to do was to get her safely back to the farm, where she could tell the Launays what had happened. If questioned they had to be telling the same story. Once there, she could change again and go back to the convent, turning up for work as if she knew nothing of the night's events. It would be a risk, but as far as she knew, apart from the three soldiers of course, no one but Sarah and Sister Marie-Marc had seen her the night before. No one there would know she had been involved, and she could find out exactly what had happened. So, half an hour later, dressed in the cotton frock and with the scarf tied over her hair, Adelaide slipped out of Madame Juliette's back door, walked down the alley and headed for the Launays' farm.

"Will you contact Marcel? Get him to come to the farm?" Adelaide asked as she paused inside the kitchen door. "I need to see him soon, so we can decide what to do next."

"I will," agreed Madame Juliette. "Now go . . . and good luck."

The Launays greeted Adelaide with relief, but listened with horror as she related the events of the night.

"You must get away from here," Gerard said. "We will say that you found the country too quiet and have gone to live with relatives in Paris."

"No," Adelaide shook her head, "I must go to the convent as if I know nothing. It'd be more suspicious if

I didn't turn up, and anyway, I have to find out what happened there."

"They were arrested," Gerard said. "You know that from Madame Juliette."

But Adelaide was adamant. "I don't know for sure that it was Reverend Mother and I must find out."

They didn't agree; they knew nothing of the close bond between their "niece", Adèle, and the reverend mother, but they accepted her decision and once she had changed into her normal working clothes, Adelaide set off to the convent.

She found Sister Elisabeth in the kitchen. The nun looked relieved to see her. "Where's Sister Marie-Marc?" Adelaide asked innocently.

Sister Elisabeth shook her head. "Not here today. Sister Marie-Joseph is helping me this morning. Now, Adèle, please bring up some coal. The range is nearly out."

"Of course, Sister," Adelaide replied and picked up the buckets. Once down the cellar steps, she hurried through to the hidden room. The door, which had been battered open, now hung drunkenly from one hinge, and the old ladder lay on the floor.

The grille had been pulled down into place and was covered with something on the outside, so that there was no daylight. It was obvious that they had discovered how she had escaped . . . but did they know who she was?

When she carried the bucket of coal up to the kitchen, Sister Elisabeth was nowhere to be seen, but Adelaide found the novice, Sister Marie-Joseph, washing up the breakfast plates in the scullery. She picked up a tea towel and started on the drying.

"Is Sister Marie-Marc ill?" she asked innocently.

The novice shook her head. "She went with Mother," she whispered.

"With Mother? Where?" Adelaide tried to keep her tone light.

"The Germans took them." The girl's voice shook and Adelaide saw that there were tears running down her face. "And Sister St Bruno, she's dead!"

"Dead!" Adelaide didn't try to hide the horror in her voice. "How did she die? Did she have a heart attack?"

"No," whispered Sister Marie-Joseph. "That German colonel, the one with skulls on his uniform" — her eyes were wide with remembered horror — "he kicked her in the head and she died."

Disbelief and rage hit Adelaide with equal force. She stared at Sister Marie-Joseph incredulously. "What did you say?"

"She was praying . . . out loud . . . the Twenty-third Psalm. He kicked her in the head and then he just walked out. The soldiers took Mother and Sister Marie-Marc and they all left."

"And then what?" demanded Adelaide. "What happened then? Nobody said anything? Nobody did anything?"

"Sister Marie-Paul told us to say and do nothing. She said we didn't want any more trouble from the Germans. She said that from now on we must keep ourselves to ourselves."

"And Sister St Bruno?"

"She's in the chapel. Her funeral Mass is tomorrow."

"Sister!" Sister Elisabeth's voice was sharp as she addressed them from the kitchen doorway. "You're not gossiping, I hope! You know what Mother said." She glowered at Sister Marie-Joseph. "You will remain silent for the rest of the morning," she ordered. "Is that understood?"

"Yes, Sister." Colour flooded the novice's face and she busied herself with the washing-up, plunging her arms into the sink to her elbows and scrubbing the plates as if they were coated in grime.

"Mother would like to see you, Adèle," Sister Elisabeth continued, "in her office."

Stunned by the news of Sister St Bruno's violent death, Adelaide turned, pale-faced, to look at the nun. "Mother . . ." she began.

"Is waiting for you in her office, Adèle. Make haste!"

Knowing that Mother Marie-Pierre was being held in the village, Adelaide approached what had been her office with great unease. When the bell summoned her inside and she opened the door, she was still half-expecting to see Sarah, but her worst fears were realised when she saw that it was Sister Marie-Paul who now sat, grim-faced, behind the desk.

Adelaide allowed her surprise to show. "I'm sorry, Sister," she said, "but Sister Elisabeth said that Mother wanted to see me."

"And so I do," Sister Marie-Paul replied smoothly. "I am Reverend Mother, now, Adèle . . ."

"But Mother Marie-Pierre . . . ?" began Adelaide.

"Mother Marie-Pierre is no longer living in the convent. In her absence, the sisters have chosen me to carry on her work." There was the faintest pause, as if Adelaide might comment, then she went on. "Now, I'll come straight to the point, Adèle, with regard to your position here. I am afraid that is terminated from today. We no longer require your help. I am sure Mother Marie-Pierre warned you that the job would only be temporary." She reached into a cash box that stood on the desk. "Here is what you are owed for this week," she said, handing Adelaide some folded notes. "Please leave the convent now, straight away. I wish you good day, Mademoiselle." Sister Marie-Paul picked up a paper that was in front of her and began reading it; the interview was clearly over.

Being dismissed suited Adelaide very well, but she gave a heavy sigh as she put the money into the pocket of her skirt, and with a quiet "Good day, Mother", she left the room.

As the door closed Sister Marie-Paul looked up again, thoughtfully. Sister Celestine, so often Sister Marie-Paul's eyes and ears within the convent, had reported to her that she had seen Adèle wandering about after curfew. Clearly the girl was up to no good, and Sister Marie-Paul wanted no further trouble with the Germans. Better to get the girl out of the way and arrange other help for Sister Elisabeth in the kitchen. The sooner she was out of the convent, the better.

Adelaide did not, however, leave the convent, not immediately. She went quietly along the passage to the chapel. When she opened the door she was hit by the smell of incense and the warm glow of candles. Despite the wartime shortage of the latter, the nuns had not stinted for Sister St Bruno. Her plain wooden coffin stood on a trestle before the altar with candles at her head and feet and more burned on the altar. Sister Danielle was the sister kneeling and keeping watch, but she did not look up when Adelaide quietly took a seat in a pew near the door. The silence lapped round her, seeping into her mind and her heart. She thought of Joseph and Janine who had been taken from this very place the night before; and what would happen to them. She thought of her aunt, Sarah, who with the faithful Sister Marie-Marc had been arrested too. What would become of them? And she thought of her Great-Aunt Anne, lying in the wooden box in front of her, dead, simply because some German soldier had casually kicked her in the head.

She thought of Marcel and hoped that he could get her out of the area very soon, but before she went, she had one thing she needed to do. Her hatred of Hoch flooded through her veins like melt water, turbulent, icy cold and powerful. Before she left she would do her damnedest to make sure he hunted down no one else.

Chapel was not the place to plan revenge, so Adelaide said silent goodbyes to her great-aunt, and getting quietly to her feet slipped out of the chapel and out of the convent.

Once outside, Adelaide hurried back to the village. It was a risk appearing in the village itself, but she had to discover what had happened to Sarah and poor Sister Marie-Marc. As she came into the square she heard the sound of an engine behind her, and turned to see a covered lorry, swastikas emblazoned on the sides of its canopy, grinding down the hill behind her. She stepped hastily out of its way and watched as it swept up in front of the town hall. A little crowd of onlookers gathered as people paused to watch what was happening. When the lorry came to a halt one soldier jumped down and went into the town hall while another circled to the back of the truck, his rifle trained on the tied-down flaps.

Adelaide joined the group watching as four prisoners were brought out from the cells beyond the town hall. More guards followed, and, covered by their comrades, two of them untied the flaps that sealed the lorry. There were shouts and cries from inside, and as the flaps were raised, Adelaide could see the pale faces of the men and women who were already crammed into the truck. Some covered their eyes at the sudden sunlight, others reached out, begging for water, calling for help.

One of the guards jabbed at them with his rifle, shouting. "Get back! Get back I say, or I'll shoot."

Adelaide stared in horror at the prisoners being brought to the lorry. The Auclons, dressed only in their ragged underwear, staggered forward prodded by the rifles of the guards, their arms round each other for support. They were followed by the two sisters. Mother Marie-Pierre was almost carrying Sister Marie-Marc, who stumbled along beside her on unsteady legs, her eyes glazed with incomprehension. Both were battered and bruised, their faces swollen and blood-smeared, and although they were still dressed in their habits,

440

neither had her head covered. Colonel Hoch, Adelaide realised with another flood of ice through her veins, had spent the night interrogating them.

Hoch had indeed had a busy night. He had come to the cell into which the two nuns had been unceremoniously tossed, and flung wide the door, crashing it back against the wall. Stepping inside he had filled the tiny room with his presence. The sisters, sitting together on the single narrow cot that served as a bed, looked up fearfully. He saw the fear in their faces and he smiled. Fear he enjoyed; fear would get him what he needed to know.

"Stand!" he barked. The two nuns obeyed, the older of the two swaying a little unsteadily on her feet. Reverend Mother reached out a hand to steady her, and Hoch, watching the instinctive gesture, knew on whom he should concentrate, who would crack.

He turned to the soldier who had followed him to the door. "Shut the door, lock it, and wait outside."

The man saluted and pulled the door closed with a clang. Hoch waited until he heard the bolt drawn across before giving his attention to his prisoners.

On his orders they had been taken through the German HQ to the police cells, and there he had let them stew for over two hours. It had given them time to consider their fate before they were interrogated, which, he knew, made interrogation more fruitful.

Hoch was angry. His raid on the convent had only been partially successful. He had received information that a family was being hidden there. A young woman and a child had been seen after curfew near the convent, and it was suggested that it might be the Auclon family. He had hoped the raid would deliver the whole family into his hands, and although he now had the parents locked up, the children seemed to have eluded him. He had hoped to arrest the young woman, whoever she was, at the same time. He'd been right, she had been there, but his idiot, incompetent men had allowed her to slip through their fingers. The cellar had quickly been discovered, disclosing where the Jews had been hidden, how they had been supplied with food, how the children had been removed and finally how the young woman had made her escape from the convent. He had sent men after her, but searching the countryside in the dark had been a waste of time. The woman had vanished, and the men concerned had only been able to furnish the sketchiest of descriptions. Good enough though for Hoch to recall seeing a young woman with the mother superior on a previous visit to the convent, a young woman who might fit. It was one of the things he intended to learn now, one way or another.

Looking at the two nuns standing before him, he realised that their habits gave them psychological protection. Somehow they would feel safe while still dressed in their black robes and white hoods; their dignity would be preserved, their feeling of self.

"You can start by taking off that ridiculous headgear," he said sharply. "Now!"

Sister Marie-Marc began to protest, but Mother Marie-Pierre simply reached up and began to remove the offending hood, encouraging mildly, "Come along, Sister. Do as the colonel asks."

Sister Marie-Marc was used to obeying Reverend Mother and without further protest, but with shaking hands, she did as she was told.

"And that cap thing!" snapped Hoch when they stood there, hoods removed, but heads still encased in the tight-fitting wimple and wide starched collar.

"Is that really necessary?" Mother Marie-Pierre asked. She remembered how Sister Eloise had looked, diminished and vulnerable with her cropped hair standing in a spiky halo about her head, and she knew it was part of Hoch's intimidation tactics. She had no illusions about his interrogation methods and she was afraid. But she had to be strong for Sister Marie-Marc, to give her the courage they would both need from now on.

"Don't make me ask twice, *Reverend Mother*." Hoch spoke softly, menacingly. "Remember, I have men outside who would be only too delighted to discover if a nun was the same as any other woman under all that black bombazine."

Mother Marie-Pierre undid the wimple, but left her collar in place, and Sister Marie-Marc did the same. Their heads were revealed, Mother Marie-Pierre's hair in tiny cropped curls, Sister Marie-Marc's scalp almost bald, with only wispy hair above her ears.

Hoch smiled at what he saw, two women, one of them old and scrawny, one in middle-age, the mystery of their calling shed with their hoods. Two very ordinary women, both afraid.

"Now I can see you properly," he began, "I'm going to ask you some questions . . . and I expect some answers." He fixed his eyes on Reverend Mother. "Where are the Auclon children?"

"I have no idea," replied Mother Marie-Pierre.

He moved so quickly and unexpectedly that she received the full force of the back of his hand across her face. Almost knocked to the floor, she staggered backwards, and it was only Sister Marie-Marc's grasping hands that kept her on her feet.

"Wrong answer! Where are the Auclon children?"

"I don't know." This time she was ready for the blow, but this time he used a clenched fist to her cheek and nose. Blood spouted and a cut opened up under her eye. Mother Marie-Pierre cried out, her hand flying to her face as the blood poured unchecked down onto her collar. Sister Marie-Marc screamed, and sat down hard on the bed, her legs having given way beneath her.

"Who brought the family to you?" Hoch demanded, ignoring the older nun's sobs. Mother Marie-Pierre pulled a handkerchief from her pocket and tried to staunch her bleeding nose, but she made no reply.

"You!" he roared at Sister Marie-Marc. "Stand up."

Sister Marie-Marc struggled to her feet, her face ashen, her eyes wide with terror.

"Who brought the family to the convent?"

Sister Marie-Marc shook her head. "I don't know," she whispered.

Hoch raised his hand again and Sister Marie-Marc flinched away, but it was not her that he hit, but her superior, another stinging blow across her other cheek.

444

"Turn the other cheek!" he mocked. "Isn't that what you do, you holy nuns? Not so holy now, though, are you? Telling lies. Telling lies to save a family of filthy Jews. Well, let me tell you, you holy sisters, your lies won't save them. Nothing you can do will save that family. *They'll* never see their children again, and when *I* find them they'll follow their parents to Germany. But I need to know where they are, and you are going to tell me." This time he did hit out at Sister Marie-Marc, knocking her to the floor and then aiming two sharp kicks at her body. The old nun moaned, curling herself into a ball and flinging her arms up to protect her head.

"Stop it! Stop it!" shrieked Mother Marie-Pierre. "She doesn't know anything!"

"Possibly," agreed Hoch, "but you do, and if you don't tell me what I want to know, it will be her who suffers." He delivered another kick, this time to Sister Marie-Marc's shaven head.

"Stop it! You'll kill her!"

Hoch looked down at the figure now lying still on the floor. "Yes, I may. But that is entirely up to you. As soon as I have the information I need, I shall leave you in peace. Now, where are those children?"

Mother Marie-Pierre's thoughts raced. Sister Marie-Marc couldn't take much more of Hoch's brutality. More kicks to the head and she would indeed die. Save her life and risk the Auclon twins? She had seconds to decide. She opted for partial truth.

"I don't know where the children are," she said reluctantly, "they were taken away."

"Who took them?" Hoch's eyes gleamed as he watched her face, searching out the truth.

"I don't know. A man came for them."

Hoch aimed another kick at Sister Marie-Marc's head, his boot connecting with a sickening thud. "You're lying!" he said almost conversationally. "It was a young woman. She was seen. Who was she?"

Mother Marie-Pierre paled, but held her nerve. "I don't know. A man brought them, a woman took them away. I'd never seen either of them before."

"Oh, I think you had," said Hoch. "I think it was that girl who was at the convent when I came before. She was seen running away tonight. I have a good description. I think it is the same girl. If you don't tell me who she is, I shall simply ask up at the convent. There's a sensible nun up there. I've dealt with her before, she doesn't want any more trouble." He waited for some reaction, but although Mother Marie-Pierre was shaken at the thought that Adelaide had almost been captured, she was relieved to know she had got away. Surely she would make good her escape from the area as fast as she could. She must know there was no future for her in these parts now her cover was blown.

"So," he said, "you might as well tell me her name now and save me the trouble of going back to the convent." Again his hand whipped out across her face, the signet ring on his finger ripping a gash across her chin. Then he glanced down at Sister Marie-Marc still and silent on the floor, and prodded her with his toe. She moaned softly. "She's still alive . . . just," he remarked. "So, now, *Reverend Mother*, let's start again, shall we? And this time don't try my patience any longer. Who brought the Jews to the convent? They'd been hiding in a derelict cottage, and then someone brought them to you. Who was that?"

Sister Marie-Marc moaned again. Hoch said, "Please answer my question, or your sister will die."

"A man from the resistance. I don't know his name. I'd never seen him before."

"If you didn't know him, why did he bring the family to you?"

"The convent is a Christian house," replied Mother Marie-Pierre. "I suppose he must have thought we would give shelter to any family in danger."

"Because you'd done it before!" snapped Hoch. "That's why he came to you! A secret room was prepared in the cellar. I saw it with my own eyes. You knew they were coming . . . or someone in the convent did. Someone prepared that hiding place . . . if not you, who? The girl? She worked in the convent. She came in each day. You had to have help from the outside. Who is she . . . the one that prepared the room?"

"I did it." The words were scarcely more than a croak. Sister Marie-Marc had opened her eyes and was staring up at the colonel. "I made the room. Mother didn't even know about it until the Auclons were there."

Mother Marie-Pierre dropped to her knees beside her sister. "It's all right, Sister," she said, "you don't have to say any more."

"Oh, I think she does," Hoch said, pushing Reverend Mother aside. "Go on, Sister, what about the girl? The

447

young woman who took the children away and then came back for the parents tonight? Who is she?"

"I don't know," murmured Sister Marie-Marc, her eyes closing again.

Hoch bent down and lifted Sister Marie-Marc's head from the floor, peering at her swollen face before letting her head drop with a sharp crack onto the stone floor. "I don't think she'll survive tonight," he remarked, glancing up at Reverend Mother. "I shall leave you to consider now," he went on. "We shall resume in the morning. I shall bring another of my men who is specially trained in interrogation. Perhaps he will be more persuasive than I am." He walked to the door and then glanced back at the figure on the floor. "It's a pity you weren't more helpful. You could have saved her a lot of pain."

Mother Marie-Pierre held his gaze. "Will you send in some water so I can bathe her face?"

"No, Reverend Mother, I will not."

"And a bucket, or something . . . for our needs?"

"You can squat in the corner," he replied cheerfully, pointing to an open drain hole. "Something you'll have to get used to, I expect. There'll be few conveniences at the camps where we send enemies of the Reich." He rapped sharply on the door three times and Mother Marie-Pierre heard the bolt being drawn back. The door opened, the colonel left, and as the door closed behind him, the light went out.

Mother Marie-Pierre bent down in the darkness and tried to ease Sister Marie-Marc from the floor onto the narrow bed. As she did so, the elderly nun murmured.

"You didn't tell him did you? About Adèle and the children?"

"No, Sister, I didn't tell him."

"Thank God." She groaned as she tried to move. "Don't tell him to save me. I'm old, they're young. Don't tell him. Evil! Evil man!"

"It's all right, Sister, stay still," soothed Reverend Mother. "When it gets light we'll have a look at your bruises. It's all right." She rested the nun's head in her lap. There was little else she could do for her until she could see, except pray.

It's all right, she'd said, but it wasn't all right at all. Mother Marie-Pierre knew that Hoch would be back in a few hours, and the interrogation would start again. Would he use Sister Marie-Marc again to try and make her talk? Would he reverse the process and attack her, Reverend Mother, in an effort to make Sister Marie-Marc tell what she knew? So far they had been subjected to Hoch's bullyboy tactics, but there were other ways of extracting information from an unwilling prisoner. And so she prayed, through the darkest hours of her life, prayed for strength and guidance, for deliverance for them all. Truly, she thought, we are in the valley of the shadow of death.

As the dawn light crept in through the grubby window, Mother Marie-Pierre was able to see the damage Hoch had done with his boot. Sister Marie-Marc lay in an uneasy doze, her face was swollen, her nose broken with one eye almost closed. Damping a corner of her own blood-soaked handkerchief with saliva, Reverend Mother wiped away some of the blood that had crusted round the old nun's nose. Sister Marie-Marc's breathing was uneven, and even in her fitful sleep she moaned and muttered with pain. Mother Marie-Pierre's own face ached appallingly. Her right eye had swollen from Hoch's punch, and she, too, was finding it difficult to breathe through her nose.

Outside she heard the sounds of a new day, men's voices and the heavy tread of boots. She urgently needed to relieve herself, and unwilling to have an audience for this, she gently eased the sleeping Sister Marie-Marc off her lap and went to the drain in the corner. When she returned to the bed she realised that Sister Marie-Marc was not asleep, but had drifted off into unconsciousness. Mother Marie-Pierre hammered on the door, trying to attract the attention of a guard, to get help, but if anyone heard her hammering, it was ignored. No one came. No one brought food or water. They were left in the cold silence of the cell. Occasionally there were sounds from outside; once she heard a piercing scream and the slamming of a door. Again she hammered on their door, but to no avail.

It was several hours before the bolts were again drawn back and Hoch strode in. He had not been idle in those hours and he was delighted with the results of his labours. He had begun by interrogating the Jews. Using the same technique, as with the nuns, he had them brought together in a cell. There Joseph was handcuffed to the wall, forced to watch as Hoch began to work on Janine. First he stripped her and then forced her to lie on her back, naked on the narrow bed, tying her wrists and ankles to the bed legs so that she was stretched out like a sacrifice. She had struggled against him, but she was no match for his strength, and a sudden punch to her head had sent her flying. She had screamed with fear and Hoch had shrugged. "You can scream all you like," he said. "No one can hear you . . . and if they can, they won't come."

He glanced across at the pale-faced man. "You only have to answer my questions, Jew, and her pain will be over." He had few of the more refined instruments of torture that were available at the Gestapo headquarters in Amiens, but Janine's shrieks of pain as cigarettes were applied to her breasts and genitals soon had her husband singing like a nightingale. Within an hour Hoch had all the information he needed. His only failure was that the children were lost to him. Even the threat to put out his wife's eyes had not produced the required information from Joseph, screaming frantically that he didn't know. Hoch had come, reluctantly, to believe that he really didn't know where his children had been taken. But Hoch now knew about everything else. About the Charbonniers, how they had let the family hide in the loft of the derelict cottage and kept them supplied with food; about the Launays, who had some connection with a girl called Antoinette who had brought them to hide in the convent; about a man called Marcel who had arrived with Antoinette to collect the children, one at a time, and taken them away. Hoch had not even needed the services of his "specialist" interrogator. He and he alone had this information. He would be the one to round up this little group of *résistants*. He would get the credit; none for the mealy-mouthed apology for a major, Thielen. He would stamp his authority on this place once and for all. And then maybe, just maybe, he would be moved from this godforsaken area to a more prominent job, in Paris perhaps. He had proved that the dreadful truth that his grandmother had been a Jew did not stop him from hunting down Jews wherever they hid, and sending them to the camps where they belonged.

This information culled was all he needed. Returning from the Jews' cell, he sat down in his office to consider just exactly what he did know. The information about the fugitives at the convent had come in an anonymous letter. Hoch got it out of his desk now to look at it again. Written on cheap, lined paper, it was scrawled in pencil and simply said, "She's *hiding them in the convent! The girl had one of the children.*" Of course it was unsigned, and the writer gave no clue to his or her identity, but Hoch, guessing who had sent it, had decided to act on it.

The information had proved correct, and Hoch was in no doubt now that the "she" must be the mother superior. Someone in the convent did not like her, the letter having been sent for private purposes; an informer who wanted some sort of reward would surely have made herself known. This fitted his theory that the letter had come from the nun he had dealt with before, Sister Marie-Something. She wanted to run the convent and was content to cooperate with the Germans if necessary, to do so. She might want to be rid of Reverend Mother, but so did he. He would tolerate no subversives in his area, and Mother

452

Marie-Pierre was certainly that. The other nun, whoever she was, had been taken simply to implement his earlier threat. His point had been made, and emphatically made at that — there would be no further participation for the nuns in this war.

Hoch contacted the HQ in Amiens and arranged for one of the lorry transports on its way to Drancy, the transit camp outside Paris, to be diverted to pick up the prisoners. He had no further need of any of them. The Jews would be off to Drancy in a couple of hours, and the nuns could go with them.

That still left the question of Antoinette. Who was she? Was she the young woman at the convent? Almost certainly she was, so he could get her name easily enough. There would be no problem bringing in the Charbonniers and the Launays, they'd soon be made to talk. The only one he had little information on was the mysterious Marcel. No doubt Antoinette could furnish that information, and who knew where that might lead to?

There was also the mysterious disappearance of the weasel informer, Fernand. Since tipping them off about the Jews in the first place, he had made no contact. Where was he? Fernand, or rather his disappearance, had irritated Hoch. He wanted to know what the man was up to, so he'd sent Weber to Fernand's house, either to bring Fernand in, or find out where he was. Weber had returned with Fernand's landlady.

"Where is Monsieur Fernand, Madame?" Hoch had asked, almost civilly.

Martine Reynaud was terrified to find herself in the German headquarters and her voice shook as she answered. "I don't know, Monsieur."

"When did you last see him?"

"I don't know, Monsieur. A few days ago. He comes and goes as he pleases."

"But you must know when he's in the house."

Certainly Martine knew when the brute was in the house, with his demands for cooked meals, washing and mending to be done, boots to be cleaned. She had relished the peace of the last few days when he had made no appearance at all. She had not dared to hope that he might never come back and she might regain the use of her own home, but now this German officer with the skulls on his shoulder was glowering at her . . . and he was far more frightening than Fernand.

"Sometimes, sometimes not. He's always out and about, Monsieur," stammered Martine.

Hoch knew there was nothing more to be learned from her and he dismissed her. "When he comes back, you're to let me know. But remember, Madame, there will be no need to tell him you have been here today."

"Yes, Monsieur, I mean no, Monsieur," gabbled the woman, and scurried out of his office.

Hoch considered what he had learned. Fernand had obviously disappeared. He, Hoch, would look into the matter later on. If Fernand were dead he wasn't going anywhere, and if he wasn't, well, he'd turn up sooner or later. He could be lying low, afraid, because his information proved to be out of date. Or perhaps something had happened to him? Hoch realised that he

454

must be known locally as an informer, and probably a lot more besides. Had he met with an accident? It was more than possible that he had been silenced by one of his neighbours. Hoch did not particularly care whether the man was alive or dead, but if he had been murdered by the cell of *résistants* he was seeking now, the murder of a Frenchman would more than justify their arrest and execution when the time came.

Today, however, Hoch was concentrating on the girl and Marcel. Once he had them he'd have time for everyone else.

When he returned to the nuns' cell, he found that the older one was in a bad way. She lay on the bed, moaning softly as Mother Marie-Pierre tried to soothe her. She had removed Sister Marie-Marc's starched collar and cleaned her face as best she could with her handkerchief. As Hoch walked in the reverend mother appealed to him again. "For pity's sake, Colonel, let them bring me some water. Sister Marie-Marc is feverish, she needs water to drink, and I need to bathe her face."

Hoch looked down, unperturbed, at the old woman on the bed. "You can have some water," he said, "and then get her ready to go."

"Go!" Mother Marie-Pierre leapt to her feet. "Go where? She's in no state to go anywhere. Let her be taken back to the convent so her sisters can care for her."

"You are being taken to a prison camp," he told her, "and she will go with you."

"In the name of God, have you no pity?"

"For enemies of the Reich, no, Reverend Mother, I have not." He walked to the door and then paused. "By the way, the Jews gave me the information I needed. I shall soon arrest all the others concerned in this little affair. You will be brought out when the transport arrives." Hoch stared at her for a moment. "You are a meddlesome woman, nun, and you have brought this on yourself . . . and on her."

"And you are an evil man, Colonel," Mother Marie-Pierre replied quietly. "May God have mercy on you and forgive you, for I never will." She turned back to Sister Marie-Marc. For a moment she thought he might strike her, but he simply gave a harsh laugh and left the cell slamming the door behind him and ramming home the bolt. Not long after that the soldiers had come for them.

Adelaide watched with mounting anguish. What right had anyone to treat another human being as Hoch had clearly treated his prisoners, as the desperate men and women in the truck were being treated? Her fury threatened to boil over, but there was nothing she could do. Nothing to avert what was happening. She willed Sarah to look in her direction, so that Sarah would know that she, Adelaide, was safe; so that Sarah would know she and Sister Marie-Marc had not been deserted. Sister Marie-Marc, her face almost unrecognisable, was clinging to Sarah, muttering incoherently.

As they reached the back of the truck, one of the soldiers grabbed Janine Auclon and simply tossed her over the tailgate. There were more cries from inside as she landed on top of those already aboard. Joseph Auclon was thrown in after his wife, and then the soldiers turned to the two waiting nuns.

Sarah began to sing in English, her voice clear and loud, a bell ringing out across the square. "In death's dark vale I fear no ill, with Thee dear Lord beside me. Thy rod and staff my comfort still, Thy Cross before to guide me!" For a fleeting moment her eyes met Adelaide's, and then she shouldered Sister Marie-Marc's weight once more, and reverting to French she said gently, "Come, Sister, it's time to go . . ."

As the soldiers still hesitated, she turned to them and spoke. "Perhaps you'd be good enough to help us into the lorry." Two of them moved forward, and clearly uncomfortable at laying hands on a nun, lifted first Sister Marie-Marc and then Reverend Mother up and over the tailgate into the crush of humanity already on the inside.

At that moment Colonel Hoch emerged from the town hall, his face dark with rage. "What the hell's going on here?" he roared and the soldiers snapped to attention. "Get those flaps closed and get on the road."

The soldiers leapt to do his bidding, but as the flaps were hauled closed and roped into place, Adelaide heard Sarah's voice, raised loud one last time. "God bless you!" and she knew that the blessing was for her.

CHAPTER
TWENTY-THREE

With the arrival of Hoch on the scene, the crowd who had been watching melted away. Adelaide moved with them, fighting the tears as she watched the lorry and its miserable cargo prepare to leave. She should not be in the square at all, she knew that. She couldn't afford to be conspicuous, but neither could she bring herself to walk away from Sarah. She could do nothing for her but be there, and so she had stayed.

The German soldiers returned to their HQ, as the lorry rumbled out of the *place*, and Hoch, with a final glance around the square, followed them inside. Once back in his office, he called for Lieutenant Weber. The lieutenant found him standing by the window that overlooked the square.

"You wanted me, sir?"

Hoch looked round. "Come here, Weber. Look out there. You see that girl crossing the square now? I want to know who she is and where she goes."

"Shall I have someone bring her in, sir?" asked Weber.

"No," snapped Hoch. "I just want her followed. I want to know where she lives, who she meets, who she

458

talks to, where she goes. But discreetly, Weber. I don't want her to suspect she is being watched. Understand?"

"Yes, sir. I'll get someone on to it."

"And Weber, when you've done that, come back. I need you to go up to the convent and speak to the new reverend mother."

"Yes, sir!" The lieutenant snapped a salute and left the colonel watching Adelaide walking slowly away. Hoch was almost certain she was the young woman who had been working at the convent, but was she the one who had escaped his men last night? If she were the young woman, Antoinette, who had taken the Auclon children away, then she was the important one now. She clearly had links with a wider network. Hoch needed her to lead him to this Marcel, whoever he was, and anyone else she had been working with; maybe to the whole network. With enough rope, he would hang them all. He would leave the minor players, the Charbonniers and Launays, for the time being. They weren't going anywhere; he could round them up later on. If he arrested them too soon, it might alert Marcel, he would go to ground and Hoch would never catch him.

Unaware of this scrutiny, Adelaide made her way slowly across the *place*. With the departure of the lorry, people began to drift back onto the square once more, carrying on their everyday business. A queue of housewives formed outside the boulangerie for the daily ration of bread, workmen called to each other as they repaired a fire-damaged shop. Two young women pushing prams across the square paused to perch on the edge of the fountain and chat; a woman was cleaning her front window, another sweeping her step. An elderly car chugged in from a side road, a man with a briefcase hurried along, consulting his watch as he went; the priest came out of the church. Life went on.

How could everything seem so normal, Adelaide wondered bleakly as she watched them? How could life go on as usual when there was such an evil presence in their midst? She wanted to weep. Impotent fury and grief boiled up inside her, knotting together, a visceral pain. Her heart and mind were in that dreadful lorry, transporting its desperate human cargo to God alone knew where, and though she knew her own situation was precarious, she couldn't give it her attention.

Hardly looking where she was going, Adelaide almost cannoned into a young German soldier heading the other way. He put out a hand to steady her, and smiled. "*Enschuligen!*"

Adelaide was jolted back to the present and with a duck of her head she muttered, "Pardon!" and hurried away.

Horrified at her own stupidity, she forced herself to continue at an even pace, though her mind reeled. The soldier watched her appreciatively for a moment before going into the café. He had not recognised her, but, Adelaide realised with a sudden chill, he could so easily have been one of those who had given chase last night, and she, too, could have been gathered into Hoch's evil web.

Focus! Focus on what needs to be done, she admonished herself. There's no time to think about

Sarah now. You must put her out of your head and focus your mind on what to do next.

But try as she would, she could not banish the battered and bruised faces of the two nuns from her mind's eye. And she was responsible; it was as simple as that. If she hadn't hidden the Auclons at the convent, Sarah and Sister Marie-Marc would be safe and Aunt Anne would be alive.

A tiny voice inside reminded her that she had saved the children. She thought of the two little boys she had passed on to Father Bernard and wondered where they were now. Were they safe or had that been in vain as well? What about Father Bernard himself? If she were to be caught now, he too would be in jeopardy. The colonel had obviously been brutal in his questioning of the four prisoners, and Adelaide knew she must be in acute danger. She had no idea what he had been able to extract from them, but she guessed that they would not have been sent on their way had they still held information that Hoch needed. She had to assume that they had told him everything.

Now, more than ever, she needed to see Marcel. She had no direct means of contacting him, she had to rely on Madame Juliette. That was a security cut-out. Indeed she realised, as she didn't even know Marcel's real name, he would be safe if she were caught, but even so, she knew that she had to get away. Madame Juliette. She was another who would be at Hoch's mercy should Adelaide fall into his hands, for if she were caught, she knew that she would be unlikely to withstand Hoch's questioning for long. If there was no message from Marcel, or if he didn't or couldn't come to the farm, Adelaide decided that she must use the fallback rendezvous he had given her in Albert.

The longer I stay in the area, the more I endanger everyone concerned, Adelaide thought. Pull yourself together, woman, and get yourself away from here.

The first thing to do was to get out of sight. There were off-duty German soldiers sitting at tables outside the café. Any of them could be among those who'd been at the convent, any of them might recognise her. Whatever happened next, she had to warn the Launays and the Charbonniers. Adelaide quickened her pace and took the alley along the side of the café down towards the river. If Marcel did not come quickly she must contrive her own escape.

As she walked she considered her options. She thought about Madame Juliette's cellar. Perhaps she could hide there until Marcel did come, until he brought news from London, but the idea appalled her. She knew she couldn't survive in that claustrophobic underground room for long, and she would yet again be putting the old lady at risk. No, that would truly be a last resort. Marcel had told her that in an emergency she should head for Albert and he would look for her in the Café Rousseau every morning at eleven. Better to go there, she decided, than put Juliette at further risk.

As she reached the end of the lane, a young man in workman's overalls came pedalling along the towpath on an elderly-looking bike. He raised a hand in greeting as he passed, and as she watched him riding on along the path, she thought about the bike she had used to

462

carry the children. Perhaps she could simply get on her bike and ride away. She hadn't used it today. After some discussion they had decided that Gerard should take the child seat off the back before she used it again, in case someone remembered seeing her with one of the boys up behind her. Still, the bike was a possibility. She might simply ride out of the area ... if the Germans weren't already on the lookout for her. Could she get as far as Albert without being picked up? And when she got there, where should she go until eleven o'clock tomorrow morning?

Adelaide reached the old stone barn and turned down the track that led to the Launays' farm. Further up the towpath, she saw that the cyclist had stopped and was energetically pumping up his back tyre. He must have got a puncture, Adelaide thought sympathetically. The path was rough enough, jagged stones bedded in rutted mud. If she did decide to use the bike to get away, she must remember to take the puncture kit and pump with her. She couldn't afford to get stranded at the side of the road.

As Adelaide turned onto the farm track, Horst Braun stood up from his bicycle wheel and looked back. Pushing the bike, he walked back to the end of the track and glanced along it. The girl was walking briskly, striding out, almost running. In the distance Braun could see farm buildings among some trees, obviously her destination. He climbed onto his bicycle and rode quickly back to the town hall, taking the direct route rather than the circuitous one he had used to disguise his approach.

"She's gone to the farm in the river bend," he reported to Hoch.

Hoch's eyes gleamed. "By the river, you say?"

"Yes, sir."

"I see." Hoch thought for a moment. Weber had been up to the convent and spoken to Sister Marie-Paul, the new reverend mother. He'd come back with the information that the girl Hoch was looking for no longer worked there, she had been sacked just that morning.

"Her name's Adèle Durant," the reverend mother had said. "She lives with her aunt and uncle at a farm out along the river. The Launays."

The Launays. Hoch had smiled with grim satisfaction at this. Launay was one of the names given by Joseph Auclon in his efforts to save his wife. So, there definitely was a connection. Joseph had said the girl's name was Antoinette, but he could have been wrong. Adèle? Antoinette? Hoch was certain in his own mind that Adèle and Antoinette were one and the same the girl Hoch had seen and recognised in the square today. And now young Braun had watched her heading down the lane that led to the Launays' farm. The problem was going to be how to keep watch on her without being seen. Hoch had no doubt now that she was the link and must eventually lead him to the man Marcel, and Hoch was sure that Marcel was a key figure in the emerging local resistance movement. He wanted them both: the girl, Antoinette or Adèle, and Marcel.

"Shall we bring her in?" Braun asked.

464

"No!" snapped Hoch. "I'm waiting for someone to contact her. For now I just want her watched."

"It will be difficult to get near and keep watch without being seen."

"What's it like there?" demanded Hoch. "Is there no cover?"

"Very little, sir, until you reach the farm buildings. There are a few trees round the house, but the fields are pretty open, just some low hedges. Oh, and there's a derelict barn at the end of the track. But that's not very near the farmhouse itself. You wouldn't see much from there."

"But you could watch the track itself? The approach to the farm?"

"Yes, sir. That would be easy enough."

"For the moment that's all that's necessary," replied Hoch. "I'm looking for someone. Take two men and watch from the barn. If anyone goes to that farm, or anything suspicious happens, you're to report back. Use one man as a runner to keep me up to date." He thought for a moment. "Who's watching the place now?"

"No one, sir. There was no time for backup."

Hoch cursed under his breath and then snapped. "Well, get back there, man. Get back to that barn and keep watch. And Braun, remember, don't stop anyone going into the farm, but let me know at once if anyone does." He thought back to Joseph's description of the man Marcel. "I am looking for a man, thirtyish, quite tall with dark hair and eyes. If someone who fits that description approaches the farm, send word immediately."

Hoch gave a malevolent smile. "And I shall come myself."

"Suppose he tries to leave again, sir? Before you get there?"

"If possible follow him, if not, arrest him. And the girl too, if she is with him. But I want them alive, Braun. Injured if necessary, but alive."

"Yes, sir." Braun saluted smartly and left the room.

When Adelaide reached the farm, Marie came running out to meet her.

"Adèle, are you all right? What's happened?"

"It's bad," Adelaide replied. "Where's Gerard?"

"In the top field, mending a fence."

"Quick, Marie. Go and get him. We have to talk."

With scared eyes, Marie nodded and set off, out of the farmyard. Adelaide went into the house and gathered up her few possessions. She was calmer now. She knew that she was on her own. The Launays could do nothing for her, and if the Auclons had talked, they would have problems of their own soon enough. If Marcel did not come in the next half-hour, she would strike out alone. She slipped her knife into her garter where it nestled comfortingly against her leg. She knew there would be no escape if she were cornered, no point in being unarmed and innocent. She had no gun, but the feel of the knife against her flesh gave her an illusion of security.

Marie and Gerard came back into the yard as Adelaide was pushing the old bicycle out of the shed. Gerard had already removed the child seat, and there was now just a small parcel carrier behind the saddle, to which she had strapped her small suitcase.

"Adèle!" cried Marie. "What's happened? Where are you going?"

Adelaide quickly told the couple what she had seen that morning. "We are all in danger now," she said. "The Auclons must have talked, so it's almost certain Hoch knows about me. So, it'll be better for you if I'm not here. You can say that I got the sack from the convent this morning, so I've gone to Paris to look for work."

"But where will you go?" asked Marie.

Adelaide smiled at her. "To Paris, to look for work. That's all you need to know. What's more important for you is to know nothing about the Auclons. Hoch will know I was involved, but you must plead ignorance. You had no idea what I was doing. Innocence and ignorance. Just stick to the fact that I came to help you out on the farm and earned some extra money working up at the convent. You had no idea that I was involved with anything else."

"You think that Hoch is going to buy that?" asked Gerard scornfully.

Adelaide shrugged. "I don't know. It depends what the Auclons were made to tell him. But you'll just have to stick to that and hope he does. We must warn the Charbonniers, too. He'll know about them as well."

"If he knows all this, why isn't he here already?" wondered Marie. "Why hasn't he arrested us yet?"

"I don't know," conceded Adelaide. "Let's just be grateful he hasn't, and take advantage of the time he has given us. One of you should go over to the Charbonniers and warn them. In the meantime, I'll leave. If a man called Marcel comes, tell him I will be at the fallback rendezvous tomorrow."

The sound of a vehicle coming along the track made all three of them spin round, and for a moment Adelaide thought it was a German staff car edging into the yard. It had, indeed, the familiar long bonnet and inverted chevrons of a Citroën similar to the one that Hoch had requisitioned, but instead of a German at the wheel, Adelaide saw, with an explosion of relief, that it was being driven by Marcel. On the windscreen was a large sign saying "Doctor". Leaving the engine running, he jumped from the car, slamming the door behind him.

"I got your message," he said. "Time to go."

Adelaide looked across at the Launays who stood staring at Marcel. "What about them?" she asked. "They're in as much danger as I am."

"Nothing we can do for them," Marcel snapped. "They can't leave their home. They'll have to brazen it out. The only thing they know about is you . . . right?"

"Yes, and the Auclons."

"Hoch already knows about the Auclons. They can tell him nothing more."

"He may think they know more," cried Adelaide.

"Adèle, there's no way we can protect them if he takes it into his head to arrest them. But it will be far worse if you are taken too . . . for everyone. Now get in the car!"

468

"He's right, Adèle," Marie said. "We'll be safer when you've gone. The only other thing we know is about Étienne and Albertine, and if Hoch knows about us, he'll know about them as well. It's a risk we all took, but please, go now before things get worse. Don't worry, we'll warn them too."

Adelaide looked at her for a moment. As always it was Marie who was the stronger of the two Launays, Marie who had defiantly fought death for her man and nursed him back to health, Marie who had faced Fernand's knife and given nothing away. Adelaide hugged her tightly, loving her for her courage.

"Hurry," Gerard urged, taking her case off the bike. "There's no time to lose."

Adelaide broke away and climbed into the car. "Thank you both," she said, "and good luck."

Marcel turned the car in the yard and then drove slowly back along the track.

"Message from London," he told her. "They want you home again. There's a plane bringing someone in tomorrow night. It'll pick you up."

He was driving up the track as he spoke, but before Adelaide could answer a man in workman's overalls stepped into the road, barring his way, and flagging him down.

"What the . . . ? Christ!" exploded Marcel as he saw two others in German uniform step out behind the first, training machine-guns on the car. "Hold tight," he rasped. "Get down when I say."

He continued towards the three men, slowing down and raising an acknowledging hand, as if complying with their signals, but as he reached the end of the track he bellowed "Down!" and slamming his foot on the accelerator the car leapt forward and he drove straight at them. As the three Germans dived clear, Marcel wrenched the wheel and took the corner onto the towpath at full speed. Adelaide ducked below the dashboard clinging to the seat, as she was nearly thrown across the car into Marcel's lap. A machine-gun rattled behind them, the bullets thudding into the ground around them as they sped away. The back window shattered showering them with glass, and Adelaide wrapped her arms round her head and face in a belated effort to shield herself from the flying shards. Even as she did so the windscreen disintegrated. Marcel grabbed a pistol from between the seats, and using the butt as a hammer smashed away the remains of the glass. They careered along the path and out into the lane, and there were several thuds and bangs as more bullets pounded into the body of the car. At one moment the car slewed drastically to one side, as a tyre burst, but Marcel, wrestling with the steering wheel, managed to keep them moving, the car slumping heavily on the flattened rim.

"Stay down!" he yelled as Adelaide shifted in the seat beside him. The machine-guns continued to blaze behind them but the turn in the road hid them from view, and for the moment they were safe. They reached the main road and Marcel swung the car towards Albert.

"You all right?" he asked without taking his eyes off the road.

470

"Yes." Adelaide's voice was shaky. "Yes, I think so." She sat up cautiously. "Ouch! There's broken glass everywhere and it's vicious!" Blood seeped from cuts to her face, hands and arms, but otherwise she was uninjured. She looked across at Marcel. Blood was streaming down his face and neck, but he continued to grip the steering wheel, keeping the damaged car limping along the road.

"Marcel, you're bleeding," she cried. "Are you hit?"

"Only glass, I think," replied Marcel through teeth clenched in pain. "They'll be after us, Adèle, we must dump the car. It's had it!"

"They haven't got a car," Adelaide said, "or a motorbike. If they had, they'd be here by now. Keep going until we find somewhere better to ditch the car."

Even as she spoke, Marcel slumped down across the wheel, his foot slipped off the accelerator and the car shuddered to a halt.

"Marcel!"

Marcel groaned, and shifted in his seat. "My shoulder!"

"Quick, swap places. I'll drive!" Adelaide leapt out of the car and rushed to the other side. "Come on, Marcel!" She opened the driver's door and hauled him out. His jacket was soaked and sticky with blood and Adelaide realised it was not just from the gashes on his face and neck. He must have been hit in the shoulder.

"Come on, Marcel," Adelaide urged. "Get in the back!" She managed to heave him into the back seat, slamming the door shut to hold him inside. A glance behind her showed her no Germans in hot pursuit, but it also showed her a thick slick of oil on the road; the car had definitely been hit.

With a curse she clambered into the driver's seat and tried to start the engine again. It coughed and died, refusing to catch.

"Come on! Come on, damn you!"

Her mind raced. They had to find some sort of cover. If the car would go no further they would have to go on foot, and, with Marcel in the state he was, that truly would be a lost cause. Capture would be inevitable. Adelaide gave one last despairing pull on the self-starter, and miracle of miracles, the engine spluttered into life. Carefully she eased the clutch and the accelerator and the Citroën began to edge forward, its blown tyre thumping and bumping on the road. They moved slowly, but at least they were moving.

We shan't be able to go far like this, she thought, and they'll be right behind us. She glanced into the back of the car. Marcel was slumped as she had left him on the back seat.

"Marcel! Are you awake? Can you hear me? Marcel! Marcel!"

The only reply from behind her was a grunt and the sound of rasping breath.

As the car limped forward, Adelaide considered their options, and there appeared to be none. She pressed hard on the accelerator, and despite the shredded tyre the car picked up some speed.

"Come on! Come on!" she muttered, willing the car forward, but as they rounded a bend in the road, a second tyre blew and the car slewed sideways. Adelaide

472

wrestled with the steering wheel, but the car did not respond and they cannoned into a tree at the side of the road with a resounding bang, and the engine died.

"Christ!" Adelaide was flung forward, hammering her ribs against the steering wheel, leaving her winded. For a moment she sat still, fighting the stabbing pain in her chest, trying to regain her breath. An ominous ticking came from the engine and there was a strong smell of petrol. Adelaide heaved herself out of the car, and jerking the back door open she struggled to pull Marcel clear. He tumbled out onto the road, and she saw that his shoulder was bleeding steadily now. This was no wound caused by flying glass, and Adelaide knew that it was bad. He was dazed but he was conscious as she reached under his arms to drag him away from the car. He was heavy, a deadweight, and she struggled to move him.

"Come on, Marcel," she snapped. "Help me! We've got to get away from here. They'll be here any minute!" She pulled him to his feet and, as he took some of his own weight, supported him against her as they made their way slowly along the road towards a gate leading into the adjacent field. Pursuit could not be far behind and Adelaide knew that they must, at least, get out of sight. For a moment Marcel rested on the gate, regaining his strength, and then they moved into the field.

"We must find somewhere to hide," Adelaide said, "while we do something about your shoulder. You're losing blood."

"Copse over there," Marcel rasped, pointing to a stand of trees on the further side of the field.

"Too far. They'll be here in a minute."

"Leave me here," Marcel said. "You could make it on your own."

"Shut up and let me think," snapped Adelaide.

Even as she spoke she heard the sound of an approaching car. Too late to do anything but hide and pray. Adelaide looked round and saw the dry ditch that ran along the back of the hedge.

"Into the ditch!" She rolled Marcel into the ditch and giving him the pistol she had brought from the car pushed him down under cover of the overhanging branches.

"Stay here," she hissed. "I'll be back."

The sound of the engine told her it was only one car, not a convoy of troops come searching. Pray God it was only a civilian car and not the Germans at all. She slipped along the field side of the hedge until she was level with the wreck of their car, then she too dropped into the ditch, and watched through the hedge as the approaching car came to a halt.

As the Citroën had disappeared drunkenly round the bend in the lane, Braun bellowed at the other two. "Hold your fire. They're out of range!" He looked round to discover only Schilde on his feet. Taube lay motionless on the verge where the lurching car had tossed him. Braun checked for a pulse. "Out cold, but alive. Right. I'll go back to HQ and tell Colonel Hoch what's happened. You do what you can for Taube, make him as comfortable as you can and I'll send help."

474

Leaving Schilde to attend to his comrade, Braun grabbed his bicycle from inside the barn and set off to the village. He was not looking forward to making his report. He had failed, and Colonel Hoch did not tolerate failure.

"Well?" Hoch growled when the unfortunate Braun came into his office.

"They've made a break for it, sir," Braun said. "Two, in a car. A man and, I think, a woman."

"What!" the colonel bellowed. "And you let them go? What car? Why didn't you report to me when the car arrived?"

"We didn't see it arrive, sir. It must have been at the farm before we set up in the barn."

"Why the hell didn't you stop it, as it came out?"

"We did, sir. We flagged it down as it drove up the track. It had 'Doctor' displayed on the front windscreen and it was slowing as it reached us. Schilde and Taube had them covered and I stepped forward to speak to the driver."

"What did he look like?" demanded Hoch.

"Difficult to tell, sir. I only saw him briefly. Dark hair. Not an old man, probably somewhere in his thirties."

"Marcel!" Hoch leapt to his feet. "Why didn't you stop him?"

"We thought he was stopping, sir, then at the last minute he put his foot to the floor and simply drove us down. Taube was knocked unconscious, he's still out. We opened fired and the car took several hits."

"But they've got away," growled Hoch.

"I don't think they'll get far, sir," Braun replied. "One of the tyres blew, and the car took a definite hit."

"Weber!" Hoch's bellow could be heard all over the building, and the lieutenant appeared at the run.

"Colonel?"

"Get the car!" barked Hoch, and as Weber rushed to fetch the car Hoch turned on Braun with a tirade of invective, damning him for his stupidity, incompetence, cowardice. "You should have stopped the car at any price!" Hoch roared. "Doctor indeed! It was a wanted resistance leader!"

Braun did not remind the colonel that his orders had been to take prisoners, to take them alive. He valued his own skin too much for that. "They drove straight into us, sir. By the time we were on our feet again they were away. But the car was damaged. They won't get far, sir."

"And the girl was with him, you say?"

"There was a passenger."

"Which road did they take?" Hoch interrupted impatiently.

"They headed north-east, sir, towards Albert. You should easily catch up with them; the car sounded in a very bad way. Shall I call for reinforcements, sir?"

Weber and the car appeared on the square, and the colonel strode out to join him. "Twenty men!" he snapped over his shoulder. "Find Major Thielen and send him after me with twenty men, along the Albert road. Warn him I want no more cock-ups. Tell him to bring the dogs. And you," he added ominously, "I'll see you when I get back."

476

He scrambled into the car. "Drive!" he ordered, and Weber, revving up the engine, roared out of the square.

Braun went in search of Major Thielen, but it took him a little while to find him, as he was off duty and had returned to his billet.

"*Résistants*, you say?" The major listened to Braun in surprise. He thought Colonel Hoch was only interested in searching out Jews, and the way he had gone about it the night before had sickened him. Thielen had heard about the night-time arrests at the convent, and although he was not unduly worried that two more Jews had been shipped out, he was concerned that two nuns, one of them the reverend mother no less, had been sent with them. Thielen had not seen them go, but he had heard the gossip that had described the state in which they had been loaded into the lorry. Making war on a convent full of nuns was not acceptable to Major Thielen, but there was little he could do about it. Hoch outranked him, and even if he had not done so, Thielen would have thought long and hard before he crossed swords with any SS officer. But *résistants*? They were another thing, and when he heard from Braun what had happened at the farm, Thielen gave brisk orders. Within minutes a truck was drawing up in the square and twenty men piling on board.

"You stay here and see to your wounded," he ordered Braun as he swung himself up into an armoured car beside two dog handlers and their dogs. "Let's go!"

The little convoy swept out of the square and headed at speed along the road to Albert.

"Looks like trouble up ahead, sir," the driver said. Thielen looked up to see thick smoke swirling up into the sky.

"Foot down, Sergeant," he ordered and braced himself as the armoured car swung round a corner.

Hoch and Weber had quickly reached the main road leading from St Croix to Albert. Although it was the main road, all of it was narrow and much of it was twisting, and Weber slowed instinctively as he approached the corners.

Hoch snapped. "Get a move on, Weber!"

"There's oil on the road, sir," said Weber. "They must have taken a hit."

As they rounded another sharp bend Weber hit the brakes and they skidded to a halt. There, in front of them, its bonnet crunched against a tree where it had slewed off the road, was the Citroën. Its doors were open, as if its occupants had fled the car in haste.

"Come on," Hoch said, "let's take a look." He drew his pistol, and easing open the car door stepped down onto the road.

Weber did the same. "Shouldn't we wait for some backup now, sir?" he suggested uneasily. "We don't know what we're going to find."

"We're going to find an empty car," snapped Hoch. "Whoever was in it isn't going to hang about waiting for us. Come on."

Cautiously they approached the car. There was the drip, drip, drip of oil, and Hoch could see it pooling under the car. The rear offside tyre had completely disintegrated, with the rim buckled and bent; the front

478

nearside tyre was flat. Clearly the driver had lost control of the vehicle as he had rounded the corner too fast and slammed into the tree. Slowly Hoch edged his way round to the driver's door, gesturing with his pistol that Weber should take the other side. The car was full of broken glass, vicious shards scattered over the floor and the seats, more in the road. The inside of the car was spattered and smeared with blood, and on the back seat was a dark stain, clearly blood and far more than a smear.

"Be careful, sir, it might be booby-trapped!" Weber was not enjoying this. He felt himself over-exposed. Here they were, just two of them, in pursuit of desperate fugitives, *résistants*, who had already mown down those who stood in the way of their escape. Weber felt it was time to await the coming reinforcements. Let them scour the area and catch or kill these dangerous fugitives. "It might blow up, sir!"

"Don't be ridiculous, man," scoffed his colonel. "They've had no time for that. Look at the blood, here on the back seat. One of them at least is wounded. They won't get far."

"They may be armed, sir," ventured Weber. He looked nervously round him, but all was quiet; there was no sign of the *résistants*. Where had they gone? Were they lurking in the hedgerow waiting to pounce? A rustle in the bushes made him spin round, his pistol levelled at the sound, but it was merely a bird, hopping from twig to twig.

"What a coward you are, Weber." Hoch's voice was icy with contempt, but even so he moved aside from the car and looked round. The road curved away in front of them, low hedges on either side, punctuated by tall poplar trees.

"They went this way," he said. "Look, one of them is bleeding." Pistol in hand, he followed the trail of blood along the road to an old gate leading into the adjacent field. He jerked his head for Weber to follow him, and reluctantly the lieutenant did so, his eyes swivelling nervously as he continued to search for any sign of the fugitives.

They edged along the hedge towards the old wooden gate. It was almost closed, hanging askew on its ancient hinges as if it had been dragged across in a hurry. The trail of blood stopped there, but there was another smear on the top bar, as if someone had leaned on it for a moment to regain his breath. Before going through the gate, Hoch surveyed the field beyond it. In the distance was a small copse, the trees standing tall from the bushy undergrowth that covered the ground beneath.

"Over there." Hoch pointed at the copse. "They'll be holed up in that wood."

Weber looked where he pointed. "I'm sure you're right, sir. But we can't flush them out on our own, not just the two of us. We need men to saturate the place."

Hoch eyed him grimly. "I know that, Weber. I'll wait by the car. You stay here and keep watch on those trees. Shout if you see any movement."

Adelaide had watched as the car pulled up beside theirs. It was a German staff car, but there were only two men in it, and as they got out to have a look, the inkling of an idea twitched into her mind.

Given enough time and a little luck, she thought, we might yet get away.

She watched as the two officers got out of their car, pistols drawn and ready for trouble. Hoch she recognised at once; the other, a younger man, she had seen before, but did not know his name. He was obviously ill at ease, his pistol unsteady in his hand as he stared round him. The two men stood talking for a moment before Hoch pointed to something on the ground and they moved slowly up the road.

Adelaide wormed her way under the hedge and out into the lane. The staff car had been pulled off the road just behind their crash. Adelaide peered from behind it and saw the two men making their way cautiously towards the field gate. A quick glance into the staff car showed her the keys still dangling in the ignition. She snatched them away and stuffed them into her pocket, before ducking back into the safety of the hedge.

The two men had reached the gate now and were looking over into the field. It would probably be moments only before they found Marcel, but she had to assume they wanted to capture him, not kill him, and she made no move.

Keep a cool head! she told herself. Wait your chance!

She watched as they went through into the field, and the moment they were out of sight she sped after them, hidden by the hedgerow, her feet soundless on the grass verge. As she reached the gateway she heard their voices and then the sound of someone coming back. Pressed into the shelter of the hedge, she waited, poised, her knife in her hand. Surprise must be her ally.

The man came through the gate; it was Colonel Hoch. As he turned back towards the cars Adelaide launched herself at him, bringing her knife up, hard and strong towards his chest. In the moment that she moved, he saw her and twisted away, striking out at her. Her knife rammed home into his shoulder, and he gave a bellow of pain, staggering away, dropping his pistol, but still on his feet. Wrenching the knife free she attacked again, aiming at his groin and this time her knife found its mark. With an agonised shriek, Hoch doubled up and Adelaide gave the final thrust deep into his side. Shots rang out, and she lurched sideways as Lieutenant Weber hurtled out through the gate, his pistol in an unsteady hand, firing as he came. The shots went wide, and Adelaide sprang to her feet, diving forward as another bullet zinged over her head. Her knife still clutched in her hand, she twisted violently, rolling away, coming again to her feet, but Weber shouted, "Halt!" A glance showed her that he had her covered. He was afraid . . . his hands were shaking, but they held the pistol out in front of him, and at that distance he could not miss.

"Now, drop the knife!" He spoke first in German and then in schoolboy French. "Drop the knife and lie on the ground."

Adelaide did as she was bidden. For the moment she had no alternative . . . maybe later, if she complied now. Her eyes flicked to where Hoch's pistol had fallen, several yards away, measuring the distance and gauging

482

her chances of reaching it before Weber shot her. They were nil.

"You are a *résistant*," the lieutenant was saying. "You will stay where you are till my men arrive, or I will shoot you dead." Weber stood well clear of her as she lay spread-eagled on the ground. He held his pistol at arm's length, clutched in two hands and pointing at her. He was taking no risk that she wouldn't attack again. His eyes flickered across to the inert body of Colonel Hoch. "And a murderer. For this killing, you will be shot."

"Oh, I don't think so." Marcel's voice was a drawl, and as Weber spun round two bullets thudded into his chest. The lieutenant fell where he stood and Marcel leaned awkwardly against the gate. "Takes care of those two," he said. "Time to move before the rest get here."

"We'll take their car," Adelaide said. "Come on, let's get you into it."

"All in good time," Marcel said. "Let's get them into ours first."

"What! Come on, Marcel! They've got troops coming!"

"So, let them find a car crash. The cars are the same. They'll realise in the end, but it will give us more time."

"The cars are the same . . . ?"

"Use your eyes, Adèle," snapped Marcel. "Come on, we have no time. Get them into the wreck."

Together they dragged the two bodies along the road to the crashed Citroën, and heaved them into the front seats. It wasn't easy. The bodies were a deadweight and Marcel was struggling with the wound in his shoulder, but somehow they managed, heaving the two men into the car and slamming the doors against their sagging bodies.

"Move their car up the road," ordered Marcel, and, retrieving a jerry can of petrol from the boot, he splashed it generously over the bonnet and inside the crashed car, before striking a match and tossing it in through the open driver's window. The petrol ignited with a whoosh and Marcel leapt backwards, almost falling over before staggering to the waiting staff car. Adelaide had the engine running, and as Marcel hauled himself into the passenger seat she let in the clutch and pulled away.

"I'll direct you," Marcel said, his voice weak as he collapsed back against the seat.

Even as they accelerated away, Major Thielen was thundering along the road from St Croix in his armoured car, the truckload of men behind him. He saw the black smoke pouring into the sky and as he rounded the corner he almost ran into the burning Citroën. His car and the following truck screeched to a halt. Men jumped down into the road and the two dog handlers with their dogs jumped out of the armoured car. There were yells of "Keep back! Keep back!", but Major Thielen ran towards the burning car. He could see two bodies inside, could make out the insignia on the burning jacket of the driver. The heat was intense, driving him back, his hands held up to shield his face.

"There are people inside!" he yelled. "Give a hand here!"

484

There were indeed hands, but they dragged him back from the burning car. "There's nothing you can do, sir," one of his junior officers shouted. "It's too late, they're gone. Keep back!"

Even as he dragged the major clear, the petrol tank of the burning car exploded and they were all thrown backwards as a fireball erupted into the air, raining burning debris down on their heads as they dived for cover. Pandemonium reigned for a few moments as the troops beat out the sparks that smouldered on their clothes and burned in their hair. Patches of dry grass ignited along the roadside, and the tree against which the car had been wedged flamed like a torch above the burning remains.

Later, when the fire had been doused and the car had cooled enough to be approached, Major Thielen peered into what remained of its blackened shell. The explosion and subsequent conflagration had incinerated the two bodies he had seen, but he had no doubt who they were. Braun had passed on orders from Colonel Hoch to follow him in pursuit of two *résistants*, and this Thielen had done.

It was clear to him, he told his men gravely, that in his haste to apprehend the *résistants*, the colonel's driver had taken a corner too fast and crashed into a tree. There was oil on the road, which must have made him skid.

He didn't believe it, of course, but whatever the cause of the accident, Thielen was glad to be rid of Colonel Hoch. He considered him a disgrace to the Fatherland. Thielen was fighting a war, but he had no time for thuggery, torture and murder, practised on civilians, and he knew that Hoch had committed all three. Life without him would be a welcome relief indeed. He was glad Hoch was dead and he was not going to look particularly hard at the circumstances; he had no intention of suggesting that the colonel's death was anything more than a dreadful accident, happening in the course of his duty. Such would be his report.

"Should we search the area, sir?" demanded Hartmann, the young officer who had dragged him back from the burning vehicle.

"Certainly," agreed Thielen. "Let the dogs loose and see if they pick up a scent."

The dog handlers did as they were ordered, and the dogs ran round in excited circles, as they discovered patches of blood in the dust of the road.

"Blood, sir," reported one of the handlers. "Looks fairly fresh."

"See if they pick up a trail," ordered Thielen. He might still find the *résistants* that the colonel had been chasing. The dogs were released again, but apart from nosing about in a dry ditch at the edge of the field for a while, they found nothing to take their interest, and after a while they were returned to the armoured car.

"I wonder how they came to crash," Hartmann said, studying the remains of the Citroën. "I suppose this is Colonel Hoch's car."

"Of course it is," snapped Thielen. "We've seen him in it a hundred times. Please see to the removal of the bodies, Hartmann, and arrange for the burial of the remains. I will report back to SS Headquarters in Amiens."

Hartmann appeared to be about to speak, but thinking better of it he snapped a salute and turned to give the orders to his men. Hoch had been feared almost as much by his own men as he had by the local population. A sadistic and ambitious man, he would be mourned by no one.

Thielen realised that the knowledge Hoch had gained from the torture of his most recent prisoners had died with him, but even so, he didn't despair of catching the *résistants*. Braun had actually seen them, so he could give a description, and Thielen himself already had one contact in the locality. He could be tapped for more information. No, Thielen didn't despair of catching them at all . . . and the credit would be his.

"Get the road cleared," he ordered Hartmann, "then report to me at HQ."

Unaware that pursuit, for the time being, was over, Adelaide and Marcel turned off the road to Albert, and, with Marcel navigating, took the lanes and by-ways, travelling across country until they bumped along a dirt track and through the gate into a farmyard. As they turned in, Adelaide recognised it as the farm Marcel had taken her to on the night she had landed. She pulled up in the yard and the elderly woman, Maman, who had looked after her the last time, came out. When Maman saw Marcel slumped in the front seat of the car, she began issuing orders to Adelaide, and between them they managed to get him out of the car and into the house.

"Put the car in the barn for now," Maman said as she took hot water from the kettle on the range and set about removing Marcel's shirt. "We'll hide it properly later. Now," she said, turning her attention to Marcel, "let's have a look at you."

Adelaide did as she was told, driving the car into the open-ended barn so that it was not immediately apparent to anyone who came into the yard. The front seat was covered in blood, and she realised that Marcel had been bleeding steadily ever since they had made their break. His wound was worse than she had realised, and the effort he had put into moving the two German soldiers into the wrecked car, and his determination to get them both to a safe house, had made it worse. She found a bucket in the yard and filling it at the pump set about trying to remove the bloodstains from the leather seat. She got the worst off, but the stain needed more than clean water and a cloth to remove it completely. Next, she found a screwdriver in a box of tools and carefully removed the number plates. There was no point in making identification of the car easy. Someone had lost his car; the German staff car was almost identical; with a little careful work it might be a replacement.

When she finally went back into the kitchen she found Maman bandaging Marcel's shoulder. Marcel was pale, his face drawn with pain, but he managed a weak smile as she came into the room.

"Where's the car?" he asked.

488

"Taken care of, for now," she replied, putting the number plates on the table beside him. "All we have to do is get rid of these and replace them." She spoke to Maman. "How bad?"

"Not good," replied the old lady, tipping the bowl of bloodied water down the sink. "He's lost a lot of blood, but he'll live. Now, what about you?"

"Me?" Adelaide sounded surprised.

"Sit down and let me look." Maman poured clean water into the bowl, and taking Adelaide's hands washed them thoroughly. The water made the cuts from the flying glass sting, but none was very deep, and Adelaide had been almost unaware of them in their flight.

"And your face. Hold back your hair."

Adelaide did as she was told and the old lady washed and anointed the cuts to her face and neck. "You're lucky, there's only one bad one here on your chin. It really needs stitching or you'll have a scar." She turned to Marcel. "Perhaps when the doctor comes . . . ?"

"No doctor until we've got Adèle away," Marcel said firmly. "Too risky."

"But you . . ." began Maman.

"I will wait until Adèle has gone."

"Surely you can trust Dr Clabot."

"Of course, I still have his car . . ." he laughed, "well, one just like it. But there are other eyes and ears, and I won't take any unnecessary risks until Adèle is safely away." He tried to stand up, but his legs seemed to buckle under him and he sank back onto the chair. "I have to contact the reception group," he said. "There's another drop coming in tomorrow night, and we have to be ready. The same plane will take Adèle out. Will you contact Rousseau for me? I need to talk to him."

"In the morning," Maman promised. "What you need now is some hot food and a good sleep . . . and no argument," she said fiercely as he began to protest. "Time enough for Rousseau then."

Adelaide was given the same bedroom she'd occupied before. As she lay in bed trying to sleep, she considered all that had happened since she was last in that bed ten weeks ago. Ten weeks! Was it really only ten weeks since she had parachuted into France, into the war of occupation? She thought of the people she would be leaving behind, everyday people who were trying to live normal lives; and the others who were living anything but normal lives as they fought against those who had taken over their towns, their homes, and in some cases their families. She thought of Sarah, quietly courageous, and the valiant little Sister Marie-Marc. She thought of Sister St Bruno, hiding a fugitive Jew under her bed; of Father Bernard sheltering those hiding from the Germans, those on the run and in fear of their lives. She thought of the Auclons, the parents prepared to give up their children in an effort to save them; of the twin boys so wary of anyone but each other. Madame Juliette, the Launays and the Charbonniers, simple folk prepared to put their own lives at risk to fight against the evil that had overtaken their country.

And then she thought of Colonel Hoch, the embodiment of that evil. She had plunged her knife into him without compunction. The memory of Sarah, battered and bruised, and of Sister Marie-Marc, almost unable to stand, flooded through her, and the tears streamed down her cheeks. She had made sure that the monster would never torture and murder again, but for so many that was too late. She had been trained to kill, to be prepared to kill, and she had done so. Fernand, rotting at the bottom of the Launays' old well, and Hoch, whose eyes gleamed as he inflicted pain; Adelaide felt no more remorse than she would have destroying any other vermin.

Next day Marcel, though still pale and weak from loss of blood, seemed a little better. Adelaide was sitting with him in the farm kitchen when a young man arrived. He was introduced to Adelaide as Rousseau.

"We have to be prepared for a landing tonight," Marcel told him. "Incoming, another wireless operator, outgoing, Antoinette. Can you make the arrangements?"

Rousseau nodded. "Of course, leave them to me." He looked gravely across at Marcel. "I must tell you though, Marcel, I am concerned about young Benoit. He's been acting very strangely these last few days. I think I won't include him in the reception party. You need to talk to him. To find out what's wrong." Rousseau grinned suddenly. "I saw him today. He came into the café and gave me one bit of news to brighten my day."

"Oh?" Marcel looked up with interest. "And what was that?"

"He said two German officers were killed yesterday in a road accident over St Croix way." He laughed. "Don't care how they die as long as they do!"

"How did he hear that?" asked Marcel sharply.

Rousseau shrugged. "He didn't say, just said he'd heard it. May not be true of course."

"Keep an eye on that young man," Marcel warned. "He's too free with his tongue. Does he know about the drop tonight?"

"I haven't told him, but it doesn't mean he doesn't know. To be honest, Marcel, the whole group chat too much among themselves. You should talk to them all."

Marcel nodded. "I'll have a word," he said. "I'll see you later."

"Surely you're not coming tonight!" exclaimed Rousseau. "Not with your arm useless and in a sling. You won't be any help and it's an added risk."

"I shall be there," Marcel said in a voice that brooked no argument, and Rousseau shrugged.

"You're the boss," he said and took his leave to go and make the arrangements.

When he had gone Adelaide asked, "Who is this Benoit? Is he a security risk?"

Marcel shrugged. "Everyone is a security risk," he said. "Benoit is probably no worse than anyone else, except that he's young and can be careless." Marcel smiled across at her. "Don't worry, *chérie*, the risks are there every time, they are no greater tonight than any other."

The night was dark with only patchy moonlight between the scudding clouds. Adelaide stood with

Marcel in the shelter of a hedgerow at the side of the field that would be the landing strip for the incoming aircraft. His arm was in a sling, but he insisted, as he had to Rousseau earlier, that he was coming with her to see her safely away.

During the afternoon they had talked, sitting side by side at the big kitchen table, left on their own as Maman had made a discreet withdrawal.

"When you arrived I wondered why on earth they had sent someone so young and inexperienced," Marcel admitted. "I reckoned you were a tremendous risk to us all."

Adelaide grinned at him. "Yes," she agreed with a smile. "You made that abundantly clear!"

He took her hand in his and held it against his cheek. "How wrong I was! You're the gutsiest girl I've ever come across . . . and the most beautiful."

Adelaide felt the colour flood her cheeks and she pulled her hand away. "Come on, Marcel. We both know there's no future in talk like that."

"Isn't there? This bloody war isn't going to last forever, and when it's over I'm going to come over to England and find you." His eyes were intent upon her face. "I love you, Adèle. Didn't think it could happen to me . . . falling in love at my age . . . far too cynical . . . but it has. I love you and when we've kicked the bloody Boche out of France, I shall come and find you." He reached out to her with his good arm, pulling her to him. Adelaide allowed herself to rest against his heart, for a precious moment feeling safe within his embrace, and each of them had drawn comfort from the closeness of the other.

"I mean it," he said. "When this war is over, I shall come and find you, wherever you are." He spoke in English, his accent, as he spoke her language rather than his own, imbuing the words with added depth. "Look for me after the war, for if I survive I will come." He kissed her then, holding her a little awkwardly with one arm, the passion in his kiss reinforcing the passion in his words.

The sound of the Lysander throbbed in the air and the reception party switched on the bicycle lamps set out to illuminate the makeshift runway.

The pilot made a single pass overhead, and then the engine note changed as he throttled back and made the approach to land. Marcel pulled Adelaide into his arms one more time and kissed her as if he would never let her go, and she, responding, returned his kiss with equal passion.

"Remember," he said fiercely, "and never doubt it, I shall come and find you, *chérie*."

The plane touched down, and almost before it had come to a halt the door was opened and the incoming wireless operator was scrambling down the ladder. Reaching back, he heaved his wireless suitcase from the plane.

For a moment Marcel stared down at Adelaide's face as if to imprint it on his memory forever, and then he gave her a little push. She ran across the grass and scrambled up the ladder into the plane. The moment the door slammed behind her, as she was scrambling

494

into the observer's seat, the pilot revved the engine and taxied round to take off again.

As he did so, there was a rattle of machine-gun fire from somewhere outside.

"Christ!" bellowed the pilot. "Ambush!"

One glance sideways through the canopy, and the pilot's face became a mask of grim determination. The plane was gathering speed and Adelaide was flung against the fuselage as the Lysander lumbered across the field before lifting into the air. The sound of gunfire continued, and as the Lysander banked away, Adelaide looked down to see muzzle flashes from the field below. The moon sailed out from behind the clouds, and in its pitiless light Adelaide saw figures running in all directions, some stumbling and falling, others diving for cover in the surrounding woodland. And then they were gone, as cloud enveloped the plane and she could see nothing.

"Just got you out in time," shouted the pilot above the roar of the engine. "Sorry for the poor bastard we just took in! He's probably bought it!"

Adelaide huddled against the throbbing fuselage of the plane, the tears flowing, unchecked, down her face. For the first time she allowed herself to acknowledge what Marcel had come to mean to her. Strong and brave, he came to the drop to make sure she got away safely . . . because he loved her, and she had seen him mown down by machine-gun fire. His words echoed in her ears. "Look for me after the war, *chérie*, for if I survive I will come."

As the Lysander droned its way home across the Channel, Adelaide knew with a despairing, aching heart that Marcel had not survived and that he would not come.

Epilogue Summer 2006

Adelaide Talbot leaned back against her pillows and sighed. "So there you have it," she said. "I came back to England and when I'd been debriefed, I was given wireless training and then sent back. Different area of course, where I was completely unknown. Normandy. I worked with the local resistance as a courier and liaison until the Allies landed."

She smiled at Rachel Elliott, journalist from the *Belcaster Chronicle*, who had come to interview her. "I was lucky to survive, hundreds of us didn't."

The old lady fell silent and closed her eyes. Wondering if she had fallen asleep, Rachel glanced across at James Auckland, sitting on the other side of the bed holding his grandmother's hand.

"What a sad story," Rachel murmured. "Sad and brave. I wonder what happened to them all, Sarah, Sister Marie-Marc, Marcel and the children."

She was just reaching forward to switch off her tape recorder when Adelaide's eyes opened again and she said softly, "It was all so long ago, so long ago."

"Did you ever find out what happened to Sarah?" Rachel asked gently, sitting back again and letting the tape continue to run.

"Yes, I did," replied Adelaide. "It took some time, of course. Everything was in chaos at the end of the war. The Allies discovered places like Bergen-Belsen and Auschwitz. Hundreds of thousands of people had disappeared and those that had survived were refugees; no homes, no families and nowhere to go. We traced Sarah to Ravensbrück, the concentration camp for women. Some of the survivors remembered her, and spoke of how she did all she could to alleviate the suffering of those around her. One woman said that 'Mother' was always wherever she was needed, nursing, encouraging, keeping her faith strong to strengthen others. Even most of the German guards treated her with some sort of respect, occasionally giving in to her demands for an extra ration of food to be shared among those too weak to collect their own portion." Adelaide gave a rueful smile. "She died as she had lived, always caring for those around her, putting their needs first. She finally caught typhus, which in her weakened state carried her off very quickly."

"And Sister Marie-Marc? Was she with her?" asked Rachel. She had been completely caught up in Adelaide's story and felt she had come to know the people who had played their part.

Adelaide shook her head. "I asked, of course, but no one I met remembered her. I think she probably died en route to the camp. She was in a dreadful state when she was loaded onto that lorry, and it's unlikely she survived the journey. I imagine they went first to Drancy, the transit camp outside Paris, where the conditions were said to be absolutely appalling."

498

Adelaide gave a rueful smile. "Dear Sister Marie-Marc, she was so determined to outwit '*Les sales Boches*' who stole her chickens."

Silence settled round them and the old lady again closed her eyes. Rachel didn't speak; her mind was teeming with everything she'd heard. There was such a story here; far more than she had ever anticipated when, at the suggestion of James Auckland, she'd asked the old lady for an interview. James had sent the book he had written about his grandmother's exploits in the war to the *Chronicle* for review, and Drew Scott, the editor, had given it to Rachel to read.

Rachel had been fascinated and had rung James up to arrange an interview.

"It's not me you need to talk to," he said. "It's my grandmother. I'll introduce you if you like."

Rachel had accepted the offer with alacrity, and here she was hearing the story, first hand, from the woman whose story it was.

"You didn't think of writing the book yourself?" Rachel had asked her.

With a laugh, the old lady shook her head. "No, I'm far too old. I'll be ninety in September. No, it was James who suggested it. I didn't think anyone would be interested, but he said they would, so I left it to him."

"And you simply told him what had happened."

Adelaide shrugged. "I told him what I knew. I don't know exactly what did happen when Sarah was arrested and questioned, but," she added grimly, "having seen her and Sister Marie-Marc and the Auclons when Hoch had finished with them, I could guess." She sighed and again lapsed into a silence broken only by the summer sound of someone mowing the grass below the window.

Already Rachel's journalistic mind was sorting and cataloguing what she had heard, the story she would write already taking shape in her head. The details of the fear and the courage that had emerged as she'd spent the afternoon with Adelaide were safely trapped on tape, ready to be replayed as Rachel worked on her story. No simple book review now; but an in-depth piece of journalism.

"But of course I did find the twins," Adelaide said suddenly as if there had been no lapse in the conversation. "Jacques and Julien."

"Did you?" Rachel was startled back to the present. "How marvellous! Where were they?"

"In the convent in Paris. Father Bernard had managed to get them there and Mother Magdalene kept them. She gave them new names and managed to get them new identity papers. When I went back to try and find Sarah, I went to the mother house in Paris in case they had news of her. They hadn't of course, but Mother Magdalene mentioned that the boys were still there and I asked to see them. They didn't remember me, but I knew them at once."

"And their parents?"

"Enquiries had been made about them, but nothing was known about either of them. Almost certainly they were sent to one of the extermination camps, but there was no record. They simply disappeared among the thousands of others."

"What happened to the twins?" wondered Rachel.

To her surprise both James and Adelaide laughed. "Well, that I can tell you," Adelaide said. "I adopted them and brought them home to England. We anglicised their name, Auclon, to Auckland. James is Julien's son."

"What?" Rachel stared at James in disbelief. "You're joking!"

"Never more serious," he grinned. "My dad, Julien Auckland, is a doctor, and my uncle Jacques is a solicitor, or they were before they retired."

"And they're both still alive?"

"And kicking!" James agreed cheerfully.

"It really is the most amazing story," Rachel said. She turned back to Adelaide. "And Marcel? Did you ever discover who Marcel really was? Did you ever find out what happened the night you made your escape?"

Adelaide smiled. "Oh yes," she said. "He told me himself."

"But I thought he was . . ." began Rachel.

"So did I," admitted Adelaide, "for the rest of the war. But he wasn't. Because he wasn't working with the reception party, he wasn't out in the field when the Germans opened fire. Only he and Rousseau survived that attack. It turned out that Benoit, the young man they had been discussing, had turned traitor." Adelaide's voice hardened. "Like Fernand, Benoit wanted to be on the winning side and had been selling information to the Germans." A shadow passed across her face as she added, "Needless to say, he did not survive the war. Anyway, Marcel managed to get away, and to gather another group round him. He continued his fight until France was liberated and the war ended. And then he came to find me." Her face lit up at some private memory. "He was a lawyer. His name was Antoine Talbot, we were married for forty years."

Also available in ISIS Large Print:

The Parish of Hilby

Mary E. Mann

When Mr James Massey moves to the Parish of Hilby and becomes the new tenant of Wood Farm he is soon the centre of attention.

Invited to events within the typical small Norfolk Village by the local residents, Massey finds himself attending village concerts, a garden party, high tea at the grange and even dinner at the vicarage.

As the residents warm to him so too do the hearts of two women, Helen Smythe and Pollie Freeman. When Pollie mistakes his affections for a proposal James realises it is Helen he favours above all. But Pollie has informed her parents of the engagement and in a small village where word travels quickly will James have a choice?

ISBN 978-0-7531-8234-5 (hb)
ISBN 978-0-7531-8235-2 (pb)

The Secret Scripture

Sebastian Barry

Nearing her 100th birthday, Roseanne McNulty faces an uncertain future, as the Roscommon Regional Mental hospital where she's spent the best part of her adult life prepares for closure. Over the weeks leading up to this upheaval, she talks often with her psychiatrist Dr Grene. This relationship, guarded but trusting after so many years, intensifies as Dr Grene mourns the death of his wife.

Told through their respective journals, the story that emerges — of Roseanne's family in 1930s Sligo — is at once shocking and deeply beautiful. Refracted through the haze of memory and retelling, Roseanne's story becomes an alternative, secret history of Ireland. Exquisitely written, it is the story of a life blighted by maltreatment and ignorance, yet still marked by a flame of love, passion and hope.

ISBN 978-0-7531-8178-2 (hb)
ISBN 978-0-7531-8179-9 (pb)

The Same Earth

Kei Miller

It all begins with the theft of Tessa Walcott's polkadot panties and a river that changes course overnight . . .

When Imelda Richardson leaves the small village of Watersgate armed only with one small suitcase, she is doing so for the second time. One of the throng of young Jamaicans who left the island in 1974, Imelda's journey has taken her to England, and a law degree. But when her mother dies, Imelda returns, choosing Jamaica over England.

The village is still dominated by the Evangelical church and the thundering voice of Pastor Braithwaite. When Tessa Walcott's panties are stolen, she and Imelda decide to set up a Neighbourhood Watch. But they haven't counted on Pastor Braithwaite and the crusading zeal of Evangelist Millie. As a Pentecostal fervour sweeps through the village, the tensions between old and new come to a head.

ISBN 978-0-7531-8174-4 (hb)
ISBN 978-0-7531-8175-1 (pb)

Playing with the Moon

Eliza Graham

Selected for the World Book Day Spread the Word promotion.

Shattered by a recent bereavement, Minna and her husband Tom retreat to an isolated village on the Dorset coast. Walking on the beach one day, they unearth a human skeleton. The remains are soon identified as those of a black American GI who, it seems, drowned during a wartime exercise 60 years before.

Growing increasingly preoccupied with the dead soldier's fate, Minna befriends a melancholy elderly woman, Felix, who lived in the village during the war. As Minna coaxes Felix's story from her, it becomes clear that the old woman knows more about the dead GI than she initially let on. Felix's final shocking confession allows her to come to terms with an event that has cast a shadow over her life, and helps Minna to begin to accept her own loss.

ISBN 978-0-7531-8170-6 (hb)
ISBN 978-0-7531-8171-3 (pb)

The Ashgrove

Diney Costeloe

In 1921, eight ash trees were planted as a memorial to the men from the village who were killed in World War One. Now the Ashgrove is under threat from developers, and the village is torn between the need for more housing and the wish to preserve the memorial.

Rachel Elliott, a local journalist, uncovers a mystery surrounding the Ashgrove. Eight men and nine trees — in whose memory is the ninth tree and who planted it? It is only when she is given a diary and some letters that she begins to unravel the truth. Written by a young girl, Molly Day, a nurse in a hospital in France, the diary and letters tell of her life in the hospital and her love for Tom Carter, one of her patients.

ISBN 978-0-7531-7383-1 (hb)
ISBN 978-0-7531-7384-8 (pb)

ISIS publish a wide range of books in large print, from fiction to biography. Any suggestions for books you would like to see in large print or audio are always welcome. Please send to the Editorial Department at:

ISIS Publishing Limited
7 Centremead
Osney Mead
Oxford OX2 0ES

A full list of titles is available free of charge from:

Ulverscroft Large Print Books Limited

(UK)
The Green
Bradgate Road, Anstey
Leicester LE7 7FU
Tel: (0116) 236 4325

(Australia)
P.O. Box 314
St Leonards
NSW 1590
Tel: (02) 9436 2622

(USA)
P.O. Box 1230
West Seneca
N.Y. 14224-1230
Tel: (716) 674 4270

(Canada)
P.O. Box 80038
Burlington
Ontario L7L 6B1
Tel: (905) 637 8734

(New Zealand)
P.O. Box 456
Feilding
Tel: (06) 323 6828

Details of **ISIS** complete and unabridged audio books are also available from these offices. Alternatively, contact your local library for details of their collection of **ISIS** large print and unabridged audio books.